LEGALLY OURS

BOOK THREE OF THE SPITFIRE TRILOGY

NICOLE FRENCH

D1519448

CONTENTS

Prologue

Brandon

My heart is about to jump out of my body. It's going to bust through the buttons of this goddamn monkey suit and sprint all the way to New York, because nothing seems to be moving fast enough.

"David!" I bark, startling my driver. "Can't this thing drive any fucking faster?"

For a second I feel bad. David's been with me a long time, since I started Ventures and it became clear that even parking my own car was a waste of my time when that time literally equaled money. He's been loyal, kind, and more importantly, discreet. I can trust the guy with the most intimate details of my life, and I do.

So yeah, I feel bad for yelling at him. But only for a second.

"Seriously!" I shout. "What the fuck am I paying you for? Should I just drive to New York myself?"

He knows I don't mean it, that I'll apologize in the morning with a fat raise or some extra vacation time. He knows I'm losing my fucking mind. But instead of driving the hundred-plus miles-per-hour down the 93 like he knows I'd be doing, David taps on the gas just enough to appease me.

I'm really starting to hate New York. More than your average Bostonian, and that's saying something. Hating New York is in our blood.

But as far as I can tell, everything shitty that's happened to Skylar and me in the last six months has come out of that cesspool. Miranda flying down out of the penthouse we owned on Park Avenue. Janette, that sick viper. And Victor fucking Messina, whose face I swear to God I'm going to cut the fuck up if it's the last thing I do.

The thought makes me shake. My fists clench, eager to hit something.

There's a different Brandon surfacing—one that hasn't been around in a long time. I felt it the second I walked into that bar last March and name-checked my old crew from Dorchester. I felt it

1

when I smelled the grease in Messina's hair, saw the greed and arrogance in his sweaty face. But I pushed that Brandon away, convinced that if I threw money at the problem, it would disappear, and this guy, the one I've worked so hard to lock away, would fade into the past where he belongs.

The angry Brandon who couldn't keep his emotions in check. Who used to hustle the schoolyard by day, suffer panic attacks by night, while he waited for his shithead dad to decide who he wanted to take his misery out on—his junkie wife or no-good son. The kid who had no self-control at all.

I shudder, a lightning-quick image of a bloodied salad tong flashing through my mind before I push it all away. The bastard used to grab whatever he could find. After I hid his toolbox from under the sink, he started going for kitchen implements. And you want to know something? Getting beaten with a whisk really fucking hurts.

But I can't think about those days now. It's better that I think about the guy who grew out of them—a hard-as-nails asshole with a hair-trigger temper and a nasty right hook. The guy who was the brains behind every scheme Mickey and the boys ever ran at the pool halls. The guy who was big enough to scare the shit out of some real-life gangsters in South Boston back when they still ran the neighborhood. The guy who could outsmart just about any motherfucker, and beat them senseless afterward.

I pull a cigarette out of my pocket and flip it around with my fingers. I haven't smoked in over fifteen years—not since I met Miranda and left Dorchester for good. It's a filthy habit, not one I ever missed, but I bummed one off Craig, my head of security, just before we left. I couldn't have told you why at the time, but I know now.

"David?"

David's kindly gaze flickers back to me through the rearview mirror. "Sir?"

"Pass me the lighter, will you?"

David can't quite mask the frown when he sees the cigarette, but he obediently pulls the electric knob from the front console and hands it over his shoulder. I light up, then hand it back before I open my window and hold the cigarette by the crack.

It feels good. Right. Like I'm going to be okay. The familiar scent of ash and nicotine drifts over me like a mask, like it's helping

2

me put on this old uniform. It's a scent I associate with the street. Of the rough-and-tumble group I used to run with. Of other lowlife fuckers like Messina. Of the hard-edged kid I once was. That I might need to be again tonight.

Messina already left a message for me with Margie, and the moron didn't bother to mask the number—a LAN line somewhere in the city. It's too easy to see where she might be. An abandoned warehouse in an outer borough. Maybe there's electricity, maybe there's not. Tied to a chair maybe, or a pipe on the ground. She's dirty, cold, probably bruised all over the place, since if I know Skylar, she fought like a feral cat when they took her. Possibly passed out, or just waking up with a nasty headache, since a woman who weighs maybe a hundred and twenty pounds soaking wet wouldn't have been able to do much before hurting herself more than the men who took her.

I consider what she might be wearing, hoping that will calm me down. I hope to God it wasn't that blue dress—the thing made me want to rip her clothes off in the middle of a benefit. It fit her like a damn glove, not to mention had a slit up the thigh that put some very dirty things in my head. I don't even want to think about what a guy like Messina would do if he saw her like that.

She changed, I tell myself. Into those god-awful jeans she likes to wear, maybe, although it probably wouldn't matter. She never wears a bra when she's home, which is why we can't work in the same room without me jumping her. She has no clue how beautiful she is when she's dressed like a slob, her sunset-colored hair tangled in a knot, kiwi-colored eyes clean and bright. Sometimes, especially right before bed, when she's in nothing but those Band-Aids she calls pajamas, she takes my fucking breath away. And then it goes right to my cock.

Fuck. I really hope she's wearing the jeans. But then again, my girl is gorgeous no matter what. It doesn't matter what she's wearing—you can't mask that kind of beauty. She's a work of art, and Messina knows it. The thought of what he might do to her before I get there only fuels my rage more.

My other hand fists as I take a final drag on the cigarette and flick it out the window. Yeah, I can be that guy again if I need to. And with Victor Messina? I fucking want to.

3

One

My head was throbbing. Like, really throbbing, as if there was something inside it trying to get out with a sledgehammer, banging at my skull from the inside.

That's because you have a concussion.

Apparently being knocked out made my conscience talk like a disapproving schoolteacher.

Great. OhmygodshutUP.

I rubbed my head and sat up to get my bearings. The room was pitch-black and smelled slightly of bleach—like it had been scrubbed clean too many times. There were no windows that I could see, but then again, I couldn't see anything. I could be at the top of the Empire State Building right now and not know it.

The floor was cold, concrete, with remnants of dust or dirt that stuck to my fingers and cheeks. I brushed the side of my face I'd been lying on. How long had I been here? Hours? Minutes? I didn't think it had been days. I was too strong for that.

Fear set in as I remember exactly where I was and why. Each memory slapped me in the face.

Brandon, finding out about the abortion.

Brandon, looking like I'd torn out his heart.

Brandon, telling me to leave.

Sitting alone in a diner while he announced his bid for mayor.

Returning home to find Victor Messina, the gangster who seemed to be doing everything he could to ruin my family's life, waiting outside my apartment.

I tried to run.

I failed.

My head throbbed harder, and as I pressed my fingers into my temples, I willed myself to see something—anything. My eyes found a sliver of light—a door. As they adjusted more, I took in the details of the room that were only slightly evident. Cinderblock walls with no window. A few pipes angling through the ceiling.

I was in a basement, then. Underground, where no one could hear my screams.

4

A shadow fell in front of the light. There was someone outside, someone moving around. Voices, but they were too muffled to understand beyond the fact that they were obviously male.

Messina.

Just as I was trying to think of something to say or do to get myself out of here, the door swung open, and the short, stubby form of Victor Messina stood silhouetted in the door frame, meaty hands on his hips like a fat Peter Pan. Behind him were the lumbering forms of the two goons who had captured me—I didn't know which one had hit me on the head, but I hoped I could return the favor.

"Well, well, well," Messina sneered over his shoulder to his cohorts. "Sleeping Beauty's awake, boys."

He turned back to the room and flicked on a light with a fat finger. The harsh fluorescent lighting made my head thump even harder, and I scooted into the corner, closing my eyes and wrapping my face in my hands. He wasn't going to kill me. Even Messina wasn't stupid enough to kill his bait. But that didn't mean he wouldn't hurt me.

"Oh, come on, sweetheart," he taunted as he stepped into the room. "Ain't you glad to see me? Stand up so I can look at you."

I cowered further into the corner.

"Have it your way," Messina said, and gestured to his men, who plodded in and grabbed me roughly by both arms. One smelled like cheap cologne; the other stank of pastrami.

I immediately started pulling and twisting as hard as I could. Somehow, I managed to slither out of their grasps once, but Pastrami Breath kicked me in the ribs, hard enough to make me double over in pain. Before I could recover, I was dragged to a chair in the middle of the room.

"Let me GO!" I shrieked, knowing even as I did that my cries were swallowed by the concrete walls.

I kicked and scrambled, but I was no match for the two refrigerator-sized men, who held me down and duct-taped my wrists together behind the chair back.

"There, that's better," Messina said once I was properly tied down. He bent down, although he was still a few solid feet from me. "Tsk, tsk, tsk," he clicked his tongue. "That's quite a goose egg you got there, Red. You shouldn't be so clumsy."

"Whatever I have is because of you and your fucking gorillas," I seethed, pulling again at my taped wrists, which only caused the tape to dig further into my skin.

Messina stood up and shrugged. "Whatever you say, sweetheart. To me, it just looks like you took a nasty little fall. High heels'll kill you."

He tapped the side of his nose and chuckled with the other two men, who had taken places against the wall on either side of the doorway. I glared. I had nothing on my feet now, but I'd been wearing flip-flops when they'd taken me.

"Well, I got some bad news for you, Red," Messina said. It was amazing how the nickname, which had always sounded so sweet out of Brandon's mouth, was positively nauseating from Messina's.

I pushed again at my restraints. The tape didn't budge, and its knife-edge only made me angrier. "What's that? Did the insurance company deny your breast reduction surgery again?"

A few eerie laughs left Messina's chest like a creaky rocking chair. One, two, three.

"We got a comedian here," he said to his goons. Then he turned to me with a face like fire. A sweaty, gin-soaked dumpster fire. "We'll see how far those jokes get you, sweetheart."

He started to pace, nibbling his nails and flicking the bitten pieces at me one by one. One stuck to my cheek. I wanted to vomit.

"You see, your boyfriend ain't responding to my messages," Messina said as he walked back and forth across the room. "I tried his office. I tried his secretary. Nothin'. I'm starting to think he don't care about you no more, Red." He turned, beady eyes blatantly perusing my body. "Did he finally wear that pussy out? Looks like it could get a little more use."

Messina approached, his odor of sweat and cheap cigars more pungent with each step. I shook in the chair.

"I could probably find something to work with here," he said as he reached out to toy with a loose lock of my hair. He gave it a playful yank.

"Is that right?" I asked, my voice quavering. I needed to hold my temper. But I wanted him closer. Just a step closer.

"You got a trade in mind, gorgeous?" he asked, fat lips grazing my earlobe.

"Yeah, I got a trade in mind," I whispered, urging him closer. He leaned in. "It's called...GO FUCK YOURSELF!"

I hefted a foot out and hit pay dirt between Messina's stubby legs. He collapsed forward, bloated face a bright red as he clutched my target. Unfortunately, my position in the chair didn't give me much room to gain momentum. Messina, however, had plenty.

"Fuckin' bitch!" he hissed, still hunched over to protect his balls. "Try that again, honey. I dare you."

Then Messina's hand hit my face with a loud smack, hard enough that I saw stars. A trickle of blood slid from a newly raw spot on my cheek: a cut from his massive diamond pinky ring. His hand found my face again and again—across my eye, at the side of my jaw, against the temples, one and two. When he was finished, my head hung limply. I was conscious, but just barely, with one eye already starting to swell shut.

"Get her phone. Take her picture. If he won't answer my calls, maybe he'll answer hers," Messina barked at his underlings, who immediately sprang into action. Still rubbing his balls protectively, he scowled from the doorway. "And you better hope he does, Red. Because if you ain't worth shit to him, you sure as fuck ain't worth shit to me."

* * *

Time stops working properly when you're locked in a room with no light or windows. It might have been hours before the door finally opened again. It might have been days. I wasn't sure of anything except for the fact that my stomach felt like it was sinking into itself, and I was in and out of consciousness. My head hurt. My ribs hurt. Everything hurt.

The door banged open against the concrete, echoing multiple times inside my aching skull.

"Well, good morning, Sunshine." A splash of cold water to my throbbing face, forced me awake. I blinked open the eye that wasn't still swollen shut.

"Good news, Red," Messina crowed as he and his cronies circled around me. "Lover boy texted back after all." He gave a nasty smile that showed his tobacco-stained teeth. His left front tooth had been capped, with a clear color difference between the fake part and the real. "It'll be there, he said." Messina nodded, satisfied. "It ain't poetry, but I'll take what I can get."

"What'll be there?" I croaked. My throat was dry and parched after going for so long without water. Droplets fell down my face and into my mouth, and I licked eagerly around my lips for more.

"Oh, you're worth a pretty penny after all, Red," Messina said as he cracked his knuckles. Each pop was like a hand grenade in my head. "A cool twenty-five mil." He winked at me. "Think he'd do fifty? I thought about it, but I'm too impatient, you wanna know the truth. Unmarked bills can take a while."

He stopped in front of me and with a fat finger, tipped up my chin so I had to look at him.

"Whaddya think, gorgeous?" he asked with a sinister grin. "You think I could get more?"

"You won't get a fucking penny," I said through my teeth. "He's too smart for you, you fucking overgrown toddler."

Messina's eyes darkened, but the nasty grin remained. "Well, then maybe I should just get my money's worth now."

He let my chin drop, and his gaze drifted over my body, hands following familiarly over my shoulders and arms.

"Stop," I croaked, finding a few remnants of strength to shake against his touch. "Stop fucking touching me!"

Messina's sweaty form just leaned closer as his hands took hold of my thighs and wrenched them apart, holding them still against the chair.

"Let me go!" I shrieked into Messina's ear, earning myself yet another slap. Luckily, that hand didn't have any jewelry.

"None of that, now," he said. He laughed, big heaving guffaws that shook his belly, and grinned with an open mouth that revealed multiple fillings. "Don't make me tape that pretty mouth shut too."

He traced a fat finger over my face, giving my cheek another tap on the side that was already hurt. The swift touch sent a river of pain through my cheekbone, still raw from his previous blows. He leered down my loose tank top.

"You're a little skinny for my taste, Red," Messina said as he continued to look me over like I was a brood mare. "But we could still have some fun while we wait for lover boy to show up. Do you think he'll still pay up for damaged goods? Would he want my sloppy seconds?"

Messina squatted down, his belly hanging over his pant buckle as he put himself just below eye level with me. He set his sweaty palms on my knees and started to tug at my jeans.

"Don't fucking touch me!" I shrieked, seizing in my chair.

I wrenched my body around, but it was no use. They had nailed the thing to the floor. My wrists were taped tightly enough that I could barely move and certainly couldn't stop Messina's pork-like fingers from unzipping my loose jeans down to my underwear.

"What do you say, Red?" Messina asked as he eyed the blue lace fabric. "Does the carpet match the drapes?"

I took a deep breath to scream as loudly as I could into his ear, but before I could let it go, the door flew open, and a shadow fell across the room.

"Skylar!"

I jerked my head up and saw Brandon in the doorway, trying his damnedest to muscle his way past the pair of Messina's goons. My stomach dropped. As happy as I was to see him, I wanted nothing more than for him to get the hell out of here as fast as he could. Both of Messina's henchmen looked a little worse for wear, but each had firm grips on Brandon's arms, essentially locking him in the door frame.

"Ah," Messina said as he straightened up. He grinned at me, a foul-mouthed mask of a man. "Too smart, huh? Guess not."

"Get your fuckin' hands off her!" Brandon thundered. He was clearly straining against his captors with every bit of effort he had, causing his face to turn bright red and the veins in both his forehead and his neck to pop visibly.

I had never been so surprised to see anyone. Or more relieved. Or, as I saw Messina reaching around his back and into his waistband, more worried. There was only one thing he would keep there.

"Brandon!" I cried out, suddenly filled with dread. I turned to Messina. "Let him go. Please, you'll get your money, I promise."

With a roar, Brandon managed to knock one of the thugs' heads into the door frame, felling him with a quick blow. He turned to the other, lightning fast, and proceeded to pummel him into the floorboards, exacting six-feet, four inches of corded vengeance until the guy fell next to his partner.

Brandon turned to me and Messina, who was now standing behind me, gun drawn and pointed at my temple. Brandon froze.

A knife tore through the duct tape at my wrists. My arms were free, but with a gun at my head, I still couldn't move.

"Stand up, Red," Messina ordered, yanking me out of the seat and pinning both of my wrists in his ham fist.

I cringed as his fingers dug into the raw wounds. I followed his orders, keeping my eyes glued to Brandon's. Stay there, I willed him with everything I had.

"Let her go," Brandon said as he took one careful step over the still bodies on the floor.

Messina cocked the gun with a loud click.

"You stay right there, Don Juan," he said as he twisted me around the room, moving in an awkward dance with Brandon.

Up a flight of stairs, I could hear voices yelling for us—Brandon's security team, obviously left behind when Brandon had jumped out to find me. Three of them toppled into the room; one even had another gun drawn.

"It's over," Brandon said in a low voice to Messina. He glanced at the felled men. "Let her go, and we'll take you to the police instead of shooting you like the fuckin' dog you are."

His South Boston accent, which usually just came out when he was emotional, was so thick I almost couldn't understand him. "Are" was so flattened that the "r" had completely disappeared.

Messina's hands at my wrists tightened as he steered me toward the door, keeping the barrel of the gun to my head.

"No, I don't think we're done yet," he said, his nervous breath hot on my neck. I swallowed heavily. "Tell your men to get out of the way. Into that room."

Brandon stepped out of my prison, but nodded at his men, who filed inside with dark looks at Messina.

"Shut the door," Messina ordered.

Reluctantly, Brandon followed his orders.

"Please," I whispered.

"Shut it, Red," Messina barked with a wicked twist of my wrists. "Unless you want me to pull the trigger."

Brandon's eyes bulged at the threat, but he stayed where he was.

"Your money is at the drop point," he said. "Pass her to me, and I'll let you go."

"Oh, I think you'll let me go, all right," Messina said as he rotated us all in that same strange dance to the exit. He stopped with his back to the open stairwell. "And if it's not there, you better believe I'll be back. And this time I won't be so nice."

He stroked my cheek, and the muscle in Brandon's neck ticked even more violently.

"Get. The fuck. *Off* me!" I shouted, and with a whoosh of energy I didn't know I had in me, I whirled around and punched Messina straight in the face. The gun went off toward the ceiling, and a shower of plaster fell down on all of us as Brandon yanked me away from Messina and into his arms.

"You fuckin' bitch!" Messina yowled, as he re-cocked the gun and pointed it directly at us.

Brandon shook his head and shoved me behind him.

"Don't," he said. "Otherwise you won't get your money. The only thing stopping my team from shooting their way out of that room is my voice. You shoot, you're dead."

Messina's hand shook as he backed toward the door and weighed his decision. He squinted at us, then turned suddenly, pointed the gun downward, and fired two shots into the temples of his cohorts before turning the gun back on us.

"Witnesses," Messina bit out. ""You follow, *you're* dead. And if you talk or the money ain't there—you're next. The both of yous."

And then he was gone, the sound of his heavy footsteps beating on concrete until he was out of the building.

"Fuck," Brandon breathed as he pulled me close. "Stay here."

He eased me down into another chair, then went to let the security team out of the room before returning. Craig immediately took a look at the men lying on the floor, then gave instructions to the other two to alert the police. But when he turned to help pick me up, Brandon waved him away.

"I got her," he said. "Let's get out of here."

"You came back," I whimpered into his neck, tears starting to flow. "You came for me."

Brandon said nothing, just drew me into his chest. His fingers pressed hard into my shoulder enough to turn his bruised knuckles white. Finally, he started to stand up.

"No," I moaned, trying in vain to keep him with me, but my efforts to hold on only resulted in him sweeping me into his arms, my legs dangling over one elbow.

"Skylar, we have to go to the hospital," he said as he started walking us toward the door.

He carried me up the stairs and into the blinding sunlight and settled me into the back of an SUV that sat in the wide gravel lot with its tires shot through.

"The ambulance will be here in a second," Brandon said as he stroked my hair.

When I finally found the courage to look at him, I found him close to tears himself.

"Your face, baby," he said in a voice that cracked.

He traced his thumb gently over my wounded eye and cheek, but drew it away when I winced. The sound of his voice breaking and the watery texture of his bright blue eyes brought more tears to mine.

"Brandon," I breathed.

It took him less than a second to gather me into his arms again, pulling me into the crook of his shoulder while we both released our emotions—me in great, noisy sobs, him in long, silent streams down his chiseled cheeks.

"How did you find me?" I hiccuped into his chest.

His hand grasped the back of my head, holding me tight. I burrowed further in.

"The picture from your phone," Brandon breathed. "He was using a burner phone that couldn't be located before that. But Craig traced the IP address of your phone. Stupid fuck didn't know you can do that with a picture."

"What about the money? Jesus, Brandon, twenty-five million dollars..." The staggering ransom choked in my throat.

"Fake," Brandon said as he pressed his mouth into my hair. "All of it. But even if it wasn't, you would be worth it. I'd pay anything just to...God, Skylar, I'm so sorry. You wouldn't be here if I hadn't..."

I shook my head viciously into his shoulder.

12

"No," I protested. "You have *nothing* to be sorry for. Brandon, I should have told you about everything, so, so long ago. I'm...God, I ruined everything!"

Brandon just gathered me even closer, stroking my hair from scalp to tip, hushing me over and over again until we had each reclaimed our cool.

"Shh," he crooned against the crown of my head. "I'm just glad...I got here in time. You're safe now, baby. You're safe."

"But, Brandon—"

"I love you," he interrupted. "That's all that matters now. That's it."

The wail of sirens could be heard approaching in the near distance. In another minute, a squad car, followed by an ambulance, pulled to a stop in front of the SUV. I was placed on a gurney and transferred to the back of the ambulance. Brandon sat beside me, holding my hand the entire time while his team gave their statements to the police. There was no more time to have the conversation I knew we'd need to have eventually. But he was right. We loved each other, and that was all that mattered right now.

Two

Beep. Beep. Beep.

A heart-rate monitor will drill into your brain when you're asleep, did you know that? Especially after you've sustained multiple head injuries.

Beep. Beep.

Ow. Everything hurt. And I mean *everything*.

Beep.

"Fuck."

The word came out like a dagger, sharp and scratchy in my dried-out throat. Ow.

"Hey there, chickie."

Slowly, I blinked my eyes open. Everything was blurry, and for a while, all I could see was something that strongly resembled a fuzzy black stick of cotton candy. Eventually my eyes focused, and there was Jane, my best friend, her short hair a shock of black against the white hospital walls.

She smiled and touched her cat-eyed glasses. "What's going on, slugger?"

I didn't say anything, just grunted. "Slugger?"

"Oh, we heard all about how you decked that guy. Brandon is *very* proud. I didn't know you had such a mean right hook."

I grunted again at the memory. My hand ached, along with just about every other part of my body. "I don't."

A chair leg screeched across the floor. Jane sat down next to me and picked up my bruised hand. I let her, but fumbled around the side of the bed with my other hand.

"You want to sit up?" Jane asked. "Hold on. They have a remote that, I swear to God, is made for someone with fingers the size of my hands."

She handed me the admittedly oversized controller that was attached to the bed with a cord. I pushed the incline so I was sitting up again.

I looked around. The room was empty except for the two of us, although a bustle of nurses paced the hallway.

14

"He went home to change," Jane said at my unspoken question. "He'll be back in a few."

"B-Brandon?" The words caught in my throat, strange and sticky, as if they hadn't been used in a very long time.

Jane gave me a small smile and patted me lightly on the arm. "That man hasn't left this room in three days, or so the nurses tell me. I made him go take a shower so he wouldn't force you back into a coma from his stink."

"C-coma?"

My eyes popped open, and I struggled to sit up completely, only to realize that there were several IV needles and wires attached to my body.

"Whoa, whoa, girl." Jane placed a hand on my chest and pressed me gently back into the mattress. "Don't make me talk to you like I'm some kind of horse whisperer. You're fine. Let's not tear the place apart just because someone said the C-word."

I chuckled, but it came out like a wheeze. The actions made my jaw hurt. I reached up gingerly to touch the sensitive skin where I'd been hit over and over again.

"Yeah," Jane said, her eyes following my fingers. "You sort of had a double-whammy there. Mafioso Shithead really fucked up your face. Cracked cheekbone plus a nasty gash. You'd make a good zombie."

"Why?" I croaked. Any more than one word hurt.

Jane folded her hands together over her knees.

"Well," she said frankly. "You got the shit beat out of you, kid. Luckily, nothing was surgery-worthy, but the doc said you sustained some brain swelling from a head injury, which was bad enough that you essentially ended up in a mini-coma to heal. Plus, you have a couple of cracked ribs, a nasty sprained ankle, and a whole mess of cuts and contusions on your face. Basically, it's like you fell down a flight stairs." She looked up sharply. "Dude. Did that fucker throw you down a flight of stairs?"

I cringed, which only made my jaw hurt more. Touching it gingerly, I wondered if I had a few loose teeth in there.

"Don't answer that," Jane said quickly. "At least, not until the police get here to take your statement."

We were interrupted by a nurse dressed in scrubs covered with multi-colored ice cream cones. He carried a chart and smiled when he saw that I was awake.

"Well, look who decided to join the living?" he said in a thick Caribbean accent. "How you doing, girlfriend?"

I gave a weak smile, and the nurse smiled back, moving around to take my vitals.

"My name is Henri, your nurse until about three o'clock today. And where is that handsome fella been living here the last three days?"

I glanced at Jane.

"He'll be back," she said, more to me than to the nurse.

I nodded while Henri continued to take my oxygen levels, blood pressure, and whatever else the charts at the end of the bed told him to do.

"Yes, yes, you're looking good for someone who's been dead to the world for seventy-two hours," he said with another bright smile. "I'll just let Dr. Gibbons know you're up and about. Can I get you anything? Maybe ice for that throat? You must have a mean case of dry mouth."

Gratefully, I nodded. Several minutes and five ice chips later, I finally felt like I could speak without cracking my throat in half.

"What happened?" I asked Jane. "What are you doing here? Why aren't you in Chicago?"

She gave me a look like I was insane. "You didn't really think I would go back to Chicago when my best friend's been kidnapped and hospitalized, did you?" She shrugged. "The SA likes me. Gave me an extra week before I start—unpaid emergency leave, of course, but I'll take it."

Her words brought back the chain of events in sudden, sensory patches. The sheath of my blue silk dress. The sparkle of the necklace I'd given back to Brandon. His face, long and heartbroken as he'd discovered I'd had an abortion and hidden it from him. The long fingers of my mother, trailing the edge of a bathroom sink while she'd tried to blackmail me with the information. The smirking lips of Miranda, his ex-wife, and Jared, my once-friend, as they'd told Brandon anyway.

The stink of the city streets as I'd wandered home. The sweat staining Victor Messina's collar. The rubbery feel of his fingers at my waist. The taut muscles in Brandon's neck when he'd somehow rescued me.

He'd come for me. And he wasn't hurt. The realization caused my chest to deflate with relief.

But where was he?

I clutched my head in my hands, suddenly overwhelmed by everything. Jane put a sympathetic hand on my shoulder and rubbed.

"Take it easy," she said. "Maybe eat some of that ice cream, since you seriously look like death. You'll be able to manage all of this, especially with my rapier wit to guide you."

I snorted, but took the ice cream Henri had brought. She was right, of course. An empty stomach didn't make anything better.

I heard the voice down the hall before I actually saw him.

"She's up?"

Closing my eyes, the cold vanilla still on my tongue, I listened to the sound of Brandon pestering the doctor.

"I want her moved to the VIP wing as soon as possible. Cost isn't an issue. She shouldn't be in a public room like this; there's too much of a security risk."

Mmmm. Bossy Brandon. Hot Brandon.

Jane snorted, and my eyes popped open.

"Well, now I really know you're not dead," she said with a shake of her head. She waved a finger over her face. "Everything, babe. I can see it all."

I flushed and dove back into my ice cream. I heard the murmur of someone's—the nurse's? The doctor's?—responses, but I couldn't understand what they were saying.

"Oh," Brandon's voice replied. "I see. Well...that's just great."

As if my brain was programmed to isolate his movements apart from the rest of the din, I listened to the sound of his footsteps, big and sure, making their way over hard tile toward the room. When he popped inside, it was like the sun entered. A tall, forlorn, extremely tired-looking sun.

His blond hair was still slightly damp from a shower, curling more than usual around his brow and at the top of his shirt collar. Even though it was the middle of the week (a Tuesday? Wednesday? I wasn't sure), he was dressed casually in a pair of comfortable black joggers, a faded Harvard Law T-shirt that clung to his broad shoulders, and his favorite old Red Sox hat, the brim curled and

17

frayed over his face. He hadn't bothered to shave, and had about three days of dark blond growth covering his square jaw.

Our eyes met, and I couldn't move. The ice cream dripped off its spoon onto my wrist until Jane took it from me and set it down on the tray. She glanced between the two of us, then stood up.

"I'll just go track down your fam, Sky," she said. "Unless you want me to..."

"No," I said, still locked in a game of owl with the exhausted blond giant in my doorway. "It's fine."

With another brief glance at me, Jane slipped out. As she slid between Brandon and the door frame, she muttered, "Be nice," and left.

Brandon swallowed, the movement rippling through the tensed muscles in his neck.

"Hi," I said meekly.

I pushed the rotating tray to the side and grabbed for the blankets over my legs, clutching them in my hands. I didn't know what to say. He was here. He had apparently *been* here the entire time. And yet, other than the few words we'd shared before the ambulance arrived, the last meaningful conversation we'd had was when he'd discovered that I'd not only aborted our child three months ago, but I'd also hidden it from him. He'd told me to leave. And I had, thinking I had lost him for good.

But now he was here. And he had said we loved each other. So, where did that leave us?

Brandon walked silently into the room and took Jane's seat. I would have been encouraged that he had sat down next to me, but it was the only chair in the room.

"You look tired," I said lamely.

Brandon gave me a dark blue look that basically said, "No shit, Sherlock."

I gave a small smile. It wasn't returned either, but Brandon's mouth twitched a little at the corners. He turned his Red Sox hat backwards and rubbed both hands over his face.

"I am," he said finally and sighed, long and hard. "Today I feel a lot older than thirty-seven, Red. But I'm glad you're awake again."

"I'm sorry," I said in a small voice, but with a heavy heart.

"You're *sorry*?" Brandon's voice was incredulous. "*You're* sorry?" His eyes turned to me, wet and wide. "Look at you, baby."

18

I reached up gingerly to touch my face, unsure exactly what he was talking about. I winced a little when I pressed on my cracked cheekbone. I figured there was probably some bruising along with the cut on my eye. But still, I could open both eyes again, so it couldn't be as bad as before.

"Got a mirror?" I asked.

Brandon rubbed the back of his neck, like he didn't want to answer the question. Reluctantly, he reached to his pocket and pulled out his cell phone, then turned it to the selfie camera and handed it to me.

My breath choked in my throat again as I saw what he saw.

It wasn't pretty. I wasn't bloody anymore, and the nasty cut on my eyebrow had been sewn up, leaving only a thin red line. When Brandon had picked me up, my face had been swollen with a nasty black eye and a gash, but now it was a mess of multi-colored bruises in various stages of healing. Shades of purple, blue, black, yellow, and orange colored my freckled skin in a nasty mosaic that spread down my neck and shoulders too. The worst were still dark purple—over my right eye and cheekbone. I touched the area again, wondering where the crack was.

I didn't even want to look at the rest of my body. My ribs, where I had been kicked. My thighs, which had been wrenched apart. The ankle that was still sore after Messina had dragged me into his car and into that dank room. Thank God Brandon had arrived when he did, because the thought of what would have happened otherwise took my breath away.

"It's not that bad," I said weakly as I handed back his phone.

"Not that bad?"

"What are you, a parrot? Stop copying everything I say."

At that, Brandon barked out a harsh laugh and wiped the tears out of his eyes. "Christ," he said through a few more chuckles. "Fuckin' parrot. Well, at least I know you're still you, Red."

The nickname was heartening. Maybe there was a silver lining to the shape I was in. If taking a beating would mean I had a chance to earn back Brandon's heart, I'd take it ten times over again.

"Brandon," I said, surprised by how creaky my voice became.

He looked up, blue eyes deep, oceanic. The crinkles at the corners were more pronounced than usual, and there were deep shadows underneath them.

"I *am* sorry," I said softly. "For...you know."

His eyes grew even wider, so deep I thought I could dive into them. They started to water again at the end of our stare-off, when finally Brandon broke away with a quick swipe.

"Yeah," he said. "Well."

"Brandon, I—"

"I don't want to talk about it right now," he said, suddenly interested in the wood grain of the chair arm.

"Brandon—"

"Skylar. Not now, all right?"

I opened my mouth, then closed it again. Even though I was encouraged by the fact that he was even here, I wasn't sure what we were doing, and it killed me. It hadn't escaped me that he had scooted the chair back to the wall, keeping a solid three feet between us. I was dying for his touch, but right now, I didn't have the right to ask for it, even in my condition.

"You can go if you want," I said quietly, working the blankets in between my hands. The thought was painful, but I didn't want him here out of obligation. "Jane and my family are here. You...you don't have to stay if you don't want to."

In return, all I got was another very dark blue look.

"Red?"

I bit my lip, then let it go when I hit the swollen edge of a bruise. I winced. "Yeah?"

"Don't do that. Don't push me away."

Before I could reply, the clamor of my grandmother's voice rang down the hall.

"How is she?" Bubbe demanded of Henri as she followed him and the doctor into the room, Jane and my dad shuffling behind her. "When will she come home? Does she know who she is? She doesn't have amnesia, does she?"

Bubbe shot to my side when she saw I was awake.

"Skylar," she demanded. "Do you know your name?"

I frowned. "You just said my name, Bubbe."

Bubbe screwed her face up tightly, then relaxed. "That was too easy. Tell me, what day is it?"

I shrugged. "I've been asleep for three days and was held captive in a room with no windows. How would I know?"

Bubbe threw her hands up as she turned to the doctor. "You see! What else could she have forgotten? *Oy*, my heart!"

"Skylar seems to be doing just fine, Mrs. Crosby," the doctor replied calmly as she glanced over my chart. "Would you mind moving a bit so that I can take a look?"

"Here, Mrs. Crosby." Brandon jumped out of his seat and hovered in the doorway.

Bubbe patted him familiarly on the cheek, and I didn't miss Brandon's shy smile as she sat down. Dad nodded at Brandon, but moved to the back of the room, taking his usual place as a wallflower. With a sharp look at Brandon, Jane elbowed her way to stand next to me. Brandon watched her closely. Was that jealousy in his eyes?

"Skylar," the doctor said. "My name is Dr. Gibbons. I'm the neuro attending on-call tonight, and I was here when you were brought in. Do you remember anything about that night?"

I shook my head. Dr. Gibbons smiled warmly.

"I'm not surprised," she said. "You were pretty out of it when your boyfriend brought you in."

I glanced sharply at Brandon, who looked studiously at the floor.

"Um, yeah," I said. "How long...how long have I been out? Someone said I was in a coma for three days?"

Dr. Gibbons smiled kindly. "Not a coma, really. More like restorative sleep. You've actually come in and out of consciousness a few times, and your brain has responded to basic stimulants. Some patients experience extended sleep for a day or so after suffering a nasty concussion."

I blinked. Concussion. Right. That was why things still felt so foggy.

Dr. Gibbons glanced around the room. "I hate to kick everyone out, but we need to do an exam to make sure everything is working right in there. One person can stay if you'd like."

Jane reached down for my hand and squeezed, but surprisingly, Brandon pulled off his hat and stepped forward.

"I'd like to stay, if you're okay with it." Brandon's voice was low, and he focused on the brim of his hat, clutched in his large hands.

Beside me, Jane tensed. Bubbe and Dad glanced between Brandon and me, clearly lost on the tension between us.

I swallowed. "Are you—are we—are you going to..."

I couldn't quite ask if he was going to leave me afterward. I wasn't sure I could bear his support now if I was only going to lose it as soon as I was well enough to leave the hospital.

Brandon didn't say anything, but met my gaze, his eyes dark, pain-riddled sapphires. I swallowed again and looked at the doctor.

"He can stay," I mumbled.

Jane squeezed my hand and followed my dad and Bubbe out of the room. Brandon pulled the heavy hospital chair next to the bed and sat down to witness the doctor's exam with me.

It didn't take long. A few checks of my reflexes, a light shined in my eyes. When she scratched a fingernail down the bottom of my foot, I winced, but the doctor nodded approvingly. Immediately, I felt my left hand captured by Brandon's and squeezed lightly. The calming effect was immediate, and my heart rate slowed.

"Well, you're looking pretty good, kiddo," said Dr. Gibbons. "Especially for someone who had the stuffing beaten out of her." She stood at the end of the bed and marked a few things off on my chart. "Your dad said you're a lawyer?"

"I—" The words clogged in my throat. "I just took the bar. I was supposed to start my job on Monday."

Shit. Did Kieran know what had happened? Was I still going to have my job at Kiefer Knightly?

Brandon squeezed my hand again.

"You're fine," he murmured. "I talked to Kieran."

I relaxed and listened to Dr. Gibbons as she rattled down the laundry list of everything that Messina had done.

"As assaults go, I've definitely seen worse," she said. "The bruising looks scarier than it really is. You've got a bunch of contusions that will fade within a week or so. A couple of cracked ribs and the fracture in your cheekbone, but there's nothing to be done about those besides rest and no contact sports. You'll have to hold off on that UFC championship until next year."

The doctor chuckled at her own joke. Beside me, Brandon huffed. Great. We got a comedian here.

"We were a little worried since you were out for so long, but honestly, sometimes that's just the body's way of insisting on its own healing process." Dr. Gibbons shrugged. "It's sort of a mystery sometimes why it does what it does. But we'll want to do a CT scan before you leave just to make sure there's no brain bleeding or anything like that. Of course, the fact that you're awake and seem to have most of your memory is a great sign."

I just stared at her. It wasn't the slightest bit comforting to hear that they weren't totally sure I was going to be okay.

Beside me, Brandon spoke up. "What about her ankle?"

My head swiveled down to my feet, suddenly recalling the way Messina had tossed me into the back of the van. I didn't feel anything right now. The IV sticking into my arm caught my eye. *Ah, pain meds*.

The doctor nodded. "Honestly, that's the worst of it. It's a decent sprain, Ms. Crosby. You'll need to stay off it for about two weeks. But really, the more you can move it, the better." She rattled off a few physical therapy moves I could do at home.

"How—" I cleared my throat, which was still scratchy. "How long do you think I'll be off work?"

The doctor frowned. "It's hard to say. I'd like to get the results back from your CT scan first, and then we'll go from there. But if nothing shows up, I'd probably suggest a week or so, given the severity of the rest of your injuries. At minimum, you sustained a nasty concussion, so jumping into a brain-heavy job like a being a new lawyer probably isn't going to help you heal. You need rest. Do you have a good place to go for that? Where someone can take care of you?"

I froze. The gravity of what had just happened suddenly hit me: I had been kidnapped by a thug. From my apartment. A man who also knew where my father and grandmother lived. Who would undoubtedly be angry when he discovered the ransom left for him was a trap. I shrank back into my pillow.

"She does. She'll be staying with me."

I blinked over to Brandon. He gave my hand a brief squeeze, and then let go. *What?* My brain wasn't working fast enough to respond. My eyelids started to droop. Already I was feeling tired again.

The doctor nodded. "Good," she said. "That's good. Well, an attendant will be by shortly to take you down to Radiology. Meanwhile, someone from the local precinct will come take your statement."

"What?" I look up to the doctor, who just smiled sympathetically.

"Matthew Zola was here," Brandon murmured. "I've already given my statement, but they need yours too."

I relaxed a bit at that. Zola, the assistant Brooklyn D.A. assigned to the case against Messina, was someone with whom I was friendly. We hadn't spoken since I'd moved back to Boston at the end of May, but I knew he was hoping my family would testify in a potential trial. So far, my father had resisted, worried about the level of protection the D.A. would be able to give him and Bubbe, but also resisting the obvious move out of New York that would happen if they had to go into protective custody.

However, three weeks ago, Bubbe had agreed to help me get Dad out of Brooklyn. Was that even happening now? Would she agree to come too, now that she knew our entire family were targets, not just her son? Brandon was sitting beside me, but I still had no idea where we stood. Was he still planning to help?

The question swirled in my head, making me feel dizzy. I pressed a hand to my forehead and grabbed for the cup of melted ice chips. Brandon watched with obvious concern.

"You okay?" he asked.

"Tired," I said automatically, and then realized it was very, very true.

Brandon's gaze flickered over me, then he turned to the doctor. "Is that normal? She just woke up."

Dr. Gibbons tucked the clipboard back into the holder at the end of the bed. "Perfectly normal. She's been through a trauma, and her body will need extra rest. They'll wake her again for the CT, but I'd say it's just fine if she wants to catnap."

I sank further into the pillow with welcome relief. Everything was so overwhelming. Sleep felt like solace.

"It's okay," Brandon was saying beside me. "Rest. I'll be here when you wake up."

Three

I woke again to voices, several of them, all speaking loudly over my body. I lay in the dark, eyes shut, while they slowly separated through the fog of pain relievers and head injury.

"Honestly, Cory, I don't even know what you're doing here. Just tell the donors that I'm caught up with a family affair. They'll understand."

"Exactly, boss. A *family* affair. This girl isn't your family. You're throwing away your political future over a good time."

"Cory, I swear to God, you need to stop right there."

After the CT, the hospital had wanted to keep me another day for observation, and I had slept for most of it. They had been weaning me off the Percocet to see if I would be more alert when I woke up next. My ankle throbbed. The shrill voice of Cory Stewart, Brandon's campaign manager, general pessimist, and one of the people I liked least in the world, lanced through my head like an arrow. Oh, I was definitely alert. And hungry. And really fucking grumpy.

My eyes opened, and I saw Brandon sitting stalk-straight in the hospital chair, still wearing the same T-shirt and baseball hat as before. His stubble was almost a full-on beard at this point, and I smiled a little, wishing I could run my fingers through it. I'd never seen him with a full beard. He looked hot. A little bit savage.

Cory stood at the end of my bed, arms crossed in a plain gray suit. His sharp, beady eyes found me looking at him, and the snide expression morphed to outright dislike. The man was a genius at maneuvering other people through public relations nightmares, but I hadn't seen any indication that he had the slightest bit of people skills himself.

"You can ask her yourself," Cory said with a nod. "She's finally awake."

Brandon swiveled toward me, and his gaze softened. He offered me a half-smile, but made no move to touch me.

"Hey," he said. "You're up."

"Ask me what?" I struggled to sit up. Wow, I was weak. I clutched the hospital gown to my neck. I had no desire for Cory's judgmental stare to evaluate my bruised body.

"Nothing," Brandon said with another sharp look at Cory. "It's nothing for you to worry about."

"Oh, right," Cory retorted. "I forgot, I'm just the fuckin' campaign manager here. And that optics doesn't mean shit in politics. Excuse me, what fuckin' alternate universe are we living in, man?"

"Cory! I said, *can it.*"

Brandon gave his manager the kind of look that would have turned anyone else to stone. I had seen that look before. It was terrifying. Cory shrank away from the bed, but managed to keep his ground.

"Fine," he said. "Just fuckin' *fine.* I'll cancel the appearance tonight, but next week, you *are* getting back out there. Otherwise you have to find yourself a different campaign manager, because *I* don't waste my time with half-assed projects." His gaze darted back to me with only slightly masked contempt. "Sorry about getting kidnapped. Hope you feel better soon." Then he left.

Brandon sighed and turned to me with a sheepish, but guarded expression. He pulled off his hat, revealing a head full of messy blond waves that badly needed to be combed. I was dying to run my fingers through them.

"Sorry about that," he said. "Cory's an asshole. But he's just trying to do his job, and I'm making it difficult for him." He gave me a rueful look. "Can I get you anything?" He nodded at a covered tray next to the bed. "They brought breakfast, but you were asleep."

My stomach growled. I had been subsisting on IV fluids for days. I was starving.

"What time is it?" I asked as I pulled the tray in front of me. I removed the lid. Cold pancakes, but not terrible, as far as hospital food goes.

"About ten. You've been asleep since yesterday afternoon."

I paused, mid-bite of pancake, and looked Brandon over. "Have you been here the entire time?"

He sighed, but didn't answer, just folded his hands together and stared out the window.

26

I chewed my pancake and took a sip of orange juice. "So, what was that about? He thinks you need to leave?"

Brandon perched his chin on his clasped palms and nodded. "You don't need to worry about what Cory thinks."

"Cory hates my guts."

Brandon's strong features softened. "He doesn't hate your guts."

"He thinks I'm going to kill your campaign. Same thing. And he's probably right."

Brandon sighed and rubbed his face with both hands. He still looked incredibly tired, as one would after sleeping for three nights in a hospital chair.

"Cory," he said finally, "isn't the boss of me. Neither are you, for that matter."

An uncomfortable silence passed between us. I took a few more sawdust-filled bites of pancake, then pushed the tray away after I took the edge off my hunger. Brandon looked at the mostly-full plate critically.

"That's it?" he asked. "That's all you're going to eat after three days?"

I just glared. "Why do you even care?"

Brandon's jaw dropped. "Are you *kidding* me?"

I opened my mouth to snap back at him, but was interrupted with the entrance of another few people: Dad, Bubbe, and Matthew Zola.

"Oh, there she is! My sleeping beauty is awake again!"

I ventured a smile at Bubbe, even though the movement pulled slightly at the stitches over my eye.

"Hey, Pips," Dad said softly as he leaned down to kiss me on the head. "Glad to see you're up and about." He glanced at the pancakes. "And eating something. It ain't Junior's, though, is it?"

I chuckled with him, but Brandon rolled his eyes.

"Maybe you need to bring something from the house, Sarah," he said to Bubbe as he stood up. "She needs to eat more than a few bites of pancake."

I quirked an eyebrow at the sudden use of Bubbe's first name. Apparently, they'd been getting much more familiar with each other.

Bubbe nodded from the end of the bed. "Blintz. I'll bring blintz." She looked up and down Brandon's large form. "You can come help. We'll be back by the time they're done here."

She turned to leave the room again, giving Brandon no choice but to follow. He clapped his hat back on, but before leaving, glanced at the tray and back at me.

"*Eat*," he mouthed.

I stuck my tongue out. His lips twitched, and then he left.

Zola pulled the doctor's stool over to one side of the bed while Dad sat in the newly vacated chair. He was the same as I remembered—the same shock of thick black hair, lean form, friendly smile. At one point, I'd thought there might be something between us, but it had been clear from the start that Zola and I were only supposed to be friends. And right now, I was glad to have a friend like him in my pocket.

"Hey there," Zola said. "You look..."

"Like shit," I supplied with a weak grin.

He just nodded, and pulled a pad of paper out of his messenger bag. "I was gonna say better than before, but yours works too." He clicked his tongue a bit and shook his head. "I'm so sorry, Skylar. We've been watching them for a while, but we haven't been able to get an arrest warrant without sworn statements from any witnesses. Now Messina's gone underground—we think to New Jersey—and the NYPD doesn't have the jurisdiction to cross state lines."

I grimaced. "It's not your fault."

"No, it's mine."

Zola and I turned to my dad, who was gripping the sheets on the other side of my bed, tightly with his right hand, but not so tightly with the left. His crippled grasp was the result of a similar beating he'd suffered last spring at the hands of Victor Messina. He looked to me, his gray eyes reddened and wet.

"It's my fault you're here, Pips," he said with a cracked voice. "If I hadn't been such a lousy, no-good, goddamn gamblin' loser, we'd none of us be here right now. Not Brandon, not Matthew here. And my baby girl wouldn't have been beaten within an inch of her life and in a goddamn coma."

"Dad, it wasn't really a coma—" I started, but he swiped away the words with his bad hand.

"No, Pips," he said, and then turned to Zola. "I'm done bein' a coward. I could've made it easier for you to arrest the bastard last spring if I'd've testified, isn't that right?"

Zola glanced briefly at me, then nodded. "The police would have had grounds, yes."

Dad sighed. "And then Victor could be locked up right now, huh?"

"Well," Zola said, "I don't know if things would have moved that fast, but..."

"That's it, then. I'm ready to testify, or whatever you need to do to put that piece of shit behind bars. He hurt my daughter. I ain't nothin' if I can't stand up for that."

Zola and I sat there for a moment. Then I nodded slowly, and turned to the handsome young prosecutor.

"Me too," I said as I reached out to take Dad's hand. "We'll do it together. But first, let's talk immunity."

Zola looked at me with some respect, then back to my dad. "Look, Danny," he said frankly. "I'm not gonna sugarcoat it for you. If you've got the dirt you say you do, you're involved in some pretty serious shit here. The D.A. might be interested in prosecuting you for aiding and abetting, especially if this fails to inculpate."

Beside me, Dad gulped audibly. I sat up fully with a wince and grabbed for Zola's sleeve.

"Immunity," I said. "Or no statement."

Zola smiled instead. "I had a feeling you'd say that." He looked back at my dad. "Danny, if you agree to testify to this in court and provide the documentation about some of these transactions, we'll grant total immunity from prosecution. To you and your family."

Dad looked like he had just won the lottery. The poor man had clearly come into the conversation thinking it was going to land him in jail. "Really?" he said eagerly.

"We'll need it in writing," I cut in, my inner lawyer turning on before Dad committed himself to anything else.

With a mild smirk, Zola just nodded at me. "Of course," he said. "I just happen to have the papers here."

We spent the next few hours recounting all of the details of Dad's and my experiences with Victor Messina while Zola recorded our statements. Some of Dad's stories were hard to hear. He'd been far more involved with the gangster than I'd realized, accruing and paying off numerous debts to the man and his ilk for most of my life. He'd done an extraordinary job of hiding his addiction for several years until he'd run up a debt he finally couldn't pay off, and we'd all suffered for it.

Zola took detailed notes and recorded both of our statements, occasionally asking a few questions to clarify or make sure we had the details. At the end, he put the recorder in his bag along with his notes and turned to my dad.

"That was...Jesus. There's a lot to verify, but that gives me a lot to work with. Thank you." Zola paused, chewing on his lip for a moment. "But Danny..."

Dad looked up.

"You got a safe place to stay?"

My mouth went dry. You didn't have to be a genius to get the subtext. We weren't safe in Brooklyn anymore—not when Victor Messina and his cronies knew exactly where to find us. But I already knew that.

"I've got it taken care of."

Brandon's voice reverberated through the room as he walked in, arms fully loaded with a giant blueberry-ricotta blintz that would serve the entire hospital floor. He set it down on the counter at the far end and turned to all of us as Bubbe trotted in behind him.

"Danny, my assistant has secured a spot for you at Maple Acres, the rehabilitation program in Natick," he said. "We've got you there under a pseudonym, if you're willing. Plus, I'll have a security detail in the program with you. You'll be completely safe."

I looked to Dad, who just nodded his consent. "I ain't leavin' until I've got this thing under control, Pips," he said with a brief squeeze of my hand. "That's a promise."

Zola looked between me and Bubbe. "Mrs. Crosby, you're a bit late to the party, but your son and granddaughter have decided to testify in the Messina case. It's my recommendation that you leave the Brooklyn area as well."

"I've got her an apartment in my building," Brandon cut in again. He looked sheepishly at Bubbe. "That is, Sarah, if you'd like it. We can find you something else if you'd prefer, but it's in the same building where Skylar will be staying."

I wasn't sure whether I wanted to kiss him or throw my water at him. This was classic Brandon: gifting by stampede. Bubbe, however, didn't seem to mind. She just strode up to him and clasped his cheeks between her manicured hands.

"You," she said fondly, and yanked him down to her short form so she could smack a kiss on both of his flustered cheeks. "Thank you."

Brandon stood back up looking adorably flushed. He rubbed his face a little, but looked pleased.

Bubbe turned to Zola. "It's all settled, as you can see. My Brandon and Skylar are taking care of everything, just like I knew they would."

I didn't miss Brandon's repressed grin when Bubbe referred to him as "her Brandon." Now, if only *I* could make him look like that again...

"Well, that's all I need from you for now," Zola said as he stood up and slung the messenger bag over his shoulder. "I'll be in touch about any progress on the trial, and if Messina is arrested."

He turned, but was met by Jane walking into the room with an overnight bag, presumably full of clothes for me.

"Hey, Sky, you really didn't have much at your grandma's house, so I just got—oh!"

Zola was staring at Jane like he'd just been smacked in the face. Immediately, Jane turned bright red, and edged around him like he was made of fire.

"Hi," Zola said. He shuffled his bag to his other side so he could shake her hand. "I'm Matthew, the prosecutor on the Messina case."

"Jane," Jane said, shaking his hand awkwardly. "Best friend."

"I'll, um, be seeing you around, I hope," Zola said awkwardly, suddenly aware of the fact that he was standing with an audience of four other people. He nodded back at me. "I'll see you, Skylar."

I watched Jane curiously as she watched him walk away. Then she turned back to me.

"Well?" she asked. "An attendant's on his way up with the wheelchair, and Brandon's got a freakin' presidential caravan downstairs to get you out of here. What do you say, chick? You ready   to   head   home?"

31

Four

I slept for most of the four-hour drive back to Boston. Brandon had wanted to hire an ambulatory car to transport me back, but I fought it tooth and nail. I had a nasty concussion and a bum ankle, but I wasn't in critical condition anymore, no matter what I looked like. So, while some of Brandon's security team stayed behind to help Bubbe and Dad pack up their things to leave the following day, I laid across the back seat of the Escalade while Brandon rode up front with Craig, his head of security.

Margie, Brandon's assistant, was clearly some kind of wonder woman. I was pretty sure she could run the entire planet if given the right tools. In a few days, she had single-handedly procured my dad a spot in the best rehabilitation program in Boston, rented Bubbe an apartment in the same secure building as Brandon's penthouse, and hired a property manager to make sure the house in Brooklyn was taken care of until Bubbe and Dad decided whether they wanted to rent or sell it.

According to Zola, Messina and his thugs had disappeared underground, somehow aware of the APB out for their arrest. With Dad's and my statements, Zola had enough to put the man and his cronies away for a very long time—if they could catch them in the first place. Until then, all of us would have permanent bodyguards, tracking our every move until the trial was over.

Before, I might have chafed at the suggestion that I needed a bodyguard. But right now, I was thankful for the hulking men who had been assigned to keep me and my family safe. Brandon hadn't allowed us to be alone together since Zola left. I was waiting for the chance to thank him—and to ask him what it meant for the two of us.

I awoke with a start when the front door of the Escalade opened and closed. Everything was dark. We were inside the underground garage of Brandon's building. My ankle throbbed and my head was pounding. The last round of Percocet was wearing off, and I was starting to feel the real effects of my injuries.

As I sat up from the carry-on bag I'd been sleeping on, my door opened. Brandon crouched down and started to reach inside the car, apparently to carry me out. The gesture was warm, but his face looked like ice.

I backed away, scooting farther into the car.

Brandon frowned. In the dim light and under the brim of his hat, his face was cast almost entirely in shadow, but I could still see the lines of his mouth turned downward. "Skylar, what are you doing?"

I glanced around the garage, groggy and unaccountably nervous. Another car had parked besides us—David in the Mercedes, along with the other two members of Brandon's new security team.

"I just..."

I pushed a hand over my face, wincing as I inadvertently touched my wounds. My thoughts were still jumbled and dazed. Jane had braided my hair back into a tight queue before I'd left the hospital, but I still felt like garbage. I found my glasses sitting in the cup holder, and shoved them on. There, that was better. At least now I could see the annoyance on Brandon's handsome features clearly.

"Where are my crutches?" I asked in a small voice.

Brandon bit his lip and cast his gaze up to the ceiling. "Christ," he mumbled. "Skylar...let's just get you upstairs."

"I can walk," I insisted stubbornly, scooting toward the edge of the seat. I thrust my legs outward, forcing Brandon to stand up and step back. I edged my way out of the car and stood up, balanced on my good foot. "See?"

As stone-faced as ever, he just gave a heavy sigh, then nodded at David, who pulled the crutches out of the back of the Mercedes.

"Here you are, Ms. Crosby," David said with a kind smile as he handed them to me.

At least someone doesn't hate me.

"Thanks."

I looked back at Brandon, who had his arms crossed in front of his chest in a way that put his biceps on display. Well, that's unfair.

"Well?" I asked. "Shall we go?"

We started to make our way to the elevator, but in my Percocet-addled daze, I was a lot less coordinated than I thought. It took me about ten steps to trip over the stupid crutches, land on my bad foot, and topple toward the ground. I was swept up by a pair of strong arms while my crutches clattered to the concrete.

"Hey!" I protested, although the feel of Brandon's warm shoulder against my cheek made my insides thrill. That smell was still there: almonds, metal, soap.

"Just stop," Brandon gritted out as he carried me the rest of the way to the elevators. "You're not alone in this. Just let me help you."

"What about my crutches?" I asked lamely, even as I burrowed into his neck.

He tensed at the movement, but held me a little closer. "David will get them."

The elevator opened on the top floor and we stepped into Brandon's apartment. I hadn't realized when he said I was staying with him, that he meant actually with *him*. I had thought he meant somewhere else in the building, although I didn't know why that had been my assumption. Why would he want me here when we were so seriously...broken?

Brandon carried me down the hallway where his bedroom was, but then turned left into a guestroom and deposited me on a large bed. He took a few steps back and flipped on the light.

I looked around. I had seen this room before, of course, on one of the few times I'd poked around the apartment. I actually hated this apartment—a rented palace in the sky where Brandon was living until his divorce was finalized and he could purchase a new house. It was the opposite of everything I knew about him and the kinds of places he loved: cold and modern, with sharp-angled furniture and dark, colorless decor. This room was no different, with stiff glass-and-chrome fixtures, a dark gray bedspread, and ceiling-to-floor picture windows that looked out over Back Bay. It was posh and pristine.

I loathed it.

"Why am I here?" I asked him, glancing around the strange room. I looked back at Brandon, who was watching me carefully. "Why don't I just stay in the same apartment as Bubbe?"

Brandon pulled off his hat and shoved a hand through his hair, which badly needed to be brushed. "I don't really want to discuss it right now. I'd just feel more comfortable if you stayed with me, okay?"

I frowned. "No, it's not okay. Brandon, we need to talk."

Brandon sighed and rubbed a palm over his eyes. "Skylar...can it wait? I'm exhausted. I've been sleeping in a hospital chair for four days. All I want to do is take a shower, have something to eat, and watch the rest of the Sox game knowing that no one I care about is going to die. Can you deal with that?"

I opened my mouth to argue that if he wanted some peace, he'd probably get more if I wasn't staying here. But his eyes, un-shuttered and blue, silenced me.

"Please, Skylar," he asked quietly. "I just need some time, okay?"

Wordlessly, I nodded. Time was something I currently had in spades. Kieran had assured me that I had as much as I needed to recuperate, refusing even to bring over case files for at least another week.

"Want some company while you watch?" I asked hopefully.

But Brandon just shook his head. "I'd like to be alone for a while. Do you need anything? Sarah is going to come up in an hour or so with some dinner."

I tried to ignore the way my heart sank at his words. "No, I'm good."

Brandon looked at me for a moment, then stepped out of the room. "Okay, then. I'll be in my room if you need something."

"Okay."

I grabbed the remote for the TV mounted on the wall, and turned on something mindless. I barely noticed what was on.

Brandon stayed in the doorway for a few more moments, watching me as I worked *very* hard not to look at him. With one more forceful sigh, he left. I listened to one footstep after another as he padded across the carpeted hall. His bedroom door opened with a creak. When it shut, it felt like it shut on my heart.

* * *

A few hours later, after two episodes of *Mad Men* and another short nap, I woke up to voices in the hall. Bubbe had arrived with dinner and was busy flirting with Brandon.

I rolled over, grabbed for my glasses, and switched on the light next to the bed. The room had changed a bit since I'd fallen asleep.

35

Someone had placed a small vase of flowers on the bureau below the TV, and my crutches and two loaded duffel bags were stacked beside the large wall closet, in which every piece of clothing I owned had been hung and color-coordinated. A few other keepsakes had been arranged on the bureau, including a photo of Brandon and me, taken less than a week ago, when we were in France together.

I traced a finger over the frame. It had been taken in Carcassonne, the big medieval castle, just a few minutes before Brandon had asked me to marry him. I hadn't said yes, although a part of me wanted to. I'd said, "not yet." Brandon had me wrapped up in his arms while he pressed a kiss to my cheek; I was grinning from ear to ear. We looked tan, bright, and impossibly happy. I wondered if we might ever be like that again.

I hopped over to grab the crutches and, upon catching a glimpse of myself in the mirrored closet doors, quickly re-braided my hair. I blanched at my rainbow-colored face. It was a far sight from the happy grin in the photo. I was still in the loose black sweats and NYU T-shirt Jane had brought for me to wear, but I wasn't about to go digging through my things just to impress my grandmother. Anyone else out there would just have to deal with my less-than-perfect appearance.

I shuffled into the large, open living space that including multiple sitting areas, a dining area, and a kitchen, bordered on two full sides by the picture windows that looked out over Boston at night. It was beautiful, but the overall effect of the apartment still made me feel like I was inside a very tall icebox, and I knew that Brandon felt the same.

Brandon sat at the breakfast bar in the kitchen while Bubbe bustled around, making herself perfectly at home. The television mounted over the central fireplace played the Red Sox game on low, but no one was watching. Sitting with his chin perched over clasped hands, Brandon conversed easily with my grandmother with a smile on his face and a twinkle in his eye. The sight made my heart warm.

"Oh, *bubbela*, there you are!"

Bubbe caught sight of me from the kitchen, and Brandon swiveled on his stool, all signs of friendliness chilled, like someone had snuffed out a fire. And, of course, that someone was me.

"Hi," I said as I hobbled in.

Slowly, I managed to get myself up on the stool next to Brandon, but he slid away on the pretense of getting a glass of water.

"Well, I brought over spaghetti and meatballs," Bubbe said with a wink at Brandon. "Should last this one another day or two, if he doesn't keep sneaking tastes of my sauce. I make it from scratch, you know."

"It's wicked good," Brandon said as he dipped a finger into the pot for another taste, earning himself a smack on the wrist from Bubbe.

He backed up, dimples out in full while he sucked sauce off his index finger. His gaze met mine with another twinkle, and I couldn't help but grin at him. For a moment, he smiled back, but then, as if he had suddenly remembered that he was upset with me, his face shuttered once more.

Bubbe turned to me with a plate full of pasta and sauce.

"Eat," she ordered. "You look like death, Skylar, and I don't mean like those models who starve themselves. That food in the hospital—terrible!"

"Well, I was asleep for most of the time, so I don't really remember," I said, but as the scent of my grandmother's food reached my nose, my stomach growled hard enough for everyone to hear.

Bubbe just gave me a look that said, "I told you so," and I obediently bent to my plate.

"And for you, mister," she said as she laid another, much larger plate of pasta on the bar next to me. "Sit. Eat. Big man like you needs to keep his stomach full."

"Thanks, Sarah. This looks incredible."

It wasn't like Brandon never had decent food around. Ana, his housekeeper and chef, usually prepared a selection of meals every other day for him to heat up as needed. I'd had Ana's food—she was an excellent chef, probably better than Bubbe. If his mood was any indication, I suspected Brandon liked having Bubbe around more than anything else. Things tasted different when they were made out of love.

"Well, that's all for me," Bubbe said as she untied the small apron from around her trim waist and hung it on a hook next to the refrigerator. It was one of many seventies-style flower patterns she owned. With its bright teal and brown fabric, it was the most colorful thing in the apartment.

"You're not eating with us?" I asked as she brushed nonexistent dust off her slacks and collected her keys from the counter.

"No, I thought I'd give you two a bit of time to...reconnect," she said. "You don't need an old woman poking around your business."

I stifled a snort. Since when did Bubbe not want to poke around other people's business? And why did she think we needed to reconnect? Had Brandon told her what happened?

She just looked pointedly between Brandon and me, clearly noticing the solid three feet between us. I felt the space as well. Brandon had never been able to sit more than a few inches from me before. Normally we were like magnets.

Bubbe patted her hair and came around to give me a kiss on the cheek. "Eat. Rest. Enjoy your man. I'll be back in the morning for breakfast." She leaned into my ear and whispered, "You take care of him, *bubbela*. These last days have hurt him, too."

God.She had no idea—not about the abortion, not any of it.

Wincing, I accepted her kiss and gave her one too. "Thanks, Bubbe. Love you."

She turned to Brandon and beckoned him down to give him the same treatment. "You take care of my *bubbela*," she instructed with a pinch of his cheek. "I'm trusting you."

"You got it, Sarah," he said.

Brandon surprised Bubbe by hugging her close and giving her a loud, smacking kiss on the cheek.

"Ah!" she cried, slapping him on the shoulder. "You devil! A shameless flirt, that's what you are!"

Brandon released her with another grin that made my heart beat faster, then turned to his food. Bubbe headed to the elevators with several more comments about Brandon's devilish ways, and then, as the elevator doors closed around her slight form, was gone, leaving Brandon and me together. Alone.

Brandon sat silently, the sounds of his chewing and the blare of the postgame report filling the room. I tooled around with my pasta, no longer hungry as my stomach tied itself into knots. *Enjoy your man*, she'd said. But was he still my man? How would I know?

Brandon cleared his throat. "Why aren't you eating?"

38

I blinked over to him, then back down at my mostly full plate of pasta. It smelled fantastic, but my gut was too clenched to care.

"I—"

I broke off, unsure of what to say. I turned and hoisted my twisted ankle on the stool between us. Sitting up for too long made it throb.

"Nerves," I said finally, folding my hands in my lap. "I lose my appetite when I'm nervous. When I'm..."

"Guilty?" Brandon set his fork down and turned to face me. He met my gaze with eyes like arrows. "You know, it's funny. I kept wondering this summer why you'd never finish your food. You'd pick at everything, every time we went out. I thought it was just the stress of the bar exam. Maybe having your mother poking around."

I stared down at my plate, twisting the noodles around my fork. "Yeah. Well." I took a deep breath and looked up at him. "I *was* guilty, wasn't I?"

Brandon didn't say anything, just leaned on the counter with one elbow.

I swallowed.

"Why didn't you just tell me?" he asked quietly. "That's what keeps getting me. It's not the fact that you had an abortion, not really. It's that you didn't tell me about any of it. Not the pregnancy. Nothing. You didn't let me in, Skylar."

"I..." I twisted my hands together, trying and failing to find the words I needed to explain. "I was scared. No, that doesn't even cover it. I was terrified."

"Of what?"

I gulped. "I was afraid you wouldn't forgive me," I said. "I knew how much you wanted a family. You're Catholic, nominally anyway. I was afraid you wouldn't be able to move past it."

Brandon stared at me for a moment. Then he snorted.

"You expect me to believe that's all it was? Give me a fuckin' break, Skylar. I'm pro-choice, and you know it. I donate to three different family planning organizations for the express purpose of preventing kids from being born into the kind of shitty home life I had. But that's not the situation here. That would have *never* been the situation between us."

"I know that!" I sputtered. "I know that. But Brandon, consider the situation. You and I were broken up—"

"Yeah, because *you* broke it off!"

He took a deep breath, pulling his temper, which was plainly balanced on a knife-edge, back into check.

"You should have told me," he said with a voice clenched between his teeth. "If that was really what you wanted, you should have at least given me the chance to support you. You should have given me the chance to be your partner through all of it."

"I didn't want you to stay because you had to, like you did with Miranda," I said meekly. "I didn't want to hurt you."

"Bullshit," Brandon barked. "You didn't want to hurt yourself. *That's* what you were scared of."

He wasn't wrong. I had been petrified to tell him. We had spent those two months trying to rebuild the beauty of what we were together. It had all seemed so fragile, and he had seemed so happy. I hadn't wanted to ruin it by dropping another bomb in the middle of the whole thing.

"All I ever wanted was to be with you. Really *be* with you," Brandon continued in a voice that was starting to shake. "Skylar, I wanted to marry you, raise a family with you! "

"I didn't know that at the time!" I cried out. Tears were starting to stream down my cheeks, and I swiped them away. I hiccuped back sobs, but the feeling still wracked through my chest. "Brandon," I said, striving to even my voice. "I didn't know that."

"Come on, Skylar. I asked you to move in with me. I wanted you to share my home. You knew I loved you!"

"I wanted those things too. But I also knew you lied to me," I said bitterly as I pushed my plate away. "I knew you had a wife the entire time we were together. Still do, right? I knew I'd expressly asked you to *stay out of my family's business, and you didn't*! Do you think I'd be sitting here, fresh out of the hospital, if you hadn't gotten involved the way you did?"

I hadn't realized I'd felt that way until the words fell out of my mouth. I felt guilty, yes, over the abortion—guilt didn't even begin to cover the multitudes of emotions that had tortured me over the last few months. But my actions had a relatively limited effect, however heart-breaking. Brandon's had landed me in the hospital, and tossed Bubbe and my dad out of their home. We were refugees now— admittedly well cared-for refugees, but refugees nonetheless— because of his actions too.

So yes, I realized. I was also angry. But still...underneath it all...I just wanted to be us again. If I could forgive him for what he'd done...could he forgive me?

Brandon just sat there, opening and closing his mouth like a fish. His gaze traveled over my body, touching on the places where he knew I'd been hurt. My skin prickled under his gaze—over my ribs, the bruises still around my neck and shoulders, the still-sutured cut on my eyebrow, my swollen ankle propped on the stool.

He closed his eyes, clearly in pain. I wanted to reach out to him, but something beyond my injuries kept me in my seat.

"Why do we keep doing this to each other?" he asked quietly.

I paused. "Doing what?"

"Hurting each other."

It was true. We had hurt each other, so very badly, so many times. But, my conscience argued, it wasn't the same as the kind of hurts we'd both suffered at the hands of others. This wasn't my ex willfully cheating on me, or my mother, who purposefully revealed my secrets or abandoned me. This wasn't Brandon's abusive father or his drug-addicted mother. We might have been dysfunctional, it was true, but we weren't malicious. If anything, our injuries happened because we loved each other too much.

The thought oddly gave me hope. Maybe it was a problem that could be fixed. Maybe we just needed to learn how to love the right way, instead of doing it like we both tended to do: like bulls in a china shop.

But before I could say so, Brandon had pushed off his stool and was walking toward the bedroom hallway.

"Where are you going?"

"To bed. It's late."

I glanced at the big clock in the foyer. It was only nine.

"But...we're talking," I said.

Brandon paused in the hallway entrance, one hand propped wearily on the doorway as his head bowed down. "I think that's enough talking for tonight, don't you?"

"But—"

"Skylar?"

He turned around, and his piercing blue gaze met my green. He looked tired again; his large body sagged with grief and stress...and maybe guilt too. Like he was literally carrying the world on his shoulders.

I bit my lip. His eyes caught the motion. A muscle in his jaw twitched, but then he sighed.

"Let's just...give it a rest for tonight, all right? We'll talk more tomorrow."

Wordlessly, I nodded.

"You need help getting back to your room?"

I glanced at the crutches behind me, then at my plate of pasta, still mostly full on the counter. "No, I think I'll try to eat a little bit more before I go to bed."

Satisfied, Brandon nodded. The idea seemed to make him feel a bit better.

"Okay," he said. "You have a good night, Skylar. I'll see you in the morning."

It was only after he was gone, and I was left alone, spooning the bright red spaghetti sauce and brooding over the fact that we were sleeping separately, that one thing occurred to me. Not once during our entire exchange had he called me anything but my given name. Not baby. Not gorgeous. And not Red.

Five

We didn't get to talk again for a while more. Brandon was gone the next morning well before I woke up around eleven. I heard someone bustling around the kitchen again, and I limped in to find Bubbe tossing pancakes onto a plate.

"Sure you don't want to just stay up here?" I asked as I approached the kitchen.

"Oh, hush, you," Bubbe said as she poured another round of batter. "I have an open invitation to use the code-thing to that elevator. Brandon said. And you know I like my privacy too."

I had to snort. Bubbe treated privacy the same way she did dust bunnies: constantly chasing it away.

In the light of my first day without pain meds, my head was finally starting to feel clear again, enough to notice some substantial changes had been made to the penthouse decor. It was still full of the cold, angular furniture that came with the rental, but a few choice things had been added. Mainly *my* things. The mid-century bureau and desk I'd purchased on consignment had replaced a few of the chrome-and-glass pieces that had been there before. One of the metallic side tables had been replaced by my antique wood one, and several pieces of the modern art prints had been replaced by the Art Nouveau prints I had collected in my room. Together it created a strange mix of my style and the rental furniture. I was oddly and hilariously moved in.

I approached the fireplace, which was now adorned with the various framed photos that used to sit on top of the piano in my room. They were all there: pictures of me and Jane, me with Dad and Bubbe, me and Brandon last winter, when we were first dating.

There were also a few new ones of the two of us from this summer: in Cape Cod with my half-siblings, Annabelle and Christoph, and another one of us in France. I touched a finger to that one.

"I set those up there," Bubbe's voice rang out. She couldn't know how the news drowned my spirits. "Brandon asked me to help put your things away when they arrived this morning. I heard him arranging it with that assistant of his when you were in the hospital.

He was very insistent about it." She continued talking as she wiped the batter off the edge of the bowl. "Kept going on and on about how it needed to be there when you came back."

I turned and looked around at the mishmash of my belongings and his. "You did this just this morning?"

Bubbe nodded while she slid a few pancakes on a plate for me. "He helped, along with that housekeeper of his. But I did most of it. Looks nice, don't you think?"

I glanced back at the photographs. I don't know why I was surprised to find my things here. Brandon was a man of action. And I obviously couldn't go back to Eric's apartment.

"Yeah," I said. "It does."

As I limped over to the breakfast bar, another change caught my eye. At the far side of the room was a black baby grand piano in one of the large open spaces.

"What's that?" I wondered, pointing as I sat down. "Did that come this morning too?"

Bubbe nodded and set my plate in front of me along with a cup of tea. "I told him he could get rid of that thing your mother sent you, good riddance to her." She pretended to spit three times, as if superstitiously warding off evil.

I looked suspiciously at Bubbe. "What did he tell you?"

"It was your friend Jane that filled me in on what that hussy did to you and Brandon," Bubbe said. She set down her spatula and gave me a hard look. "One day, I'd like to know why you didn't talk to me about everything yourself, missy, since you and I both know I was already very aware of the baby. But we'll let that rest for another day."

I stared down at my plate, feeling guilty all over again. Of course she knew. And in a way, I was glad she did. There was nothing worse than keeping secrets from the people I loved.

"I-I'm sorry, Bubbe. It was...the last several months haven't been my best."

"Well..." Bubbe trailed off, her small, birdlike form stilling for a moment. "I won't say you didn't make mistakes, *bubbela*," she said finally. "But your father and I still love you. And I think this man still does too."

I gazed back at the piano, which stood like a shining black beacon in the morning sunlight. Without even looking at it, I knew it would be the best Brandon's money could buy. Anything less wasn't his style. But I wasn't quite ready to think about what it might mean for us, particularly since he was going out of his way to avoid me at the moment. Would he move someone in whom he didn't love anymore? Or was he just doing it to be nice while he figured out what he actually wanted?

I shook my head as my headache returned. Stewing about it wouldn't help. I'd just have to wait until he was ready to talk again.

"Where's the army you're feeding?" I joked as I started in on my breakfast.

"Brandon's housekeeper is very nice, but she doesn't know how to keep enough food in his kitchen," Bubbe said as she poured several more palm-sized discs onto the pan. The sizzle filled the room.

"Ana's been his housekeeper for a few years now," I said. "I'm pretty sure she knows what he likes."

Bubbe just snorted. "Come now, *bubbela*. A man that size eats nothing but the nuts and coffee he has stashed in his cupboards? What does he exist on, air?"

I would have pointed out that there was a lot more than that in Brandon's extremely well-stocked cupboards, but Bubbe kept talking.

"Skylar, did I teach you nothing about manners? That boy is saving our family's life right now. The least I can do is make sure his freezer is full. Besides," Bubbe added with a pat to her hair. "He said he likes my cooking. 'Tastes like home,' he said."

I rolled my eyes, but still smiled at her. "It *does* taste like home, Bubbe."

"I'll pack some for your father too. I'm going for visiting hours tomorrow, and who knows what they're feeding him in there?"

I chewed my pancakes and didn't point out that for the money that place cost, they probably had a five-star chef.

"Dad's been there barely twenty-four hours," I said instead. "Don't you maybe want to wait a little bit? Let him get settled?"

Bubbe scoffed. "Please. What kind of mother would I be if I didn't make sure my son was all right?"

"Um, the kind who doesn't smother her forty-five-year-old son?"

In response, I got the kind of dirty look only my grandmother could provide. So I shoved another large bite of pancake in my mouth and stopped talking.

"So, I assume the iciness between you and Brandon isn't just about your accident," Bubbe remarked while she wiped down the countertop.

I set my fork down on my plate and swallowed. "Yes."

"And from the way he's looking at you, I assume you're not the one who broke the news to him. Jane told us your mother tried to blackmail you, but not whether she succeeded."

I sighed. "She...well, no, it was Maurice, I think. One of them basically sold the information to Brandon's ex-wife, and she was the one who told him, just before he announced his run for office."

Bubbe clicked her tongue and shook her head while she turned off the stove and started cleaning up the counters. "So, his pride's been damaged, as well as his trust. That's quite the mess you made there, *bubbela*."

"Yes," I agreed as I stirred my tea. "I honestly don't know if he's going to forgive me for it."

Bubbe huffed. "Of course he will. Why else would you be here, with all of your things moved in? Why would any of us be here right now?"

I looked up. "Because he feels guilty about his role in the accident. He knows that if Messina hadn't clued in on our connection to Brandon, I wouldn't have been kidnapped. Brandon likes control. And he's too nice to just abandon us, even if he doesn't want anything to do with me anymore."

Bubbe tipped her head from side to side, as if weighing the possibilities.

"Perhaps," she said. "But then why aren't you staying with me, not up here?" She turned back to the counter, talking while she worked. "You know, in my day, a girl in your situation...well, let's just say I know more than one girl who would have gone to that clinic if she could have."

She paused, lost for a moment in some distant memory. Then she looked at me, her wise eyes suddenly full of passion.

"I'm not saying you did or did not do the right thing, *bubbela*. But a baby...is women's work, whether we want it to be or not. We give up so much of ourselves, especially in those first few years.

More than any man will ever know. Brandon can be angry all he wants, but he will never truly understand what he would have asked you to give up in order to keep that child, whether he was in the picture or not. And when I think of it, of all you've given in your life to get where you are..." She trailed off, clicking her tongue loudly. "It would have been a shame. We would have loved that child, but it would have been a shame, nonetheless, to see you become a shadow of yourself when you are on the cusp of such wonderful things."

I wasn't sure I agreed with her, but I said nothing. It was, at least, nice to know that Bubbe didn't hate my decision. I knew she hankered for great-grandchildren and was dying to see me get married, so it was a bit surprising to hear her voice this particular opinion.

I gulped, and she turned away to finish cleaning up. Then she packed up her apron and grabbed for her keys. I cocked my head curiously.

"Bubbe," I said as she walked around to give me a kiss good bye. "Where are you going in such a hurry? You don't know anyone in Boston."

In return, I got another scoff. "*Bubbela*, do you think I've spent seventy-two years on this earth and not learned how to make friends?"

I bit my lip. "Sorry. So where are you headed?"

Bubbe grinned. "What, you think we're the only Jews in Boston? There's a temple around the corner. They have a mah jongg group too."

With a quick kiss to my brow, she popped her purse over her shoulder and headed toward the elevator.

"You think about what you're going to say," she said. "And come up with something good. You and Brandon are too good for each other to lose what you have."

* * *

So I did think. I thought for most of the day while I flipped through the TV and bored myself watching the news and HBO. I thought while I emailed Kieran requesting case files to work from home this week instead of waiting until the next (she refused). I thought while Bubbe returned with a casserole for dinner, and I thought while we ate it together at the breakfast counter, and I thought afterward, when she went back to her apartment on the fourteenth floor and I was alone again in the penthouse.

I thought while I watched the sun fall below the other tall buildings of Boston, while I lay alone on the stiff couch until well past dusk. And I thought some more from my equally isolated bedroom until finally, I fell asleep.

* * *

The room was still black when I lurched awake. I glanced out the picture windows. This was an empty shell of a place, no matter the pictures that were scattered around. Boston twinkled in the black of the night. I checked the clock. Three a.m.

I rubbed a hand across my eyes. My head and ankle hurt, but I didn't want to take any more Percocet. Ibuprofen would hopefully take care of it.

My heart was pounding, as if something had startled me awake. I held a nervous hand to my pulse and listened, but the apartment was still. One of the benefits of living in an ice palace in the sky was the quiet. I'd never lived anywhere so utterly silent my entire life.

Was Brandon home? I didn't know, and I wasn't about to go check. He'd said he needed space, so that's what I would give him until he was ready for me to be close again. I laid my head back down on the pillow and closed my eyes, willing sleep to come again. But then:

"NO! GET THE FUCK OFF!"

Brandon's deep voice reverberated across the hall, followed by a half-scream, half-shout that froze my bones. I shot out of bed as fast as my hobbled ankle would let me, ignoring the pounding in my head at the sudden rush of blood. I hopped across the room, grabbed a crutch off the wall, and limped frantically across the hall, not even knocking before bursting into Brandon's bedroom.

He was corkscrewed around the sheets, sleeping as he usually did in nothing but a pair of black boxer briefs. The sight of him, all lean muscle and sinew cast with moonlit shadows, would have stopped me in awe had he not been covered in sweat and seized in what looked like agony.

Brandon's blue eyes were wide open, but he was clearly asleep, staring through me in abject terror.

"No," he moaned loudly. "Stop! Don't..." His voice drifted lower and into unintelligible babbling, but equally fraught with pain and dread.

My chest ached as I approached his writhing form. What was I supposed to do when people sleepwalked? I couldn't remember. Wake them up? Let them sleep?

But I didn't need to decide, because with one more vicious twist of his big body, Brandon slammed his head into the wooden headboard, waking himself with a howl. I dropped my crutch to the carpet and was on the bed in two more hops.

"Brandon," I said, setting a hand on his shoulder, slick with sweat. "Hey. It's okay. I'm here."

He rubbed a hand on his forehead as his pupils focused. "Fuck. Wha-where?" He looked to me with an expression that was half annoyed, half terrified. "What's happening?"

"You were having a dream. A nightmare, I think."

I scooted closer, so that I was leaning into the stack of pillows against the headboard. He was only sleeping on one side of the bed—the right side, the side he'd adopted when we were together before. My side was practically untouched.

Brandon curled into himself and began to shake, a minor shiver that soon started to vibrate through his whole body.

"F-f-*fuck*," he muttered to himself. "M-make it stop."

He clutched his head, like it hurt. Whatever was going on in his mind hadn't totally disappeared when he woke up. Immediately, I scooted even closer and rubbed a hand up his back, which seemed to calm him. Hesitant at first, he allowed me to pull him against my chest with a strangled groan, and his big arms wrapped around my waist so tightly I could barely breathe myself. His breaths were shallow, stunted.

"Ssshhhh," I crooned, weaving my fingers into his thick curls and stroking over his shoulders.

It seemed to work. The shaking subsided, and his breaths, while still shallow, gradually became longer and longer.

"Skylar," he whispered into my chest.

His arms hugged me tighter; I felt like he was squeezing my heart. Despite the pain shooting through my broken ribs, I knew this was where I belonged. Was he in as much pain as I was, sleeping across the hall from one another, knowing that I'd put that gargantuan space between us? He continued to tremble, and his big body clutched to mine like a buoy in whatever storm he saw.

"Brandon, what can I do?" I asked as I continued to stroke his shoulder, his hair. "Tell me how to help."

"S-s-sing," he stuttered. It was the only word he seemed to be able to get out. "Sing."

Sing?

But I started humming the bars to the first song I could think of: "My Funny Valentine." My voice, wobbly from sleep, cracked at the high reach at the end, but Brandon didn't seem to notice. He just grasped the hem of my T-shirt and listened.

"I got you," I said after, continuing to stroke his hair, repeating the words he'd said to me only a few days before. "I got you."

Eventually, his shaking subsided. The white of the moonlight seemed to fill the room, and the sweat that had covered his body evaporated into the night. Brandon's arms began to relax around my waist, and his head grew heavier and heavier on my chest. His breathing became deeper, and mine did too as I pressed my nose into his hair and inhaled. Almonds. Soap. Brandon.

But just when I thought he was asleep, his arms loosened, and he pulled his hands out from under my back.

"You sang that song with your dad," he mumbled.

I nodded into his hair. "You remembered."

He sat up. His eyes were now clear, and much calmer. Traces of whatever frenzy had been gripping him still flickered, but now he seemed to have regained control.

"I remember everything that night," he said clearly. "It was the night you started to let me in."

I remembered everything too. I remembered the way he had shown up in New York unbidden, escorted me to my dad's jazz club and then walked me back to the house in Brooklyn. The way I'd fought his presence at first, but then how we'd talked and laughed all

50

over the subway and the city streets. The way he's kissed me, slow and soft in the cold outside my family's house. It was the night everything really started between us.

I was just about to hug Brandon, to pronounce my apologies yet again, when he started to pull away.

"It's okay," he said as he slipped off my chest. His fingers lingered a moment on my stomach, but he pulled them back into his chest while he laid on his pillow. "I'm okay now."

"Are you sure?"

My hand crept out to the new space between us. I was dying to pull him close again. A week ago, I wouldn't have given it a second thought. Anyone could see that Brandon needed comfort, and it was killing me not to give it to him.

He shut his eyes as if in pain, but turned onto his back to look up at the ceiling.

"I'll be fine," he said. "They...it won't happen again tonight."

The last word hung off his sentence like a threat. They? Tonight? Just how long had this been going on? I'd just spent two weeks straight in France with the man, and countless other nights in the months before, but he'd never done anything but snore.

"Skylar."

My name broke through my thoughts.

"Yeah?" I whispered.

"Just go."

He turned again onto his side, so that he was facing the windows, his back resolutely to me. It was everything I could do not to scoot next to him and wrap my arms over his big shoulders.

But.

Slowly, quietly, I pulled back the comforter and got out of bed. Brandon didn't move a muscle, barely even breathed while I picked my crutch off the floor and slowly shuffled out of the room. I paused at the doorway to look back.

"I'll be here if you need anything," I said in a small voice. "I— good night."

Brandon said nothing. I closed the door behind me.

Six

The next several days progressed similarly. While my injuries healed, I was alone, spending a few meals a day with Bubbe, but by myself in the empty apartment until night fell and sleep came. After a few days of watching everything on HBO (reading still made my head hurt), I was bored out of my mind.

Brandon was a ghost, leaving around sunrise each day for workouts with his trainer, and returning most nights after I was already asleep. He had one more nightmare, but woke before I could limp into the room. He met me with a look that was a cross between pain and desire, but then shook his head and asked me to leave. It felt like I was tearing myself in half, but I did what he wanted and stayed in my room.

By Friday, when I called Kieran to beg for some work files to be sent over—just to have something to *do*—she had given me another unequivocal "no" on the matter. When I'd argued I could prove I was fine by coming in, she had just snapped that no one needed to scare off clients with a face full of bruises. She had a point. Although the bruising had faded considerably, there were still several purple and yellowing spots, not to mention the angry scar over my eye.

In the end, Kieran agreed to allow me to work from home the following week, and said she'd bring over case files I needed to get started, as well as a laptop to attend meetings remotely. It wasn't the start I wanted to make at my new job, but I was grateful for the flexibility.

Jane had gone back to Chicago once it was clear I was going to be okay and was in the capable hands of Brandon and Bubbe. She had felt guilty that she couldn't stay, but I had insisted she go. There was no reason her career should suffer along with mine. Being a new lawyer was brutal under any conditions.

So it was to my surprise when the elevator rang open Saturday morning, and Jane walked in with a giant bouquet of flowers.

"Hey!" I greeted her from the couch, where I had my foot propped on a pillow. "What are you doing here?"

My best friend grinned as she dropped her messenger bag and the flowers on the foyer table and raced to sit next to me on the couch.

"Hey," she said with a quick embrace. The leather and silver bracelets stacked on her wrist clinked in my ear. Then she pushed me back to get a look at me. "It's my day off. I found a cheap flight. You look good, babe. Better. Less *Night of the Living Dead*. How are you feeling?"

"Better. I'm mostly off crutches, and the stitches fell out, so no more Franken-face."

Jane nodded, then released my shoulders. "Good. Are you off the Percocet? Because I brought mimosas."

She stood up and walked back to retrieve the bag she'd left in the foyer, then went to the kitchen to start making our drinks. I pushed myself up from the couch and limped into the kitchen to join her.

"Where's Richie Rich?" she asked, looking around the apartment.

I shrugged and held up a hand. "Who knows? He doesn't spend much time here these days."

Jane quirked an eyebrow. "What do you mean? Wasn't the point of having you here so he could keep an eye on you?"

I shrugged. "I thought so...but I don't know. He has the security team for that—they have a whole office downstairs that monitors everyone who comes into the building. And he has Bubbe to cook and Ana to clean. He's been avoiding me."

I accepted a drink from Jane, and we went back to the couch to sit down.

"So how's the job?" I asked. I wasn't in a hurry to start talking about Brandon's and my standstill. Sometimes it felt like it was all I ever thought about.

Jane took a long drink of her mimosa, then poured another tot of champagne into the glass.

I watched. "That good, huh?"

She took another long drink, then smacked her lips. "It's...fine. Busy. Interesting. The hours are long enough that I don't have to answer my mother's phone calls."

"But..."

She didn't answer for a moment, then finally shrugged. "I miss it here," she admitted. "There, I said it."

"Just the city?" I wondered suggestively.

A few months ago, Jane and Eric, my other good friend and recent roommate, had restarted the fling they'd had during our first year of law school. I'd watched as it had turned progressively more serious over the summer, to the point where they'd even gone to Brandon's last political event together, the one that had turned so disastrous. Neither of them was willing to admit they were a couple, but it was obvious to me that was exactly what they were.

Jane gave me a dirty look. "Don't start on that." She sighed. "The truth? I'm not just here to see you."

"I see how it is," I teased. "My broken bones are just an excuse for your booty call."

"No, no," Jane said. "It's..." She sighed despondently. "I have to break up with him. Not that there's anything really to break off. But I have to do it."

"Oh." I held my glass and looked at my friend sadly. It had taken her a lot to admit she even liked Eric at all, and that wasn't very long ago. This was a massive step backward. "Can I ask why?"

She pulled off her glasses and rubbed her brow for a moment before replacing them. "Well, there's the distance, for one."

"That never stopped you before."

"I know, but that's when it was just..." Jane trailed off, leaning her head on a pillow. "Now it's different. I actually like him. But Sky, I don't have time for a real relationship, and neither does he. What are we going to do, trade flights between Chicago and Boston while we both work eighty-hour weeks? Where is this going? Is someone going to move and retake the bar all over again? Who's that going to be?"

She shook her head and drank more of her mimosa.

"I just don't see how it's going to work out," she continued. "Long distance is hard enough without all of the other pressures. We're not serious. It's better we break it off now."

I didn't say anything for a bit, just reached out and patted my friend's shoulder. I couldn't exactly argue with her, nor was I in any position to be giving relationship advice at the moment. Not when I couldn't even figure out my own.

"Will you look at us?" Jane said with a half-snort. "What a pair of tools we are. Moping around after a couple of dudes."

"Yeah," I agreed.

"Hey," Jane said sharply as she sat up to refill both of our glasses. "This is the part where you tell me what the hell is going on with Brandon that he would basically abandon you in this condition. That is exactly the opposite of literally everything I know about the man."

I pressed my lips together and hugged a throw pillow to my chest. "Well, you know. You were there when he had that bomb dropped on his lap. I'm not sure what to do. He asked for space, but that was almost a week ago now. I...I'm trying to give it to him, but it's driving me nuts. He's so hurt, that much is obvious, and I don't know what I can do to make it better."

Jane examined me for a moment, rubbing her chin. Then she pushed her bright, red-framed glasses further up her face.

"I'm going to say something you're not going to want to hear," she said as she crossed a thin leg over the other.

I grimaced. Jane's reality checks could be brutal, but they were often what I needed. "Shoot."

"I'm not sure you can come back from something like this, Sky."

At first I wasn't sure if I had heard her correctly. Jane had been Brandon's and my biggest champion, even in the early days when he acted like an ass and tried to buy my affections. But now Jane's face was long, her eyes honest and sad. She didn't want to say it to me; that much was clear.

I stared hard at my hands.

"But..." I stumbled. "Don't you think..."

It was pathetic. I couldn't even finish my own sentences. Angrily, I swiped at a few tears that rose unbidden.

"Don't you think he'll forgive me eventually?" I asked at last.

"Not like this, he won't."

Jane's voice was uncharacteristically sharp. It's not that she wasn't blunt—if anything, her candor was often what got her in trouble with most people. That was something we had in common. But she wasn't heartless, and right now her tone had shifted into frustration.

"Real talk, my friend?" she asked.

With a face that felt like it might crack into pieces, I nodded.

"Right. Skylar, that man has done nothing but love you, done nothing but try to give you the fucking world. And from the beginning, you just kept throwing it back at him."

"But—" I started, but Jane shoved her finger across my lips to stop me.

"Nuh-uh," she said. "Just listen."

My mouth was still held shut, so I just nodded.

"He's not coming back to you this time," Jane said bluntly. "You crossed a line when you did what you did. I'm not talking about the abortion. You were in a shitty place, and you were scared, and you had your reasons for it. I'm talking about the fact that you cut him out of the decision, and the fact that you kept it from him for months. Not days. Not weeks. *Months*. And then he had to find out from his ex-wife? You fucked up majorly, Sky. You know I'm right."

She took her finger from my mouth, and I blew out a long breath I hadn't known I'd been holding. Every word she said was true, but that didn't make it easier to hear. With Bubbe coming around every day, pointing out the nice things Brandon had done for me around the apartment, it was easy to believe that eventually he'd come around. But maybe he was just making it easier for him to leave eventually. Maybe he was just setting things up so he wouldn't feel guilty upon cutting me loose.

"So that's it then," I said to myself after I tipped back the rest of my drink. "It's over."

"Can you just stop the fucking pity party for once?" Jane said as she swiped my glass away from me. "You're not listening to what I'm saying!"

"What am I not hearing?" I choked out. "You're saying we're done!"

"I'm saying you're done if you just sit on your ass and don't *do* anything, Sky!"

I gulped. "What are you talking about?"

Jane rolled her eyes, then cracked her knuckles. "Skylar, think about all the ways Brandon has tried to win you over. The big crazy gifts. Showing up unexpectedly. The flowers, the letters."

"They were...insane," I said. "Those kinds of things don't tell people how much they love you."

"Not for you," Jane countered. "They just weren't the right way to talk to *you*. But this isn't about *you* anymore. It's about him. And right now, *he*'s the one who's hurt, Sky. You want to win him back, maybe it's time for you to start speaking his language, buttercup."

I sat back into the couch, feeling like I'd just been hit over the head.

"His language," I repeated to myself.

"That's right," Jane said. "Time to stop moping and start plotting. Because, my friend, coming back from this fuckup is going to take something *big*."

* * *

We tossed ideas back and forth for the rest of the morning, trying to determine something that would mean as much to Brandon as he wanted his gifts to mean to me. It couldn't be something generic, obviously. His first attempts at wooing me had been entrenched in sleaze—a trip to Paris I'd turned down immediately, a diamond necklace from Tiffany's that I doubted he'd even picked out himself.

But he'd learned soon enough to give from his heart, and it had made all the difference. The bracelet around my wrist was just one example: a simple, hand-pounded cuff with words from a Yeats poem engraved on the inside:

One man loved the pilgrim soul in you.

"What does he want more than anything in the world?" Jane kept asking as she paced the living room in front of me. I would have been pacing with her, but I still couldn't walk for too long on my foot.

We kept circling back to one thing. Family, and the symbols that went along with it. Between his parents and the strange relationship with his foster parents, Brandon had never had a real one, but had wanted one his entire life. It was why, we decided, he was fine with having my nosy grandmother living just a few floors down from him. It was why he had no problem putting my dad through rehab, why he had stuck it out in such a horrendous marriage for as long as he did. And it was why what I had done hurt him so very badly.

Family.

57

So we came up with a list of things I could do that would be out of the ordinary that would give something of that to him. I would begin with the smallest, easiest of them first. And before Jane left, we had a plan in place for Operation Grovel. She was right: I couldn't save my relationship, couldn't win back the love of my life if I didn't put myself out there. And I was done being passive.

Now was time for action. And surprises. Unlike me, Brandon loved surprises.

Unfortunately, waiting for him to come home wouldn't work, since I had no idea what kind of hours he was keeping. So under Jane's supervision, I pulled out my phone and typed out a quick message.

Me: Do u think u will b around for dinner tonight?"

The interminable ellipses hovered at the bottom of the screen for what seemed like forever, but finally, I got a response. *Good.* At least I know he's listening.

Brandon: I don't know. Why?

I paused, then tapped out my response.

Me: I'm making something. Was hoping you'd be here to test it out.

This time the reply was instantaneous.

Brandon: YOU'RE cooking?

I rolled my eyes. Okay, so I wasn't the most domestic person in the world, but that didn't mean I couldn't perform basic tasks in the kitchen. Still, this was part of the point. I'd never done anything remotely domestic for Brandon—never cooked or cleaned, since he had a housekeeper, and whenever we stayed at my place, we always just ate out. It wasn't my strength, and he knew it. Which, hopefully, would make it mean more.

Me: they used to call me julia child back in brooklyn.
Brandon: I'll believe it when I see it.

I grinned. He was joking with me. That was a good sign.

Me: you just wait. I'll blow your socks off. 7 okay?

It took a few more minutes with those infuriating dots, but eventually his response came.

Brandon: See you tonight, Red.

The familiar nickname turned my smirk into a full-on grin. He hadn't called me "Red" once since I'd woken up in the hospital. It was his endearment for me, one that now meant so much more than the color of my hair. In this moment, it was progress.

Except now I needed to figure out how to cook something that would make him call me that again.

* * *

"I can do it! Stop hovering!"

The rest of the afternoon had turned into a battle of the wills between the two stubborn Crosby women while Jane got day drunk on a bottle of wine, presumably to prepare for her impending breakup. After recovering from her shock at my request that she show me how to make Brandon's favorite meal, eggplant Parmesan, Bubbe had jumped into the fray with the authority of a drill sergeant. Jane wasn't much help, basically egging both of us on throughout the afternoon.

"You're doing it wrong, *bubbela*. Let me, let me."

Bubbe elbowed her way in front of me at the kitchen island. For such a small person, she was surprisingly strong. She tried to snatch the round piece of eggplant, dripping with egg wash, out of my hand. I, however, held it high enough that she couldn't reach it.

"Oh, *snap*!" crowed Jane as she poured herself a third glass of wine.

"Skylar!" Bubbe cried with her hands on her hips. "Is this any way to treat your grandmother?"

I just stuck my tongue out at her. This wasn't the first time today she'd played the guilting grandma card. I stepped out of her reach instead of handing it to her. Bubbe continued to follow, and I hobbled around the kitchen, holding a dripping piece of eggplant over a paper towel while Jane giggled into her wine glass.

"This is better than Real Housewives," she commented as she watched the chase. "Seriously. You guys could be the next Kardashians. Irish-Jew edition."

Bubbe huffed, then finally gave up. "That's too much egg, Skylar. If you do it like that, it's going to be mushy. You'll be serving Brandon slugs."

"Slugs!" I cried out with faux horror. "Slugs, I tell you!"

Bubbe just huffed, although I could see her fighting not to smile. "*Bubbela*, really, why don't you just let me make it? I'll have it breaded and fried in a half an hour, and then all you have to do is put it in the oven before he gets here. Easy." She snapped her fingers.

But I shook my head and returned to the shallow bowls of flour and bread crumbs.

"No," I said. "I have to do this myself. It's important."

Bubbe threw her hands up in the air and clicked her tongue in disapproval. "*Oy*, it's your funeral, girl."

She pulled off her apron and surveyed it critically before hanging it up on the hook. I never understood why Bubbe wore aprons to begin with—she never got a thing on them.

"Well, I'm going to leave you to it, since you refuse my help. I don't stay where I'm not wanted," she said after washing her hands in the sink.

"Come on, Bubbe, don't be like that," I said as I dipped the eggplant back into the egg a few times, and then set it into the flour. I held up my goop-covered fingers and wiggled them at her. "You know I love you. Come on, stay. Help the crippled girl make her eggplant slugs."

My grandmother cracked a smile, letting me know she wasn't really that angry.

"No, no, it's fine. You've got Jane to help you, and you know what to do. Just don't overcook them. They need to be crispy." She picked her keys off the counter and patted me fondly on the cheek. "You can tell me how it went in the morning. Call me when you're up. I don't want to disturb anything."

And with a mischievously raised brow that had Jane and I giggling all over again, Bubbe left us to our own devices.

Seven

Two hours and three batches of fried eggplant later, I was sitting alone at the breakfast bar nursing a glass of wine with Sade playing in the background. My finished concoction sat in the oven. It was almost nine o'clock, and I was feeling ridiculous and a little bit drunk, having polished off most of the first bottle of wine by myself.

Jane had helped me do my makeup well enough to cover the remaining bruises over my face and neck. We had chosen an outfit that was both comfortable and sexy, something I knew Brandon liked: a short black sack dress with spaghetti straps and a back that was low enough I had to go without a bra. It showed off the parts of my anatomy Brandon favored: my ass and my legs. Jane had helped me blow out my hair into tousled waves, which we'd clipped back onto one side and allowed to flow down my other shoulder.

So, I felt like I looked as close to the best version of myself as I could considering my injuries. But inside, I was a ball of nerves.

This was ridiculous. He was two hours late and hadn't even bothered to call. So, he'd called me "Red." It was a nickname, probably just used out of habit. Did I really think making him dinner was going to solve everything?

I should just go to my room, I thought. That stupid fucking room, with its stupid fucking walls that felt like they were closing in on me every night. Leave him a plate on the counter and call it a night.

So wrapped up was I in doubt that I barely noticed when the elevator doors rang open at 9:03. But then Brandon's footsteps filled the room, and I couldn't have not looked at him if I tried. He was dressed in a dark blue suit and lavender shirt, with his tie partially undone and his jacket slung over his briefcase. His golden hair was rumpled, and he had just a taste of five o'clock shadow that sent all sorts of very inappropriate thoughts through my head. His blue eyes, though tired, glowed.

"Had a rough day?" I asked.

I swayed a bit on my stool. Several glasses of wine on an empty stomach wasn't doing much for my bodily control.

Brandon practically jumped at the sound, dropping his briefcase in the foyer. He was clearly not expecting me to be sitting there. But when he caught sight of me, his surprise quickly turned heated as he took in my bare shoulders, legs, and back, plus the stiletto heels I'd put on despite the fact that at the moment, I couldn't walk in them to save my life.

"Hey," he said softly, too tired, it seemed, to put up the mask he'd been wearing around me most of the week. "Sorry I'm late. Fundraiser went over. You, um, look nice."

I glanced down at my dress, then back up. "Thanks."

It was a garbage apology. He hadn't tried to call, and we both knew it. This was a test.

The thought angered me, but I shoved it aside, choosing instead to focus on how delicious his forearms looked where they tested the fabric of his rolled-up sleeves.

"You look nice too," I said as I slid off the stool.

I landed on my good foot and stood there for a moment, basking in the interest he couldn't quite mask as he took in my simple outfit, my exposed legs. He hadn't forgiven me—not even close—but it was good to know I could get at least some reaction out of him this way.

Then I tried to take a sultry step forward and fell spectacularly toward him as my bad ankle twisted.

"Jesus!" Brandon yelped as he caught me just before I smacked my face on the hardwood floors.

He swept me up in his arms, but before I had time to enjoy his sweet, masculine scent, he deposited me on the island countertop. He kept his hands on my arms to make sure I was stable.

"What are you thinking with those things?" he asked, nodding at my heels. "You can barely walk without them as it is."

I looked lamely at the shoes, then kicked them off. They clattered onto the floor, leaving me barefoot, one knee crossed over the other in a way that bared most of my thighs.

"That better?" I asked with a raised brow.

Suddenly we were both acutely aware of the fact that we were touching for the first time in days.

"I need to get away from you," Brandon said suddenly. He took a step back and loosened his tie even more while he swallowed heavily.

I pressed my lips together and sighed. This was definitely going to be a one-step-forward, two-steps-back process. I gestured toward

63

the plates I'd carefully set up around the dining table, the candle that was now sadly burned out.

"Dinner's ready."

Brandon walked to the table curiously. "You did all of this for me?"

His tone of voice made me hopeful and sad all at once.

"You sound like no one's ever made you dinner before," I joked as I slid off the counter and limped into the kitchen.

He had been married for fifteen years. I found it hard to believe that in all that time Miranda, his wife, had never done something as basic as this.

"Not like this," he said as he circled the dining table, which I'd set carefully with the white Italian dishes in the cupboards, along with a few candles (now burned down) and a spray of late-blooming sunflowers.

I'd made a Caesar salad to go with the dinner, and Jane had helpfully brought over a cheesecake from Mike's before going to break up with Eric. I made a mental note to call her about that tomorrow morning. She had said she had a red-eye flight that night; otherwise, I would have invited her to stay here.

"I don't think I've ever seen you make anything more than boxed macaroni or warmed up soup," Brandon remarked good-naturedly as he poured himself a glass of wine and refilled mine on the counter.

I limped over to pull the sizzling pan out of the oven. Okay, it didn't look horrible, and it stilled smelled pretty good. Maybe a little overcooked on the top, but I didn't think it would be that bad. I stood up with a satisfied smile and set it on top of the stove.

"I still have a few tricks you haven't seen," I said. Bravado. Yes. That was what I needed here.

Brandon carried the pan to the table so that I wouldn't have to on my bum ankle. I followed with a serving spoon and then took a seat while he dished both of us up. I watched as he took a bite, chewed once, and stopped, his face suddenly stuck in one position.

"What?" I asked. I picked up my fork and eyed the meal dubiously.

His blue eyes glinted in a way I hadn't seen in a while, in that way I yearned for. He held his lips still, then carefully, forcefully, swallowed the bite in his mouth.

"It's...ah..."

My face fell. "It's no good, is it?"

Brandon chewed on his lip for a moment, clearly forcing back a grin, although he couldn't stop his dimples from appearing. "It's...different."

"You're so full of shit."

I threw my napkin at him, which he dodged with a chuckle. As embarrassed as I was, the sound made my heart warm. I'd make a thousand shitty dinners if I got to hear him laugh with me again.

"Okay, you try it, Red," he said with another grin that lit me up inside.

"Fine," I said. "I bet it's fine. Bubbe gave me the recipe."

"But you cooked it?"

I rolled my eyes and speared some of the eggplant, which immediately fell off the fork, unable to keep its shape. Brandon watched with mirth as I shoved it in my mouth defiantly.

I chewed. Once.

"Well?" he asked.

"Oh my God," I said through a mouth full of complete and utter mush. "That's absolutely *terrible*."

This time Brandon laughed, a full-throated laugh that filled the entire room. I forced down the offending food, and started laughing with him. Suddenly the entire setup seemed hilarious and neither of us could stop laughing. The slightly wilted flowers, the burned-out candles, the overcooked food. Who was I kidding? This wasn't me; it never had been. I was closer to Bettie Page than Betty Crocker.

"Bubbe was right," I said after I forced the bite down. "It really does taste like slugs!"

"Can I—can I get something Ana made now?" Brandon gasped between heaves. "Unless...no, Red, I'm sorry. I can't eat it."

"Are you kidding? I slaved over this all afternoon!" I cried out, causing him to laugh even harder, me right along with him.

It wasn't until I was wiping tears from underneath my eyes, trying not to smear my carefully drawn eyeliner that we finally stopped laughing. I set down my fork and stood up to clear away the offending dish, which Brandon quickly scooped out of my hand again and took to the kitchen before returning with cheese, prosciutto, and a cutting board.

"You didn't have to do that," I said when he returned. "I offered to make you dinner."

"Well, there's still the salad," he said as he sat down and took another drink of his wine. He dished himself up some greens, then stopped with a quirked eyebrow. "You didn't make this dressing, did you?"

I almost threw my napkin at him again, but the dimple in his cheek made me stop. It just felt so good to joke with him again. That is, until I noticed the slightly darkening skin underneath his left eye, and a fresh scrape on his cheek bone, partially camouflaged by stubble. It wasn't the same bruising that he'd gotten during his scuffle with Messina's men. This was something new.

"What happened to your eye?" I asked, pointing my empty fork at his face.

Brandon touched a hand to the puffy skin and blanched, all signs of merriment gone. "Oh. Nothing. I just ran into a door at work yesterday."

I frowned. "Seriously? That's the best you got? You sound like a bad domestic violence PSA."

He didn't answer, just took another stoic bite of salad. Whelp. There went the mood.

We continued to eat in relative silence, the sounds of our forks clinking on the plates while we plowed through the salad, charcuterie, and the second bottle of wine.

"Thanks for this," Brandon said after eating the last of the salad. "It was nice."

He collected my plate and started to take the empty dishes to the kitchen. I followed with the rest, and we began cleaning up together. Brandon was as messy as always—I had literally never seen the man do dishes without getting water and soap all over himself.

"Here," I said, trying to edge in between him and the sink. "Let me. You're making a mess of your nice shirt."

"No, that's okay, I got it."

"Seriously," I said as I grabbed for the sponge and started scrubbing out the salad bowl. "I wanted to do this for you."

"Yeah, but you shouldn't be standing on your leg for too long," Brandon argued back as he continued to spray food off the plates, causing a bit of water to hit him and me at the same time.

"Stop!" I cried. "It doesn't need to be that high! Turn it down!"

"Jesus, can you just give me some space?"

Brandon turned off the sprayer, but still reached into the sink irritably for another glass to load.

"What?" I asked, confused even as I crowded him even more. "I'm just doing dishes."

"Skylar, seriously. I need you to back the fuck *off*!"

I stopped scrubbing and narrowed my eyes. "Why? What's wrong with me?"

"Well, to start, you smell too damn good!"

Brandon exploded backward, stepping away against the island behind us. The move put three feet between us. It might as well have been a mile.

"And then there's that dress—you knew what you were doing with that, prancing around with your legs all long and..."

He yanked at the collar of his shirt, swallowing heavily as his eyes landed on the aforementioned body parts. The look made a flush bloom over them, and I squeezed my thighs together. Brandon's eyes bulged.

"And on top of that," he continued, his voice suddenly strained, "I can't fuckin' think straight with all that water plastering your dress to your chest like that, when you're looking at me like..."

Slowly, I leaned against the counter, facing him. With his water-spattered shirt pressing the fabric over his defined chest, he looked like he'd stepped out of a wet T-shirt contest. A really sexy wet T-shirt contest for men in five-thousand-dollar suits. I looked down at myself. He's gotten water all over us both, and the thin cotton of my dress, now damp over my breasts, was making my current state of mind pretty obvious.

"Like what?" I asked coyly as my insides clenched.

Brandon glared at me, but it was full of a different kind of heat. "Like you want to tackle me."

Maybe this evening wasn't a total wash after all. I slid my hands provocatively down the edges of the counter, arching my back slightly. Brandon watched the movement with dilated eyes.

"Maybe," I said, "I do."

Slowly, because I couldn't actually walk very well, and also because I didn't want to rush it, I crossed the space between us, doing the exact opposite of what he had asked me to. Brandon inhaled sharply as I stepped into his personal space. I raised a hand and laid it gently on his damp chest. When he made no move to step away, I stood up on my tiptoes, balancing most of my weight on my good foot.

"You're mad," I breathed against his ear.

I wasn't planning to seduce him tonight, but since I was here, I might as well go for it. We both clearly wanted it, needed it. Maybe that was the path toward healing.

"So fucking mad," he agreed. He closed his eyes as if in pain, the strain causing the muscles at his neck to bunch. On the counter, his fists clenched tightly. "And you're mad at me too."

"Incredibly," I agreed as I undid his tie and slowly pulled it the rest of the way from his neck. I folded it up and smacked it lightly against his chest. "Furious."

His eyes blinked, full of blue fire. "I don't think this is a good idea."

But the clear desire all over his handsome face said exactly the opposite. And so did a week of sleeping in separate bedrooms, not to mention the two empty wine bottles on the table. My underwear was drenched, the front of his pants looked uncomfortably tight, and I was pretty sure I couldn't stop myself from doing this if I tried.

I popped up on my toes again, then slipped the tie around his neck so I could pull him down to me. He didn't stop me. Slowly, tentatively, I pressed my lips to his. When he didn't pull away, I tugged on the tie a little more, encouraging him closer. I opened my mouth, inviting his tongue to mingle with mine, luxuriating in the wine-flavored taste of him.

We kissed like that for what seemed like hours, bodies rigid, mouths moving slowly. It was gentle, yet tense. But then I captured his full lower lip between my teeth and sucked. Hard.

He froze. And then his reaction was almost instantaneous.

Suddenly I was scooped up, pivoted, and set on the kitchen counter, my legs wrapped around his waist, his strong arousal pressed to my core. His hands were everywhere, grasping at my bare legs, my ass, sliding over the damp fabric of my dress to cup my breasts.

"Fuck," he breathed in between furious, torrid kisses that were almost more teeth than tongue. "*Fuck*."

"Brandon," I moaned as his mouth found my neck.

He bit down. I yanked open the buttons of his shirt, sliding my hands across his chest before I tore the entire thing off him. It was easy to forget just how beautiful he was when I hadn't seen him like this in nearly two weeks. Tall, tan, lean, and muscled, all of it pressed against me.

"You want me to fuck you, Red?" he asked in a low, almost menacing voice against the sensitive skin behind my ear. He licked me there, then bit the spot again, making me writhe.

Something in his tone should have scared me. Every muscle I could see was pulled taut: his forearms, his neck, the twitching muscle in his jaw. I should have seen he was a ticking time bomb.

But instead, I just said, "Fuck, yes."

In a flurry, I was carried over to the sofa, where I was dumped on my knees to rest my body over the back of it. The tie was yanked out of my hands, and my arms were pulled in front of my face.

"Clasp your hands together," Brandon ordered. "Hold them there."

Slowly, I did what he said. Immediately, my wrists were captured in silk, and I watched while Brandon jerked his tie into a rough knot. He doesn't want me to touch him, I thought just before he finished. I was too turned on to care.

"Don't move," he ordered.

I obeyed, and my dress was yanked over my hips, and my underwear torn away, flung to some unknown place in the apartment. Brandon's hand brushed over my bared legs, taking handfuls of my ass and squeezing.

"Fuck," he muttered as he squeezed again.

One hand slapped me lightly across one cheek, and I jumped slightly. Brandon squeezed the other, harder this time, making me jump again.

"Mmmph," I grunted at another light slap. I pressed my face into the cushion. God, I was wide open and dying for him.

"You want it rough, baby?" he asked me, rubbing a coarse palm over my cheek before smacking it again.

I couldn't answer. I didn't care how he took me, I just wanted *him*.

His hands left me then, and I heard the jangle of his belt buckle as he undid his pants. I tensed, even though I was more than ready for the size of him. He wasn't allowing me to be tender, but if he'd let me close this way, I'd take it. Maybe we'd be able to find our way back to one another.

I arched my back, ready to take him. But instead of filling me as I was expecting, instead I felt the warmth of his mouth. He bent voraciously to his task, pressing his face fully between my legs from behind, his tongue slipping inside me while his fingers reached around to find my clit. He licked, nipped, sucked, nipped again before he suddenly pulled away.

Oh no. Brandon had a track record of withholding orgasms when he was angry.

"No!" I whimpered. My hands stayed where they were, tied in front of me, but I clenched my thighs tightly around his head, holding him in place. "*Please* d-don't leave me hanging, Brandon."

He said nothing, just forced my legs from around his head. It wasn't fair, really, that he was so much stronger than me. But just as I had resigned myself to going without, he dove back, licking and sucking and biting, just on that edge of pain and pleasure.

"Is this what you want?" he growled as his hand found my ass with another, harder smack. My back arched in response but the hand on my hip kept me still.

His tongue traveled over me, through me, as fervently as any other part of him could. Then he pulled back as his hands took control, one at my clit while the other thrust one, two, then three fingers inside me and fucked me mercilessly.

"Is this what you want, baby?" he demanded. "To fuck you with my tongue? Make you scream with my hand?"

My hips writhed, jamming into his face while my hands clenched in front of me. I hurtled toward a complete loss of my senses.

"Yessssss," I hissed. "Do it. Make me...oh, God, Brandon, fuck me!"

"Scream it, Skylar. Scream my motherfucking name!"

His order wasn't hard to follow. He withdrew his hand and suddenly replaced it with his long length. He filled me completely with one harsh thrust as he reached around to work my clit even harder. His other hand smacked me again, the crack of skin on skin filling the room. The sound of my screams filled the air, seemed to undo him as much as they did me, and it didn't take long before we were both falling apart completely.

"FUCK!" he cried as he came in a fury, emptying himself into me completely.

"Brandon!" I cried out.

We fell forward together into the couch, my hands still bound over the cushions. Eventually I wriggled out of the tie—clearly Brandon wasn't a knot-making expert.

"Brandon?" My voice was slightly muffled in the pillows.

"What, Skylar?" he mumbled into my neck.

His big body covered mine completely, his warmth pulsing through the clothes we were still both wearing. I reached a hand behind me to comb through his curls. He was still gasping and seemed to calm a little as I clutched his soft hair.

"I love you," I said. Then, after a few more breaths: "I'm sorry."

It was the wrong thing to say. A split-second later, Brandon pushed off me, eyes closed as if in pain. I twisted around to look at him, but he wouldn't meet my gaze.

"Fuck," he muttered to himself, pushing his hands over his face violently, then tugged even harder at his hair. "*Fuck.*"

Then he started to move in a frenzy, yanking his shirt back over his shoulders, refastening his pants. He ducked around the couch toward the elevator, still swearing to himself over and over again as he grabbed his keys and wallet from the entry table and pounded the elevator button so hard I thought he might break it.

"Where—where are you going?" I asked. I now stood next to the sofa, pulling my dress back down. I had absolutely no idea where my underwear ended up, and my body was still flushed from the effects of our union.

Brandon finally turned to face me, struggling to close his shirt. Two buttons were torn off completely. He had scratch marks down one side of his face. The combination of that, the wild blond riot of his hair, and the slightly crazed look in his eyes, made him look like some kind of marauder.

He took one look at my own disheveled state, and seemed to lose it completely.

"FUCK!" he shouted.

He turned and swiped at the flower vase standing on the entry table. The glass shattered all over the dark wood floors, scattering the petals of red and white roses.

I stood stock-still while Brandon's chest heaved. A lone tear slid down his reddened cheeks, and he seemed to be struggling for breath. But I couldn't move. Who was this person? Had I created him?

The elevator doors number continued to light up higher, although they hovered at twenty for a while. Brandon took one look at them, and shook his head violently.

"Fuck it," he said, more to himself than to me, and opened the door to the stairwell instead.

I just watched in a trance as the heavy door banged shut and the quick echoes of Brandon's sprinting footsteps grew faint. All I was left to wonder was about how desperately he needed to be away from me that he preferred to jog down twenty-eight flights of stairs instead of waiting a few more minutes for the elevator.

I stared at the broken glass for several minutes, wondering whether I should clean it up. But in the end, I just hobbled to my bedroom. I shut the door and leaned against it, keeping my eyes shut for   a   very   long   time.

Eight

But I didn't last long in my room either. Midnight arrived, then one, then two, with still no sign of Brandon. After taking a shower and changing into a cotton slip, I tossed in my bed for several hours until I finally gave up and hunted down the closet where Ana kept the cleaning supplies. I grabbed a vacuum to clean up the glass and petals that littered the foyer. I didn't know where Brandon was, but he probably wouldn't want to clean up a shattered vase when he got back.

Just as I was curling up on the sofa under a blanket and watching the gas fire burning in the fireplace, the elevator bell rang. I could hear Brandon's voice, loud and unintelligible, before the doors even opened.

I sat up.

"Skyyyylaaahhh," Brandon crooned with a goofy, pained expression. "Where aaaaaahhhh you?"

His left side was draped over the slim frame of Cory, whose face was practically engulfed by Brandon's bicep. Cory steered his boss into the living area, which couldn't have been easy, considering that Brandon was clearly piss-drunk and could barely walk.

My eyes opened wide as I observed them. Brandon was normally a temperate drinker. He had probably left the apartment a bit worse for wear to begin with after all the wine we had earlier, but now, even from clear across the room, he smelled like he had gone swimming in a cask of bourbon. His South Boston accent, with the open-ended r's and flattened a's that usually stayed hidden most of the time, was out in full, like he was straight out of a Ben Affleck movie.

"Come on you gorgeous, stubborn, ridiculously beautiful minx," Brandon called out, pushing Cory's thin arms off him, and stumbling further into the apartment. He circled around like a dog chasing his tail, colliding with a pillar next to the kitchen. "You're the only girl who could break my heart, you know that? The only one!"

Then he spied me sitting on the couch, and made a wavering, feet-thumping beeline for me. After teetering around the couch arm, he collapsed at my feet and buried his face in my waist.

73

"Gawd, you smell good."

His voice was muffled by the flimsy fabric of my slip. His hands started to fumble their way up my bare legs, and he squeezed my thighs before just laying his head on my lap with a sigh.

"I love you so much, baby. I keep tryin' to stop, but I can't." He looked up with bright blue eyes that were glazed from the alcohol. "Do you know why I can't, Red?"

Was it awful how much I loved hearing him call me that? Even if he was drunk as a skunk?

"Why?" I murmured, running a hand through his hair. He leaned into my caress, squeezed his eyes shut, then opened them again.

"I dunno," he said. "S'was hopin' you could tell me. You put a spell on me, woman."

And before I could reply, he laid his head back in my lap and started crooning the song of the same name: "I put a spell on you...cuz you're miii-eeeennnn."

I added to the mental list of things I was discovering about Brandon Sterling: the man was completely tone-deaf. I looked up at Cory, who was now standing by the fireplace, arms crossed over a wrinkled beige suit while he watched us with disgust.

"What happened?" I asked.

"What *happened*?" Cory's face screwed up like a wad of tissue. "You mean, besides *you*?"

"Hey!" Brandon blared from my lap. "You need to talk to her with res-*pet*!" His words were becoming increasingly slurred. "Otherwise I'ma kick your ass, jus' like I did'a that other guy."

Brandon continued crooning his song into the folds of my skirt.

I glared back at Cory. "What is he talking about?"

Cory pressed his thin lips into a frown. "He got into another fight. I had to tear him out of a bar in Savin Hill. It took me, David, and two security guys to get him into the Mercedes."

"*Another* fight?"

Of course. The bruises around his eye and on his hands. I looked down at even more scrapes on Brandon's knuckles, some of them clearly days old, others obviously brand new. There was an additional scrape over his nose, but otherwise he wasn't too much the worse for wear. Still, this was a lot more than running into a door, and obviously not a result of his scuffle with Messina's thugs. How could I have missed this?

Because you've barely seen him.

"What's wrong with me?" Brandon muttered into my slip. "I try an' I try. But you always say no. I ask you to move in wi' me— nothin'. Ask you to marry me—big fat no way. I'm only good for one thing, ain't I? *Ain't I, Sky-lah?*"

"*What* is he *talking* about?" Cory spat. "He asked you to *marry* him? When? What the *fuck* is going on?" The little man was sputtering like a kettle about to boil over, and it looked like his small head was about to pop off his body from the pressure.

"Relax," I said sharply. I started to stroke a tentative hand through Brandon's hair again. "It was in France, before...everything. And I did say no, so you don't have to worry."

"Tha's right," Brandon said, rearing back up on his knees to look at Cory. "She said, NO SIR!" Then he pivoted back to me with a face like a sad, drunk puppy. "Why don't you wanna marry me, Red? Don't I make you happy?"

He leaned back and started yowling more tone-deaf lyrics up to the ceiling. If I hadn't already known the lyrics to Springsteen's "Brilliant Disguise," there was no way I would have recognized the song.

"LOOK AT ME BABY!" he sang-shouted in a way that made me want to cover my ears.

Cory actually did. I cringed at the unusual high note that practically cracked the windows just before Brandon collapsed again into my lap. Cory looked at him, completely repulsed. Then his sharp gaze snapped back to me.

"This is the second fight this week," he informed me.

He yanked his tie off of his neck and shoved it violently into his pocket. Vaguely, I wondered if Cory had ever had his blood pressure checked; half the time, the guy looked two seconds from a heart attack.

"He's lucky the other guys were just as drunk and no one got any video. Just like he's lucky I'm so fuckin' good at my job." Cory glared at me again, pulled his phone out of his pocket to check the time, then shoved it back in. "Listen, Orphan Annie."

I blanched at the name. "You know my name, Cory. Can you please just use it?" Why couldn't this guy ever just acknowledge me as a person?

Cory continued as if I hadn't said anything. "If he's going off the deep end, I can't help him. He's not listening to me, so maybe you can get his ass to straighten out, since you're the one who fucked it up in the first place. But this kind of shit can*not* continue. I can only pay off so many people to keep it out of the press, and he's been lucky so far. But seriously, he gets into one more fight—*one more*, you hear? I'm gone. When he's sober again, can you manage to tell him that?"

The condescension in Cory's voice made me want to start throwing some punches myself, but right now I had a snoring giant pinned to my lap. Besides, this *was* genuinely alarming. Two fights? Nightmares? Coming home fall-down drunk? What was happening to Brandon?

Was it really all my fault?

"I'll tell him," I said quietly, pressing a hand gently to Brandon's shoulder.

"You better," Cory said, and turned to leave. But when the elevator arrived, he held the door, tapping his lips for a moment. Then he turned to me with one more thing to say.

"If you care about him," Cory said, more slowly than I had ever heard him speak before, "you might want to think about what's best for him. Whether *you* are really what's best for him."

I opened my mouth with a sharp retort, but was interrupted by a long, loud snore from the man passed out in my lap. As the elevator doors opened, I stroked the thick mane of blond, giving tenderness that he wouldn't accept earlier. Brandon hummed and smiled, and melted further into me.

"I love you," he muttered in between another throaty exhale. "So fuckin' much."

"I love you too," I whispered. My heart squeezed in my chest. "So much."

* * *

We stayed there the rest of the night. Eventually Brandon found his way onto the sofa so that we were stretched out on it together, with me leaning against the arm and a folded blanket, him a heavy weight between my legs while he used my stomach as a pillow. It wasn't the most comfortable night of sleep I'd ever had, but I wouldn't have traded it to be anywhere else.

At one point, he woke us both with an unintelligible shout, but when his sleep-glazed expression found me, his arms wrapped around my midsection like a vise, and he burrowed back into my body. I wove my fingers through his hair, and he fell back asleep quickly.

But in the morning, I woke up alone. Without the benefit of the blackout curtains that outfitted the bedrooms, I rose practically with the sun that shone through the massive picture windows like a bullet to my brain.

Brandon was up, and I had been draped with the blanket. Pushing myself up, I looked around the apartment. His keys, wallet, and briefcase were still sitting in on the foyer table. So, he hadn't gone yet.

I pulled myself up, massaging out a kink in my neck. Testing my weight on my bad ankle, I limped to Brandon's room. The door was shut. I knocked, but there was no answer.

"Brandon?"

No answer.

Tentatively, I opened the door and pushed it open. I walked into the room and nearly ran into a giant, dripping wet, completely naked Brandon.

"Whoa!"

"Christ!"

We both cried out together as our bodies came into contact, the wet of the shower water seeping through my flimsy nightgown. The electricity was instantaneous, and we jumped apart in shock.

"Jesus, did you forget how to knock?" Brandon gasped after he sprinted to the bathroom and grabbed a towel to wrap around his waist.

I crossed my arms over my chest, but that didn't stop him from looking at me up and down. He pressed his full lips together, then grabbed a blanket off the bed and tossed it to me.

"Put that on," he said gruffly.

"Why?"

"Because that dress thing was already almost see-through, and now it's completely transparent."

I looked down and gasped when I saw the outlines of my nipples and the shadow of hair between my legs visible through the wet cotton. I wrapped the blanket around me and quickly sat down on the bed, earning a quick chuckle from Brandon, who had pulled on his underwear and tossed his towel onto an armchair.

With his back to me while he pawed through his dresser, I had an opportunity to ogle him openly. The boxer briefs left little to the imagination, hugging the taut curves of his ass and leaving the rest of his skin, still tanned from our two-week vacation on the French Riviera, bare. I could appreciate how the lines of his trim waist spread to the broad expanse of his shoulders, how his long legs seemed to go on forever. As he rifled through his drawer for something, the ripple of muscle over his shoulders practically made me drool.

Seriously, no one should be allowed to look that good, especially not when they are hung over.

"It wouldn't have bothered you before," I said without thinking, suddenly wanting nothing more than to strip off my clothes and lay myself down on the bed for the taking. Little more than a week ago, that's all it would have taken to get him to stop whatever he was doing.

He turned back around, several T-shirts in hand, and caught me staring, open-mouthed, at his washboard abs. His mouth quirked a little, but then turned stern.

"Careful."

I blinked and shook my head. Then I frowned. "I'm sorry. How terrible of me to forget that I'm a pariah."

The quirk turned into a scowl. "Skylar, don't. I'm really not in the mood."

I stared down at the carpet. "Fine. Then the least you could do is cover yourself up too."

That earned me another partial smirk, but Brandon made no move to put anything else on. Bastard. It was then that I noticed he was pulling more clothes out of his drawers and putting them inside a small suitcase that lay open on the ottoman next to the armchair.

"Where are you going?" I asked.

Brandon bent over the suitcase to pack in some underwear, giving me another excellent view of his underwear and the ass underneath it. When he turned around and caught me gawking at him again, he rolled his eyes, but grabbed a pair of sweatpants out of the dresser and tugged them on. It didn't matter. The man would have to cover himself in a trash bag to dim that light, and he was still shirtless. Did he really think I was going to be able to focus on anything besides those washboard abs?

"I have to go to LA for a few days on business," he was telling me.

That startled me out of my staring. This was the first I'd heard about this trip. It certainly wasn't out of the ordinary for Brandon to travel on business; he did it enough that his company had its own plane. But for some reason, this trip stung a little. Leaving now, when things were so...uncertain.

"Oh." I gulped. "Okay then." I stared down at the carpet, focusing on the flecks of white in the dark gray.

"Is there something you needed when you came in here?"

When I looked back up, his eyes were cold, although they seemed to soften again when he saw my uncertainty.

"I...I just wanted to know you were okay," I said. "After last night, I mean."

The new bruises on his face had turned darker, and a scab had formed over one of his knuckles. With his shirt off, I could also see what looked like fingernail gouges at his collarbone. He was a bit scratched up, but didn't—quite—look like he had gotten the shit beat out of him. I hated to think what the other guy looked like.

"Yeah, sorry about that," Brandon said, interrupting my examination. "It won't happen again."

"That's not what I'm asking," I pressed. "I'm asking if you're okay."

"So *now* you're worried if I'm okay?"

His eyes iced over, and when he turned them on me, I stiffened.

"I-I-" I could only stutter.

"I'm fine, Skylar. You don't need to worry about me, all right?"

I bit my lip, willing away the tears that threatened to fall.

"Okay. Well..." I paused, looking out the window at the sun cast over Boston. It was a legitimately beautiful day, just not in this apartment. "I'll look for a new apartment while you're gone, then.

So that Bubbe and I can get out of your hair. We might be able to find something reasonable in Jamaica Plain. Maybe Roxbury."

If I'd felt like the room was frozen before, suddenly it turned into a damn tundra.

"What?" Brandon was stone-still, eyes like ice.

"I just thought I'd look for an apartment so I can, you know..." I trailed off, frigid like a scared rabbit.

"No, I don't know."

I sighed. "Brandon, it's obviously time for me to leave."

"Says who?"

"Says *me!*" I replied, frustrated. "The doctors said I would be able to walk unassisted in two weeks, and I'm almost there now. My ankle is going to be fine, and so will my ribs. *I'm* going to be fine. And since you clearly don't want me here—"

"Who said I don't want you here?"

His expression was heated and his pectorals rippled, like I had insulted him in some way. He crossed his arms, and the movement made the muscles in his forearms stand out.

I looked at him like he was crazy. Maybe he was. "Um, *you* did."

"I never said anything like that."

"You didn't have to," I said, getting a little more than exasperated. Was he trying to humiliate me? "You treat me like I have leprosy. You barely talk to me. If I enter a room, you leave it. Aside from last night, which basically turned into a disaster, you've barely been here. I'm making you so angry that you're fighting other people. That, and the nightmares—Cory's right! I'm obviously making you miserable, and you'd probably be better off without me!"

The tears that had been threatening now fell freely down my cheeks, and I swiped at them angrily, trying to head them off as everything I'd been thinking spewed forth. I didn't want any of it to be true, but maybe it was. Maybe the best thing I could do for Brandon would be to let him go.

Brandon exhaled a long, low sigh, then threw a handful of socks into his suitcase.

"What do you mean, 'Cory's right'?" he asked as he came to sit next to me. The mattress dipped under his weight, and my shoulder leaned into his. He didn't move away.

"Just...something he said last night. He suggested that maybe...maybe I'm not good for you."

We sat there for a moment, shoulder to shoulder, while Brandon worried a T-shirt in his hands.

"Skylar, your dad is safe in rehab, and we've got a full security team basically living with your grandmother. But there is still an open case against Messina, who is on the lam. And until that fucker is locked up, I just..." Brandon trailed off as he thrust his hands into his hair and pulled. He set his jaw and looked at me. "You're staying here. That's it."

"I'll be *fine*—" I started to say.

"Look, I'll be nicer," he broke in.

He gave me a wide, fake grin that made him look like a drunk lion. It was a far sight from the thousand-watt smile that usually lit me up inside, but it still made me chuckle.

"If I'm nicer to you, you'll stay?" he asked, taking a demeanor that was once-again painfully business like.

It wasn't even just the indifference that was killing me, although it was terrible in its own way. It was the mood swings, the back and forth. As much as I wanted to stay and try to work things out with him, I wasn't so sure that was actually what *he* wanted.

"It's really not—" I started again, this time pushing myself up to standing.

"Skylar," Brandon interrupted. "Fuck!" He stood up and paced to his bedroom window.

I froze. "What?"

Brandon shoved his hands back through his damp hair and groaned.

"It's like I'm caught in a fucking time warp here," he stated. "I think about what happened, what you kept from me, all the time. When I'm around you, my heart feels like it's being trampled. But the thought of you gone fucking tears the whole thing out!"

I stood there silently, unsure of what to say. I could feel his ambivalence in every one of our interactions. I understood what he was feeling because I felt it too. He was just trying to keep his heart pieced together. The heart I had smashed apart.

"We'll still have security," I said again, this time more quietly. "We'll be safe...and you can...move on with your life. If that's what you want."

81

I couldn't bear to look at him when I said the last words, couldn't bear to see if that was really what he wanted. My voice choked in my throat, and I sat back down on the bed to get my bearings. When he joined me, his heavy weight on the mattress caused me to tip into him again. Brandon balanced his elbows on his knees, rubbing his forehead with both hands. At long last, he sighed.

"Just give me the week," he said quietly. "I'll be back on Friday. We can figure everything out then, okay?"

I sat there a few more beats, letting the words sink in. It wasn't a denial that he wanted to move on, but it wasn't a confirmation either. So that was something.

I huffed. Brandon gave another smile that was more like a grimace, and we both broke down chuckling. He reached a hand out like he was going to touch my knee, but then pulled it back. I closed my eyes and inhaled. He was close enough that his sweet scent of almonds, soap, and metal was fresh and intoxicating.

I wondered if I'd ever smell it again.

"All right," I relented. "If it means that much to you, I'll stay."

Nine

On Sunday, I managed to get out of the apartment for Family Day at Maple Acres, the rehab facility where Dad was undergoing his treatment. He was now one week into his four-week program, in one of the few centers in the country that even provided in-patient services for gambling addiction. Bubbe had apparently been coming to visiting hours so often that the therapists suggested that she take some distance, so I was the only one coming to Family Day this week.

The center felt more like a boutique hotel than a treatment facility. They only housed fifteen patients at a time, all in separate rooms, so they could spend the time detoxing from the relationships that had cost many of them their self-control. It included a meditation room and a sauna. When I entered the posh house after my personal bodyguard, Lucas, parked on the expansive grounds, I thought it really looked more like a spa than a rehab center.

Along with several other family members who had shown up for the group therapy session, I was guided into a large room where we all sat in chairs on the periphery, facing the circle of patients in the center. I quickly found Dad, his small form hunched over while he chewed on his nails. When he realized I was there, he gave a cautious wave, but resumed biting. I offered what I hoped to be an encouraging smile.

It started out with the lead doctor of the facility introducing himself along with his staff. We then listened a bit about the philosophy of the center, which included a fairly standard approach of requiring its patients to publicly recite their mistakes to their loved ones.

"It's not about shaming," stated the doctor. "It's about owning what we've done so we can move forward productively." Then he looked around the circle of patients, all of whom happened to be men. "Gentlemen? Shall we get started?"

One by one, each man (there were about ten of them) stood up and addressed their families. Their stories were hurtful, some of them detailed, some not. Some of them clearly made confessions their families hadn't known before; nearly all of them provoked tears.

I gripped the edges of my seat when they came around to Dad. He stood up, massaging his bad hand, as had become his habit when he was nervous.

"Hi everyone. My name is Da—Robert," he started out, the same as all of the other men.

He stumbled a bit over his middle name, clearly forgetting he was supposed to be here under a pseudonym. I smiled, offering encouragement.

Then he did something different when he picked up his chair and came to sit directly in front of me instead of speaking from the group. I gulped, sat back as Dad's nervous gaze flitted around the room before resting on me.

"Heya, Pips," he said softly, invoking my childhood nickname, taken from Pippi Longstocking.

"Hi, Dad," I said, just as low.

He squeezed his hands together and looked around. "This is my daughter, everyone. Ain't she beautiful?"

Confused, the rest of the room murmured their agreement, and I blushed slightly. Dad picked up my hand and started to brush over the knuckles lightly.

"Yeah, she's beautiful," he repeated, almost to himself. "Most beautiful thing I ever made, and that's the truth."

I knew the people in the room didn't understand that statement like I did. But my father was a musician, someone capable of communicating poetry on the keys. Or at least, he used to be, before his addiction cost him his hands. But to be told I was the most beautiful thing he'd ever made...that was really something, coming from him.

"She also almost died," Dad continued. "Couple of weeks ago, my baby girl was kidnapped by the same asshole—er, sorry, kids, excuse my French. By the same jerk who did this to my hand." He held up his scarred paw so everyone could clearly see the damage. "He did it for one thing: because of my gambling addiction."

"Dad—" I started to argue that Messina had only targeted me because of Brandon, but Dad held up the same hand, stopping me.

"Please let him speak," said the doctor from the back of the room.

84

"No matter how you look at it, Skylar, none of this would have happened if I'd been able to stay away from the track. Then I wouldn't have had to borrow money from that low life. Brandon wouldn't have had to pay him off for us. Me and Ma wouldn't have lost our house—the house I wanted to give you one day, you know. You wouldn't have had to get rid of...well, you know."

I gaped, glancing quickly around at the people who were watching us, then back at Dad.

"You think I didn't know about that, Pips?" he asked with watery eyes. "I knew. And I did nothing, did I? I still got involved with a woman who was in Messina's pocket. And all she did was dig for information on you. How do you think that good-for-nothing low-life knew where you lived? It was *my fault*, baby."

His voice cracked at the end, and I watched as my father, so normally easy-going and implacable, swiped at a few tears that trickled down his cheeks. I gulped again and dabbed at my own eyes. For once, I was unable to speak. As much as I'd wanted to treat my dad purely as a victim, everything he said was true. And there *was* a part of me that was angry at him for all of it.

"I wasn't there for you, kid," he said. He ran a hand back through his hair, but the two sides just flopped forward again. Then he clasped one hand to his chest, like he was finding it hard to breathe.

"It's okay," said the doctor. "Tell her what you need her to hear."

I clenched my teeth, willing myself not to break down with him in a room full of people.

"I'm sorry," Dad said in a low, shallow whisper. "For everything. And if it's the last thing I do, Skylar, I will be a better man. I *will* be a better father to you, someone you'd want your own kids to know, if you ever have them."

It was the final statement that finally broke down the last wall I had. Tears started to stream down my face as I shook in my chair. Dad reached out to grab my hands, squeezing them both, albeit not quite as tightly with his bad left one.

"Daddy," I whispered, unable to say anything else but that.

Dad just let his own tears keep flowing freely, then reached up to pushed a strand of hair back from my face before he pulled my head down to his thin shoulder.

"I'm sorry, Pips," he said as he stroked my head. "I love you, and I'm sorry."

* * *

Another hour and many more tears around the room later, Dad and I had eaten a brief lunch in the cafeteria and were strolling the grounds of the center while he enjoyed a much-needed cigarette.

"You look good, Dad," I said as I observed the decent-sized plot of land. The center was a converted colonial house on two full acres, most of it lush grass. "They're treating you well here, huh?"

He pulled out his cigarette and lit it carefully, but I was surprised by the scent, which actually smelled sweet.

"Is that herbal?" I asked as the smoke wafted around me.

Dad gave me a wry grin, one I hadn't seen in a while. He took a long pull that hollowed out his cheeks, then exhaled two faint rings.

"Well, it ain't pot, if that's what you're asking," he said.

I rolled my eyes. "I know *that*. I know what weed smells like, Dad."

"Yeah, yeah, yeah. Don't remind me you're old enough for that." He took another drag. "It's a placeholder, they say. I'm here to beat one addiction; I might as well beat 'em both."

I looked dubiously down at the cigarette in his hand. "Is it a good idea to be adding that kind of stress on your life?"

Dad just chuckled. "I never thought *you*'d be trying to get me to smoke, Pips, since you've been nagging at me to stop since you first found out it causes cancer." He snorted. "You always thought the best of me, kid. Better than I deserved. Took good care of me, too."

"Did I?" I asked softly. "I'm not so sure."

"Aw, kiddo."

Dad stopped walking when we reached a big oak tree at the top of the hill. He sat down on the grass, and I plopped down beside him, laying my crutches beside me. I was off them around the apartment, but found I still needed them for longer walks.

"You know, I meant everything I said in there," he said. "Every word." He peered at me with sad eyes. "I've been a shitty father to you, Pips."

86

"That's ridiculous—" I started to protest, but Dad held up his hand, the left one, which still had dark scars crisscrossing over the top.

"No," he said. "I've put myself before you too many times to count. How many times I practiced piano instead of playing with you growing up? How many times I packed off to Nick's for the weekend, let Ma take you to your music lessons and your swim practices? I don't even wanna get into the mistakes I made with your mother."

My shoulders dropped at the mention of Janette. "Dad—"

"Let me finish, Pips," he interrupted gently. "You know, we do this thing in here where we look at accountability. Me and this guy from Atlantic City—boy, does *he* have a gambling problem, let me tell you—we calculated all of the money we'd spent at the track and the interest built up from all those bad loans. And when I did, it was like someone punched me in the gut, kid." He turned and looked at me straight on with a sad expression. "I could have put you through college twice over, baby. You wouldn't have had to take a red cent from Janette, that viper. And she would have had no reason to invite herself back into your life. Even that's my fault. I see that now."

I opened my mouth again to argue, but then closed it. I wouldn't have asked him to pay the kind of money Janette had to put me through school, but then again, if he had had the money, my dad probably would have just done it. And I couldn't argue with that fact that my life now would certainly be better if my mother hadn't come back into it, even if the secret she'd used to blackmail me shouldn't have been a secret in the first place.

"So, what now?" I asked finally as we stood up and kept walking.

"We talk a lot about what's next," Dad said. He gazed toward the canopy of trees at the bottom of the hill and played with one side of his mustache before sucking again on the end of his fake cigarette.

"What does that mean?"

"Honestly, Pips? I got no fuckin' clue." Dad turned with a crooked half-smile. "Excuse my French, kiddo. But you're a big girl. You can handle it."

I bit my lip. Dad was scared—that much was clear. He had literally had everything taken from him in the last six months, all of it from his own folly. For now, he was safe, under the careful guard

87

of his assigned bodyguards and the watchful eyes of the center. But in three more weeks, when he finished the program, he was looking at nothing.

No band.

No job.

No house.

Nothing.

"The doctor makes me play every day," he said as he kicked a few fallen leaves out of his way. I looked up hopefully. He shrugged. "Says it's therapeutic. I don't know about that. I sound like shit. But he says an hour, or as long as my hand don't hurt. Makes the gorilla over there watch."

He nodded backward toward the hulking bodyguard standing just outside the center.

"Is Kyle really that bad?" I wondered.

"Nah," Dad said. "I'm bein' a baby. Besides, I'm sounding better all the time. Who knows, maybe one day I'll actually be able to play for real again. Even if it's just for you, Pips."

I smiled. If that wasn't progress, I didn't know what was. Dad gave a bashful shrug.

"And you?" he asked. "What's next for you, kid? You got that job? How about you and Brandon?"

I grimaced, and Dad laughed outright, hard enough that he started to cough.

"That good, huh?" he asked.

"I tried to make him eggplant parmesan."

Dad burst out laughing, hard enough that he had to clutch his bad hand to his stomach while he bowled over. "You're kidding. You? *You* cooked?"

I folded my arms and scowled. "I can cook."

"*Pop Tarts* ain't cookin', Pips." Dad nudged me in the shoulder, still chuckling. "You tell Ma about it?"

"No, and don't you dare," I replied stubbornly. "She'll never let me hear the end of it. Bubbe was mad enough when I kicked her out of the kitchen."

I proceeded to recount the disaster of an evening. I left out the dirty sex over the back of the couch while keeping the part where Brandon left angry. Dad snickered a bit in the beginning, but soon

88

just listened quietly, still stroking his mustache meditatively as we walked.

"I just...I don't know what to do," I ended. "He's so angry, Dad. I want to make things better, but I don't know how. I honestly think he'll come back after this trip and realize he's done for good."

"Well, I can't speak for Brandon, Pips." Dad kicked another cluster of early fallen leaves away, and they burst through the air in an array of red, orange, and yellow. "But it's hard for us guys. We're already so separated from the action when it comes to kids, right from the beginning. But we want to be a part of it. I know how it feels to have that choice taken from you."

I cast a curious look at him, wondering if he was talking about me. Had he wanted Janette to get rid of me when she was pregnant? Had she, headstrong, impetuous Janette, forced my birth on Dad?

Dad just squeezed my hand for a second as we walked, his way of telling me to stop thinking so hard. The gesture worked. My dad might be a weak person, but I had always known he loved me. That was never in doubt.

In rehab," he kept going, "they talk a lot about communication. And there ain't nothin' to do here but read the books they got in the study. I read this one last week about, what're they called...love languages. You ever heard of them, Pips?"

I couldn't hold back my snort. "The *Five Love Languages*? Really, Dad?"

"Hey, hey, hey, isn't that what you stuck me in here for? To learn about how to deal with my family and all?"

He was joking, but only a little bit. His head ducked down, and immediately I chided myself for teasing him. Who was I to be stuck-up about a book? If it helped him stay clean and healthy, it was doing a better job than I could anyway.

"You're right," I said. "I sound like a snob."

Dad shrugged, but smiled in acknowledgment. "Yeah, well. You come by it honest, so I can't blame you too much for it."

"So what does it say, the love language book?"

He shrugged as we stopped at the top of the next hill and looked down over the center and the rest of Natick at the bottom of the valley.

"Sure ain't like New York," Dad murmured as he took a final pull of his cigarette, then stubbed it out on a tree trunk.

I didn't answer, just waited for him to speak. He sat down on the grass with a thud, and I took a seat beside him, laying crutches beside me.

Because he was my dad, it was easy to think of him as old, but he wasn't. Despite the threads of early gray that had streaked his floppy hair since I could remember, he was still a relatively young man, only with a face weathered by stress and hardship. He rested his thin arms onto his knees and observed his hands.

"It's simple," he said as he turned his wrists over and back. "You want to love Brandon the right way? Forgive you for what you did? You just have to figure out his language. And know it might not be the one you speak." He gave me a knowing look. "But also, he needs to learn yours. Has he tried to do that too?"

First Jane, now my dad. Why was everyone able to see this solution besides me? I looked at my hands clasped over my knees, at the hand-pounded bracelet that encircled one wrist. A gift from Brandon, one that demonstrated a moment when he'd learned how to get through to me. Our affair had started with so many of his missteps, many of them rooted in miscommunication. Big grandiose gestures to me, a girl who hated material gifts. But he'd learned how to speak to my heart—much more, I realized, than I'd ever learned to speak to his.

I'd just assumed he knew how I felt—how could anyone not love Brandon? How wrong I was.

"I think they're teaching you some stuff in here, old man," I said, nudging Dad's bony shoulder.

In return, he gave me another one of his patented shy grins.

"Ah, well," he said. "It could be worse."

Ten

On Friday, after nearly a week without any word from Brandon, I looked at my face in the mirror and decided to go into work. The bruising around my cheek and eye was almost completely gone, and the cut across my brow had faded to a small red scar. Nothing a little concealer couldn't hide. My ankle was doing well; I still walked with a limp, but nothing too terrible. And even though my ribs were still pretty tender, I could sit up just fine.

Screw waiting until Monday. I was bored stiff.

Considering everything that had happened, it was a relief to have something else to do besides sitting around brooding. For the first time in months, I knew that Bubbe and Dad were safe. I had a stable job waiting for me, one I'd been working toward for three years of law school and studying. Even if my personal life was currently in shambles, I still had this. I still had my future.

So I entered the office almost two weeks late, and I couldn't have been happier to be there. I started by spending an hour in HR, and then spent the better part of the morning orienting myself with Marina, the assistant I now shared with another new associate, and a senior partner to whose case I'd been assigned. Before noon, I found myself happily drowning in boxes of depositions. I wouldn't officially be able to practice law until my bar exam results came in next month, but there was still plenty for me to do.

It was sometime past eight that I was disturbed by a knock on the transparent glass door of my office. I jerked my head up from the mess of papers and the empty salad container on my desk to find Kieran striding in, looking her severe, impeccable self in a slim black pantsuit with red loafers. She took a comfortable seat in one of the chairs that faced my desk and crossed one foot over her knee.

"Are we going to have a problem with authority?" she asked bluntly, although the quirk of her eyebrow showed she was partially joking. "I thought I said next Monday. At the earliest."

I swallowed. "Yeah, well. I was getting bored. Recovery isn't all it's cracked up to be."

"You look like you're doing all right," she said, as she looked me over frankly. "The bruising's gone, at least."

"I won't scare the clients," I said with a wry smile and polished off the last of my iced tea.

Kieran barked a short laugh. Then her expression turned serious. "You still don't look like you're up to being here until eight at night. You look exhausted."

I leaned an elbow on the brief I was currently working on. "You say that like every other first year isn't still here too."

Kieran shrugged. "O'Keefe and Swanks are gone. Nirmal's not on this floor, so I don't know about him." She tipped her head. "Then again, none of them were abducted two weeks ago. I meant it when I said you should take it easy."

I pulled my glasses off and set them on the desk so I could rub my forehead. Between Bubbe and Brandon, I was getting *really* tired of being micromanaged. I was also tired of being inside my own head. I knew that eventually I'd have to process everything that happened to me, but work was a welcome respite from all of the drama.

"I'm fine," I said. "To be honest, it's better than the alternative of sitting around the apartment by myself day and night."

Kieran pursed her bright red lips sympathetically—or at least as sympathetic as she ever looked. One day I'd have to ask for her cosmetics brand. She didn't seem to wear any other makeup, but that slash of red was always there, no matter what.

"He's upset," she stated. It was a fact, not a question. "It's that bad?"

I sighed and set down my pen so I could lean back in my chair. "He's...yeah. It's bad. He's gone for the rest of the week on business. Said we were going to 'figure things out' when he gets back tonight. Whatever that means."

"So what are you doing here?"

I pursed my lips and blew out a long breath. "Well, he hasn't exactly been getting in early lately. Most nights he doesn't show up until I'm already asleep. So I wasn't in a huge hurry to run home and wait."

To my surprise, Kieran scoffed. "Fuckin' Brandon. Men. I swear to God."

I frowned. "You think? I don't know...I think he's got every right to be upset after what I did."

"Please." Kieran looked at me, suddenly serious. "Look, it's none of my business. But I would have done the same thing. About the baby."

I froze, then reached a hand to the far corner of my desk to press the button to frost the walls and the door. My transparent face wouldn't do me any favors with this conversation. Kieran watched with some approval.

"Christ, sometimes I don't think he really understands how complicated his life makes other people's," she continued. "What were you supposed to do? Put your entire life aside for a junk show who may or may not be able to get his shit together? As his friend *and* his lawyer, I feel I can say that with more authority than most. His life was a complete mess."

I sat back in my seat and started toying with my pen, unsure of how to respond. She wasn't saying anything new, but I didn't necessarily feel the same way. Kieran tended to be less than generous with her best friend. I thought Brandon was complicated, not a screw-up. And on top of that, the way Kieran talked about him—about us—made us sound like we were totally separate, like the decisions we made didn't affect each other. But that couldn't be further from the truth.

Somehow, some way, Brandon had crept so far into the heart of me that sometimes I couldn't tell where he ended and I began. That was the real reason why all of this was so painful. His hurt was my hurt. My pain was his. We couldn't lose each other without losing ourselves.

That was the other reason I'd had to come into work. There was a very real possibility that when he got back—tonight or tomorrow—he was possibly going to tell me it was over. And I definitely wasn't ready to deal with that.

Then something occurred to me. "You were recording when he found out. What happened to that? Is Miranda going to sign the papers now?"

Kieran screwed her thin brows up in confusion. "You didn't know? She signed them two days after he made his announcement. I handled it while you were in the hospital."

My eyes bugged out of my head. "*What?*"

Kieran shrugged, like it wasn't that big of a deal, even though we both knew it meant everything to Brandon's and my relationship.

"You know as well as I do that no Massachusetts judge would ever admit that recording into evidence," Kieran said as she examined her nails. "But the court of public opinion is a very different thing." She smirked. "She wanted to play dirty. She forgot who she was dealing with."

Suddenly I couldn't feel my legs.

"Jesus," I breathed, "Kieran, you're not going to...you're not going to release that thing, are you?"

I could just see the headlines of *Page Six*: "Bye Bye, Brandon's Baby!" or something equally trite yet pithy. I'd be the abortion girl for the rest of my life. And in a city that was half Catholic, Brandon's political career would be as good as gone.

But Kieran shook her head. "No, no, no. Brandon has it now anyway, and you know he'd never do anything like that to you."

Did I? I thought so. Or, at least I used to think so.

"It's just leverage in case Miranda ever tries anything again. But I don't think she will. Last I heard, she went back to New York."

For the first time in several weeks, a weight lifted from my shoulders as one of the many complications that had thwarted Brandon and me over the past few months disappeared. A chain, unbound. That chapter of Brandon's life was finally over. The question was, would I be in it as he moved on?

"Anyway," Kieran interrupted my thoughts. "Like I said, I would have done the same thing. Single, wrapped up in whatever drama you were obviously dealing with, with an uncertain relationship to boot?" She nodded with each list item. "You made your choice, and that was your right. If he's making you feel bad about it—"

"He's not," I interrupted. "He's not doing anything."

Kieran looked at me like she didn't believe me. "If you say so. But that would be a first."

My hands gripped the edge of the desk. Suddenly I wanted to get back to the apartment as fast as I could. I didn't want to hide anymore. I wanted to face things with Brandon—whatever they were going to be—head on. The real question was how. How could I fix things? How could I help us heal?

Kieran sat forward, tapping her mouth for a second, as if trying to figure something out. Then she looked up.

"I don't know if I should tell you this, but honestly, I don't give a shit what he thinks." She looked up. "You know Brandon's birthday is next week, right?"

I blinked in surprise. "What?"

I was sure I had seen his birthday somewhere—a *Wikipedia* page or something like that, long ago. But Brandon had never mentioned it to me, and I had clearly forgotten the date.

"He doesn't usually make a big thing of it. I have him over for dinner. Sometimes his parents come, sometimes not. Miranda used to throw him these ridiculous parties out at her parents' place at the Cape, but he always hated them."

I nodded with complete understanding. For Brandon, those kinds of parties were about business, not pleasure. They were so far from the person he was on the inside.

"I haven't planned anything this year," Kieran said as she stood up. She dusted off her immaculate black pants and gave me a grin as she turned to leave. "But you know where to find me if you decide to do something."

I pursed my lips, thinking. "Okay. Although I don't know if he would want me to do much for him either..."

Kieran scoffed. "Don't let him tell you what to do. And Skylar?"

I looked up.

"He loves you. And you love him."

There was nothing mushy about the statements. Kieran was as matter-of-fact as they came.

I smiled. "Kieran, you're so sentimental."

She rolled her sharp eyes and knocked on the door frame. "Don't get used to it."

"Hey," I said just before she left. "Can I ask you something else?"

Sometime in the past few weeks, I'd stopped feeling so shy around Kieran. She knew most of my secrets, if secondhand, and she had turned out to be one of my biggest advocates with Brandon. She was definitely on my team. But there was something missing from her investment in my relationship with her best friend.

"What?" she asked, as sharply as always.

"Why did you and Brandon never...you know? You're so close, I would have thought you'd be a good match. Especially since you're single."

Kieran raised a thin brow. "Who says I'm single?"

I frowned. "Aren't you?"

She gave me a sharkish grin. "Of course not. I've been married for five years."

I balked. What? Kieran didn't wear a ring; then again, I didn't think I'd ever seen her with any jewelry or ornamentation—only that dash of red across the lips.

"Brandon's always saying he wants us to have a double date. He thinks you and Pushpa would get along, and we could have dinner parties. I'm not sure why he thinks you and my wife would get along other than you're both female." She rolled her eyes. "I swear to God, sometimes he's the biggest girl in the room."

And with not just one, but *two* minor bombs dropped, Kieran left as quickly as a shadow. The door closed behind her, and I was left wondering just what kind of *woman* Kieran had decided to spend her life with.

But before I could wonder any more, my cell phone buzzed loudly on the hard wood of my desk. I picked it up and smiled.

"The Lord is alive!" I answered with a grin.

"Hilarious." Eric's dry voice filled my ear. "Especially since you're the one shacked up like Rapunzel in her tower. What are you doing right now? I'm just getting off, and I could come pick you up in a few minutes. It's been a long damn week, and I need a drink."

I hadn't heard from Eric or Jane since last weekend, when she had informed me of her plans to break it off. From the sound of my former roommate's voice, it sounded like he needed someone to talk to, and I wouldn't mind a sounding board myself right now, particularly from a man's perspective.

"I'm actually at Kiefer right now," I said. "Just leaving. Where should   we   go?"

Eleven

Twenty minutes later, I found myself sitting at a booth at Manny's with Eric, Cherie, and Steve, the three other interns I'd worked with at Sterling Grove, Brandon's firm, in the days before I'd actually met him. Now they were all first-year associates there, while I had ended up at Kiefer Knightly. Lucas, my bodyguard, sat a few tables away watching people like a Rottweiler, but as the bar filled up, his bulky presence became less obvious.

"You know, you could tell your man to lay off us a *little* bit," Steve said as he returned from the bar with a pitcher of PBR, pint glasses, and a whiskey soda for me. "Sterling is ruthless. Seventy hours I put in last week!"

I smiled as I accepted my drink. It was sweet of him to remember.

"We haven't even passed the bar yet," Steve grumbled.

"Are you kidding?" Eric said. "That would only make him come down harder. He barely lets me call him Brandon, and I've seen the guy half-naked."

He blanched at the memories, and I giggled, earning a sharp, gray-eyed glare.

"Oh, you think it's so funny," he said. "I should have slept with Kieran just to get even with you. Then *you'd* see how freaking awkward it is to be that up close and personal with your boss's sex life."

"I think you got plenty even," I replied. "I seem to remember walking in on you and Jane at least once, isn't that right?"

"No way, man. You hit that? Jane is *hot*," Steve said, earning a slap to his arm from Cherie. He looked apologetically at her through his smudged glasses. "Sorry, babe, but it's true!"

I glanced at Eric—I hadn't known that Cherie and Steve were dating. He just shrugged, as if to say, "It happens." Then I rolled my eyes at Cherie, and she chuckled.

"I wouldn't mind running into Sterling in his underwear," she admitted. "I'll bet he fills them out pretty well. What does he wear, boxers or briefs?"

I didn't answer, just shook my head and took a drink of my whiskey.

"Come on, woman," Steve said as he stood up and tugged Cherie out of the booth. "Let's dance, and I'll help you fill something else out later."

Eric and I both made twin faces of disgust at Steve's awkward double entendre, but it was hard not to smile as he and Cherie took off for the tiny dance floor by the jukebox. Steve was a terrible dancer, but Cherie was so clearly into him that it didn't matter. I balanced my chin in my hand and watched them, remembering the only time I'd ever actually danced with Brandon—in the kitchen of Eric's apartment, swaying slowly to a Springsteen song. It was the night I'd let him back into my life, and a night when he'd decided to let me back in too. And yet here we were, hurt by each other all over again.

"Arrrggggg." Eric leaned his light blond head onto his crossed arms and groaned.

I turned to look at him. "Somehow I doubt that's about work."

"She...drives...me...*crazy*," Eric groaned again into his shirt sleeves. He sat up, red-faced and eyed me suspiciously. "Tell me something. Has Jane always been so goddamn cagey?"

I raised an eyebrow, somewhat surprised. Eric was usually so stoic; this was the first time I'd actually seen more than a flicker here and there of what he was actually feeling. Since he and Jane had gotten involved again, he'd barely mentioned her, although what little he had said made it clear she was definitely more to him than just a good time. Eric was extremely good at keeping his cards close to his chest.

"What's going on?"

Eric pushed a hand back through his short hair and rubbed at the back of his head while he polished off the rest of his beer. I helpfully poured him another pint from the pitcher on the table.

"Last weekend she came," he said.

I nodded. I had seen her on Friday.

"We had a great weekend," he continued. "We *always* have a great weekend. When we're together...I don't know...it's like, things just work." His gray eyes turned surprisingly solemn. "D'you know what that's like, Crosby? When things just *fit*?"

Brandon's blue eyes flashed through my head, and my heart squeezed. I smiled sadly and patted Eric on the shoulder. "I do, friend. I do."

Eric nodded and sat back. "I thought so. You and Sterling—" He made another face at the memory of walking in on Brandon and me one too many times. "When I wasn't completely skeeved at catching my boss with his hands all over my roommate, I remember thinking, that's what I want." Eric looked at me again with those same sad eyes. "You looked happy, Cros. Both of you. And when I'm with Jane, even with her crazy hair and the fact that she *won't shut the fuck up*, I feel that way. I feel happy." He chewed on his lip for a moment. "Actually, I like the hair. And I like all her dumb comebacks. I even like it when she calls me Petri Dish." He looked up sharply. "Do *not* tell her that."

"Awww, Eric. I think you're in love with my best friend."

He made another face. "Jesus. Is that what this is? Shit."

I nodded with a grin, rubbing his shoulder. "Yeah. You're pretty much fucked."

"I just wish she weren't so goddamn difficult!" he cried, shaking his hands at the ceiling like some kind of crazed marauder.

I cocked my head. "What exactly happened?"

"She didn't tell you?"

I shook my head. If she hadn't actually followed through on her threat to break it off with him, I wasn't about to blow her cover.

"Of course she didn't," Eric muttered. "The one time she keeps shit to herself." He sighed. "I asked her to meet me in New York over Labor Day instead of coming here. Go to lunch with my family. Take in the sights. Have a lot of kinky hotel sex."

My eyebrows practically flew off my forehead. "Whoa, whoa, back up. You asked her to meet your *family*?"

Eric came from the same stock as my mother—Upper East Side royalty who substituted nannies and a trust fund for human touch and familial bonds. While Eric wasn't much for divulging secrets (this was something we had in common), I did know that for whatever reason, he had left New York primarily to get away from those people. The fact that he wanted Jane anywhere near them meant one thing: he really was head over heels.

Eric just clapped his hand to his cheek and started massaging his temple like he suddenly had a vicious headache.

"I—yeah. And then last weekend she comes over for an hour. And it's normal. We're all over—um, yeah. We're normal. Until the end, when she tells me she doesn't think it's going to work out anymore and jumps in an Uber for the airport. Now she won't answer my texts, won't take my calls. And if it were anyone else, I'd be over the moon to get out of doing the break-up myself. But this time...I don't know. Am I crazy to want to get on a plane and shake some sense into her? Am I?" He looked at me with an exasperated grin. "I guess I am in love with her, aren't I?"

I held my glass up in a mock toast. "Cheers, friend."

We clinked glasses and drained them together.

"I'm going to do it!" Eric announced to the room as he poured himself another beer. No one in the crowded bar looked up, so he turned back to me. "I'm going to do it. I'm going to buy a ticket and go see her tomorrow. Because I'm tired of this 'will they, won't they' bullshit, and I sure as shit don't want her screwing some other guy in Chicago."

"What are you going to say?" I wondered.

"I don't know," Eric said as he whipped out his phone and started thumbing to a travel site. "I love you, I guess." He looked up and grinned that smile that so curiously transformed his face from being almost plain to downright gorgeous. "Hey, you know what? That actually felt pretty good."

I punch him lightly on the shoulder. "Way to pop your cherry."

Eric smirked and looked back at his phone. "Maybe I should ask her to move back to Boston. She hates Chicago anyway. She's always talking about how she should have just stayed here since her mother drives her nuts."

He thumbed over his screen and whipped out his credit card, then punched in the numbers while he stuck his tongue out of the side of his mouth in concentration. A minute later, he looked up in triumph.

"Done. Tomorrow morning, that psycho is going to talk to me whether she wants to or not." He looked at the empty pitcher and frowned. "I'm going to need more liquid courage."

I grinned as Eric went back to the bar for more drinks, but I couldn't help the twinge in my chest. I was happy for my friend—I really was. I only wished I were as certain about the steps to save my own crumbling relationship.

* * *

After a third watered down whiskey soda, I left Eric at the bar while he rehearsed his speech. Watching him brainstorm his big overtures for Jane made me want to do some problem-solving of my own.

Eric and I were cut from the same cloth—both of us New Yorkers with the same reticence, the same fear of letting go. But Eric was willing to do it, to make a damn fool of himself for someone he loved. Did I need to do the same thing to win back Brandon? What would that even look like?

I tossed my briefcase into the back of Brandon's Mercedes after Lucas escorted me back to the car, but I stared for a minute up the street in the direction of the apartment building. It was still relatively early for a summer night. At just eight, dusk was barely hitting the city, and a few last glimmers of sunshine seeped through the buildings to the West.

"Ms. Crosby?" Lucas beckoned. "Everything all right?"

I blinked as I came back to the present moment. "Yes. I think so." I looked straight at him. "I'd like to stop by the river on the way home, if you don't mind."

If he was surprised, the big man didn't show it. He just nodded and whispered in David's ear. David caught my eye as I slid into the backseat of the Mercedes. And just before I looked away, he winked.

* * *

A few minutes later, David pulled into Magazine Park, one of the many parks that bordered the Charles River on the Cambridge side. I recognized the trails that Brandon ran almost daily (and sometimes forced me to run with him), and immediately got out of the car.

It was one of those late summer nights that was actually perfect for walking around. After a sticky August day, I was comfortable

101

walking around in nothing but a skirt and a tank top, and the number of people who were also enjoying the cool night breeze made it seem more like eight o'clock than ten p.m. I limped down one of the paved paths, nodding at a few other people walking on the river path.

One of the perks of having security following me around, I realized, was that in a way, I had more freedom. I was alone, but I no longer had the same fear of being alone I'd carried with me my entire life, the same way anyone—especially a woman—who grows up in the city has to be afraid. I didn't have to hold my house keys in my pocket like weapons when I passed strange men on the street. I didn't have to avoid dark corners or poorly lit blocks. I could just walk.

With Lucas following about thirty feet away, I made my way through the park, past the baseball fields where I knew Brandon had played Little League when he first moved in with Ray and Susan, and down to a bench near the water's edge. There was only a slight breeze coming off the river, and there were even still a few boats gliding past the bank.

This was one of the few places that Brandon came to find peace, almost daily. Despite his tendency to be slightly impulsive, the need for stability was something we had in common. We were both creatures of habit, with set routines that just happened to work well together—except when they didn't. Then things tended to blow up.

Besides helping him maintain a drool-worthy body, Brandon's daily running habit was also indicative of something else: that when he made a decision, it was a decision he made every day, not just once.

I shook my head, feeling incredibly stupid. What had I been thinking? He wasn't the kind of man who needed an apology dinner, gifted like a bouquet of flowers that would wilt. Nor was he the kind of person who wanted to be manipulated into makeup sex, even if by accident. Brandon needed permanence. Safety. Things he'd never really had. He needed to know that when I and anyone else said they loved him, we meant it, not just right then, but always.

I put my feet up onto the bench and pressed my knees into my chest. Dad was right. I'd been content to let him learn how to speak my language, never once thinking how to talk to him, to let him know just how much he truly meant to me. Brandon had rescued my heart from a place where I thought it might be permanently broken.

Actually, it was more than that, I realized. He had taught me how to love in the first place.

I thought back to the spring, after I'd broken up with him the first time. I'd thought we were broken irreparably after I discovered that Brandon was both married and going behind my back to deal with Victor Messina. But instead of sitting around waiting for me to forgive him, Brandon had taken action. Letters, every day. About his childhood. About growing up with Ray and Susan. Letters about the kind of person he was and the person he wanted to be for me. And, of course, so many, many words about why and how he loved me.

I want you, I'd always said.

So he gave me him.

They were gestures that hadn't worked at first, but had played a major part in breaking down my defenses. Because in the end, I'd believed him. In the end, I'd come to realize that I couldn't be without him.

Every letter always ended the same:

Do you love me yet, Red?
I love you. Always.
B

Always. My fingers toyed with the bracelet on my wrist, the one with the engraving from Yeats on it. *One man saw the pilgrim soul in you.* Well, I saw the pilgrim soul in him too. I just needed to show him how.

Across the park, the echoes of voices laughing filtered through the night air. I watched a group of teenage boys loping through the still-lit baseball field in an impromptu game. One of them, a lanky blond kid, was clearly the star of the group. His athletic ability surpassed the rest, and his friends clearly worshipped him.

The ball hit the kid's bat with a sudden crack through the air. I watched it sail over the field. By the time it had sailed over the fence, I had a new plan in order to show Brandon just what I mean by love too.

Twelve

When I got back to the apartment, I had a head full of ideas after texting and emailing furiously the entire ride back. Something had shifted inside me. I couldn't just sit around passively and wait anymore for things to get better. Not for my job, not for Brandon, not for anything, despite the fact that everyone seemed to be telling me to do just that.

The nervous energy followed me back up to the penthouse. I took one look around the cold, empty space and I knew I couldn't stay there. But since it was close to midnight, there wasn't a lot more I could do. I just needed a way to get rid of my nervous energy.

"Lucas," I called out just before my bodyguard disappeared into the elevator.

"Ms. Crosby?" he asked kindly.

"Hold on a sec," I said as I limped toward the bedrooms. "I'm going to go for a swim."

* * *

I liked swimming at night. It was one of the reasons I belonged to a twenty-four-hour gym. I never had to share lanes with anyone, and I could meditate in the water the same way many people do in the wee hours of the morning. With the flurry of thoughts running through my head at the moment, I wasn't as tired as I should have been after a long day at work and the evening out. I suddenly had a lot of excess energy to burn off.

But despite the fact that it was so late on a Friday, the twenty-five-meter pool on the twentieth floor of Brandon's building wasn't empty.

To my surprise, I walked in to find Brandon's big form hunched at the water's edge. His jacket, shoes, and socks had been neatly cast on a lounge chair, but he still wore a white dress shirt and black vest, his black suit pants rolled up to his knees while he dangled his feet in the water. The pool's reflection cast a halo around his dark blond head, making him look like a tortured angel.

"We'll be all right, Lucas," I said softly, but it wasn't until the door slammed shut that Brandon turned around.

"Jesus," he said, clearly surprised. "What are you doing here?"

I held up my goggles and swim cap as I walked to join him. I tossed my cover-up and flip-flops on the lounger next to Brandon's clothes. Brandon cast a sideways glance down my bared body as I lowered myself beside him, but he was clearly too caught up in his own thoughts to do more than that.

"What are *you* doing here?" I asked as I dipped my feet into the water.

The backlighting of the pool glowed through aqua-colored waves, brightening Brandon's face as he gazed down.

"I came back to the apartment, but you weren't there. I—it surprised me, was all."

I raised a brow. "So you decided to hang out by the pool?" Brandon wasn't exactly an avid swimmer.

He tipped his head. "I guess...it's one of your places, you know? I thought it might help me understand you a little better." He looked at me with eyes that were as blue as the water. "What were you doing out so late?"

"I went for a drink with Eric, then for a walk."

He frowned skeptically, and glanced at my ankle. "A walk?"

I returned his lopsided smile. "Okay, it was mostly a drive. I had David take me to Magazine Park."

Brandon peered at me curiously. "Why did you go over there?"

I smiled shyly. "I thought it might help me understand you better."

His dimples emerged a little at the repeated line, but they disappeared quickly as we both gazed into the water, hypnotized by the ripples of light.

"You know, for a second, I thought you'd left," Brandon said finally. "I thought you'd gotten another apartment after all."

I looked up. "I told you I'd stay. I would never just go—"

"I'm not done," Brandon said gently as he placed his hand over mine on the edge. "Okay?"

I opened my mouth, then shut it again, transfixed by the feel of his wide, warm palm. "Okay."

He twisted his foot around in the water, and the sound of the trickles filled the room. But he didn't take back his hand.

Oh God, I thought. This is it. He's going to break it off, going to tell me we're done. My heart started thumping wildly, and a hundred different ways to beg him to take me back flew through my mind, each more ridiculous than the next. This man was the only person in the world who could really and truly smash my heart apart, and I was going to have to watch him pull out the hammer.

"I want you to stay, Skylar."

It was like I hadn't heard him as I barreled into my defense. Words poured out of me like vomit, babbling in that way I did whenever I was nervous.

"Please don't do this, Brandon, you and I can make it work, I'll do anything, really. I am so fucking sorry—for everything! I'll stay at home and do all of your laundry and I'll come work at Sterling Grove or be your date to as many stupid functions as you want, or I'll hide behind the couch until your campaign is over if that makes things easier. Anything to make it all up to you, I swear, I—"

"Skylar. *Skylar*," Brandon interrupted. The hand over mine squeezed, silencing my outburst. "Did you hear what I said?"

I bit my lip as his word finally landed. And when I looked up at him, his dimples were out. Just a little. "I—"

"I was miserable this week without you," he continued, holding my gaze with his penetrating blue one while he spoke. "Look, I'm still hurt. I'm still angry. But the truth is...it's so much worse when we're not together. I just don't work without you, Red."

My mouth opened and closed, over and over while I processed his words. All of my crazy plans flew away as I realized what he was handing me. Not a promise that everything was fine. A chance.

"You want me to stay?" I repeated in a small voice.

Brandon nodded, his eyes wide and vulnerable. "I want to try. I don't know what that looks like...but I still want to try."

A sob I didn't know I'd been holding in escaped my throat and echoed through the room. I covered my mouth with both hands as I hiccuped back a few more. Brandon watched cautiously, although he made no move to touch me.

But he wasn't backing away from me. I'd take it.

"You...you have no idea," I choked out. "How much I've...how badly I felt...how much I wanted..." I couldn't get my words out properly. I took a deep breath. "Brandon, would you...would you let me kiss you now?"

It was a familiar request—the same one he'd made other times when he knew I needed control, needed to know he cared about what I wanted. I didn't want to cross his line if he wasn't ready to go there, but I wanted to be close to him more than I'd ever wanted anything in my life.

He stared at me for a moment, his big eyes unblinking. Then, with little more than a grunt, he pulled me into his lap so my thighs straddled him. His hands unerringly found my waist and started to stroke lightly down my back and over my thighs, and back up again as we watched the reflections of the lights bouncing through each other's irises. His chin jutted out slightly, offering his mouth in response to my request, but waiting for me to take what I said I wanted.

So I kissed him. His mouth welcomed me as one of his hands slid up to gather my hair at the nape of my neck. My arms wrapped around his head, pulling him closer as I sucked his lower lip between my teeth and delighted in the feel of his tongue twisting around mine. This was so far from the fury of the other night. It was tentative, but still a homecoming of sorts.

"Skylar." He slipped a hand over my sport bikini top to palm my breasts, one, then the other. "I...Jesus. Baby, I need you. I don't want to...but fuck, I do."

Something in me stilled at his frank admission. Although I wanted nothing more than to let myself melt into his warm touch, I pulled back, clasped his face between my hands, stroking his cheekbones with my thumbs.

"Oh, Brandon," I said as I touched my forehead to his. "I need you too."

It occurred to me just then that I'd never said it before. Not so plainly, without anything else. Brandon stared, face unmoving, but my face reflected in his oceanic eyes with a mix of torture and elation.

"Say it," he whispered even as his fingers tightened around my waist. "Say it again."

"I love you," I pronounced slowly and clearly. "And I need you."

I touched my lips to his again, and it was like a lightning bolt struck through us. Brandon jerked me closer, and his mouth opened hungrily. But as his body lunged toward me, we both lost track of exactly where we were. One moment we were intent on consuming each other; the next, we were toppling into the pool with mutual squawks.

We fell apart, splashing around in the water, finding our bearings. When we surfaced a few feet apart, I was trying to sort my masses of wet hair out of my face, and Brandon held out his arms like a bird as water streamed from his soaked white shirtsleeves. Our gazes met, and suddenly we both started laughing uncontrollably.

"Jesus!" Brandon crowed as he shook out his arms, raining water all around him.

I held my belly and fell back into the water wheezing. "You look like a wet albatross!"

One blond brow arched, even though Brandon's belly was still shaking.

"You think?" he said as he started marching toward me. "I'll show you a wet albatross!"

He dove toward me, grabbing my legs before hefting me over his shoulder and then tossing me back into the water while I shrieked.

"You!" I cried as I swam back to him. "You're going to pay for that!"

I went to splash at him, but he caught my wrist and captured my further cries with another kiss that blew all further thoughts of revenge out of my head. When he released me, I couldn't feel the chill around my shoulders. I could only feel the warmth of his hands at my waist, the pull of his lips on mine

"Please," he said, his voice low and guttural. "Please."

I didn't need to ask what he wanted. Quickly, I undid the buttons down his chest and at his pants, and pulled the sopping fabric from his shoulders. He shimmied out of his pants under the water, and we threw his clothes onto the pool's edge with a splat.

"Your turn," he murmured as his gaze seared over my bikini top. "Off."

Wordlessly, I obeyed. It was another perk of having a bodyguard outside the door, I realized. There was no fear of anyone disturbing us.

Brandon chewed furiously on his lower lip as I peeled off the rest of my suit. As soon as I had tossed it behind me, I found myself backed up to the pool's edge. Brandon ducked his head down and licked, then nipped at one perked nipple, then the other, sucking hard enough that I squeaked at the pain that just bordered on pleasure. His big hands reached under my thighs, and with a splash, I was lifted bodily out of the water and set on the ledge.

"Sit back," he ordered. His palms moved down my legs and gently pushed my knees apart. "Spread your legs."

"Wait," I said with a hand on his chest. Droplets of water hung from the smattering of golden hair there. "I—"

He cut me off with another long, thirsty kiss, one that brought both of our bodies together. There was nothing between us now, and I shuddered at the length of him pressing against my stomach.

"What, Red?" he asked darkly as he let go. He pushed my legs wider apart so that I could feel all of him teasing between them. One hand drifted closer to that meeting place, tickling and testing my patience even as my hips tilted involuntarily toward him.

"I—oooh!" I stuttered as his thumb found my clit.

Brandon sucked again on my lower lip, and most of the blood drained from my head.

"Spit it out, baby," he growled into my ear, biting lightly on the lobe as his thumb moved with a more insistent pressure.

"I-I-I want to—*shit*—I want to please—Jesus!"

"You want to please Jesus?" Brandon said, breaking me out of my reverie just enough to glower at him. He chuckled and leaned in to bite my lip again.

"No," I said with a light shove to his chest. "I want to please *you*."

Without waiting, I reached down and took him in my hand, enjoying the silky feel of him, solid in my palm, and the way his eyes rolled back into his head when my thumb brushed over the tip.

"Fuuuuuck," he moaned, and leaned his head onto my shoulder, both of his hands dropped to the pool's edge to he could maintain his balance. His hips tilted further into my hand, urging me to stroke harder. I turned to kiss him, just as he had kissed me earlier, sucking on his full lower lip until he was moaning in my mouth.

"You like that?" I asked as my hand moved faster. "What else do you want?"

Brandon bit down on my shoulder, and then, with a speed I wasn't expecting, jerked away and lifted my legs up, pulling them over his shoulders instead, forcing me to lie back completely on the pavement.

"What I want," he said once he had my legs pinioned under his forearms, "is to feel you come on my face."

I sat up on my elbow, ready to protest even as the rest of my body opened willingly for him.

"But—" I tried again.

He swallowed my protests when his tongue swiped up my center, and then back down again, forcing me to collapse onto my back and take his ministrations. There was no way I could do anything else.

"Brandon," I moaned as he slipped one finger, then two into my slick heat.

"Shhhh," he vibrated against that most sensitive spot. He sucked and nipped, his stubble rubbing deliciously against my inner thighs.

A third finger entered me, and all three curled upward as he continued his work, building me up, stopping, then building me up again.

"Brandon." Totally oblivious to the concrete floor, I could only say his name as my back arched upward and I gasped toward the ceiling. "Please."

He said nothing, just hummed slightly as he worked, causing a vibration whose effect was instantaneous. The man could seriously play me like an instrument.

"Oh, *fuck*!" I cried out as the first spasms shot through my body. Brandon pressed harder with both his fingers and his tongue, and I started to shake. "Oh, Jesus...*Christ*...Brandon, I'm com-*coming*! Bran—DON!"

But before I could completely shake out my orgasm, he had pulled back both his hand and mouth, and entered me suddenly with one rough thrust. He filled me completely, one rough hand grasping the flesh of my thigh, the other sliding behind my back to lift my tensed body up so he could crash his lips to mine as he moved. The effect simply drew my orgasm out longer, causing me to shake uncontrollably in his arms while his hips thrust furiously toward his own release.

"That's it, Skylar," he growled as he bit into my neck. "Keep coming for me. Keep squeezing me, baby. Just. Like. *That*!"

My fingers wove into his hair, clutching the damp curls for dear life as he plunged into me, thrust after unforgiving thrust. My cries filled the room as he pounded once, twice, three more times, until finally he found his release with a long, low shout. My heels, hooked around his waist, squeezed and shook, and I held on for dear life as both of our bodies trembled together.

"You okay?" Brandon said a few seconds later.

He pulled back, releasing me from the vise-hold against his chest. He slid a hand over my cheek, brushing lightly over the spot where a few slight remnants of my injuries still showed. I winced a little, but his touch was light enough that it didn't hurt.

His eyes were still wide, still a little bit afraid. But they were tender too, and for the first time in a while, warm.

I smiled and nuzzled into his chest.

"I'm fine," I said. "I love you."

Tentatively, he wrapped his arms around me and sighed, although he didn't respond in kind. The omission hurt, but I was okay with that for now. I couldn't expect to get all of him back in one night.

A few moments later, he released me with a kiss to my forehead, then hopped up onto the ledge and padded to the stack of courtesy towels on a shelf by the door.

"Come on, Red," he said as he wrapped one around his waist, covering himself up just enough to make it down the hall to the elevators. "Let's go home. It's late, and we still have some more making up to do."

* * *

"No! Stop!"

Just as my eyes were starting to get used to the pitch-black room, I was rammed off the mattress onto the carpeted floor with a thud.

"Ow!" I yelped, rubbing my head as I pushed myself up.

Brandon was asleep, writhing, muttering pained gibberish while the sheets twisted around his body.

"No!" he cried out, bracing himself against the mattress like he was defending a blow. "Skylar!"

111

He stared out at some invisible phantom, his blue irises dilated and the color of a night sky, glassy and crazed. His chest rose and fell, the muscles in his neck ticked.

"Brandon?" I asked in a small voice.

At the noise, he jerked his face in my direction, but saw without seeing.

"Skylar?" he asked in a low, slight voice that was terrifying for the fear in it.

"Brandon?" I asked again. "I'm here. I'm safe."

It was like a veil was lifted. He blinked, once, twice, and his pupils shrank to their normal size as he regained full consciousness. He found me on the floor where I was peeking over the mattress edge, and then confusion, followed by shock, registered on his face.

"Shit," he said, lumbering across the bed to help me up. "Did I push you off?"

"It's okay."

I climbed back on, and the bed sank slightly under our combined weight. The comforter was dark gray, like most of the other furnishings in the apartment. I was reminded once again of how much I hated this place—how cold it was, how unfriendly. Brandon sat up and leaned back against the headboard, his hands thrust into his hair, elbows balanced on his knees.

"Shit," he muttered, the voice muffled through his forearms. "I'm so sorry." He looked up. "Are you okay? Your ribs, your ankle—"

"I'm fine," I cut in, laying a hand on his arm.

He looked down at it and laid his head on my fingers for a moment.

"Brandon," I said quietly. "What is going on? You never did this before. Is it—is it because of...what I did? Is it because of the abortion?"

The word hadn't actually been uttered out loud between us. It was always other people saying it, along with plenty of other things.

He took my hand, and played a moment with the delicate bones. I didn't notice it most of the time, but his hands swallowed mine.

"No," he said quietly. "It's not that. I mean...it doesn't make it any easier, of course. But I told you, Red. I forgive you."

Relief washed over me, but it was quickly overtaken by a different concern. If our problems weren't the main source of his sleep problems, then what was?

"Then what's going on?" I asked.

Brandon sighed.

"I used to get them before," he admitted. "When I was a kid. They would come and go. They didn't stop until I had been at the Petersens for a year or two, after they forced me to see a counselor." He blanched. I already knew that Brandon wasn't the biggest fan of therapy, but I wasn't totally sure why.

"What—what are the dreams about?" I asked, hoping he would keep talking.

He shook his head, but lay back on his pillow. I followed him, and we faced each other in the dark.

"All sorts of things," he said. "There were always a few recurring ones. When I was a kid, it was mostly my father, the things he would...do. To my mom and me."

He lay there for a moment, then turned onto his back and stared up at the cold, white ceiling. I didn't know the specifics, but between Kieran and Susan, I had been told enough about Brandon's childhood to know he'd had it bad. Really, really bad.

"He was big," Brandon said in a low voice that was almost a whisper. "Taller than me, if you can believe that. When he'd come home from the bar, I'd see his shadow coming up the stairs before he appeared. I remember crying to my ma, scared that a monster was there. She's just say, no, it's just your pops. And I'd be even more afraid."

"Why?" I asked. "What happened?"

Brandon closed his eyes and shuddered. "Which time?"

I was silent now, afraid to even breathe. There was nothing I could say or do to make those memories disappear. Most of the time I wouldn't choose to erase Brandon's past, since it made him who he was. But this pain, I would gladly vanquish.

Brandon squeezed my hand a little tighter, then turned to me with eyes that were one part sad, one part hopeful.

"They'll go away, Red," he said. "They always do." He pulled my hand to his lips and feathered them softly over my knuckles.

"Come here," I said softly.

I tugged on his hand, and Brandon scooted the rest of the way across the bed so that he could lay his head on my chest. He sighed, long and contentedly as his other arm wrapped about my waist and he buried himself into me.

"God, you smell good," he murmured, his voice already slurring toward a hushed sleep. "I missed you," he rumbled into my ear.

His big body wrapped itself around me, his arm around my waist tight. But slowly, slowly, he relaxed, his breaths growing longer, his limbs heavier. I wove my fingers through his thick hair over and over again, and he sighed.

"I missed you too," I whispered. "I love you."

But he didn't answer. He was already fast asleep.

Thirteen

I woke up the next morning alone. Still, I could feel, rather than see Brandon's absence. When I turned over, he was standing at one of the picture windows, looking over Boston like a king.

He wore nothing but his usual black boxer briefs, the ones that slung just below his hip bones and perfectly set off the ridiculously cut muscles of his lower abs. His arms, crossed over his chest, bulged slightly, and the lean muscles in his legs were flexed all the way to the floor.

I might have tried to lure him back to bed if it hadn't been for the look on his face. His brow was furrowed, and the late morning light cast shadows over the notched scar and tiny frown lines above his eyebrows and at the side of his eyes. His hair looked like he'd spent most of the morning tugging on it, but for now, he was obviously lost in thought.

As if he sensed my gaze, suddenly he turned his head, and his blue eyes, now the color of the sky behind him, zeroed in on mine and brightened.

"Hey," he said. "You're up."

I pushed myself up, propping my head on one elbow. "Just barely. You okay? You looked awfully deep in thought over there."

Despite his size, Brandon moved with the grace of a cat. In a few brief steps, he slid back into bed and lay on his side, facing me. I lay back again, allowing him to drape an arm over my torso. His hand drifted over my collarbone, between my breasts. I thought I knew where he was going, but his fingers stilled just over the flat expanse of my stomach, right over my navel.

"I was just thinking," he said quietly. "Of what could have been."

My breath caught in my throat. Oh. Was he rethinking everything? Maybe forgiveness was still too much to ask, no matter what he had said last night.

"I think..." he started low, so quietly his voice almost blended in with the rustle of the covers. "I think I understand now. Why you...didn't keep the baby, I mean."

Terror tore through me. Was this the part where he told me he couldn't get over it after all? I tried to move, but his hand stilled my hips, and his penetrating blue gaze pinned me in place.

"Just listen?"

I took a deep breath and obeyed, staring up at the ceiling. Maybe it was better that we didn't look at each other. I didn't think I could handle the depths of that stare right now. Maybe he couldn't handle mine either.

"Okay," I said.

He grazed his fingernails over the length of my forearm, the shimmer of light hair there.

"We...weren't together," he said, stumbling a little over the words. "And you...you were afraid. Of our kid being caught, like you were, between parents who wouldn't always be there for it. I mean, *I* knew I loved you, Skylar, but I *was* still married. And I did keep that from you. And how I went about dealing with that shit with your dad...Jesus. You must have been so scared. So confused."

Wordlessly, I nodded. There was nothing I could say. I wasn't interested in defending myself, even if he did speak the truth. I had been scared—terrified, in fact.

"Do you regret it?" he asked softly.

Brandon's thumb lightly stroked just below my navel. The tenderness of the small gesture made me choke up.

"I..." I started softly, entranced by the movements of his fingers. "Sometimes."

It was the best I could do. I cleared my throat, determined this time not to internalize everything. I had made this decision for the both of us, in my own way railroaded him the same way I was always accusing him of doing to me. In so many ways, our problems often came when I kept things to myself.

"I regret losing that potential, that future," I said, "I love you so much now, and I loved you then too. And that part of me, the part that does want to raise a family with you one day, Brandon, that part regrets it a lot. That part mourns. Will probably always mourn."

We stared together at the space below his hand, entranced by the fickle quality of his rough calluses stroking the smooth skin, tickling my navel. A tear trickled down my cheek. I didn't wipe it away.

"Mostly," I continued, "I regret not telling you. Not letting you decide with me. I took that away from you, and... Jesus, Brandon, sorry doesn't even begin to cover it. I *never* should have done that. I should have told you from the start. From the second I knew I was pregnant."

I hiccuped over my own voice, the tears falling faster now.

"I'm so sorry," I choked out. "More than you'll ever know."

His hands were so gentle, more than I deserved.

Brandon said nothing for a long time, just let me cry, his hand remaining on my stomach. I turned my head into his neck, letting the tears come, letting both of us be vulnerable together in a way we never had before. For the first time since I'd met him, everything was out on the table, good, bad, and ugly. There were no secrets, no lies. Just us, imperfect as we were.

Eventually, all of the pain from the last several months apart, the yearning, the guilt, flowed out, until all that was left was the warm length of his body next to mine, and the complete and utter love I still felt flowing between us. It gave me hope.

"Shhhh," Brandon finally murmured into my ear. He placed a slow kiss at the edge of my earlobe and pulled me into his chest. "I already told you, Red. I forgive you." Then, after another pause: "I'm glad you did it."

Wetly, I blinked, completely taken by surprise. "Wha-what?"

"I'm glad you did it," he repeated. He pulled back to look me in the face. Even though his eyes were wet and fathomless, they were also kind. "I know what it's like to be raised by parents who don't have it together, Skylar. So do you, for that matter."

"Brandon, I wouldn't have been like your—"

"I know," he cut me off. "I know, baby. I know that even if you were living in a dumpster, you'd be a better mother than mine ever fucking was. But the fact is, our lives, our relationship, was a mess."

I gulped. The vitriol of that statement wasn't intended for me, but it hurt anyway.

"But I'm glad you didn't have to go through it alone," he continued quickly, still stroking my back. "Because if we have a kid, we're going to do it right. Together."

I didn't miss the emphasis on the word "if." His uncertainty stung, but I couldn't blame him for it.

"But what if it doesn't happen again?" I wondered.

117

I knew that in all likelihood, I'd be able to get pregnant again one day. But by the time I was ready (likely not for another three-to-five years, once having a baby wouldn't essentially mean career suicide), there was definitely a chance it would be a lot harder.

"Honestly?" Brandon said. "It doesn't really matter. When we're ready, we'll try. And if it happens, great, but if it doesn't, then we'll do what Ray and Susan did for me. Only this time, we'll do it without any strings attached. We'll love that kid like it's really our own."

His body tensed, and once again, I found myself wondering what sorts of demons were circling around his mind. If I asked, I wasn't sure he would tell me, so I decided not to press. Not now. The time would come for that catharsis another day.

Until then, I knew I had more work to do to earn back Brandon's trust. The plan I had come up with sitting by the river swirled around in my head again, and I nuzzled his shoulder, ready to get started. Love was just one step toward healing.

* * *

It was close to noon when Lucas pulled the Escalade in front of the small colonial house in Somerville. I sat there for a moment, taking in the house where Brandon spent ten years after social services had placed him with his foster parents, Ray and Susan Petersen. Having missed his morning workout, Brandon had taken a few hours with his trainer later in the morning before going to a meeting with Cory and the rest of his campaign staff.

"Everything all right back there, Ms. Crosby?"

I looked up at Lucas and smiled, although I was a little sad. This was going to be a hard conversation.

"I hope so," I said, and got out.

"I'll be out front when you're ready to go, Ms. Crosby," Lucas said as he ushered me up to the porch.

He glanced suspiciously from side to side while we waited for the Petersens to answer the doorbell. Two weeks ago, I would have rolled my eyes at his protectiveness, would have fought it tooth and

118

nail. But after being kidnapped—an experience I still hadn't even started to process—I was grateful to have the big man with me.

"Oh Ray, keep your hat on!"

Susan's voice rang through the oak, and a second later her birdlike form opened the door. She looked the same as the last time I saw her, albeit dressed in casual jeans and a flowy blue shirt instead of the equally flowy dress she had worn to Brandon's campaign announcement.

The Petersens, I knew, weren't particularly happy with Brandon's sudden decision to run for mayor. While at first enamored by the idea of Brandon becoming a statesman, even the president, Susan had clearly been overwhelmed by the press attention she'd received at the fundraiser. Ray, on the other hand, simply thought politics was a waste of Brandon's keen mind. Of course, the man wouldn't have settled for anything less than his own profession, an MIT professor and researcher.

"Skylar!" Susan cried out with her arms held toward me. She pulled me in for a quick, tight hug, and with an uncomfortable nod at Lucas, shut the door behind us.

"Gets a bit tiresome, doesn't it?" she asked. "Having them around all the time. Ray's about had it up to here, let me tell you."

I shrugged off my jacket and allowed her to take it, looking around curiously. "You have a security detail too? Where are they?"

"You didn't see the van across the street?" she said waving a hand toward the door. "They watch the house like hawks." Then she put a hand on my shoulder. "But of course it's necessary, after what you went through, dear. Just awful—Ray and I were terrified when we heard the news."

Something in me stilled. Susan was one of the few people who had actually mentioned out loud what I'd been through. I took a deep breath and smiled.

"Yes, I'm afraid that's my fault," I agreed grimly. "I'm so sorry my family's troubles are causing so much frustration for everyone."

"Oh, hush," Susan chided as she led me down the hallway. "You're not the hooligan bullying everyone, now are you? And after what they did to you..." she clucked her tongue, looking me over carefully. "You look amazing. I'd be an absolutely mess if someone abducted me, good lord. Thank goodness you're all right, and thank

119

goodness for Brandon, is all I can say. We might grumble about the security, but the truth is, I'm glad I don't have to worry."

I followed Susan into the kitchen, where her husband, Ray, was enjoying a soda and scratching notes on a pad of paper. They were clearly math notations, much like the ones I'd seen in his office (and the similar pages of notation Brandon occasionally tinkered with from time to time). The table was covered with them.

Not for the first time, I wondered if the man ever stopped working. Like father, like son, I supposed. Which, of course, was why I was here.

"Lunch is almost ready," Susan said as she bustled over to the stove. "I made my famous chicken pot pie. Can I get you a drink while we wait, Skylar? A glass of wine, maybe?"

"Why can she have wine in the middle of the day, and I'm stuck with soda?" Ray piped up, although he didn't lift his head from his work.

"*She's* not the one on blood pressure medication," Susan rejoined.

"I'm fine, Susan," I said. "Water is great."

She poured glasses of water for all three of us, carried them to the table, and sat down beside me. "Ray, put that away. We have company now."

After Ray grumbled and stowed his work on the cluttered counter behind him, he turned to me curiously.

"So, you didn't die," he said gruffly, looking me over. He eyed the still-red scar over my eyebrow. "Got you good, I see."

I gulped, ignoring the rising panic that shot through my system as I recalled the blows to my face. I'd worked hard to shove it all away for the past few weeks, but it was going to be harder when people I knew commented on it every time I saw them. I reached up and gingerly touched the scar across my eyebrow.

"I'm alive," I said simply.

I closed my eyes, remembering the look on Brandon's face when he busted through the door. The fury. The desperation. Thank God, I thought. Thank God he had found me.

Ray grunted. "This is exactly what I feared," he said to Susan. "And it's just the start. He goes into the public eye, and what happens? We all have bull's eyes drawn on our foreheads."

I opened my mouth, prepared to tell them just *why* Messina had chosen to target me, but Susan spoke up first.

"We've always been targets, Ray," she said. "Brandon has always attracted the attention of all sorts of people—you know that. Or have you forgotten what it was like when he was a teenager, getting into all that trouble? Or when the Keiths took a liking to him. Stan Keith could see his potential when he was still basically a street thug. Why do you think he was willing to marry his daughter off to a boy he hardly knew?"

"And you don't think this kind of pressure is going to get to him?" Ray retorted.

But Susan just sighed impatiently. "I think it doesn't matter, you idiot. We love him and support him. That's all that matters."

Her words were encouraging, considering what I was there to do. I took a deep breath. I might have been overstepping, but I didn't care. This was more important than whether or not Ray and Susan decided to like me.

"That's good to hear," I said as I pulled a slim file from my bag and set it on the table.

"What's this?" Ray flipped through the papers and darted a suspicious glance at me through his smudged glasses.

"They're adoption papers," I said evenly, ignoring Susan's sharp intake of breath while I maintained eye contact with Ray. He was the one I needed to win over anyway.

"Adoption..." muttered the gruff older man. "Adopt who? Brandon?" He snorted and his white brows furrowed, like two crooked caterpillars. "Why would this even be necessary? He's almost forty, for Pete's sake."

"It's not necessary," I said as they continued to page through the document. "It's a gesture. A way to tell Brandon that, well, you really consider him family. Your son."

At that, Ray flipped his sharp gaze back to me.

"Well, *of course* he's my son," he snapped. "Why the hell would anyone think otherwise?"

"Probably because we never did anything like this," Susan said wearily. The look on her face made me wonder if this had been a conversation they'd had before.

Ray swiveled to his wife. "What are you talking about? Brandon knows we're his family."

"That's the thing, Ray," I said gently. "I don't think he does."

I proceeded to detail all of the things Brandon had told me about his relationship with the Petersens—his uncertainty regarding Ray's affections, his suspicions that they had allowed him to live permanently with them more because of his mathematical aptitude (and its potential to help Ray's scholarship) and less because of their genuine affection. His constant feeling like all of his considerable accomplishments were never enough for Ray. His guilt over choosing to live with them instead of his abusive, drug-addicted mother, and her subsequent death by overdose soon after.

Then I told them about the kind of stresses he was really under now, or at least what I knew of them. I came clean about everything—the fact that I had only found out about Miranda last spring, and following that had left Brandon, but discovered I was pregnant soon after. The fact that my father, a recovering addict, had brought Messina down on all of us. The fact that I had had an abortion and hid it from Brandon. And the fact that he had found out an hour before announcing his candidacy for mayor.

Under the critical eyes of Brandon's foster parents, coming clean about my contributions to Brandon's anxiety was the hardest thing I had ever done. But by the end, I was relieved. I wanted to help unite this family, and I could never hope to be a part of it if I wasn't honest about who I really was.

By the end, Ray sat there, clearly dumbfounded, and Susan had tears streaming down her face. She swiped back one, then another, but they kept falling.

"I never knew," she kept whispering to herself as she folded her hands together in her lap. "He never said a word about any of this. He talks about you, of course, Skylar. Every time we speak. But he never...nothing in the last few weeks, or even months. Oh, my poor boy."

"Well, at least one of you had the smarts to do the right thing," Ray muttered.

I looked up. "Excuse me?"

"About the baby," he said, pointing a knobby finger in a very professorial way, as if indicating I should have known. Ray had a way of talking to everyone as if they were stupid. "You and Bran met, what, last February? And he thought it would have been a good idea to raise a child with someone he hardly knew?" He snorted. "Typical Brandon. I swear, Susan, he never thinks things through."

"My decisions had nothing to do with him," I protested. "To start, it could have happened to anyone. We were using protection. It failed. And maybe what I did makes logical sense, but the reality is that I love your son, Ray, and he loves me. But I hurt him badly, and he's suffering because of it."

Susan blinked with concern. "Suffering how?"

"Nightmares," I said plainly. "Almost every night now."

Susan and Ray both straightened immediately.

"What?" Susan asked as she held a hand to her lips. "After all this time?" She looked at her husband. "Do you remember what they were like?"

Ray said nothing, just stared hard at me. "Is he taking anything?"

I frowned, confused. "Not that I know of. Should he be?"

Ray sighed and shook his head. "No. The group homes used to put him on all sorts of terrible antipsychotics for the terrors because they thought he was a threat to the other kids. The social workers wanted us to keep him on them, but when our arrangement became permanent, we took him off. Paid for a real therapist, not just some state quack."

I swallowed and decided to make my move.

"I wonder...I wonder if it's because he's scared again. What I did...well...you know about that now. And with everything else that's happened, the threats to me and my family, the kidnapping, and, of course the pressure on him right now with his run for office...I think he's lost that feeling of safety again. In a different way, of course, but still...lost."

I reached out to the papers between us. "I was hoping something like this would help. I want to do what I can to show him that he isn't alone in this—any of it. I want to show him the people who love him, who can still offer safe harbor." I paused, drifting my fingers over the plain black-and-white text. "I just want to make him happy."

"Oh, sweetheart," murmured Susan as she reached across the table for my hand. "He's very lucky to have you."

I was surprised by how quickly her statement brought the glimmer of tears to my eyes. I genuinely wasn't sure how the

Petersens would respond to my revelations. I had honestly been prepared to be kicked out of the house at the end of everything.

"Thank you," I said quietly, squeezing her hand back. "Truly."

Ray just stared at the documents for another few moments, then back at me.

"And you think this...would tell him he's my son?" he asked. "Without a doubt?"

I shrugged. "It takes more than a piece of paper to make a family," I admitted. "But yes, I think it will help. It can't hurt."

Susan bit her bottom lip and watched Ray. The older man peered at me with sharp eyes that glinted through his smudged glasses. His jaw was clenched as he considered the decision. It was the most focus I'd ever seen Ray Petersen put on someone without criticizing them.

"Where do we sign?" he asked finally.

I released a breath I didn't know I'd been holding.

"Start here," I said, flipping a page in front of him. "And I'll take care   of   everything   else."

Fourteen

"I don't know," I said after I swallowed a bite of chicken salad on Monday. "They signed the papers, but it doesn't seem like enough. Like, 'here's some proof your parents actually love you, so can you love and forgive me too?' Meh. I need more."

On my desktop computer screen, Jane cocked her head. She looked about as conservative as I'd ever seen her, in a stolid gray shift dress and matching jacket, her black hair tamed respectably. The only thing about her regular style, which usually looked like something off a Sex Pistols poster, were the vintage red frames resting on the end of her nose while she scanned over the adoption papers I had just emailed.

"Looks good to me," she said finally. "But you're the family law expert, chick. I just go after the bad guys."

She took a massive bite of ramen, enough that she had noodles streaming out of her mouth in a way that made her resemble Cthulhu. I laughed when she tried to speak.

"What's that?" I asked. "I don't speak noodle."

Jane swallowed and rolled her eyes. "I said, what does Eric think?"

I narrowed my eyes, and she studiously looked at her desk. I set down my fork.

"Don't play coy," I said. "It really doesn't suit you. *Eric* doesn't think anything because *Eric* is not my best friend in the world and the only other person on the planet who knows I am doing this. And correct me if I'm wrong, but I believe that *Eric* was too busy in Chicago this weekend to talk about this, wasn't he?"

Jane bit at her thumbnail and gave me a grimace. "What do you want me to say?"

I pressed my lips together and said nothing at all. Jane sat back in her chair and groaned up at the ceiling.

"Yes, fine, *fine!*" she cried. Then, pointing at me through the lens of the video camera: "Okay, *Clockwork Orange*. Stop staring at me like a psycho."

I sighed, but still cracked a smile. "So what happened? I take it not good."

Jane just closed her eyes and sighed. "So you knew he was going to show up this weekend?"

I nodded. "Yeah. I was there when the light bulb went on."

"Why didn't you stop him?"

I grimaced. "It was really that bad?"

Jane toyed with her noodles. "No. It was just...awkward. He showed up at my cousin's apartment at noon. And I..." she trailed off. "Okay, so I might have had another guy in my room with me."

My jaw dropped. "Jane..."

"What, like that's a surprise. I'm single, Sky. And you *were* my roommate for three years."

"Yeah, but..." I shook my head. "Poor Eric, though. I mean, you guys just barely broke up."

Jane tucked a piece of hair back behind her ear and shrugged, looking guilty. It wasn't an emotion I was familiar seeing on her face.

"Yeah, well," she said. "It's for the best, I guess. You know I'm not the type to sit around in relationships past their expiration date. Neither is Eric for that matter. I'm sure he'll be back to fucking Aryan Barbies in no time."

I bit my lip. The way my friend was twisting her lips told me there was a lot more to her denial than just a fear of intimacy. But before I could answer, the phone on my desk rang.

"Skylar Crosby," I answered on speaker with a know-it-all grin at Jane.

"There's a Janette Jadot here for you," said Peter, the front receptionist. "Are you expecting her?"

I froze. On the screen, Jane's jaw had dropped completely, revealing another mouthful of half-chewed noodles.

I hadn't heard from my mother in weeks—not since that horrendous moment at Brandon's candidacy announcement, when she and several other people had watched Brandon's and my relationship implode with the revelation of my betrayal. It was a revelation for which Janette was responsible. She and her backstabbing husband, desperate for cash to support Maurice's downtrodden career, had actually had me followed by a private investigator in the hopes that he would dig up enough dirt to blackmail me. In the end, the photos and the record of the abortion had gone to the highest bidder: Miranda Sterling née Keith,

126

Brandon's ex-wife. And she, of course, had gone straight to Brandon, hoping to lasso his attention back to her.

So in a very real way, my own mother was directly responsible for the tenuous condition of my relationship (not to mention the fact that I had fled the party and immediately been abducted). And now she was here. The question was why.

"Send her back, please," I told Peter. "Thanks."

"Don't you *dare* take me off this screen, Skylar," Jane reprimanded, sticking a finger into the webcam. "Tell that bitch to go back to the seventh circle where she belongs."

"Jane...I gotta go."

"No, Sky—"

"Byeloveyoutellyoueverythingafter," I said quickly enough that my friend couldn't get a word in edgewise before I exited out of the chat window.

A few minutes later, I watched through the glass office walls as Peter escorted Janette down the hall. She was dressed as impeccably as ever in a pair of white summer pants and a blue-and-white-striped blouse. With her light brown hair twisted back, she looked a little like Audrey Hepburn.

She caught sight of me through the walls and waved Peter away. I stood as she entered.

"Skylar," she said cautiously, hovering near the doorway, then taking a few more steps in.

"Janette."

"Thank you for seeing me."

I tapped my fingernails on the desktop. "You didn't really leave me a choice."

"Skylar, please. I wouldn't have made a scene."

She looked me up and down, her bright green eyes—the same exact shade and almond-shape as mine—perusing me. "I heard you were...hurt. Your grandmother called to tell me."

Bubbe. I shook my head. Of course she wouldn't have been able to resist rubbing everything in Janette's face. She hated her with a passion, and wouldn't have hesitated to lay all the blame for my kidnapping straight at Janette's designer-shoed feet.

"I'm glad to see you're all right," Janette continued. "You haven't answered any of my calls."

I didn't say anything, just glared until she had the decency to look away.

"Skylar," she started again as she trailed a delicate finger up and down the back of the chair. "I'm so sorry, darling—"

"I don't think so," I cut her off. I pushed my glasses up my nose and crossed my arms. "After what you and Maurice did, you should be glad I haven't already filed a restraining order. And if you don't leave me alone, that'll be the next step."

That's right. Don't fuck with your daughter when she's a lawyer.

Janette paled visibly, grasping at the edge of the office chair.

"That's all," I said as I sat back down. "I have a lot of work to do. You should probably leave now."

"I was wondering if I could take you to lunch," Janette said, pivoting completely, although when she looked at the half-eaten salad on my desk, her expression fell.

I gaped. "Are you kidding? Did you hear a word I just said?"

Janette rolled her eyes, the first sign I'd seen that broke through her carefully crafted elegance. "Of course, Skylar, my ears work perfectly well." She looked at me, her green eyes flashing. "I'd like to talk to you about Annabelle and Christoph. I know you want to see your brother and sister."

I pursed my lips. Annabelle and Christoph, Janette's children with her husband, Maurice, were a delight—in other words, nothing like their parents. I had only just met them this summer, and the thought of losing them all over again did hurt. Before things had all gone south, Brandon and I had been trying to convince Maurice and Janette to put their children in boarding school in Massachusetts instead of Switzerland so that I could see them more often.

Finally, I sighed and tossed the rest of my salad in the trash.

"Fine," I said. "Thirty minutes. But that's it."

* * *

We walked in relative silence, letting the buzz around Copley Square and our steps on the sidewalk fill the space between us. Lucas

128

followed several yards behind, but every so often, Janette would glance back at him, as if his presence unnerved her.

"Must he follow you everywhere?" she asked. "He's so...conspicuous."

I glanced back at Lucas and waved. He continued to survey the scene.

"He helps make sure no others psychos have secret photographers following me," I retorted.

There was a long silence. We continued to walk, and Janette gave a few more half-hearted attempts at small talk.

"That's a nice suit," she said some time later. "It's good to see you in something more tailored. You have such a nice figure—it's a shame when you cover it up."

I rolled my eyes. Between Janette and Bubbe, I would always have someone trying to get me out of my favorite old jeans. The only person who seemed to like me in them was Brandon.

"Those shoes are...an interesting choice with that outfit," Janette continued.

I looked down at my flats. They were polished, though obviously not the standard choice for a suit. But I still couldn't walk in heels with my ankle the way it was. I frowned. I wasn't really in the mood for Janette's passive-aggressive bullshit.

"How about here?" I announced, stopping in front of a cafe that had an al fresco seating area. It was across from the Common. Through the trees, I could actually see the black iron gate and the gray stone exterior of Brandon's old house. The house where we'd met.

The cafe was quiet. We could sit outside, where no one would overhear our conversation easily, and I could leave quickly if Janette was too much to deal with.

Janette looked over the restaurant skeptically. "Here? I was thinking we could go down to the Martin or someplace like that. It's only a few blocks away."

"Janette, aren't you broke?" I asked bluntly. "I mean, isn't that why you tried to fuck up your daughter's life?"

"Wel—I—not entirely..." she replied with slightly reddened cheeks. She stood up straighter. "Mother is helping with an allowance."

Ah. So she'd used her kids to get back into her parents' good graces. I rolled my eyes and turned into the restaurant.

"Well, I'm going in," I said over my shoulder. "You can come or not."

We took a table outside, just under a hanging pot of overflowing petunias past their prime. Lucas sat a few tables away, giving Janette and me some relative privacy. A waiter brought some water while we perused our menus.

"I'll just have the garden salad," Janette said.

"The tortellini for me," I said as I handed him back the menu.

"Really?" Janette asked. "It's so heavy."

I didn't respond, just gave her a look. She held up her hands.

"Far be it from me to worry about my daughter."

"Seriously," I said. "Don't bother."

The waiter walked away with an expression that made him look like he'd rather stay to watch the show. After he was out of earshot, I leaned across the table. Janette leaned back slightly.

"I agreed to this lunch for two reasons," I said in a low voice that I hoped was menacing. "To get you off my back and to figure out a way to see my siblings. Beyond Christoph and Annabelle, you and I are *never* going to have the kind of relationship that allows you to comment on my clothes, my food, or, really, any other facet of my life. If you can't handle that, I'll leave right now."

Janette's green eyes widened, but she didn't move other than to take a slow sip of her water and then set it down.

"I understand," she said quietly. Her gaze finally blinked away, taking in the green landscape of the Common across the street. "Boston really is a lovely town," she said. "Some parts, anyway."

I glanced back at the park. "Yeah, it is."

"I've left Maurice, Skylar. Or, I suppose I should say that he left me, and I chose not to follow."

I jerked my head back in surprise. "What?"

Janette nodded, shoulders hunched, as if the admission made her uncomfortable with her own body.

"I-I hated it. What he—what *we* did to you." She folded and unfolded her napkin.

For the first time, I realized that this was potentially one of the only times in her life Janette had had to deal with legitimate guilt. It wasn't like she hadn't done her fair share to hurt me and my dad over the years, between toying with Dad's emotions and essentially abandoning both of us when I was twelve. But for the first time, she had hurt someone she couldn't just leave or forget about. Not without real consequences, for her and for her family.

At least, I hoped that was what she was thinking.

"Are things really that bad for Maurice?" I asked.

Janette sighed and look another long drink of her water. "Goodness," she said as she glanced behind her. "Will they *ever* return with the wine?" Then she looked back to find me watching her frankly.

"Yes," she replied. "The answer to your question is yes. He...well..." She shook her head, clearly having a difficult time getting the words out. Then she blinked at me. "He was extradited last week."

At that I genuinely gasped, holding my hand to my face. Whatever shit Maurice had gotten himself into in France must have been truly bad if the French government had negotiated for extradition. Brandon had called him a shark and Janet had compared him to Bernie Madoff, but I had thought it was an exaggeration. Apparently not.

"What about Annabelle and Christoph?" I asked immediately. "Are they staying..."

"With my family in New York," Janette confirmed. "As am I."

My heart sank a little at the thought of those kids living on the Upper East Side. I had never met kids more in need of normalcy and affection in my life—two things they were sure not to receive with the Chambers family.

"You could come visit them there..." Janette trailed off as she caught my disbelief.

I had been the Chambers family's dirty little secret since I was born. None of the members of Janette's parochial Upper East Side family had ever wanted to meet me or talk to me. I had gone through the normal stages of rebellion as a preteen, shirking my father and Bubbe in the occasional attempt to crash the Chambers' large apartment up Lexington. But each time I'd been told by the Dominican doorman that I was not welcome, and they had eventually thrown money at my father (who generally took it to the track) and later into a trust fund to pay for my education in exchange for me maintaining my distance.

That had been close to fifteen years ago, just after Janette and Dad had also broken up for the last time.

"Where will they go to school?" I asked, turning the conversation back to Janette's children.

"Well..." Janette trailed off. "I thought...I remembered that Brandon mentioned a boarding school near Boston. Andover, wasn't it?"

I quirked an eyebrow, but didn't respond.

"Maurice didn't like the idea, but I think it's splendid," she rushed on. "And if you want to see them as much as you say you do...well, I thought it might be a good *mea culpa*, as it were. My way of making this mess up to you."

I blinked, somewhat flabbergasted. Only Janette, the world's most self-absorbed person, would think that asking someone else to watch over her children was a way of making an apology.

And yet.

"And you'll stay away," I said. "For good. You won't try to weasel your way back into my life? Brandon's life?"

Janette shook her head solemnly. "I may not be a very good mother," she said, as plainly as Janette could ever say. "But *you* are an excellent sister. Anyone could see that. I believe...no, I *know*, that they would receive far more love from you than they ever could with me or my family."

"Can I get that in writing?"

It sounded like a joke, but it wasn't. I wasn't willing to do this unless she would sign something in the way of formal custody, but also that she wasn't going to harass me or Brandon again.

"Anything you like," Janette said. "As long as you promise to take care of the children. It will be a win-win, really. You'll be able to see them as you like, and I'll be free to leave Mother's house. I'm positively dying for a fresh start, and I simply *can't* last a moment longer with that old gargoyle."

I looked at my mother curiously. I knew she didn't enjoy her mother much, but I wasn't aware of that level of bitterness. Then again, I hardly knew Janette, and had never actually met my maternal grandmother.

"Is that what attracted you to Dad?" I suddenly wondered. "Was it just that he made your mother so angry?"

Janette twirled her bright diamond ring around her elegant finger. At first I thought she wasn't going to respond. It wasn't until I was about to stand up to leave that she started to speak.

"For a long time I wouldn't have anything to do with him," she admitted.

Her doll-like face had taken on a dreamy quality as she looked back to the Common. For a moment, a few strands of her hair fell across her cheeks in the breeze, and I could imagine what she must have looked like to Dad: beautiful, childlike, with a deadly combination of entitlement and naiveté.

"Back then we were so young, and your dad...oh, Skylar, he was so talented. He still is, of course, but then he was writing all of his own music, so young, so vibrant. He would be up on that stage, and he would sing and play, and you just couldn't take your eyes off him. He absolutely transformed."

She closed her eyes, as if she could hear the lilting melodies from way back when. I could imagine them too; his music was the soundtrack of my childhood. And she was right—Dad really did transform on stage, from a homely, mustachioed garbage collector into something magical.

Janette's green eyes popped open, sudden the color of ripe apples as she recalled one particular memory.

"He asked me out so many times," she said. "He had no shame. It didn't matter that he came from nothing. He saw me and wanted me and wasn't afraid to say so. For six months he tried, and six months I said no. And then one night, I said yes."

"He just wore you down?"

Janette smiled sweetly. "In a manner of speaking." She leaned her head onto her hand, propped up on the back of the chair, and drew the scene into the air with her other hand. "Every year the school put on a gala, a performance that attracted donors from all over the city. It was such a big event, conservatory reps, recruiters, even agents came. The school would only allow the best of the best to perform."

"And that was Dad?"

She nodded with a fond smile. "That was Danny. He got up on that stage, and he was supposed to play, I don't know, some jazz thing with his quartet. But before they played, he performed a song he had written for me, and sang it with that sweet, raspy voice of his.

133

And he said my name in front of all those people. This boy from Brooklyn was willing to risk his whole future to tell the world he loved me."

She covered her mouth as her smile grew even bigger with the recollection, and her eyes twinkled with some unspoken memory.

"You know, that might have been the night you were conceived."

I gaped. I hadn't realized how quickly that mistake had happened.

"I wasn't going to keep you," she admitted. "You should know that. But Danny wanted you so badly. He said no matter what happened between us—if I stayed, if I left—he always wanted his daughter." She looked at me with a sad smile. "You know, for all that you look like me, you're really so much more Danny's daughter than mine. You've got that goodness of his. That light, and that willingness to give everything you have to something you love. I was never like that. I could never—love—like that."

I gulped, but didn't say anything. Across the street, a pair of kids was riding bikes in the Common. From this far away, they almost looked like Annabelle and Christoph, and suddenly I was filled with regret and also empathy for my younger siblings. Even as she tried with her second go-around at family, Janette still couldn't find it within herself to love her children more than herself. To give of herself completely.

At least she knows it, I thought.

"Don't lose that goodness," Janette said as she looked toward the kids in the park. "It's the best thing Danny gave you. It's the best thing   you   have."

Fifteen

"Goddamn it, god*damn* it!"

I hurled a fourth dress across the guest room, and the zipper hit the picture window with a smack. I was standing in the middle of the spare room, where my clothes were still hanging in the closet. Well, at least the ones that weren't scattered all over the bed and the floor.

"Whoa there, chickie. Don't take it out on the clothes. Never take your frustrations out on the pretty, pretty clothes."

I turned toward my laptop screen and glared at Jane. She ducked out of the frame, like I was throwing something at her, then popped back up with a smirk through her leopard-print glasses.

"Sorry," I said lamely. "Everything looks the same, the same stupid shit I wear every day. Black. Gray. Boring." I sat down on the bed with a thump that shook the computer. "Janey, this isn't like any other night. I can't *look* like any other night." I groaned. "Why did you have to move to Chicago? I need my fashion guru!"

Jane tapped a finger on her mouth meditatively. "I think you're forgetting one important thing here, Sky."

I cocked my head. "What's that?"

"That it's not about YOU, you pixie-faced narcissist!" she exploded.

She made a big show of fanning herself, as if she'd been forced to lose her cool. My mouth just dropped open, but before I could argue, Jane held up a finger.

"You're not doing this for you," she clarified. "You're doing this for him. So think about it that way: what does *he* like to see?"

"Legs," we both said in unison, and laughed.

"Okay," Jane said. "That narrows it down. It needs to be short, and it needs to be a dress."

I looked woefully back at the closet and the clothes all over the floor.

"Think, Sky," Jane said. "What has he commented on? What have you worn that made him go wild?"

It was hard to say. Before my colossal fuckup, Brandon usually went "wild" no matter what I was wearing. He was as likely to have me up against a wall when I was dressed in flannel pajama pants as when I wore lingerie. The thought brought back all sorts of memories, including our first date. While it had been a disaster, it had literally started when he had walked into my apartment, caged me against a wall, and hoofed me into my bedroom to have his way with me.

It was the first glimpse I'd had of just how talented Brandon really was in certain ways. Unfortunately, he hadn't shown me those talents since last weekend. Our "makeup" was much more gradual than I'd hoped. I hadn't been kicked out of the bedroom again, but he was still home most nights later than I'd like, and had used fatigue as an excuse to get away from my advances.

I brightened at the memory of our first date. "I have an idea."

"Atta girl," Jane said. "Then let's figure out shoes and makeup. I'm thinking Bridget Bardot meets Debbie Harry. I have a couple of tutorials I want you to watch."

* * *

The bar I'd found for the party, simply called Pub, was tucked into a Brookline street off Washington Square. After scouring different venues for a week, it was one of a few that fit the requirements I had for this shindig: casual, spacious, and available on short-notice. Lucas and the additional security team that had been hired for the evening were also happy since it was small enough to keep secure.

I arrived about an hour before everyone else did to help set up. Eric, thank God, had also come early to help me prepare, which, for him, mostly meant sitting on a stool drinking beer while I oversaw the kitchen staff and made sure the Springsteen cover band I'd hired was ready to go.

"How much is all of this costing you?" he asked as he watched me rearrange some appetizer platters across the bar top.

I grimaced. "Too much. But it will be worth it."

Eric looked around the room approvingly. "I'll say. This is exactly the kind of thing I'd want."

"I'll remember to tell Jane," I said slyly.

Eric's face dropped. "Yeah. Well. Don't worry about that. She's...I think we're done, Cros. If you see her, it'll probably be without me there."

I turned from where I was hanging a streamer from the ceiling. I couldn't decide if the balloons and crepe paper looked too cheap, but in the end, I decided that Brandon kind of liked that sort of thing anyway. This was the guy who thought Susan's roast chicken was the tastiest thing in the world, who thought my family's decrepit old house in Brooklyn looked more like home than anywhere he'd ever been. While he certainly had a taste for nicer things, Brandon was also just the kind of guy who would wear the same baseball hat for fifteen years out of sentimental value, and who would keep the old furniture in his vacation home just because it reminded him of the nice family who used to live there.

"She mentioned the trip a little bit to me, but I was hoping you had a Plan B," I admitted. "I gathered it didn't go well."

Eric rubbed a hand over his face and groaned. "You could say that. She...fuck. She has a way of stomping on a guy's heart, Cros, I'll tell you that."

I got off the stool and sat down next to him. "It's just because she's scared, you know."

Eric shrugged. "Scared right into another guy's bed, huh? Or maybe it's just because she's onto something." He stared out the window, toward some unknown scene playing out in his head. "She said monogamy wasn't either of our thing, and we knew that from the beginning. She's never wanted a long-term relationship, and neither have I. She said I might not feel it now, but eventually we both would want out. We'd feel trapped."

"And you think she's right? What about the whole 'I love you' thing?"

He shrugged again and polished off his beer before setting the pint glass on the bar behind him. "I was just kidding myself. This is the longest relationship I've ever had, and it's been, what, two months? Jane doesn't exactly make it a secret that she doesn't like commitment. Plus the long-distance thing..." he trailed off as he twisted his hands together. "I just got caught up. It's for the best that we break it off now."

I watched my friend for a minute while he sat. I suspected he was wrong—that they were both throwing away something special—but

I couldn't urge him to do more than he'd done. If Jane wasn't open to big gestures, they wouldn't work.

"Sometimes it's just timing," I said lamely, and Eric nodded, although the look on his face told me he didn't like that reality.

"Sometimes," he said.

* * *

Slowly, people began to filter into the bar. With the help of Kieran, I'd chosen a relatively small guest list that was comprised mostly of some of Brandon's colleagues, friends from law school, and of course, the respective members of our families. Dad wasn't able to leave his rehab program, but Bubbe had shown up carrying three large casserole dishes full of her brisket, Brandon's favorite of her specialties.

I watched with amusement as my tiny grandmother elbowed her way into the kitchen and gave the cook instructions on the proper way to keep the brisket warm without drying it out. At one point the cook, a young man in his twenties, looked to me with a distinct "HELP ME" expression, but all I could do was raise my shoulders and laugh. Bubbe was a force of nature, and there was no stopping her when it came to food.

Before I knew it, it was nine o'clock, and I was stepping up to the bar's small stage to address the crowd after Lucas told me that Brandon was en route to the bar with his campaign and security staff. Kieran had managed to coerce Cory into cooperating, and I was grateful, since I doubt he would have helped me alone. Apparently Brandon thought he was on his way to a meet-and-greet with a local teachers union, which at least guaranteed he wouldn't be overdressed.

I gripped the microphone and tapped the top, wiping my other palm on my skirt as the crowd quieted and faced me.

"Um, hi, everyone," I said, searching out the familiar faces I knew: Bubbe, Kieran, Eric, Susan, and even Ray. Their kind smiles buoyed me against the other, more skeptical faces who only knew me from newspaper headlines as the person who had broken up Brandon's marriage.

But they were here, and that was all that mattered.

"So, security tells me that the guest of honor is due to arrive in a few minutes. If I could ask everyone to find places that face the bar entrance. Once that's done, please wait for Lucas, our security advisor over there"—I gestured to Lucas's large form at the door, and the big man gave a brief wave—"to give the signal, and then we can shout surprise. Thank you so much for being here."

And with that, I stepped off the stage and let the musicians take their places while I filed to the back of the crowd next to Eric and Bubbe.

"Shouldn't you be up front?" Eric wondered as I hopped onto a stool next to him. He nodded to where Kieran stood in front of the crowd, in a prime spot in front of the door. She would be the first person Brandon saw when he arrived.

I just shook my head. "No. This isn't about me. He'll see me later."

"Head's up!" Lucas's loud voice boomed through the crowd, and everyone went silent.

I could hear Brandon's deep voice filtering through the door before I saw him. It pushed open, and his blond head was turned outside toward his campaign manager, who was looking beyond toward the crowd.

"Fifteen minutes," Brandon was saying. "I'm tired, and Skylar's probably wait—"

"SURPRISE!!!"

The shouts of the crowd yanked Brandon around with utter and complete shock. His tanned face was stretched in astonishment as he looked around, bright eyes gleaming with recognition as they touched on the faces of each and every person in the room. Slowly one dimple, then another made their appearances, until a wide grin that raised the electricity wattage of the building lit up the entire room.

"Holy shit," he finally pronounced to my utter relief, and around him, the crowd laughed.

"Happy birthday, asshole!" yelled a man on the side of the room, one of Brandon and Kieran's law school cohorts whom I had only met about thirty minutes before.

And with that, the crowd consumed him, drawn to his orbit like the star he was.

"Hey, Springsteen!" Brandon crowed when the band started up with "Dancing in the Dark," a guaranteed crowd-pleaser. His massive grin when he registered the tune was enough to make the whole thing worth the trouble.

After Brandon swept her up in a bear hug, Kieran tried to wave me over to them, but I just shook my head and took a drink of my whiskey soda.

"Don't you want to go over there?" Eric said. "You put together this whole shindig. He should know."

I shrugged, transfixed with the happiness in front of me. Brandon couldn't stop smiling as he accepted hugs from person after person. As he turned away from one tight embrace, his gaze finally landed on where I sat across the room.

"Hi," he mouthed as he leaned down to accept a kiss on the cheek from someone else.

I just raised my glass toward him before he turned away, beckoned by another party guest.

"He'll figure it out," I said, and took another drink.

Twenty minutes later, the party was in full swing. People were dancing, enjoying the bar food and brisket, and Brandon was finally able to make his way over to where I stood chatting with Ray and Susan.

"Hi!" he greeted us, stooping down to embrace his foster mother and even slinging a casual arm around Ray's thin shoulders for a quick hug. Then he turned to me with a shy smile. "Hey."

"Hey," I replied, suddenly self-conscious. We made no move to connect, and Ray and Susan both glanced between us curiously.

"Kieran, ah, she said that you were the one who organized all of this."

I glanced around at the people, who were all clearly having a good time, and nodded, slightly embarrassed. "Yeah. I did. Happy Birthday."

"Thank you, Red. I love it."

I looked up to find Brandon's blue eyes filled with nothing but clear gratitude. I exhaled with relief.

"You've been going to so many parties with strangers lately," I said. "I thought you might enjoy one with just people you actually know. People who really love you."

For that I was rewarded with the crooked half-smile that I swore was only reserved for me—the one that meant I saw something others didn't. The one that meant he was mine, or so I hoped. My chest tingled in response.

Beside me, Ray cleared his throat, and the momentary spell was broken.

"Um, we've got a little something for you," he said, pulling out a file.

My eyes bugged when I realized what it was: the adoption papers I'd brought over last week. I hadn't expected them to give them to Brandon here. My chest suddenly felt like it was on ice. What if he didn't want this? What if he thought I'd overstepped?

With a curious glance at me, Brandon took the file from his foster father and started to page through it.

"What is this?" he asked. "Adoption papers?" His sharp eyes drifted over the places where the names had been entered into the document. "*My* adoption papers?"

"It's a little something," Susan spoke up. She was already dabbing at tears in her kind eyes. "Something we should have done a long time ago, Brandon. We should have done it when you—when you made the decision to stay with us for good."

I bit my lip as I watched Brandon read the document. His blond brows furrowed in slight confusion.

"But...it's not like I'm a kid," he said as his eyes darted over the legal jargon. "You could have done the same thing with a will, if that's what you wanted."

Ray cleared his throat again, pulling Brandon's attention.

"This isn't about when we're dead," said the gruff older man. "It's about while we're alive. And Bran—Brandon. Susan's right. We should have done it before. But we're doing it now because you should know the truth: that you *are* our son, and always have been. Sign it, don't sign it. But that's the truth."

We all three of us took a deep breath as Brandon finished reading, but when he looked up, his eyes were bright, shining stars. Susan choked back a sob. Brandon grinned.

141

"Where do I sign?" he asked, feeling in his empty shirt pocket for a pen.

"Here." I thrust a pen toward him, which he accepted with another curious smile my way.

But just before he brought his pen to the paper, his eyes caught my name on a few of the pages. He looked up.

"You did this?" he asked, his eyes full of wonder.

Again, I shrugged, suddenly bashful.

"She did," Susan jumped in. She reached across her husband to grab my hand and squeezed. "She did *all* of it. Came to us. We had lunch. Convinced us it was the right thing to do—and she was right, wasn't she, Ray?"

Ray just grumbled his agreement, but I barely noticed, lost as I was in the swirl of emotions on Brandon's face.

"You hold on to this one, Brandon," Susan was saying. "She's a keeper."

At that, Brandon looked up to his now-parents. "Susan, I'm not sure—"

"I told them everything," I cut in, the words rising out of me before I could stop them. His reticence to accept Susan's sudden endorsement was so clear. I couldn't bear for him to refuse it simply because he thought I had earned it under false pretenses.

"I told them everything," I repeated quietly. "After all, we can't be something we're not with the people we love, can we?"

Brandon just studied me for a moment more, and I forced myself to meet his inquisitive gaze head on.

"No," he said finally. "We can't."

Then he turned back to the bar and signed the document with a flourish, then handed it back to Ray and Susan. All three of them beamed—even Ray. Actually, this might have been the first time I'd ever seen the man smile.

"There," Brandon said. "It's official. Should I call you Mom and Dad now?"

But the joke didn't last long, since Susan launched herself at him, and Ray was soon pulled into a bear hug as well. I dabbed at my eyes with a cocktail napkin, while Brandon scrunched his eyes shut, clearly overwhelmed by the moment.

I slid off my stool, prepared to let the new-old family have a moment to themselves, but was stopped by Brandon's hand tugging me back.

"Wait," he said as he stroked his mother's hair.

With a brief smile, I stood by while they finished their tight embrace, and then waited as Ray pushed away awkwardly and Susan wiped the tears out of her eyes.

"Oh, you sweet boy," she said as she reached up to frame Brandon's shining face between her hands. "We love you always. Happy Birthday."

"Happy Birthday, Bran," Ray said gruffly as he put the document back into his bag. He cleared his throat for what must have been the twentieth time in five minutes. "I need a beer. Susan, can we make an exception tonight?"

"Oh, Ray, it's a party. Let's all celebrate, shall we?"

And with that, she chased him to the other side of the bar, leaving Brandon and me alone. We both leaned against the bar top, nothing touching, but our fingertips less than an inch apart.

"You did this," Brandon said again. "All of this. For me?"

Wordlessly, I nodded and took a long drink of my whiskey soda. Brandon followed the glass from my lips back down to the bar, then lifted his gaze back to my eyes.

"Why?"

"I just...you always do so much for everyone else. I guess I just thought...I thought you deserved it, that's all."

As I said the words, I found they were truer than I thought. Most of this had started out as a massive apology—a plan to win back the love of my life, to make him trust that I truly loved him. But now I realized how little of it had to do with that. I hadn't done it to see the look on his face when he walked into a crowd of people who so clearly adored him, or to watch as he realized just how much the people who had taken him in as a troubled teen truly loved him and wanted him for always.

None of it was for my own gratification. I had done it just to make him happy, whether I could see it or not. And that, I realized, is what you do when you love someone.

"Do you mind?" I asked suddenly. "Is it too much?"

Brandon's face softened. "No, of course I don't mind." He looked me over, his eyes lighting on the dress. "I always liked this dress."

"I thought you did."

Thank God, he remembered. The black knit fabric was a little warm for the end of August, but the look on his face was worth it. Brandon fingered the cap sleeve for a moment. Even the distant touch of his fingers on my shoulder sent a shiver down my arm, but in the best possible way. This close, after another week of barely touching...I could smell him, could feel him. I wanted nothing more than to sink into him, to help him forget everything that had happened, to forget myself.

He was looking at me like he wanted to do the same thing. His fingers slipped a bit closer and drifted down my arm, over the top of my hand, fingernails tracing over the smooth skin, up and down a few times. I leaned closer. His blue eyes dropped, suddenly zeroing in on my lips.

"Brandon," I whispered. "Please."

He inhaled sharply, slowly opening his mouth. But then he blinked abruptly, and shut it just as suddenly.

"Not now," he said, taking a step back. "Let's just...enjoy the party, okay?"

I watched him turn abruptly and weave his way through the crowd, finding a familiar face in it and join a conversation with the ease of a practiced politician. Which, of course, he very nearly was. When I turned, I found Eric watching me sympathetically. He had clearly seen the whole exchange, and I obviously looked pathetic.

He slid down the bar and patted my back.

"Don't worry," he said. "He'll come around. In the end, he knows who loves him. And that's obviously you."

I picked up my drink and took a long sip, watching and yearning for the golden-crowned man laughing across the room. I hoped that Eric   was   right.

Sixteen

The rest of the party continued without a hitch, and seemed like a welcome release for a lot of the people there. I guessed I wasn't the only one who got swept up in the whirlwind of Brandon's life. I recognized some of the members of his campaign, for instance, leaving their phones in their pockets for once while they tipped back pints and goofed around to the Springsteen covers. The band was doing a good job of keeping everyone going, and they sprinkled in a good mix of other songs along with the Springsteen stuff to keep people dancing long into the night.

Brandon was in the center of it all, cutting a rug with his co-workers with absolutely no rhythm whatsoever. For a long time, I watched with amusement from the bar, amazed by the fact that I could have gone this long knowing the man without discovering his horrendous dance abilities. I loved the fact that it didn't stop him from twisting his big body around with whatever beat he perceived.

But now things were calming down. We'd sung "Happy Birthday" with a cake brought out by the kitchen staff. Some of the older attendees had gone home, although the younger crowd clearly intended to stay for as long as the music continued.

I was getting antsy. It was edging on two a.m. "Later" had turned into "never," and Brandon was clearly doing his best to avoid me.

I'd tried everything I could think to get close. Asked him to dance a few times, although he'd begged off for the bathroom or the bar before returning later to dance with other people. Brought him drink refills, only to have them set aside when he took one from someone else.

I was tired of all of the sad, sorry looks my way. I felt pathetic. The adoption papers, the party—this plan was the best I had, so if it wasn't going to get me back into Brandon's good graces, maybe it was time to accept the inevitable. He said he wanted things to work, but right now, I didn't see it.

I'd already paid the band generously to play for as long as they could, and had rented out the bar for the entire night. With one last swallow of beer, I slipped off my seat in the back of the room and wove my way to the dance floor where Brandon was resting between songs. As if on cue, the band launched into a slower song, and the crowd dissipated a bit.

I tapped Brandon on the shoulder, and he swung around.

"Hey!" he said with a smile, which dropped into a frown as he realized that I had my purse slung over my shoulder. "What's up?"

"I just wanted to say Happy Birthday again," I said, my eyes darting around as I tried and failed to keep my voice from warbling. Do not cry, do not cry. "I'm going home. It's late."

Brandon didn't answer, just crinkled his eyebrows in confusion.

"Okay then," I said quickly. I stood up on my tip toes and pecked a quick kiss on his cheek, trying to ignore the way his unique scent, even overlaid as it was with beer, made me tremble with want. The tears rose again. I wasn't sure how long I could really do this limbo game. "Bye."

Before he could answer or brush me off again, I started making my way through the crowd. I had done my best, but I couldn't stay around being ignored any longer. At some point, it just hurt too much. He wasn't the only one who had been through trauma, and I was doing everything. Bending over backwards trying to please this man, trying to prove I loved him. I'd made mistakes, sure—big ones. Huge. But he had too, and I was present. *I* was the one who had come back completely. Where was he?

"Skylar, wait."

Just before I reached the exit, my hand was grabbed and I was turned around.

"Where are you going?" Brandon snapped. "I though you said you weren't going to run anymore."

"I'm not running," I insisted, even as my voice cracked. "I'm just..." I sighed, and started again. "Tell me this, Sterling. Are you ever going to come back to me completely?"

At that, the glare wiped completely from his face. His face screwed up in total confusion. "Skylar...Jesus."

I watched carefully. It wasn't like Brandon to lose his articulation.

"You have my forgiveness," he said finally. "You always did."

"Then why won't you talk to me tonight for more than two minutes?" I demanded. "When will you stop treating me like some kind of castoff?"

"When I know you're actually in this for good!" he shot back, the volume of his voice just barely below the chatter around us, but still causing more than a few people to glance curiously our way.

We bristled at each other across the doorway, but his words hit me like a slap in the face. A few seconds later, Brandon had dipped his head down, covering his brow with clenched hands, and my chest felt like it was caved in. How could he not know by this point that I was in this for good?

But of course, it made sense.

Hadn't I run when it got even a little bit hard?

Hadn't I lied?

Hadn't I turned him down?

Hadn't I pushed him away, time and time again, whenever he really tried to get close?

Marry me, he'd said less than a month before, in France. I'd thought he was half-joking, had brushed it off, then told him in no uncertain terms that I wasn't ready. But looking at him now, I understood the seriousness that was hidden under the joke. Humor was a mask for Brandon, one he wore to protect himself at his most vulnerable. How could I not have seen it directed at me?

"That's all you need to know?" I stood straight, my body suddenly full of action. "All right, then."

Brandon watched curiously as I brushed past him.

"Bathroom?" he asked when I didn't say where I was going. But now I could hear the slight fear in his voice—the fear that yet another person he cared about in his life wasn't coming back.

I turned and gazed straight at his big blue eyes. "No," I said. "But I'll be right back."

My heart thumping loudly in my chest, I slung my purse over my shoulder and marched to the bar, fueled more on adrenaline than anything else. Conscious of Brandon's inquisitive stare drilling into me, I waved over the bassist, who was on a break in between sets.

"Five minutes at the mic and the keyboard," I said, handing him another fifty.

He just nodded, and stepped back to speak to the lead singer. He nodded as well, and gestured for me to come onstage.

Having performed occasionally with my dad for most of my life, I didn't get stage fright. But as I looked out at the crowd of faces, in

147

the center of which stood the tall Adonis who had captured my heart so completely, the stakes had never been this high.

"It's all yours," said the keyboardist as we traded places. He raised a skeptical brow. "Hope you know what you're doing."

"Me too."

I leaned into the mic above the keyboard, sounding a loud blare, and winced with the rest of the crowded bar. Immediately, everyone stopped talking and looked right at me. Brandon's eyes were about twice their normal size as he watched, transfixed by whatever I was about to do.

Well, that was one way to get everyone's attention.

"Hi, everyone," I spoke into the mic.

A few people raised their hands, but most of them were looking at me like I was nuts. Maybe I was.

"So, I won't take up much of your time before the band comes back," I said. "But I have something I need to say. See that guy right there?"

I pointed to Brandon, and about fifty heads turned and stared at him. He wasn't one to blush, but right now his face was a bright, ruddy red.

"I love him," I spoke clearly, willing my voice not to shake, even though I knew my face was already flaming red. "Who here's been in love? You know, the all-consuming, do-anything, give-them-your life kind of love?"

Several people raised their hands. There were a couple of shouts of approval in the back.

"Well, that's how I feel too," I said with a smile.

In front of me, Brandon was stock-still, but his lips quirked slightly at the edges as I spoke. It sent an arrow of warmth into my chest, urging me on.

"But the thing is," I continued. "The thing is, I did some things recently that made him doubt it. And when you love someone, you have to let them know it. Don't you agree?"

A few whistles and claps spurred me on.

"So I'm going to play a song for him," I said as my hands rested over the keys. "You can sing along if you know the words."

I'd never been much of a Springsteen fan before I met Brandon. Sure, I knew the big hits. Anyone in the Tristate area knew the singles from New Jersey's golden boy. But after I found out how much his music had changed Brandon's life, starting with a cassette tape from Susan when he was just twelve, I'd unconsciously started listening to him more, learning about him. It was funny how much his story actually overlapped with Brandon's and mine. He'd met his wife while he was trying to escape a bad marriage. They'd both worked in the same industry (she was his backup singer in the beginning). She was even red-haired too.

Although I knew Brandon preferred Springsteen's earlier stuff—especially *The River*, the album Susan had given him—I found myself drawn to his later stuff, the stuff he'd written for his wife. I'd even learned a few of the pieces myself, though I couldn't have told you why at the time.

Maybe somewhere in my soul, I knew it would come to this. Somewhere, I was always doing it for him.

My fingers pressed lightly across the keys, feeling my way through the opening chords of "If I Should Fall Behind," the ballad Springsteen had written for his wife in the early days of their marriage. It was a song about commitment, a song about redemption. A song that he wrote to show her that he understood what it meant to be there, thick and thin. To show her what love meant.

In the corner of my eye, I saw Brandon collapse into a seat in the middle of the room, then lean forward to listen. The chatter of the bar had started again, but quieted down when I lifted my face to the mic, closed my eyes, and started to sing.

I wasn't a natural singer; never had been. But in a way, the song fit that too. Springsteen wasn't known for his voice either. I crooned the simple lyrics that spoke of images of love, the kind that lasted, not because a couple magically stayed together, but because they worked to make up the distance that sometimes grew between them. I played the simple chord progressions that matched the melancholy message: that everyone screws up sometimes, everyone falls behind. But, as Springsteen wrote, if Brandon fell behind, I'd wait for him. And that if I did the same, he'd wait for me to catch up too.

Somewhere in the middle, I lost myself in the music in a way I'd never been able to do before. All I saw was Brandon, and Springsteen's poetry spoke to his handsome face so clearly. I poured my heart out, and by the time I was done, the entire bar was silent. Behind me, the band's musicians stood still with their instruments. People held their drinks like statues.

But I didn't see any of them. All I saw was Brandon, who still sat at his table, knees fallen open, hand loose across the table top, jaw dropped completely. Even from twenty feet away, I could see his eyes glistening with unshed tears, two glittering blue stars in the sea of bodies. It didn't matter that there were still probably a hundred people in the room. In this moment, there was only this, there was only us.

It was embarrassing to be up here, to sing so awkwardly in a room full of strangers. I was never the type who liked having people's attention. I wasn't like either of my parents that way. I didn't seek the spotlight; I never wanted to be the center of attention. But I was willing to do this for Brandon. He spoke a language of large gestures, and worked so hard to scale them back for my sake. How many times had he tried to give me the world, only to have me shove it back in his face?

I didn't have the world to give him. But I had myself. I had my dignity. I had my comfort. I had my heart. So, I could do this for him. I could put myself out there, just like he had done for me, time and time again.

Slowly, without breaking eye contact, I pulled the mic down from the stand and stood up, moving with actions that didn't belong to my conscious mind. He was my sun, and I couldn't step out of his orbit if I tried. I was his, and if I should be so lucky, he would be mine.

"Brandon?" I whispered, but the mic amplified my voice through the still-silenced room.

He nodded, and mouthed "Skylar," although it was clear his words were stuck in his throat.

"I love you for the way you leave the fireplace on at night for visitors who might stop by unannounced. I love the way you get lost in science and numbers and leave your scratch papers all over your house. I love the way you've taken on my family like they were your own, protected us when you didn't have to."

My voice cracked as I put the mic back in its stand and took careful, wobbly steps off the stage toward Brandon. I didn't need the microphone anymore; the entire pub was a tomb. The crowd parted as I made my way to Brandon, ankles shaking, palm sweating. He must have seen my nerves on my face, considering the way everything showed there, but unlike other times, he did nothing to assuage them. He just listened.

"I love you because you're the kind of person who will send a woman flowers for six straight weeks to say you're sorry. I love you because you're the kind of man who will show up in the middle of the night just to walk a girl safely home. The kind of man who will rescue someone even when they've broken your heart."

I gulped again as I came to stand directly in front of him. Brandon tugged slightly at the collar of his shirt.

"You are *everything* to me," I said in a voice that shook, but I didn't look away. "And I know we've made mistakes. I know mine have been huge. But there's one thing I don't ever want you to doubt. I love you. I'm yours, body, mind, and soul."

Brandon took a deep breath, and before he could swipe it away, a lone tear fell down his ruddy cheek. The sight of it caused one to fall down mine as well.

And then slowly, I sank down to one knee in front of him. There were more than a few gasps around us, along with a few oh-*my*-Gods.

"Skylar," Brandon finally spoke, low and almost panicked. "What are you doing?"

But I had nothing to lose. This wasn't a way to live, in this strange limbo between us. I had to give him my whole heart or nothing. It was what he had always wanted from the start. And since I had met him, it had never really been mine anyway.

Now I was ready to let it go.

"Brandon," I said slowly as I looked up at him. "I swear, all I want to do is make you happy. I want to make you smile again. I want to make you laugh. I want to help you reach your dreams, whether it's the mayor's mansion, the White House, or the moon. And I will do anything—*anything*—to make you happy."

"Red—"

"I know you might not be ready for this. I know you might say no, and that's okay. But you deserve to know that I'm not going anywhere. If you want me, you have all of me. Always."

I took a deep breath. Brandon took a step forward.

"Red," he tried again, but I wasn't going to be stopped.

"Brandon, will you marry me?"

151

The loudest thing in the bar was now the ticking of the clock. There wasn't another sound—not a scrape of a chair, a clink of a glass. Not even anyone's breathing.

The seconds ticked by. Or were they minutes? But eventually, the silence broke down. I could hear the people behind me starting to whisper to each other as Brandon's silence extended on and on.

"That poor girl," I heard someone say.

"So sad," said someone else.

Summoning the last bit of strength I had, I stood up.

"I understand," I said, trying and failing to keep the shake out of my voice as tears flooded my vision. I stared at the beat-up floors. I couldn't look at him; I couldn't bear to see the pity I knew must be in his wide blue eyes.

I turned to leave, zigzagging through a crowd that parted easily. People murmured to each other. A few even reached out to pat me on the shoulders as I walked out. I barely noticed. I just needed to escape so I could crumple in privacy.

But before I reached the door, the deep voice that spoke to the inner recesses of my soul stopped me.

"Wait! Red!"

I froze in place, stilled by Brandon's call. Then, slowly, I turned around, hearing, rather than seeing, his footsteps move across the bar.

"You didn't even let me answer."

My hands were pressed into my face, trying to hide the tears threatening to spill over. I had to get out of here. His *answer*? His interminable silence had been answer enough.

"Oh God," I mumbled to myself. "Oh God."

I was wrong. This was so much more painful than limbo.

"No, Red, it's just me."

It was a familiar line that, much like my dress, echoed the not-so-distant past. A joke he'd made the first night we'd met, with a snowstorm whirling around us in the middle of the Boston Common. The first time we'd touched.

I dropped my hands and hiccuped back a sob when I finally saw him. No, this couldn't be real.

He was the one kneeling now, a bright beacon in the middle of a crowd who had covered their mouths in surprise. He was holding a box, the kind that every woman knows—small, square, and open to reveal a delicate circlet of diamonds that gleamed.

"You didn't think I was going to let you take this away from me, did you?" he asked with a good-humored smile that managed to brighten the entire room even though his eyes were also wet with tears.

I choked back another sob, unable to speak, although somehow I managed to step closer. Was I dreaming?

"This is real, Red," he said, with that uncanny ability to read my mind. "Skylar Ellen Crosby, you're the love of my life. You didn't just give me love; you gave me back my heart. All the things I have, any direction I go, none of it means anything if you're not there with me. So I'm asking you too...will you marry me?"

It was one of those moments where it felt like time stopped. I knew I'd always remember everything from that night. The dark wood walls of the bar. The hazy air laced with smoke from outside. The rows of clustered faces, all eagerly awaiting my response. I remember it all with crystal-clarity, but in that moment, I genuinely didn't know whether or not it was real.

"Red," Brandon whispered, interrupting my reverie. This time his voice was shaking. "Think you can answer now?"

A dam inside me broke.

"Yes," I whispered, as the emotion bubbled up from within me. A tear slid down my cheek. Then another. And then another.

"Yes?" Brandon's voice was, low, incredulous.

I exploded. "Yes-yes-yes-YES!!"

I was swept off the ground by Brandon's strong arms, and the room erupted in loud, raucous applause as Brandon covered my mouth with a kiss, the kind of kiss I'd been craving for what seemed like forever. I returned it back in full, wrapping my arms around his head, wanting to feel his love with every part of my body. When he finally pulled away, it was with a grin I hadn't seen in a very long time—a million-watt smile that seemed to make the entire room glow.

"Drinks on us!" he called out without breaking eye contact with me.

I grinned back, and the entire room cheered, congratulating us both with slaps on the back and raucous whistles. But we paid no attention, lost to anything but each other.

"You know that I paid for an open bar, right?" I said with a grin.

"I don't fuckin' care." Brandon pressed his forehead to mine. "Do you love me yet, Red?" he asked, low enough that only I could hear.

I smiled at the familiar question. The same question that had been at the end of every letter he'd sent me. There was only one answer now.

"Always," I said, and kissed him again.

Seventeen

It was past four by the time we got back to the apartment, since turning the birthday party into an engagement party gave the night a second wind. We had spent the majority of it wrapped up together on the dance floor, alternating between jumping around while I laughed uncontrollably at Brandon's hilarious lack of rhythm, and folded together like one person while we swayed during songs fast and slow.

When the elevator doors opened into the penthouse, we practically fell into the huge space, tripping over each other's feet even as we couldn't stop touching. For the first time since I met him, things with Brandon felt truly free. There was nothing between us—just the complete and utter adoration we had for each other.

"What a fuckin' great night," Brandon remarked for the fifth time as we stumbled into the kitchen for some much-needed water.

Both of us looked like we had just come back from the gym. Still sweaty with an absurdly healthy glow, Brandon was down to his undershirt, and his dampened hair curled around his brow and at the nape of his neck. He looked delicious.

"Up you go," he said as he hoisted me onto the counter next to the refrigerator—mostly, it seemed, so he could keep his hand on my thigh while he rustled around the fridge.

He hadn't stopped touching me during the rest of the night, and I loved it. It was like we were making up for lost time, and the glow burning deep inside me like the embers of a fire told me I had done the right thing. Maybe now we were finally speaking each other's languages.

"What?" Brandon asked through a mouthful of salami. "Why are you smirking?"

I just grinned as I accepted a bottle of water. "I was thinking of this conversation Dad and I had last week. It was so corny, but he was right. We just needed to learn each other's love languages."

Brandon pulled leftover pasta from the fridge and started eating it right out of the plastic container like he hadn't eaten for days—the stress of the last two weeks had been taking its toll on him too, in more ways than I'd thought.

"Don't eat it like that," I said as I hopped down and took the pasta.

"Hey!" he faux-yelped as I popped the noodles into a proper bowl and then put them in the microwave.

"Drink your water," I ordered with another smirk as I pointed at the bottle on the counter. "You need hydration."

"But—"

"Let me take care of you, birthday boy."

Brandon raised one blond brow, but obediently opened his bottle and drank half of it in one go.

"You sound like your grandmother," he said.

I just propped a hand on my hip. "There are worse things."

"You know, it's not my birthday now. It's not Friday anymore."

"It's your birthday until we go to sleep," I replied.

Behind me, the microwave beeped. I pulled out the pasta, sprinkled a bit of extra Parmesan on top, and handed it back to Brandon. He took it with a smile, and his thumb grazed over my newly adorned ring finger before he turned back to his food. I looked down at my new addition, in awe of the perfection of the ring.

"How long had you been carrying that around with you?" I asked as I hopped back up on the counter.

After he swallowed another massive bite, Brandon grinned bashfully. "Longer than you want to know, Red."

"Since France?"

He took a long drink of water and just grinned.

"The Fourth of July," I ventured again.

Brandon just shook his head, the apples of his cheeks gleaming with slight embarrassment. He polished off the rest of the pasta and deposited the bowl in the sink with a clink.

"When?" I demanded, kicking my heels against the cupboards impatiently. "Tell me."

He rubbed the back of his neck nervously. "The truth?"

I nodded eagerly.

"I bought that ring the day after I walked you home in New York."

If it physically could have, my jaw would have hit the floor. Brandon just chuckled, then leaned over and pushed it closed with one finger.

"But how could you...we barely...I didn't even...*what*?"

156

His grin widened to reveal one dimple. "What can I say? When you know, you know."

"But...*how*?" I asked again, still completely and utterly dumbfounded.

Brandon shrugged. "I *thought* it might be the case when I saw you on stage with your dad," he said. "But I knew for sure after you let me walk you home. Do you remember what you said about your house?"

I tried to recall the conversation last January and found that it returned easily. Everything about that night was stamped permanently into my brain.

"'It's no mansion on the Common...'" I recalled.

"'But it's home to me,'" Brandon finished with a smile. "And then you let me kiss you again, and I knew you were home to me, Red."

I reached out and fisted his shirt, pulling him close so I could kiss him. Like they belonged there, his arms wrapped around my waist and he returned the kiss with the promise of forever. When he let go, he was grinning, and I was out of breath.

"I'm surprised you still thought that after I slapped you on the tarmac," I said after taking a long drink of water.

"Don't forget about in my office. Although I probably earned that one."

I considered. "I would have deserved it if you had written me off." The lightness in my heart dimmed a bit as I thought about how hard I had made our beginning. "Maybe I still do."

Brandon just shrugged and gazed at the sparkling addition to my hand. "Honestly? I think it just made me want you more."

I quirked an eyebrow. "What does that say about you?"

Brandon came close again, caging me on the counter with his long arms.

"Probably," he said as he nipped one ear lightly, "that I'm a glutton for punishment."

My breath picked up as he captured my mouth again, lips sliding over mine. I honestly thought I could kiss him forever.

"Or maybe," he said as he suddenly swept me off the counter, "*you're* the masochist here."

"Maybe we both are," I murmured into his lips.

Before I knew it, I'd been carried into the bedroom and my feet were set back on the ground so that we faced the mirror over the bureau, Brandon standing behind me. I watched, transfixed, as he reached behind his shoulders and pulled his T-shirt over his head to reveal the set of chiseled abs that made my mouth water. The shirt was quickly followed by his pants, so that soon he was literally in his birthday suit, albeit blocked in the mirror by my still-dressed body.

"I can think of some ways to relieve your guilt," Brandon said as his lips met my neck. "Starting with your clothes."

He bit softly, and I arched back against him, already feeling the clear evidence of his arousal pressed against my back. His hands slipped around my waist and urged my hands up around his neck, then drifted back down to unbutton my dress from the front while I watched, completely transfixed. His touch was tender, but his eyes sparked—like the smallest piece of tinder would set the room on fire.

Once the knit fabric was undone to my waist, he brought my hands back down and slipped the dress over my shoulders, then let it pool by my feet. I heard, rather than saw his sharp intake of breath at the sight of me standing in my lingerie—black lace, his favorite.

"Fuck," came the low whisper behind me.

His eyes met mine in the mirror.

"Take it off," he ordered softly. "Slowly."

Without breaking eye contact, I brought a hand up to my shoulder and started to toy with one strap, tugging it over my shoulder. I stopped and bit my lip.

Brandon's hand pinched my hip suddenly, and I yelped as I jumped.

"Don't stop," he said evenly, his hands squeezing my waist, a bit more gently. My thighs clenched.

I bit my lip again, but this time followed his orders as I removed my bra, and then my panties, shimmying my hips slightly from side to side until they dropped to the floor with my dress.

"You really are a goddess," Brandon murmured, his eyes dilating as they drifted over my now-naked body. "Hold your hands above your head," he ordered. "Don't move."

Obediently, I did as he said, still mesmerized as he moved closer behind me, pulling my hair over one shoulder to give him access to my neck. His hands continued to play all over my body, tickling the undersides of my breasts and the delicate skin over my rib cage in a way that had me squirming in no time. Just as his hands started to dip below my waist, I closed my eyes in apprehension. My hips jerked against his feather-light touch.

Then, in a sudden twist, I found myself picked up and tossed onto the bed, then quickly covered by Brandon's big body.

"I said to stay still," Brandon rumbled in my ear. "You're not listening."

He grabbed both of my arms and held them by the wrists more roughly over my head, forcing me to arch my back and hold my breasts out on display for him.

"If you're not going to listen, baby," he said, "Then there are going to be consequences."

I sucked in a deep breath as he bent low and took one of my tautly pebbled nipples into his mouth and began to worry it between his teeth. Gradually his bite began to ride the line between pleasure and pain. I was shocked to find that line was apparently directly connected to the tingling spot between my legs, which was currently being tortured by the presence of his thick erection.

Suddenly, he released my nipple and flipped us again in a single, smooth movement so I was straddling his waist and his big hands rested firmly on the swell of my hips. He drifted one hand up to continue teasing my breasts while the other fell to the sensitive spot between my legs.

"Ahhhh," I cried as he found my clit.

He pressed it, pinched slightly between his thumb and index finger, and began to rub it in a way that had me grinding into him, simultaneously trying to rid myself of that blissful pressure and get more of it. Brandon spoke so clearly with his body; every touch, every kiss was full of nuance and complexity. It was one of the reasons why, I suspected, unlike every other sexual partner I'd ever had, he had never failed to keep my attention, never failed to stimulate me, never failed to capture my mind alongside my body in that way I needed to find pleasure with him.

His other hand pulled me down for a kiss, and he teased my mouth open, sucking on my lower lip, then the top before slipping his tongue around mine in a delicate tangle. It was a kiss that wasn't hurried or needy, but it took my breath away just the same. It spoke of tenderness. It spoke of fear. It spoke of love.

His hand finally loosened its grip in my hair and moved down the back of my neck, cupping me briefly there before sliding over my shoulder, dipping over my waist, and finding my ass with a light squeeze. He continued to stroke over my thigh, relishing, it seemed, in my bare skin.

"Skylar," he whispered into my lips. When he released me, his eyes watered like two bottomless pools of love and sorrow.

"Oh, Brandon," I said, my heart breaking all over again.

"No, baby," he said as he rolled us over.

He moved over me, pressing me into the pillows and sheltering me with the wide expanse of his shoulders. He cradled my face with both hands, staring with wet-lidded adoration over the planes of my face as he stroked my chin, my cheekbones, my lips.

"Do you know why I know we are meant to be together?" he asked in a voice so low I almost couldn't hear him. His voice was deep, thickly laid with that South Boston accent that only ever came out with me when he was too overcome with emotion to control it.

"Why?" I whispered. I was dying to kiss him again, but I couldn't move. I could feel tears welling up, not out of sadness, but from the intensity building between us.

"Because I see you, Skylar," he said, continuing to stroke my face. "I see you. The good, the bad, the ugly, the beautiful. I see you, and I love you for all of it. And you see me too."

We stared at each other, blue eyes to green, both of us stilled in each other's allure.

"Yes," I whispered. "I do." It was the only thing I could say or think. "I see you, Brandon."

A long, slow tear made its way down his stubbled cheek, and when he leaned down, his kisses were salty with the evidence.

"Skylar?" he asked as he brought my hands up to his lips. "Will you marry me?" He blinked good-naturedly at my confusion, though his expression remained intense. "I know you said yes already. I just...need to know it's real."

Next to his lips, the ring he had bought me glinted in the moonlight. Everything with Brandon had always seemed on one hand like a dream, but on the other more real than anything I'd ever encountered.

I'd rejected him two weeks ago, but everything had changed since then. Everything that had held me back just seemed stupid, inconsequential. My life would be only a shadow of its potential if I didn't have this man in it. He was truly the only person in the world who saw me for exactly what I was, and loved me for it.

"I'll marry you," I said with a soft kiss. "I'd marry you today, I'll marry you tomorrow. I'll marry you every day for the rest of our lives if that's what you want. Brandon, look at me."

He did, and this time his eyes were wide and curious.

"Don't you always say I have a glass face?" I asked.

His mouth quirked up on one side in that adorable half-smile that melted my heart every time. "Yes."

"Then what do you see?"

The other half of the smile emerged. Brandon kissed me softly.

"Love," he said, almost so low I couldn't hear it. "I see love." He closed his eyes, almost as if it was too much too bear.

"I'm yours," I said before pressing a kiss to his cheek. "Always." To the other cheek. "And." To his forehead. "Forever." To his mouth.

"Mine," he hummed against my lips. Then, just a bit more ferociously: "*Mine*."

And then it was like we couldn't get close enough. We were skin to skin, hands roving over each other's bodies as he slipped inside me, into the place that was already slick and ready. His hips kept a slow, luxurious pace, but I could feel his biceps tense with effort to maintain control.

"Lift yourself up a little," I said. "Just a little." I loved the feel of his big body, but I needed to be able to reach between us to find my high along with him.

Obediently, he pushed himself up on his forearms, providing enough of a gap between our bodies to slide my hands down.

"I want to see," he said as he looked down eagerly, even while his hips continued to move.

I placed two fingers on my clit while my other hand found one of my nipples and started to tweak the sensitive nub, both hands matching the slow, forceful rhythm Brandon set. He watched the hand at my breast with darkened eyes.

I had never been able to do this with anyone else. With others, sex had always felt like such a spectator sport; the watching psyched me out, made me feel like I was on display. I could never relax enough to find a rhythm, never felt at ease enough to find my high, never felt engaged enough to rise to new heights. But Brandon was so all encompassing; I was immersed in him. I could truly let go, do whatever I needed to do, because in the end, my pleasure would help him find his. With him, I could do no wrong.

His blue eyes, bluer than the summer sky that was starting to lighten with the sunrise, gleamed with love and longing as we drove on further. I couldn't look away. There was nothing else to see but him.

"Brandon," I gasped as his lips brushed mine.

"Take it, baby," he rumbled against my neck. "God, Skylar, I...I can't...fuck, I'm so close."

"I'm ready," I moaned, my hips rising to his, grinding as I pushed myself closer. I was so full I thought I would explode.

"Come, Red," he said, low and ragged. "Come with me."

I shattered. The hand at my breast grasped the soft flesh as every muscle tensed and lost complete control. Brandon took my mouth, fierce and unforgiving as his body shook over me, as we shook together, falling over the cliff of light and love and intensity and togetherness   that   we   were.

Eighteen

"Babe. Babe, wake up. Brandon!"

Another unintelligible shout echoed through the bedroom before Brandon jerked awake. "What? Who?" he asked, his eyes wide and glazed until they found me and slowly came back into focus.

"Hey," I said as I sat up with him. "It's okay." I rubbed his big shoulders. "You just had another nightmare."

Brandon said nothing and slowly regained his breath. His skin, completely bare after we had fallen asleep naked together, was covered with a thin layer of sweat. That might have been normal for mid-September in Boston if we hadn't been in a sky-high apartment with central air. Under my fingertips, I could feel his heartbeat pounding through the carotid artery. The tremors vibrating through his muscles slowed down as I lightly massaged his deltoids, biceps, and painfully tight trapezius muscles.

It was a process that had become routine. Eventually, he began to relax, and I laid back into the pillows stacked against the headboard so he could lay with me, head on my stomach. He slid an arm around my waist, then sighed deeply.

"Thank you," he murmured sleepily. It was the same thing he said every night.

I continued to stroke down his back and up through his hair. "Of course."

The flutter of his eyelashes blinking over my bare stomach told me he wasn't going to fall asleep this morning. No surprise there, since we'd already done this once tonight. The sky was already lightening over Boston; the sun would be up in another hour, and with it, Brandon would go for the several-mile run that seemed to get longer every day, before returning with his trainer to spar in the gym he'd set up in one of the spare rooms.

He rolled onto his pillow and rubbed a hand over his face. "God, I hate this place. I feel like Gordon Gecko living up here. It gives me the creeps." He sighed. "Have you found anything worth buying yet?"

In the month since we had gotten engaged, life had managed to calm a bit. I had immersed myself in my new job while Brandon continued the long process of selling his stake in Sterling Ventures while he stepped up his campaign appearances. Overall, it had been good to have a bit of calm and normalcy while Brandon and I adjusted to being engaged.

It only made sense, for instance, that I move in completely instead of putting my furniture in storage. But even that hadn't been a completely smooth process since Brandon, in his stubborn, misguided way, had hired movers to bring the rest of my furniture over, including the double bed swapped out for the king we normally shared. It took three nights of sleeping with his feet hanging off the end and me elbowing him in the gut before Brandon finally conceded that his bed was superior.

I gave him a look that, even in the dim light, would clearly say, "Are you kidding?" I was currently putting in around sixty hours a week at Kiefer Knightly. When was I supposed to have time to house hunt?

In response, he just held up his hands in surrender.

"Sorry, sorry," he said. "Margie can do it. She has good taste."

"Didn't Margie choose this place?"

"Yeah. But that was because I told her, and I quote: 'Find me a place as heartless as I feel.'" Brandon glanced up with an impish smile. "Too dramatic?"

I rolled my eyes. "A little. But I can't talk. I was literally a mad woman in the attic at about that point."

Brandon sighed as he toyed with my engagement ring.

As calm as things had become, I couldn't shake the feeling that we were in the eye of a storm. Other changes were afoot. Primary season was kicking into gear, and Brandon had his first debate with the other five mayoral candidates of his party scheduled next month. His campaign staff frequently made house calls to the apartment in the evenings, and he had been splitting his time between divestiture negotiations in LA and Washington and the campaign headquarters in the bottom floor of Sterling Grove.

The trial was also moving forward. Zola had called three days ago to inform us that Messina had been arrested at last, and they were proceeding with the criminal charges. The arraignment was today, and despite Brandon's strong opinion that I leave it alone, I wanted to be there. The therapist I'd been seeing recently thought it was a good idea to face my attacker. I agreed, and so did Dad, who had been released from his program last week and was now living with Bubbe while he continued physical therapy for his hand and looked for a job.

I tried to push my hair off my face, but Brandon held tight to my hand, not yet willing to relinquish his hold.

"Just a few more minutes," he murmured, his eyes shuttering as he leaned into my fingers. "God, I love you."

I smiled. "I love you too. But if we're not going back to sleep, there are things to do before we leave."

Brandon groaned into my thigh. "Well, at least waking up in a cold sweat is good for something today."

Before I could answer, he heaved himself up, ab muscles flexing ostentatiously. I ogled him openly as he moved about the room, heading into the walk-in closet and coming back out dressed in his running gear.

"I'll be back in a few hours," he said as he leaned in for a brief kiss. "Stay here for me? Naked?"

I glanced at the clock. It was just before five a.m. I was tempted to pull him back into the sheets, give him another kind of exercise to help him expel the demons he was trying so hard to fight. But I knew it would be temporary, and since he had woken me up once tonight already, I was happy to get a few more hours of sleep.

"Be on time," I joked lightly. "We're leaving at nine, with or without you."

For that, I received a light smack on the side of my thigh.

"Just try it," Brandon growled, and with another enthusiastic kiss, he bounded out the door, leaving me to my sleep.

* * *

At nine a.m. sharp, Dad, Bubbe, Brandon and I sat in the back of the Escalade. Zola had taken statements from all four of us over the last month, along with a number of other potential witnesses, so that when the police were finally able to locate the man (who turned out to be much more slippery than they anticipated), the D.A. would be ready to pounce.

"But it cannot be between us...cannot be..." Brandon murmured as he went through a speech that Cory had sent him. He looked up, brows furrowed adorably. "Cannot be between. Be between. Does that sound funny to you, or have I just read this too many times?"

I shrugged. "It's a little awkward. You say 'be' twice, but it's not grammatically incorrect."

Brandon gave me an irritated look as if to say, "Yes, I know that," and went back to reviewing the speech. His early morning run hadn't done much to lighten his mood. He was missing a breakfast event with some kind of union this morning, and wouldn't be back in time to prepare for another fundraiser at a hospital tomorrow night. Cory was predictably furious.

"You know you don't have to do this," Brandon said as he stilled my nervous hands. "We can turn around."

He smiled at my dad in the very backseat, looking for encouragement, but Dad just played with his mustache and looked out the window. Bubbe didn't respond, lost in an audiobook.

I sighed. "Yes, we do. *You* don't have to do this. Really."

Brandon just gave me a half-smile and cocked his head. "Yes, I do."

Today was a formality—the arraignment that would determine whether or not a trial would move forward. Zola was of two minds about what might happen. They had amassed enough evidence to lock Messina up ten times over on different charges, with Dad's and my statements as the cornerstone of the entire prosecution. It was still possible Messina would take the plea bargain the DA was offering: twenty-five years instead of the potential life without parole. But at the same time, Messina had proved to be unpredictable in his responses. We had no idea what he would do.

"The good news is, he's a flight risk since he evaded arrest for so long," Zola had said over the phone. "So, the judge likely won't grant bail if he decides not to take the plea."

But he didn't state the worst-case scenario: that the judge would be paid off somehow, or by some strange twist, the defense would manage to get the case thrown out. At which point Messina would be back on the streets, and my family would be on his shit list.

We arrived at the courthouse just before one, with enough time to file through the metal detectors and take our seats in the courtroom. Various people sat in the gallery, waiting while the court took a lunch recess; many others were held in the jail connected to the courthouse. I didn't see Messina. Part of me wondered if I'd actually blocked out what his face looked like, but when I closed my eyes, I saw it clearly. The sweaty, flabby jowls and lips that smacked over stained teeth just before he hit me—these things would never leave me, and I hated him for that.

Brandon glanced at me again from where he was studying his phone.

"Hey," he said.

I looked up, eyes wide.

"They won't throw it out," he said, with that uncanny ability of his to read my thoughts. "There's too much at stake here. They won't throw it out."

I took a deep breath and nodded. The rational side of me knew that was true. It was the other side of me that was still petrified about the possibility of this man back on the streets, looking for my family.

After a few more minutes, Messina himself was escorted into the courtroom wearing a bright orange jumpsuit like he had stepped off a bad crime drama.

"The Kings County Criminal Court is now in session. The Honorable Judge Leland Reynolds presiding."

The bailiff's voice rang through the courtroom, and everyone stood while the judge filed into the room and took his seat behind the bench.

"Please be seated, everyone," he said in a low, monotone voice, and we followed. After a few moments, he glanced over the files prepared for him, and then called up the Messina case.

Zola stood and introduced himself, after which a short, greasy man in an ill-fitting brown suit announced himself as Messina's lawyer: Primo Cipolla.

"I see he didn't go with a public defender," Brandon whispered, trying to make light of the situation.

I pursed my lips, unable to smile. Appearances could be deceiving. Cipolla looked like he modeled his personal styling right out of *Goodfellas*, down to the slicked-back hair and the oversized suit. But that didn't mean he wasn't a good lawyer.

A rustle behind us sounded, along with a few clicks. A group of cameras had noticed our presence, and when I glanced over, one of

167

the photographers was nudging the other, then pointing at Brandon. Shit.

"Mr. Messina," the judge spoke. "I'm going to have you stand next to your attorney, if you please."

Messina didn't answer, but the room was silent. The chains of Messina's handcuffs clinked loudly against the larger one wrapped about his hips as the bailiffs escorted him from his place by the door of the jail to where his lawyer stood, just in front of us. Bubbe took a sharp breath beside me, and Dad wrapped his fists together so tightly his knuckles turned white around the scarring. The scars that had been put there by Victor Messina.

All I felt was rage.

"Mr. Messina," the judge spoke, "these proceedings are being recorded. You have the right to remain silent, and anything you say may be used against you in this and any subsequent proceeding. You have the right to be assisted by a lawyer at every stage of these proceedings. You have the right to a public defender should you qualify, though it looks like your personal counsel is assisting you for this hearing. Is that right?"

"Yes, your honor," Messina's lawyer answered with a thick, East Brooklyn accent.

The judge continued: "Mr. Messina, do you understand these rights as I have explained them to you?"

Messina bent over the desk to speak into the microphone, and the chains on his hands clinked loudly through the speakers. "I do."

The judge read the charges in a low, bored voice, even though the gallery perked up a bit with each of the thirteen separate counts of racketeering, kidnapping, aggravated assault, tax fraud, attempted rape, and murder. Messina just stood stony-faced until the end, when he turned around at glared at me and Dad.

Beside me, Brandon tensed, and I was glad that Messina couldn't see past the bar to where I grasped at Brandon's hand. Brandon squeezed it tight, rubbing his thumb again over my ring.

The judge turned to Cipolla. "Counsel, do you wish to be heard on the issue of Probable Cause?"

Cipolla shook his head, "No, your honor."

"I have reviewed the charges as well as the information submitted by the State. I find that there is probable cause for these charges. Counsel, are you prepared to move to arraignment?"

Both the prosecutors and Messina's attorneys nodded. The judge proceeded to read Messina's rights regarding arraignment, which were then confirmed by Messina.

"Please state your true and correct name, and spell your last name for the record."

"Victor Salvaturi Messina. M-E-S-S-I-N-A," he said clearly, and the name made my blood boil.

The judge handed something to his clerk. Messina's lawyer came forward and took the document from her.

"Thank you, your honor. We'll waive the reading of the charges." Messina's lawyer walked back to his client, standing by his side.

"Mr. Messina, these charges, if proven, have a maximum penalty of life in prison. If you are not a United States citizen, these charges may carry additional penalties to your immigration status and may result in your deportation. In addition, these charges may carry with them restitution to the victims, based on the effect of these crimes on their life."

It wasn't a statement of guilt or anything close to a sentence. After all, according to the law, Messina was innocent until proven guilty. But the promise of that kind of penalty caused everyone in my family to exhale. Maybe, just maybe, there would be justice served at the end of all of this.

"Mr. Messina, do you wish to enter a plea at this time?" asked the judge.

"Take it," I muttered to myself. "Take the deal."

If he would just take the plea, this would all be over. No more hulking security, no more worrying if something terrible was going to happen to me or my family, no more trial clouding Brandon's campaign or my career.

But Messina turned his chunky head around and stared at Dad, Bubbe, and then at me with dark, hollow eyes that made my chest constrict. He smiled, a slow, evil grimace that bared his tobacco-stained teeth like some kind of demented jack-o-lantern.

Messina's lawyer started to speak, "Your honor, my client pleads guil—"

Messina whipped around, cutting off his attorney. "I ain't guilty," he pronounced so emphatically I thought he might spit on the ground.

"Counsel, do you need a minute with your client?" asked the judge, this time more impatiently.

Beside him, I could see Messina's lawyer shaking his head, trying to get his client to cooperate. He was never going to win this trial. He knew it, and so did everyone else in the room. His only chance would be to get rid of the witnesses. My heart dropped. My family and I would be living in fear for another several months.

"Mr. Messina, how do you plea?" asked the judge once more.

"Not guilty," Messina replied and stood as tall as his stubby form would allow him. Then he looked back to us again and leered.

The courtroom rustled in response, and the photographers behind us started snapping away. This was news: a mid-level New York gangster versus, by extension, a golden boy of Boston. If we had managed to avoid the public spotlight before, we were definitely in it now.

"Everyone, please be quiet!" called the judge, banging the gavel to overcome the commotion. "Order in the court!" When the room calmed again, the judge spoke to Zola. "Does the state wish to be heard on pre-trial release?"

Zola stood up, shuffling through his papers. He was surprised, but I knew he was prepared.

"Yes, your honor. We would request pre-trial detention. Mr. Messina is a flight risk. He actively worked to evade arrest in this matter, and given Mr. Messina's significant resources, any amount of bail would be insufficient to secure his return."

"Your honor, Mr. Messina is a model citizen!" Cipolla recovered from the shock of the plea deal quickly. "He is a long-time member of this community. He has always shown up for any prior proceedings, and there is no risk he would do anything different here."

Zola shot a steely-eyed look at Cipolla. "Mr. Messina has never *had* charges this severe. His avoidance of arrest shows he considers these differently. He should be confined while we await trial."

The judge thumbed through the police report. "I'm inclined to agree with the State on this. Mr. Messina, you are to be confined in the city jail pending trial. What are we looking at for trial here? Is there an agreement on waiver of a speedy trial?"

"No, your honor," said Zola. "We are ready to proceed."

"Very well. The trial will begin next Monday, the eighteenth. I have a morning status calendar. But that shouldn't affect getting a jury. We'll start after the morning recess, at ten-thirty. If there is nothing else..." The judge paused and shifted his glance to each attorney. "We are adjourned."

The judge banged the gavel, and the bailiff again called for everyone to rise as the judge stepped off the bench and retreated to his chambers.

* * *

We were ushered out of the courthouse by a pair of security guards and the rest of Brandon's security team. Bubbe and Dad made it easily to a rented car; from there, Tony was taking them both to meet with the real estate agent selling the house in Brooklyn. We all knew there would be no going back there; Brandon had long ago hired a company to put our belongings in storage.

But as soon as Brandon and I exited the building, a mob of press descended on us like flies, the bulbs of their cameras flashing as reporters clamored for interviews. Apparently, the photographers inside had summoned their hounds.

"Mr. Sterling! Do you think being a part of a criminal trial will get in the way of your campaign?"

"Do you think Messina is guilty?"

"Will Ms. Crosby's connections to the mob affect your ability to govern the city of Boston?"

It was on the last one that Brandon finally swung around and faced the reporter, who stuck a microphone up to record his response.

"Ms. Crosby doesn't *have* connections to the mob," he said clearly. "She's a victim in all of this, same as her father. Same as me. We're just here to make sure justice is served."

He gripped my hand tightly, and I forced myself to meet the lenses of the cameras head-on while they clicked away. Brandon's palm was slick with sweat—he hated this kind of attention, maybe even more than I did. But I wasn't about to look guilty right now.

171

"Was justice served when Ms. Crosby broke up your marriage?"

The question came from a man in the back, one clearly not part of the standard press corps. Brandon and I both turned toward him, and I cursed the telltale flush that immediately bloomed all over me as cameras continued to click and flash. Brandon began to shake, and he stepped toward the man as if to attack.

"No comment," I managed to call out before things could escalate anymore.

I tugged hard on Brandon's arm. The muscles in his neck were tensed to the point where I could see a vein pulsing on one side; his eyes flashed dangerously. I held them with mine, barely able to control my own nerves.

"Please," I murmured. "Let's just go."

Somehow, even with the questions that continued to fly through the air around us, Brandon managed to nod.

"Okay," he said, and continued to usher me toward the Escalade.

It wasn't until we were on our way back to Boston that the terror in my heart started to dissolve. It faded the farther we drove from the city of my birth, a city I'd always though would feel like home, but had somehow become a stranger to me. It faded, but never completely   died.

Nineteen

"I'm telling you, no one is going to follow up on it." Brandon tried to convince me again the next morning while we moved about the kitchen fixing breakfast.

After the arraignment, Dad had been eager to contact his sponsor, and Bubbe had just wanted to watch the *Murder, She Wrote* DVDs I'd bought her last year for Christmas. Brandon and I had holed up in the apartment, watching *Star Wars* while we both worked. It would have felt normal if I hadn't been so obsessed with scouring the news for our names.

"Fuck," I muttered under my breath as I leaned against the kitchen island.

My phone had about twenty Google alerts on it. Since I'd started keeping track of Brandon's and my names in the news, that in itself wasn't a surprise. Brandon was becoming a public figure, so he was going to be in the papers, especially during the campaign. In the space of a few months, Brandon had gone from a notoriously private citizen to the hottest thing on the Eastern seaboard. Everyone in Boston wanted a piece of him, not to mention a sizeable contingent outside the New England area. He had the clout of Michael Bloomberg with the charm of Brad Pitt. The guy was a unicorn, a political gold mine, and everyone knew it.

But it was this moment that I had been bracing myself for—the moment where the connection between my name and face was finally made.

"What is it?" Brandon asked as he gathered things to make scrambled eggs.

After he set the eggs and milk next to the stove, he slipped an arm around my waist and lifted me easily onto the countertop so I was sitting next to him. I barely noticed—he did it almost every day. I suspected he liked having me at eye-level, since it made it easier to sneak kisses.

He had just gotten back from his morning run, which had been even earlier than usual, since another second nightmare had woken us both up at just after four. If I hadn't already been so absorbed by the headlines, I might have been distracted by the way his sweaty tank top clung to his six-pack. But instead, all I could see was the news, and the fact that after yesterday, my name and face was in it.

Most of the headlines were nothing new, rehashing the timeline of Brandon's and my relationship. Apparently, Cory had decided to take a foot-first tactic with the fact that Brandon was still involved with his "mistress", although I thankfully couldn't be called that anymore now that his divorce had actually gone through. The campaign had released a formal press release about me a month ago, highlighting all of the parts that would make me most palatable: my elite education, the fact that I was the daughter of a city worker, my interest in nonprofit and family advocacy. Our engagement wasn't announced yet, but it would only be a matter of time until someone spotted the ring on my finger.

But then I scrolled down to a headline that made my heart stop. It was a two-bit tabloid, something probably run out of some random person's basement. But it was there, just like I'd known it would be.

"Red?" Brandon took one look at me and set down the bowl of eggs he was whisking. "What is it?"

I set the phone down on the counter, buried my face in my hands, and crumpled into his shoulder.

"What the..." Brandon trailed off as he read the headlines over my shoulder. "Oh, *fuck*."

"It's official," I said through my fingers. "I'm a baby-killing whore."

"'Our sources have confirmed that Skylar Crosby was seen entering a free clinic on the morning of May twenty-seventh'," Brandon murmured as he scrolled through the article. "'And just last night, *Wikileaks* posted actual documents of the visit, including a treatment plan that included "the abortion pill." Crosby might be a family lawyer, but she isn't family friendly.'"

I cringed at the last line, and my stomach dropped about ten stories. Brandon just stood there, silent for a moment, until he set the phone down. Finally, I looked up.

"I'm so sorry—" I started to say.

"Stop," Brandon cut in gently. He pushed my legs apart so they dangled loosely on either side of his waist, then cupped my face gently so I couldn't look away. "We're past it. Don't go there."

"But this...I'm...this is going to cause so much trouble for your campaign."

"You think I give a shit about the campaign?"

I blinked, confused. "Well, yes. I mean, it *is* your dream, right? That's what you said."

Brandon clenched his jaw, but eventually shrugged as he released my face. "I care about *you*, Red. I care about us. This...yeah. This is bad. But that's what I hired Cory for—a shark to deal with sharks. We knew this might happen eventually, so let's just let him do his job." He twisted his full mouth around in thought. "What do you think about getting out of here for the day?"

I scrunched my eyebrows. "Don't you have that event this evening? Cory's going to go nuts if you blow off something else."

Brandon shrugged. "I've got the speech dialed, and we can be back in time for the dinner."

"Where were you thinking?"

Brandon scratched his head. "I don't know. Nowhere far, just out of the city. Clear our heads before the chaos finds us—if it even does. I'm still not convinced anyone will pick it up."

I tipped my head to one side. "You do realize we literally just got back from France six weeks ago."

Brandon gave me a look. "You do realize that the emotional equivalent of a tornado just happened to us? And another's about to hit? Even if this doesn't get picked up, you've seen the primary schedule, Red. The next six months are going to be crazy."

I bit down a grin. "Point taken. Are you thinking the Cape?"

He'd managed to keep his favorite property on Cape Cod in the final divorce agreement, deciding instead to give Miranda the rest of their joint properties and a large cash settlement in order to keep her out of his business affairs. With the threat of Kieran's recording being released publicly, Miranda had suddenly been quite amenable to Brandon's still-generous offer.

But Brandon shook his head. "No. I was thinking...what if we just got in the car and drove? No David, no security. No nothing."

I raised a skeptical brow. "No security? Really? Do you think that's safe? Zola said just because Messina's in holding doesn't mean we're not targets. Not until the trial's over."

He bit his lip. "Well, maybe just one. You want Craig or Lucas?"

It was then I wondered if he was feeling as trampled by his security as I was. It couldn't be easy being someone people followed around all the time, an easy target as the pressure mounted. I was starting to get used to Lucas's perennial shadow, but that didn't mean it didn't chafe.

"Lucas," I said as I pulled him close. "He's quieter. First breakfast. Then let's go."

* * *

So Brandon steered the Mercedes out of the city, followed by the Escalade at enough of a distance that I almost forgot it was there. We meandered through the low foothills of Massachusetts, taking exits and getting back on, seeing parts of New England I hadn't known were there. Eventually, we ended up in Vermont, where mountains started to rise out of the green countryside, set off by quaint brick towns that recalled an era from maybe two hundred years ago or more.

"I'm starving," Brandon said as we started driving through Woodstock, a small town about two hours northwest of Boston. "What do you think about getting something to eat and then finding a hike? I need to get out of the car."

After sharing a burger for lunch, we decided to hike up Mount Tom on the advice of the restaurant owner who had served us our lunch. There were surprisingly few people on the trail for a Saturday afternoon—apparently, there was some sort of festival going on in a nearby town. While I did notice a few hikers glancing curiously at Brandon as we passed, no one stopped us (possibly thanks to Lucas lumbering about twenty paces behind us).

When we reached the top of the small mountain, we stood overlooking the valley on the other side. While some of the trees were starting to turn yellow here and there in the mid-September sunshine, most of the trees remained a lush sea of green that covered the landscape for miles.

"So, I don't want to wait too long," Brandon said as we sat down on the bench at the summit. The trail hadn't been empty, but right now we were the only ones at the top of the mountain.

He pulled off his frayed Red Sox hat and shook out his loose, slightly sweaty waves.

I looked at him. "For..."

"The wedding."

We'd barely mentioned the topic of our marriage since the night I—well, *we*—had proposed. There hadn't seemed any point, since according to a red-faced Cory, we had to keep it secret a while yet anyway. But I'd meant what I'd said that night. I'd married him today if that was what he really wanted.

We hadn't even talked about what kind of wedding we wanted to have. I knew that Brandon had already done the big church wedding. Months ago, a quick, painful Google search had revealed archived photos in the Boston society pages. He and an impossibly beautiful Miranda had been married at Trinity, the sprawling Episcopalian behemoth in Back Bay, in front of an audience of five hundred.

It was the last thing I wanted. But what did Brandon want?

"I just want our life together to start," he said, taking my hand in his.

He brushed his thumb over my ring, rubbing the tiny stones that circled my finger. The eternity ring that was so different from what most women received.

If I hadn't already known he loved me, the ring would have told me. Subtle and small, although no doubt the finest craftsmanship money could buy, it was a far cry from the usual splendor of Brandon's life—splendor, I had come to realize, he usually allowed others to choose for him. This was a sign that before he even realized it, he understood who I was—someone who didn't need or want that kind of opulence.

"It has started," I said as I looked up at him. "It started the day we met, didn't you know?"

For that I got a shy smile, the kind that warmed my heart whenever I saw it. He closed his eyes for a moment, long lashes shadowing the tops of his cheeks in the afternoon sun.

"I do know," he said. "But...I want everyone else to know it too."

"Cory will say it's terrible for your campaign."

"Cory knows what to do with the fuckin' campaign."

I blanched, a little taken aback. It was the second time today that he had brushed off his run for mayor. Wasn't a future in politics what he wanted?

Brandon sighed, the afternoon shadows highlighting the dark circles under his eyes. For the first time since I'd met him, he

177

actually looked his age. Sure, he still had that ruddy glow that came from running several miles every morning. I had yet to find a single gray hair in his thick blond hair, and the rest of his body...forget about it. But right now, I could see the way the wrinkles at the edges of his eyes seemed a little more pronounced than usual, the way the creases on his forehead seemed slightly deeper, and the way the skin underneath his eyes was darkened and a bit puffy.

When he opened his bright blue eyes, they just looked weary.

"Please?" he asked, more up to the trees that towered over us than to me.

"Are you hoping for a big affair?" I wondered.

To my immediate relief, Brandon shook his head. The movement caused the hair over his forehead to flop around. He really needed it cut.

"Not unless you want it," he said. "Miranda and I had that kind of wedding. It was like a charity event: full of strangers and stiff shirts."

He slung an arm around my shoulders and pulled me close to him while he talked. I laid my head on his shoulder, content to bask in the sunlight.

"That was the whole life I had with Miranda," he continued as he played with the ends of my ponytail. "It made sense we would have that kind of thing. But I felt like a stranger at my own wedding. I knew maybe ten people there out of five hundred. We were all dressed like penguins, and the caterers served beef tartar and goose liver."

He wrinkled his long nose at the memory. I had to laugh. Brandon was more of a meat and potatoes kind of guy, albeit he now paid for the best cuts of meat and the fluffiest potatoes.

He looked at me. "Is that what you want, Red? I wouldn't have pegged you for a big society wedding, but if you want it—"

"I do *not*," I said emphatically. "If it were up to me, we'd call the Justice of the Peace and be done with it."

Brandon snorted. "You make it sound like we're doing your taxes."

I nudged him in the ribs. He braced my head against him for a second with a brief kiss in my hair, then let me go.

"I don't mean it like that," I said. "Just...I'm not really the type for much spectacle, you know?"

178

"You wouldn't want your family and friends to be there? Bubbe and your dad? Jane and Eric?"

I considered for a moment. "Yes, I'd want them to be there, even though they might kill each other. Annabelle and Christoph too, although that means Janette would probably have to come. And Bubbe would probably fry me for breakfast if she didn't get to help me pick out a wedding dress." I turned to Brandon, who was chuckling. "But that's it. My circle of people is...small. What about you?"

Brandon cocked his head, thinking. "Ray, Susan. Kieran and Pushpa. Mark. Cory, I guess. Probably Harvey, David, and Ana too."

I grinned. "You might be the only billionaire in the world who would put his trainer, driver, and housekeeper on the shortlist for his wedding."

Brandon snorted. "Miranda would have hated it. She never liked it when I 'fraternized with the help'." He rolled his eyes. "But I see them more than almost anyone."

It struck me, not for the first time, how very lonely Brandon's life had become as he'd become more successful. Most of the people Kieran had rounded up for his birthday hadn't heard from him in years. Most of his friends, it seemed, had either been made through Miranda, or were people from his old neighborhood whom he'd lost touch with over the years. He still supported his friends from Dorchester financially, the ones who had gone to jail when Brandon had managed to go free. But now, he didn't seek much social interaction, content just to be on his own, around people he trusted.

And yet, looking at him, it was clear just how much it meant to him that we would stand up in front of that short list of confidantes. I wondered too, if he needed to hear it from me: hear me take him as mine, pronounce myself his, in front of the small circle of people that the two of us would do anything for.

Without hesitating, I crawled into his lap so my knees straddled him on the bench. My arms fell easily over his broad shoulders, and his hands slid up my thighs naturally, palming my ass briefly under the hem of my shorts before encircling my waist more innocently.

"I just need you," I said to him solemnly, keeping my green eyes wide so he could see the truth in what I said. "It's always been you, from the very beginning."

179

Brandon raised a dark blond brow, and his thumbs stroked my hipbones through my shorts. "Has it? You were running pretty hard there for a while, Red. Sometimes I wonder if you'll ever really stop."

I leaned in and pressed a soft kiss to his lips. When I tried to pull back, he brought a hand to the back of my head, keeping me there while he took his fill. I didn't argue. I never stopped wanting him either.

"Mmmm," he hummed as he finally let me go.

After I caught my breath again, I smiled. Then I cupped his face, stroking my thumbs over the sharp lines of his cheekbones. Sometimes his beauty really did take my breath away.

"I'm all yours," I said softly, touching my nose to his. "Now I'm staying put. For always."

Brandon hummed again, low and content, and pulled me down so I was lying on his shoulder. He wanted me—that much was obvious through his shorts. But for now (and perhaps because we were sitting in a place that could be discovered at any point by other hikers), it seemed he needed a different kind of comfort. His fingers threaded into my hair at the base of my skull, while his other hand wrapped tightly around my waist, keeping me flush against his big body.

"Always?" he asked again.

I smiled into his shoulder. "Always."

Then I sat up again. "What about at the Cape?" I suggested. "We could have a small ceremony on the lawn, or maybe in the grove by the tire swing."

The mention of the latter had me blushing slightly, to Brandon's clear delight. The last time we were in that grove, he had made love to me in the grass under the summer sky.

The more I thought about it, the better the idea sounded. There was more than enough space for a wedding on the expansive lawn, and the place meant something special to both of us. It was Brandon's favorite place in the world, one of the only places that was truly him, stripped of societal pretensions. For me, it was the place where I'd bonded with my brother and sister, where, despite Janette and Maurice's ulterior motives, I'd felt like I had a complete family.

"The Cape," Brandon repeated, testing out the words. Then he looked at me with a grin that lit up the entire forest. "I like it."

* * *

We arrived back in Woodstock to a crowd of cameras. Someone had apparently tweeted our arrival, and now photographers were trolling the streets of the small colonial town.

My head started to spin.

"Shit," Brandon said under his breath.

He grabbed my hand and pulled me behind him so I was sheltered by his big form as we made our way down the main street. The car was a few blocks down. Now that we were outed, there was really no other choice but to brave the storm and hope they missed us in the pedestrian crowds.

"Here," he said, fishing the Mercedes keys out of his pocket and handing them to Lucas. "We'll be in the gelato shop up the block. Can you pull up the car?"

Lucas looked at the keys doubtfully. "Sir, I really don't think I should leave you and Ms. Crosby by yourselves. It would be safer if I escorted you there."

"We'll be fine," Brandon said through clenched teeth as he thrust the keys out again. "I'm not exactly a pushover."

It was a tone of voice I remembered, although I hadn't seen it much lately: the one that allowed no argument. But there was a flash in his eyes I had never seen before—something angry, almost violent.

Despite the obvious fact that he disagreed completely with his boss, Lucas took the keys and gave a curt nod. "I'll be back in a minute. Stay in the shop. Go out the back door if you have to exit. Keep your cell phone on."

He glanced back and forth, as if checking for any possible assailants among the camera-bearing tourists who were strolling up and down the brick sidewalks, and then left.

181

"Come on, Red." Brandon said, pulling the brim of his cap forward and low. Then, with a glance at my flaming red ponytail, he took it off. "On second thought, you should probably take it."

With a faux grimace, I allowed him to clap the grubby old hat on my head. It was too big and fell over my face, but once I stuffed most of my hair into it, it stayed put.

"There," I said, glancing back at the cameras. "How's my disguise?"

"Sexiest disguise I ever saw," Brandon said. He squatted down and stamped a kiss on my lips.

"You're going to attract more attention doing that."

I was rewarded with a wide grin that caused more than one passerby to double-take. As much as I loved it, Brandon's smile wasn't exactly incognito.

"Worth it," Brandon said. He pushed a hand through his hat-flattened waves. "Come on, let's get some ice cream and go back to Boston before Cory sends out bloodhounds looking for me."

We walked into the gelato shop, where a line of customers was waiting to be served. For a while, it seemed like we wouldn't be recognized at all, just like we'd been able to go incognito for most of the day. But then:

"Hey, aren't you that guy who's running for mayor of Boston?"

"Shit." Brandon looked down at me with a hooded expression. "You should go. Out the back door before anyone recognizes you."

I took one look at his fists, clenched so tight his knuckles were turning white, and shook my head. "Absolutely not. I'm not leaving you here to deal with this alone."

"Skylar—"

"Hey, it's his girlfriend, too! That redhead from the papers!"

Slowly, we turned around to the owner of the voice, a squat, middle-aged man with pasty skin and a jiggling belly. He elbowed the woman next to him who looked like she was his wife. "I told you," he said to her. "It's him! That Brandon Sterling you were talking about!"

"It's nice to meet you," Brandon said, extending a hand and turning on a smile I'd only seen at banquets. It was several degrees cooler than the one I'd just seen outside, but one that charmed the shop regardless. A politician's smile.

I hated it.

The man pumped his hand enthusiastically, looking around the shop as if to show everyone else in it that he was really touching a famous person—if Brandon could actually be called famous. With a sinking feeling, I realized that was exactly what he was now.

"I know you," his wife said, and it took me a few moments to realize she was talking to me. Her finger jabbed through the air. "You're that little tramp from the pictures. The one that broke up his marriage." She looked at her husband. "His poor wife was traumatized, as she had every right to be!"

"Now, wait just a minute, ma'am—" Brandon broke in.

I placed a hand on his flexed arm—tension vibrated through it like a guitar string.

But the lady paid no mind as she stepped closer to me with angry, beady eyes. "I read that interview in *The Globe. He's* just a man—they can't help it. But you, you little hussy, you should know better than to step into another woman's marriage!"

"I—I—" I stuttered, stepping backward into Brandon's chest.

The room suddenly felt like it was caving in on me, and my New Yorker bravado was nowhere to be found. Behind me, Brandon was shaking, a dynamite stick ready to go off.

"Whore!" the woman hissed angrily as she took another step forward. A wave of whispers filtered through the shop. "Homewrecker! You leave him alone, you little slut!"

"That's enough!" Brandon erupted.

He proceeded to tow me away toward the back of the shop, out of the angry reach of the deranged woman and the rest of our audience. Unfortunately, even that exit was no longer available to us. The commotion had caused several photographers to surround the shop on both sides, and when we stepped into the alley, we were immediately hounded.

"Brandon!" they called. "Mr. Sterling! Skylar! What are you doing here? Are you hiding from your constituents? Are you ashamed of your relationship? Does Miranda know you're out?"

"No comment," Brandon said through teeth clenched so hard I thought his jaw was about to break.

"What's that ring, Skylar?" another photographer shouted, causing another frenzied round of clicks to spark off. The rest of them started shouting questions about the ring. I shoved my hand into my pocket.

"Don't hide it, honey!"

"Are you engaged?"

"Did he give you his wife's ring?"

Someone—I couldn't have said who—grabbed my arm in an attempt to pull my hand out of my pocket.

"Hey!" I yelped, yanking my arm back. "Don't touch me!"

Brandon reared back, looking very much like a bull that just saw red. "Get the fuck off her, man!"

He swiped over me toward the photographer while at the same time pulling me in front of him. Lucas stood at the end of the alley, waiting next to the Mercedes. I ran toward him.

"Whoa there, Brandon, are you assaulting the press?" jeered another photographer.

Another round of clicks and flashes went off. Brandon's hands clenched and unclenched at his sides as he glared at the cameras.

"Brandon, come on!" I called as I slid into the car. I reached out a hand, beckoning him to me.

Chest heaving, he glared at the cameramen, who were enjoying nothing more than taking even more pictures of the upset giant. These pictures, this story would be all over social media by the end of the day. Brandon needed to come now before it escalated even more.

"Come on, sir." Lucas clapped a hand on his boss to steer him back to the car.

For a moment, I thought he'd have to fight him, but finally, Brandon allowed himself to be shuffled into the backseat with me. The door shut behind him, and Lucas scurried around to the front to drive. Someone else would have to come back for his car later.

It wasn't until we were safely out of town, past the last of the stop signs and news trucks, that Brandon finally started to breathe normally again. He sat forward, with his elbows on his knees, and buried his head in his hands for a very long time.

* * *

184

That night, hours after he returned from his event, where he was peppered by members of the press following a speech on union rights, Brandon had another nightmare. It only ended when he shouted so loud I thought my ear drums burst. Wide awake, we stared at each other in the dark room. Even in the moonlight, I could see the tear tracks down the sides of his face, the creases even deeper over his eyebrows. Tears welled up in my eyes too, and we watched each other shake for a few seconds before Brandon suddenly hauled me into his chest. It was only when we were wrapped in each other's arms, breathing our mingled scents of almonds, jasmine, sweat, and tears that sleep was finally able to claim us for a few more hours.

Twenty

"All right, damage control."

Cory paced in front of us like a caged cat, back and forth in front of the couch where Brandon and I sat together, our knees touching and heads bent like derelict students. After being lugged out of bed at seven a.m. on a Sunday to listen to the guy berate us, I was really starting to hate that Cory knew the security code to our apartment.

"I guess we got sent to the principal's office," Brandon said with an impish smile at me.

I grinned back, and Brandon squeezed my hand just as Cory whirled around at us so fast his thick red tie hit him in the face.

"Oh, you got *jokes*," he said as he batted the fabric away. "It might seem funny right now, but your numbers just took a goddamn nose dive during the last twenty-four hours. Did you know there's a video? This isn't some fuckin' joke, man. You can't go assaulting members of the fuckin' press!"

"Come on, Cory, you weren't there," Brandon protested lightly. "He was tabloid paparazzi at best, not exactly the *New York Times* or anything. And I hardly assaulted him. If anything, *he* assaulted Skylar."

"You think that *matters*?" Cory exploded. "You and the Little fuckin' Mermaid over here were caught on tape pushing a paparazzo, and you think it matters which fuckin' *publication* he works for? You think it matters that he grabbed her? *They're* the ones with the cameras, Brandon, *not you*!"

I leaned back as a few droplets of spit launched through the air.

"*Cory*," Brandon barked.

"It's okay," I said. "I'm actually impressed he knows the Disney canon that well. You got a thing for Ariel, Cory?"

Brandon chuckled, and Cory shot me another death glare. I shrugged.

"Okay, okay, we get it," Brandon said. "But how does it not matter that the guy grabbed Skylar first? What was I supposed to do, sit back like a chump?"

"You're supposed to let the team of fuckin' gorillas you hired do their fuckin' jobs, not sit on their asses one-hundred-and-fifty *fuckin'* miles away from you!" Cory exploded. "Jesus *Christ*, Brandon! I swear to God, sometimes I really do think you're trying to sabotage this whole fuckin' operation!"

Then Cory turned on his heel and headed toward the foyer, blowing past the elevators and stopping at the stairwell door. "I'm going to cool the fuck off," he said when he got to the door.

"But you just got here," I said over the sofa.

Beside me, Brandon snickered. Apparently being treated like naughty high schoolers made both of us act like them.

"Yeah, get your giggles out now," Cory snapped. "Thirty minutes. And when I get back with Hope and Omar, we're going to strategize, goddammit. And you two are going to fuckin' *listen*." And with another long stream of profanity, Cory blew out of the room.

Brandon and I blinked at each other for a few seconds, then we burst into laughter together.

"Come here," he said in between chuckles. "I think we just gave Cory a heart attack."

"Oh my God, did you see how his eyes were bulging out of his head?" I said as I wiped tears out of my eyes.

Brandon's chest vibrated as he pulled me against him. Then he tipped my head up to his and pulled me close for a long, thorough kiss. When he was finished, no one was laughing anymore.

"I'm sorry," he said as he brushed his nose back and forth against mine. His thumb lightly stroked my cheek.

I pushed up to kiss him again. "It wasn't your fault."

"No," he agreed, "but I'm still sorry."

He stood up, pulling me with him, watching appreciatively as I adjusted the top of my leggings.

"Damn," he said regretfully. "Those...are really working for you."

I raised a playful brow and cocked a hip out. "You think so?"

He chewed his lip, then tore his gaze away from my legs. "Aaah, I *really* wish I could take advantage of you right now and make yesterday disappear."

"Stop," I said. "It wasn't all bad."

I bit my lip, thinking about the image of our wedding we'd built for ourselves. Brandon groaned.

"Cory's right," he said regretfully, rubbing his neck as he stepped away. "I need to call Hope before he does and start damage control."

"Okay. I have a therapy appointment, and then I need to get some work done myself. I'll probably just go to the cafe down the street, and then pick up some—"

Before I could finish my sentence, Brandon yanked me to him for another deep kiss. I melted into it, my fingers clenching at his hair as I opened my lips to his. But just as quickly, he let me go with two more short kisses and a smack on my ass.

"Go," he said with another quick peck. "Before I can't stop myself anymore."

* * *

Several hours later, I returned to the apartment with a bag full of read depositions and a growling stomach. I dropped my bag on the foyer table and walked into the living area, where Brandon, Cory, and two people I didn't recognize were all sitting around the uncomfortable sectional with empty takeout containers littering the coffee table. All four faces turned to me, but Brandon's was the only one that smiled.

"Hey, beautiful," he said, beckoning with a long arm stretched over the back of the sofa.

I went to him obediently. Brandon wrapped his arm around my waist as I gave him a brief kiss in greeting, which he extended just a second longer than was strictly necessary.

"Mmm," he murmured when he finally let me go. "Damn. Four hours really wasn't enough."

"Enough for what?" I whispered

He smirked. "Enough to get those dirty thoughts out of my head."

I blushed, glancing at the other three people in the room. I loved that Brandon wasn't shy about showing his affection for me, but every now and then it took me off guard.

"Um, thanks. I think," I said as I toyed with my hair, willing the blush in my cheeks to fade. "What's going on?"

"Oh, just a little strategizing for the campaign," Brandon said. His hand lingered at my waist as he turned back to the guests. "You know Cory, obviously, but we recently hired some other folks to help us out. This is Hope, our Communications Director, and Omar, who's in charge of social media. Guys, this is Skylar, my fiancée."

Still pinned to the couch by Brandon's arm, I waved awkwardly and ignored Cory's glare from the facing armchair as Hope and Omar said their hellos.

"Nice to meet you," I said. Absently, I stroked Brandon's hair, and he smiled up at me. "I'm going to change and get something to drink. Is there anything in the fridge?" I looked over the empty takeout containers and wrinkled my nose.

"Bubbe just brought beef stroganoff up for later," Brandon said. He rubbed his still-flat belly. "She's going to make me gain twenty pounds, I swear. Will you still marry me if I have to roll down the aisle?"

"Any day of the week," I said, earning another bright grin. It's the dimples, I thought. That was what made his smile sink into my soul every single time.

When I reemerged in a pair of harem pants and a loose gray T-shirt, the four of them were all deep in conversation.

"What about conversion?" Cory was asking. "That might help, you know?"

As I walked into the kitchen, I could feel four pairs of eyes watching as I poured myself a glass of water and pulled a plate out of the cabinet. The room went silent as I heated up some food, and when I turned to look at them, they were all staring at me.

"What's going on?" I asked, feeling under examination. I supposed I was.

"Nothing," Brandon said too quickly.

"Come on, man. She can make her own decision."

"It's not the worst idea in the world," Hope added. "The optics would probably play well in Catholic Boston. Reformed sinner atones! It's an easy headline to feed the smaller papers and blogs."

Omar remained quiet, studying his laptop.

"What's not the worst idea?" I asked as I carried my food over to the dinner table.

189

I took a seat at the corner closest to the group. Brandon came to sit next to me.

"We were just talking about the wedding," he said, almost regretfully. "They...think it would be a good idea to do something different with it to draw attention away from the video."

I frowned over a bite of noodles. "Like what?"

Brandon sighed. "It's nothing. These guys were just floating the idea of capitalizing on it for the campaign. Which we're *not* going to do."

I glanced at Hope and Cory, who were watching our interaction curiously. "Um, what were the suggestions?" I asked.

"It doesn't matter," Brandon said as he crossed one ankle over his knee and rubbed a hand through his hair. The familiar tell immediately made me more curious.

I looked to Hope. "You going to tell me?"

Beside me, Brandon groaned, but Hope just smiled.

"Everyone loves a wedding," she said. "And that goes double for a city full of romantic Irish and Italians."

"We think a church wedding would be a good idea," Cory cut in sharply. "You know, flowers, big puffy dress, altar boys, the whole fuckin' nine yards."

Only Cory could make a nice Catholic wedding sound vulgar. My stomach dropped as I looked back at Brandon.

"What about the Cape?" I asked in a small voice.

Brandon opened his mouth to speak, but Hope started talking instead.

"It's up to you," she said. "But marriage is a sacrament to a lot of people in Boston. We could get you in at Holy Cross. It would be amazing. Beautiful, really."

"Um, problem," I said. "I'm not Catholic."

"Well, that's where the reformed sinner thing comes in, doll," said Cory, earning a sharp look from Brandon. He held his hands up in mock-surrender. "Sorry, sorry. 'Skylar'," he corrected himself with mimed quotation marks. I resisted the urge to throw my fork at him.

"You would have to convert," Hope said plainly. "Brandon's already baptized Catholic, so that's not an issue, but you would have to go through confirmation classes." She sighed dreamily, as if imagining me in a white confirmation gown. "I can just see it:

190

Converting for the love of your life. Brandon would be the man who saves you from sin."

Then her eyes drew sharp as they zeroed in on me, and I saw a ruthless streak that would make Brandon hire her over the many others I'm sure were in line for this position. Alarmed, I looked back at Brandon. Suddenly my lunch seemed really unappetizing, and I reached for my water, wishing it was something stronger.

"Is this what you want?"

Brandon snorted. "Of course not. You know exactly how pious I am."

"That doesn't matter," Hope broke in again. "You're courting votes in a city full of people who keep rosaries on their rearview mirrors and only attend Mass at Christmas and Easter. They won't be checking up on all your Sunday habits, but a wedding that's not in a church will stick out."

"It'll also get rid of the abortion narrative," Cory piped up.

A chilled silence fell across the room. Now my food definitely tasted like sawdust. I pushed the plate away and walked back into the kitchen.

"*Cory*," Brandon said sharply while I pulled a bottle of white wine out of the fridge. Hell, it was five o'clock somewhere.

"Want one?" I asked Brandon as I held up a beer.

"Absolutely," he said before turning to glare at his campaign manager.

Cory shrugged, like the menace in his boss's voice was an everyday occurrence. "It's a problem, and you know it. We've been trying for weeks to figure out how to spin it when things come out, and now they are out for sure, because Miranda is a backstabbing bitch."

"*Cory!*"

Cory frowned. "Seriously? I heard *you* use that exact expression *three days ago*."

Brandon blew a long, frustrated breath out of pursed lips and took the beer I brought him gratefully. "Just...tone it down, will you?"

"What do you mean, it will get rid of the abortion narrative?" I asked quietly as I sat back down with my wine, causing everyone to look at me again.

191

I blushed immediately. The whole disclosure was still so new. I didn't think I'd ever feel comfortable talking about it, but it was particularly bad now. Still, my own discomfort needed to come second here.

"It's out," Hope said. "*The Globe* picked it up today. Second page."

She handed me a copy of the newspaper, and I flipped to the article with the clear headline: "Mayoral Candidate's Girlfriend Has Abortion." My hands started to shake, and immediately, Brandon took one in his lap.

"Well, in a way, it's a good thing you're not Catholic," Hope said. "Makes your reform clearer that way. If you converted, you would be taking on the Catholic church's stance on abortion. As in, it's wrong, and you regret it." She shrugged, as if the truth of the narrative meant little. "We could show your first communion and everything. 'Reformed sinner makes good.' You get absolved by the church, Boston forgives you. It's perfect."

"But I'm pro-choice," I said in a shaky voice. "That's not going to have to change, no matter how badly I feel about what I did." I looked worriedly at Brandon. "Is it?"

He shook his head vehemently. "Nothing about you needs to change, Red."

Behind him, Cory rolled his eyes, but Hope smiled.

"That doesn't really matter anyway," she said. "Massachusetts is one of the most liberal states in the country. And you don't actually have to say anything; that's what I'm for. Just look pretty eating the bread and sipping the wine, and it'll all go over great."

"Op-tics," Cory said slowly, like he was talking to a person hard of hearing.

I glared at him.

"I still think it's a ridiculous idea," Brandon said to them as he squeezed my hand a little harder. "I'm not running a sham campaign here. Skylar's not going to fake-convert just to make me look good."

Hope shrugged. She was obviously as cutthroat as Cory, although she managed to couch her razor-sharp pragmatism in nicer words. I supposed that's why she was the communications director.

"The reality is this," she said, looking at us both directly. "This is the kind of scandal that's really hard to recover from. You turn around and marry the girl who just terminated her pregnancy with you? Right after we've just finished putting out fires about your divorce and today's video? It doesn't get much worse than that."

"It's on *Slate*," Omar called out from his place on the hearth. "And *Vice*. It also looks like #brandonsbaby is trending on Twitter."

"*Fuck* me!" Cory groaned.

Brandon pressed his lips into a tight line, and my stomach dropped another story. Even though the truth was out there, I knew it still hurt him, and would for a long time.

"We could try to distract the press," Hope continued. "Flip the news cycle. But unless there's a terrorist attack or something, it would be hard to beat this story unless we have a competing narrative. Conversion and a big church wedding fits the bill." She smiled at us. "I mean, look at you two. You look like you just walked off *The Bachelor*. Who wouldn't want to be you?"

"This is ridiculous—" Brandon started to protest again.

"I'll do it," I cut in quietly.

Immediately, everyone looked up, including Omar, who had been mostly engrossed with his computer.

Brandon sat up straight and gawked. "*What?*"

I took another long, measured drink of wine, although my hand was still shaky.

"Skylar," Brandon said as he sat forward, still holding my other hand. "No. You don't need to do this."

I looked at him directly. His blue eyes gleamed, unwavering. God, I loved him so much.

"Do you want to be mayor?" I asked gently.

He paused, glanced at Cory and Hope, then back at me. "Yes."

"And these guys know what they're talking about, don't they?"

"Well, of course," Brandon admitted. "I wouldn't hire anyone but the best. But Skylar—"

"Then I should do it," I said simply, much more calmly than I felt. "I did something that hurt you, and keeping it to myself almost ruined us. I want to help rebuild. Maybe this is just the price I pay for doing that." I shrugged. "I can be nominally Catholic. It's no different than converting for marriage or something like that. It's not going to hurt anyone."

Even as I spoke the words, I felt a little sick to my stomach. This went against everything I believed in. But if it would help Brandon, keep him from losing his dream, I'd do it.

193

Brandon's rolled his lips together, stunned into silence. "Skylar..." he tried again.

"It's fine," I said. I pulled my hand away and turned back to my lunch.

The noodles still tasted like sawdust, but I ate them anyway, determined to put on an unaffected front. After several more minutes of silent chewing in front of my awkward audience of four, I finally got up and carried my plate to the kitchen sink. Then I grabbed my bag off the entry table and wove my way back through the room.

"I'm going now," I said with a kiss to Brandon's still-stunned cheek. "Leave you guys to your strategizing. Just let me know where I need to go and when." I turned to Hope and Omar. "Nice to meet you. Cory, nice to see you again."

The chatter rose again as I made my way out of the room, but I could feel Brandon's eyes boring into me the entire time. I didn't turn around. I knew the doubt in my heart would be all over my face.

Twenty-One

A week later, I found myself standing outside a wedding shop with Gloria Epstein, the wedding planner that Hope and Margie had booked for me, and Jane, who had insisted that she would rather cut off a finger than miss watching me try on a bunch of poofy dresses.

I'd met Gloria the day before, and the woman was both one of the preeminent wedding planners in Boston and a complete whirlwind. The massive binder she had smacked on the coffee table in the apartment had been full of concept ideas for our wedding, and after she had managed to tease a few words out of me for a "style brief," she had assured me she'd take care of the rest.

In a way, it was fine. This wedding was already starting to feel like it didn't belong to me, and I knew Brandon felt the same way. Only once did I think of the small ceremony we had imagined in Cape Cod, but the idea made me so sad, I buried it under the guilt I still carried. Things between Brandon and me were mostly fine now, but my actions had repercussions. I needed to own them.

"Do you think your grandmother will be here soon?" Gloria asked me as she tapped her stilettoed foot on the pavement. "Jenna is really very strict about her appointments."

I glanced down the street, hoping to see one of the other security cars in the line of traffic on Newbury. "She should be here any second. I think she had a brunch or something this morning." I glanced back at Lucas, who was standing as unobtrusively as a six-foot-six giant could against the building. "Are they on their way?"

"Just parked, Ms. Crosby," he said with a nod.

As if on cue, I could hear Bubbe's voice coming around the corner before I actually saw her.

"Come on, come on! They're waiting for us!"

I looked down the block to see my tiny grandmother trotting down the sidewalk, another linebacker-sized security detail jogging behind her. She waved her hand as she approached.

"I told you to take Marlborough, not Beacon, Mario," she finished chiding her bodyguard. "Next time, listen. I know what I'm talking about here."

I had to smile. Less than two months living here, and Bubbe already thought she knew the streets better than the locals.

"You should be nicer to Mario," I said as I accepted her kiss on the cheek. "He's making sure no one snatches you off the street."

Bubbe waved my comments away even as Mario gave me a grateful look. From the look of him, guarding my grandmother was a tough job.

"Shall we?" Gloria broke in as she rang the buzzer on the door.

"Yes," I said. "Let's go."

* * *

The shop was called Le Rêve, and I could see why: it was like walking into a giant, white, wedding-shaped dream. The small shop catered to clients on an appointment-basis only, providing couture dresses for the most exclusive buyers in Boston.

It wasn't a place I would have ever ended up on my own. For one, there was the ridiculous fact that one dress here could potentially cost the equivalent of more than a year's rent at my old apartment with Eric. It was a preposterous amount of money to spend on something I would wear only for a few hours, particularly when I could just get a knock off for a tiny fraction of the price. David's Bridal was fine with me.

But Gloria had insisted I rethink that instinct, considering the potential for wedding photos to make the papers. "Dress for the job you want, they always say," she had told me in her office. "If the job you want is First Lady of Boston, then we've got some work to do."

I wondered briefly if she had been chosen as a channel for Cory. His words from my last public appearance with Brandon—*Michelle Obama, not Marie Antoinette*—echoed in the back of my mind. So I had sighed, but conceded the need for a fancy dress.

Jenna, the shop owner, led us to the large tufted bench in the middle of the room, which was otherwise outfitted with racks and racks of white and off-white dresses, organized by designer. Despite the fact that I had absolutely no idea what kind of dress I wanted to have, Gloria had insisted that choosing a dress was the first thing I should do, and we weren't leaving here today until that had happened.

"Aside from the time it will take for fittings and everything within the next few months, it's the centerpiece of the whole shebang," Gloria said as she handed me, Jane, and Bubbe each a bridal magazine. "Choose the dress, and we know exactly what kind of wedding you're having. And I *really* need to know that. Like, yesterday."

"What's the rush?" Bubbe asked. "You know, if you don't mind waiting, I'm sure they would have space at the temple next year."

"Well, we want to get married before the primaries," I said, unable to meet Bubbe's eye.

"Not to mention you can't have a Catholic wedding in a synagogue," Gloria put in kindly. "As soon as Skylar's finished with confirmation classes, they'll be able to take the premarital counseling at Holy Cross. We've got the date booked for March."

"Confirmation *what?*"

Bubbe's voice rang out clearly through the shop, and all four of us were suddenly very quiet.

"Uh-oh," Jane muttered next to me.

I toed the light blue carpet uneasily.

"Skylar, for goodness' sake, stop fidgeting with your foot!" Bubbe snapped. "That's why your shoes are always scuffed like a bum's. Now look at me in the eye, and tell me this again. What confirmation?"

I sighed again and faced my tiny, yet incredibly intimidating grandmother. Even Jane had nothing to say as her fascinated gaze bounced between us, and Gloria was suddenly engrossed with her phone.

"It's just for show," I said lamely.

"But-but you're *Jewish!*" Bubbe sputtered. "How can you cross over? Just like that?" She snapped her papery fingers with a pop that cracked through the air.

"Bubbe, I am not Jewish," I protested weakly.

"You're my granddaughter. That makes you as Jewish as anyone."

"Bubbe, you're Conservative," I pointed out. "You have literally never called me Jewish until exactly this moment."

"I took you to temple all the time."

"You took me to temple maybe five times in my life. The only thing that makes me Jewish is growing up with your cooking."

We were both exaggerating, I knew. She had never had that much investment in my religious preferences beyond occasionally wanting to set me up with nice Jewish boys. And I probably identified with it more than anything else simply from growing up around her.

Before Bubbe could answer, Jenna popped out with a bright smile on her face.

"All right, ladies, let's get started! Who's got some gorgeous gowns picked out?" she asked in a sing-song voice that withered once Bubbe and I both turned our glares on her.

Jane cleared her throat. "Just call us the Macbeth witches instead. 'Double, double, toil and trouble,' and all that."

"Um, all right then," Jenna said, confused as she took a seat on the tufted ottoman in front of me. While I avoided the daggers of guilt from my grandmother, Jenna paged through a Vogue Weddings magazine with me.

"Let's talk about what you like," she said. "How excited are you for your wedding?! Gloria mentioned that you were planning a traditional ceremony at Holy Cross. What a beautiful venue!"

I tried to look excited while beside me, Bubbe scowled.

"It *is* a lovely venue," Jane piped up. "So many...pillars."

I shot her a dirty look, and she stuck out her tongue. She was enjoying this way too much.

"The venue itself is worth celebrating, don't you think?" she asked Jenna sweetly. "Maybe with champagne? Or, you know, anything alcoholic? We'll take moonshine if that's all you have."

Jenna perked up. "Oh! Would you like some champagne? I hadn't thought, since it's so early—"

"We would," Jane cut her off. Then, as an afterthought: "Please."

Jenna scurried off to dig up the drinks while I paged through the magazine and Bubbe glowered. Finally, I sighed up at the ceiling and set the magazine aside.

"Bubbe," I said. "Please. Can you just...let it go?"

Bubbe opened her mouth, clearly ready to release the onslaught of commentary that had been building up for the last ten minutes. But something on my face stopped her, and she closed her mouth with a look that was significantly more sympathetic.

"Will the reception be kosher?" she asked at last.

I cracked a smile, and I could hear Jane mutter, "thank God" to herself behind me.

"Of course," I said as I kissed my grandmother on the cheek. "I wouldn't have it any other way. You got that, Gloria? I want the reception to be kosher. Bubbe's in charge of planning food."

"Finally, a detail I can work with," Gloria said with a smile. "You and I are going to get to know each other very well, Sarah."

"I guess this is what I get for encouraging a relationship with a *goy*," Bubbe muttered as she picked up a magazine. "Oh, Skylar, look at that one! I tell you, *bubbela*, you have to get one with a beaded bodice. I always wanted a dress like that!"

* * *

Thirty minutes later, all of us except Gloria were half-drunk on champagne, and Bubbe had elbowed her way into the storeroom with Jenna to look at the "secret gowns" she insisted were kept back there (despite Jenna's insistence they were not). That left Jane and me to look at the inventory up front while Gloria chattered with other clients on her Bluetooth.

"Why don't you just tell him that's not what you want?" Jane asked after I'd made yet another sarcastic comment about the giant church wedding.

I pulled out a princess-shaped hoop skirt with about twenty layers of tulle and shook my head. "I can't. I'm trying to make his life easier right now, Jane, not harder. After all the shit I'm bringing into his life, I kind of owe him that, you know?"

Jane gave me a look that clearly said she did *not* know.

"You've done a ridiculous amount to make up for your mistakes, Sky. You can't keep sacrificing everything about yourself just because you feel guilty."

"You sound like my therapist," I muttered. Now that I was in fact seeing a therapist, I had been hearing that particular sentiment a lot.

"Smart minds..." Jane replied. "We're talking about your religion, not compromising on dinner reservations. Have you considered the fact that the majority of the problems you and Brandon have come when the two of you are not one-hundred-percent honest with each other?"

I flipped through another row of tulle-lined dresses and avoided my best friend's sharp gaze. "I'm being honest. I'm being honest about the fact that right now, I'd rather keep my reservations to myself in order to make him happy. That's my choice."

Jane rolled her eyes. "Jesus Christ. You are the Queen of Denial, lady; they should call you Cleo-fucking-patra."

"Hey! I resent that."

Jane just snorted. "Whatever you say, Cleo. But I'm not buying it." She pulled a dress off the rack and snorted. "I swear to God, I'm going to make you try on the ugliest dresses in this shop just to blackmail you later." When I wasn't full of pithy comebacks, she looked at me with concern. "You all right? I didn't want to say anything in front of Bubbe, but you don't look so good. Are the hours at Kiefer horrendous?"

I sighed and tipped back the rest of my champagne. "They're long, but nothing terrible. It's...Brandon's still having those nightmares. They...yeah. I'm not getting the best sleep."

Jane grimaced. "Jesus. Every night?"

I nodded. "Sometimes twice. I don't know, Jane...I don't think it's the abortion stuff. We've pretty much moved past that. It's just this drama in the press that keeps it going, maybe. And...I don't know. Something else I haven't figured out yet."

"Has he seen a therapist?" Jane paused, clicking her ring-laden fingers on the side of the champagne glass.

Now that she had been forced to curb her edgy fashion sense at work, outside of it she had started dressing even more like a punk video extra than before, as if to balance it out. The only thing she couldn't change was her hair, which no longer had its characteristic streaks of color through her black bob.

"From what you said, it sounds like something is triggering him," she said. "I mean...PTSD is a real thing, and it can come back with the right triggers. My dad works with guys who deal with that for decades after the fact sometimes."

Jane's father was a psychologist who often worked with veterans. I sighed. Brandon wasn't a vet, but he had grown up in a war zone of sorts. He had mentioned that he had gotten nightmares sometimes like this when he was a kid. Was that what this was?

"Not so far," I said, shaking my head. "He's pretty averse to therapy."

I don't need to be fixed, he said, over and over again. This was a man who had been running from his imperfections since he was a kid, who carried an immense amount of self-blame for the people who had neglected him, which included his mother's death by overdose. It was why he was so apt to making massive, even inappropriate gestures meant to earn the love of people around him—which I sometimes suspected was at the heart of his bid for mayor.

But other people in his youth had seen those anxieties and treated them the wrong way. He'd had terrible experiences with therapy and medication in the past. I genuinely doubted that I could get him to try that path again.

Jane interrupted my thoughts when she yanked out one of the dresses and held it up to me. "You have to try this one on."

I looked down and made a face. The "dress", if you could call it that, was absolutely covered with sequins and had a skirt that was about ten feet wide.

"Absolutely not. I'd look like a marshmallow. I wouldn't even be able to fit through a doorway."

"Precisely the point, Strawberry Shortcake. I didn't fly here on my precious weekend off to watch you be all tasteful and chic. I came here to drink champagne and heckle you in layers and layers of sequins, so let's get to it, shall we?"

With a roll of my eyes, I indicated to the assistant sales girl that I wanted to try on the marshmallow dress, then smirked back at Jane. "And here I thought it was also to make up with a certain former roommate of mine. After all, it's not like you're staying in the penthouse right now."

Jane pursed her lips, and for the first time, her normally mocking facade disappeared. Immediately, I rushed to her side.

"Hey, Janey," I said. "I'm sorry. What happened?"

She sighed and collapsed on the pink couch. "I...shit. I just...well, you know we sort of made up."

I nodded. Eric had mentioned it during Happy Hour one night after Brandon's birthday party. All I knew was that he and Jane were talking again. They were like magnets, drawn back to each other no matter what happened.

"We decided it would go back to the way it was. Like that ridiculous weekend—"

"The one when Eric said he loved you?"

Jane shot me a dirty look. "Yes, the one that we don't talk about anymore. That one."

I just raised my eyebrow and fingered a silk dress. This one I kind of liked. "So, what happened?"

"I came in last night. Things were back to usual. Hot dinner. Hot sex. The works."

I whistled. "Sounds like what you wanted."

"Yeah." Jane heaved a big sigh. "Except when I changed the sheets this morning, I found a pair of underwear in his bed. And not the kind he buys in six packs, if you know what I mean."

I winced. It wasn't like they had anything serious going on, but that had to hurt Jane's pride. "And you didn't like it."

"Of course I didn't like it!" Jane exploded, sloshing her champagne around in her glass. "Ugh, I'm *pathetic*. I stormed out this morning without saying a word." She paused and rubbed her temples. "Can I stay with you guys tonight? I just don't think I can go back there and face him."

I sighed and sat on the back of the sofa next to my friend.

"You're always welcome to stay. But you guys haven't seen each other for a month. Didn't *you* break it off with him?"

"Yes, yes, *yes*." Jane scowled and took another long chug of champagne. "Obviously trying to be monogamous was never going to work. And clearly I was right. I mean, Eric's...*Eric*."

"Also, you're *you*," I added, earning a dirty look from my friend.

"Hey, I could be a one-man woman if I wanted to," she retorted. "I just haven't wanted to."

"Before now?"

There was a very long silence.

"What makes you think that Eric couldn't do the same for you?"

"Give me a *break*," Jane spit out. "The guy is a walking erection. We broke up for all of two *seconds* before he was out banging other girls."

"Haven't you been getting around too?" I asked gently. "I seem to recall him walking in on you with another guy in Chicago..."

202

"Totally different," Jane bit out. "For one, we didn't even do anything. Like I couldn't. I could not have been less attracted to another man. All because of a fucking *petri dish.*"

"And why do you think that is?" I wasn't joking anymore as I reached out to touch my friend's shoulder.

"Oh, cut the cross-examination, Counselor," she snapped, although her comeback was weaker than normal. She lay back on the couch and groaned up at the lavender-painted ceiling. "All right, *fine!* I like him, okay? I actually like Eric and his cocky, infuriating, promiscuous, sexy, bedroom-talented ass. But I already told him I didn't want monogamy, and I'm not going to jerk him around anymore. *Fuck.*" She tossed back the rest of the champagne, then looked around the shop. "Yoo-hoo! Fancy ladies! Fill 'er up, please! I seriously need more booze here if I have to have these kinds of epiphanies."

I looked on sympathetically. I knew how hard it was for my friend to admit this out loud, and I suspected that if she could get up the guts to be honest about it, she'd probably find that Eric still felt the same way.

"All right," she said as the salesgirl brought over another two glasses of champagne. "Enough of this Gossip Girl bullshit. Now grow up and try on some froufy dresses."

So I got to work. It quickly became apparent that Bubbe, Gloria, and I all had extremely different ideas as to what kind of dress suited me, and the situation. I tended to gravitate more toward simple silhouettes—slip dresses or column gowns with delicate straps, the kind of thing I would wear in reality, just in different colors. Gloria vetoed all of them, saying those sorts of dresses were more suitable to a beach or outdoor wedding, and that the affair I was planning required something formal. Bubbe just liked anything with a lot of beading on it.

Jane was supposed to be there for moral support, although the more she drank, the uglier the dresses she picked out for me to try on, much to Gloria's increasing annoyance.

"See, now isn't that beautiful!" Bubbe crowed when I emerged from the dressing room in what must have been the thirtieth dress so far.

I looked down. It was a mermaid gown absolutely *covered* in sequins with puffy sleeves that strongly resembled meringue

203

cookies. Gloria had told me that if I wanted to dress the part for a conservative Catholic wedding, I would need to have my shoulders covered. Bubbe apparently thought that meant with giant clusters of ruffles.

Jane took one look at me and snorted champagne through her nose.

"That's your shape, *bubbela*," Bubbe said, clearly a little worse for wear from the champagne. All three of us were a bit unnecessarily red in the cheeks.

I glanced over my shoulder at the mirror. I looked like a Coke bottle that had been attacked with a glitter gun. I looked back at Bubbe and started to shimmy toward her and Jane.

"I can't even walk in this, Bubbe," I said, nearly falling off the platform as I moved to the dressing rooms. Thankfully, Jenna was there to grab my hand to steady me. "Thanks," I said, gratefully as she steered me back.

"Hold on here, hon," she said as a phone call rang in the back room. "I'll be back in a sec to help you out of this thing."

I stood in the small, mirror-lined room awkwardly while I waited, wondering how many more of these things I was going to have to try on today. Gloria was clearly getting impatient, and I was running out of patience myself. Maybe today just wasn't going to be the day I found my dress.

"God, and did you hear her grandmother's accent? She sounds like an impression from SNL or something. They should just go with that tacky beaded one. It would fit the family."

The voices fluttered over the tops of the curtain. There were two other shop girls working here. I saw them briefly when they'd helped Jenna bring out some of the gowns.

"What's that saying? Lipstick on a pig?" the other one whispered loudly.

The first girl snorted, and the two of them tittered for a bit. It was obvious whom they were referring to. I clenched the five-thousand-dollar beading, suddenly wanting to tear every bit of the finery off.

"Isn't the wedding in, like, four months or something ridiculous like that?"

"I bet she's pregnant again. That's the only way someone like that would land someone like him. Have you seen his picture? OMG, he is *gorgeous*."

That was *it*. Something in me clicked at their voices, and I swept back the curtain dramatically and stepped out, tacky beading and all. For the first time, I was actually glad I was wearing the ugly dress my grandmother had picked out. I needed to channel her attitude.

The girls froze like deer. Petty, stupid, self-absorbed deer.

"To start," I said more calmly than I felt, although the Brooklyn accent that I usually managed to keep repressed was shaking through. "The only lipstick-wearing pigs in this shop are *you* sorry bitches."

One of the girls opened her mouth. "Oh, we weren't talking about—"

"Yes, you were," I interrupted with a finger held up. "Just like you were talking about my grandmother, who has more character in her finger than you do in that anorexic body of yours."

The girl opened and shut her mouth while the other stepped forward, hands held up in surrender.

"Ms. Crosby," she said weakly, "I don't know what you thought you heard, but—"

"Uh-uh," I said, waggling my finger in a way that mimicked Bubbe perfectly. Her particular brand of no-bullshit was coursing through me, and I felt stronger for it. "Don't fucking lie to me. I heard every word."

"Is everything okay here?"

The three of us turned around to see Jenna, who had appeared from the front room with a concerned look.

"It could be." I looked down at the ugly dress I was wearing. "I'm done here. These ladies thought it was appropriate to make a bunch of derogatory comments about me and my family when they thought I couldn't hear them. Unfortunately for them, I could. Loud and clear."

Jenna's face immediately clouded as she shot murderous looks at her employees. "Oh, goodness. Skylar, I am so sorry. I assure you, this *will* be dealt with."

"It will," I said with more authority than I felt. But it felt good to take charge of something. "I'll take the first Vera Wang, the one with the train. But only if these two are done working here, starting now."

It was a twenty-thousand-dollar gown, which would fund the shop for months. I could barely remember what it looked like, but I knew that Gloria approved because it came with a shawl, and that I'd liked it because it was so simple. It certainly wasn't worth the paltry salaries of these two employees.

"Done," Jenna said without hesitation. She turned to her stunned now-former employees. "Get your things and go. I'll send your pay in the mail."

I looked to the girls with a smugly raised brow.

Don't fuck with me, I thought, surprised by just how good it felt to take back control of *something* in my life.

Twenty-Two

The priest smiled. He was a kindly older man with snow-white hair and a slight belly, patrician and grandfatherly in the way I'd expect from a man heading up the largest church in Massachusetts.

"You know," he said as he leaned back in his creaky office chair. He had spent the last thirty minutes listening to me talk about why I wanted to convert. It wasn't as hard as I thought. It seemed like the church was hungry for new converts, especially high-profile ones. "It's possible the Cardinal might want to be involved." He cocked his head knowingly. "The church has had its own share of PR problems in the last ten years, as I'm sure you know. Someone like you openly joining might be...helpful. If you're willing to scratch his back, he might be willing to scratch yours, so to speak. Expedite the process, if that's what you're looking for."

I frowned.

"The conversion process takes most converts eight-to-twelve months," he continued calmly as he picked a paperweight in the shape of a bowling ball off his desk and started to rub it meditatively. "But potentially, we could speed things up. You could do an independent study of sorts with me instead of attending the standard catechism classes."

My frown deepened. "Are you talking about money?" Was this guy for real? Was a priest actually shaking me down for Brandon's money?

"No, no, no," he chortled. "I just mean a few photo-ops, maybe your picture in the paper. Human interest stuff."

"Oh."

As much as I found the conversation distasteful—after all, shouldn't the man be more interested in saving my immortal soul than building the public profile?—it *was* sort of the whole point of this exercise. Maybe it was better that we were all on the same page about it anyway.

"I think that will work," I said. "You have Hope McGaughey's information, right? She can set up whatever photos, etc., we need to do."

Father Garrett nodded. "Yes, that's all in order. I have a few hours free now. We'll do the Rite of Acceptance during Sunday Mass if you like, but there's no reason we can't begin instruction tonight. Would you like to get started?"

I sighed. So much for getting home at a decent hour.

"Sure," I said. "I'm a quick study."

"Good," said Father Garrett approvingly with a smile that for some reason made me want to cringe. "Good girl."

* * *

I came home to an empty apartment after two hours of listening to Father Garrett lecture me on the various elements of Christian prayer. He had seemed content to talk on his own with his hands folded over his belly, occasionally asking me questions, and generally responded with "good girl" to whatever I said. I had never felt more like a diminutive schoolgirl, not even when I *was* a schoolgirl.

Brandon had gone to LA again and didn't expect to be back until late. The apartment, suspended as it was above the city, was deathly quiet.

After a late dinner of leftover chicken and salad (with a hefty glass of wine), I collapsed grumpily into the big bed alone and stared at the ceiling while I waited for sleep to come. I couldn't shake the notion that I was lying all over again. While I knew that many people converted for their spouses, it seemed like such an intensive process to go through if you didn't actually have any religious convictions to start with. It would be one thing if I had grown up in some other kind of Christian denomination, but I was singularly without faith, and until now, hadn't really been looking for it either.

Father Garrett had spent a good part of our time talking about bearing witness—the expectation that as a new convert, I would go forth and proselytize my faith to others and spread the word of the Church.

Was that what I was going to be expected to do from now on? Be a good pious wife who attended Mass every Sunday? Baptize my

208

future kids into a religion I didn't truly believe in? Was this really only going to be for the optics of the election, or would it never stop?

I twisted onto my side and found myself eye-to-eye with the framed picture of Brandon and me, taken recently in France. It was a selfie snapped on one of our long day-trips to one of many small towns around Provence. We were standing in front of a beautiful Gothic cathedral, me visibly laughing, while Brandon kissed my cheek.

I gazed at the picture for a long time. We had been so happy there, and we were starting to be happy with each other again, the stresses of this campaign notwithstanding. There was no reason we couldn't continue down that path.

People converted every day for their loves. I'd just have to do it for mine.

I padded back out to the foyer and retrieved the six-hundred-page catechism book I had brought home with me from my "independent study." Heaving it into bed, I flipped on the light and started to read.

* * *

"No!" Brandon shouted, jarring me out of sleep again.

Maybe it was the fact that I was living in an ice palace I hated and had to be followed wherever I went by a character from *Men in Black*. Maybe it was the ongoing lack of sleep and the fact that various types of immortal sins were still dancing around my brain from the reading I'd done before bed. Or maybe it was because it was only two a.m., and this was the second nightmare since Brandon had crept into bed sometime past midnight.

I didn't know what it was, exactly. But something in me broke.

"Get up!" I shouted, yanking the covers off both of us as I jumped out of the bed and flipped on the overhead lights.

"Who-wha!" Brandon yelped as he was suddenly exposed to the air-conditioned room. His eyes blinked open, and as he fully came to consciousness and registered the fact that I was awake and had turned on the lights, he turned to me with an angry blue glare. "Skylar, what the fuck? I was sleeping!"

"Well, *I* wasn't," I retorted, crossing my arms and returning the glare.

Brandon scowled more deeply, but the fierce expression lessened as he realized what I was talking about.

"Oh," he said. "Shit, Red. I'm sorry." He looked back at me hopefully. "But now you can come back to bed, since it won't happen again tonight."

I bit my lower lip. "Wrong." I huffed out a sigh. "That was the second one tonight," I said. "And it's only two. Chances are there's going to be a third now."

Brandon frowned. "What?"

At his obvious confusion, I immediately crossed back to the bed and sat next to him. Like a magnet, his hand found my knee. Normally I never wanted to stop touching him, but I wondered if tonight I needed some space. He wasn't going to like what I had to say.

"Brandon," I said. "This isn't getting any better. It's getting worse."

The hand left my knee, and instead Brandon rubbed it over his face so he wouldn't have to look at me.

"It's fine," he said into his palm. "They'll go away. They always do."

"You've been saying that for over a month. They're not going away. They're getting *worse*."

He pressed his lips together into a thin line and glared at me. "They'll go away."

I huffed and stood up, grabbing my pillow.

"Where are you going?"

"To sleep in the guestroom."

I looked at the pillow, realized it was stupid to take and chucked it at the bed, only narrowly missing Brandon's head. He ducked, and his frown deepened.

"Skylar," he stared to protest.

"I need to get some actual sleep," I said. "And since you're not interested in doing what you obviously need to do to stop waking both of us up every single night with screaming fits, then I'm going to start sleeping in the guestroom until you do."

I turned and walked out, leaving Brandon sitting there with an open jaw.

I was just starting to climb into the bed in my former room when I heard his heavy footsteps shuffling across the hall. The bedroom door banged open, and his wide shoulders filled the frame. Naked except for his briefs, with his blond waves ruffled from disturbed sleep, he looked like some kind of deranged Viking. A very, very sexy Viking.

Unfortunately, I wasn't interested in anything else but sleep.

"*What*?" I spat from the bed. "Did you *want* me to stay awake?"

"What the hell, Skylar?" Brandon demanded. "You wake me up just to walk out on me? You said you weren't going to run anymore!"

"I'm not running! I'm in the next fucking room!"

"You belong in *our* room!"

"I woke you up to make you confront your problem—"

"I don't have a problem—"

"—and since you won't do that, I need some fucking sleep!"

Brandon slammed both of his palms into the door frame and growled. "Goddammit!" he shouted. "Why do you always have to be so damn difficult?"

I looked at him like he was absolutely crazy, which in that moment, he was.

"*I'm* the one who's difficult?" I retorted, flinging back the covers so I could stalk toward him.

We bristled, nose to nose despite the fact that he stood almost a foot taller than me. Christ, I thought to myself, inwardly smirking at the fact that my new priest probably wouldn't like me thinking that way. We really were like magnets.

"I'm not the one who is living in a fucking *ocean* of my own denial," I said through my teeth.

"Are you kidding me?" he said. "Who convinced herself that a guy trying to do every fucking thing he could think of to love and protect her was some kind of scumbag?"

"Still," I seethed. "I'm here now. I'm present. *I* got down on my knees in a room full of people and asked you to marry me, for Christ's sake! *I'm* the one converting to a religion I don't believe in for you! *I'm* seeing a therapist and owning the shit that's happened to me. Is that what you call denial?"

211

To his credit, he said nothing as I rushed on.

"*I* am not the one who is waking up nightly in cold sweats with bad dreams I refuse to talk about! *I* am not the one who thinks he has to be everything for everyone all the fucking time and is DRIVING HIMSELF CRAZY DOING IT!"

"I'm not crazy, Red!"

"Well, you're getting close!" I yelled. "If I'm going through all of this to fix myself for you, then the least you could do is see a therapist to fix whatever shit is going on in your head! You clearly have some kind of PTSD from your childhood, and *something* is triggering it, and—"

"I DON'T NEED TO BE FIXED!" Brandon roared, so loudly that I jumped back.

Silence fell over us, the sounds of our breaths heaving filling the small room. Brandon's naked pecs tensed and bulged in the moonlight that striped through the blinds, making him look almost tiger-like. His eyes, which seemed to glow extraterrestially, skimmed over my body, which was scantily clad in just a light camisole and underwear.

"Oh, *no* you don't," I said, scrambling backward and around the other side of the bed.

"Come on, Red," he taunted in a low voice that had me half-turned-on, half-terrified. "You want a little crazy, baby?"

He crawled over the bed, moving his shoulders up and down like the big cat he resembled, and a split second later, he had me cornered against the cold glass of the picture window. I shook my head vigorously, although I couldn't fully look away. There was nowhere for me to go.

"Come on," he purred as he leaned down and drew his nose up the side of my neck. His hot breath caused goose pimples to rise there, and he grazed the edges of his teeth over my artery, like he was a predator getting ready to kill his prey.

"Please," I whimpered, although now I wasn't sure what for.

"Please what, Red?" Brandon rumbled against the delicate skin. He bit down, lightly. "God, you taste good. You *always* taste so damn good."

As my chest heaved, my breasts tested the confines of the camisole. Brandon looked me over, a smile playing across his lips as he zeroed in on my nipples, visibly hardened through the thin cotton.

With a light touch, he pulled one strap of the camisole over one shoulder, then followed on the other side. Then he hooked a finger in the center of my shirt and tugged until both breasts bobbed over the material, naked in the light.

His finger drifted downward, also hooking on the edge of my underwear and pulled enough so that it eventually slid down my legs of its own accord. Brandon slipped his finger in between my legs, toying with the delicate skin there. I shifted, and his finger entered me.

"You're always so wet for me," he murmured as he gently pushed it in and out.

"Ummmm," I murmured, arching me back lightly against the glass. I could barely speak when he touched me like this.

With his other hand, Brandon palmed my right breast, then gently dragged all five fingers over my flesh until they closed over my nipple. He pulled on the sensitive nub while his thumb found a slightly more insistent rhythm.

I couldn't do anything but watch.

"You get so turned on by me, don't you, baby?" Brandon asked in a low, husky voice.

"Mmmmm," I said, my eyes falling closed as his hand switched to play with my other breast. "I do."

"Do you want me to make you come, Skylar?" he asked.

"Yesss..." I said as I arched backward again, my hips rocking into his hand as if of their own volition.

As the pressure mounted and I started to approach my edge, he stopped, holding his fingers still within me.

"Ssss!" I hissed. "Don't stop!"

Brandon chuckled, but obediently moved his hand back to what it was doing before. Just as I was about to explode, he stopped again, much to my bitter disappointment. What kind of game was this? As he continued to tease me, pulling away just as the sensations really started to mount, he held me firmly in his grasp. I couldn't think of anything else.

"Goddamn it," I spat between gritted teeth. "Don't do that!"

"Makes you mad, doesn't it, baby? Go ahead," he taunted me, pulling his hand away yet again and sliding it back, over and over again. Then he pulled his hand out, and in a few sudden movements, lifted me up and pulled me on top of him on the bed. He started to rock his hips, creating delicious friction between us.

"Still mad?" he asked as he moved.

I rocked into him and moaned, unable to speak coherently.

Then, just like before, he stopped.

"Hey!" I cried out as my eyes flashed opened. "I said *stop* that!"

"Slap me for it. You'll feel better, and so will I."

I looked down at him, unsure. What? He wanted me to do what?

He started to move against me again from below, never entering but continuing that delicious friction. His thumb found my clit, bringing me once again to the point where I was starting to vibrate with the need to come. Then just like before, he stopped moving, and his thumb disappeared.

"Please," I gritted out, my hips jerking against him. "*Stop.*"

"No."

His movements began again, harder this time as he rocked into me, as he pinched that sensitive bundle of nerves. I started to moan, feeling my body tensing up, prepared to fall over that familiar cliff. Then his hand pulled away one last time, and hips froze.

"STOP!" I yelped, reaching a hand back and smacking him across the face before I knew what I was doing.

The sound echoed through the room. I sat there, stone still, staring at him in shock over what I had just done.

"Oh, shit, I'm sorry!" I blurted out. I reached out tentatively to touch the angry red handprint left across his cheek.

"Don't be." Brandon grinned up at me devilishly. "I wanted you to."

Both hands lifted my hips, then pulled me back down onto his erection, which, if it was any indication, showed just how *much* he wanted that slap. He slid into me easily, and my eyes closed in ecstasy as my body finally got what it wanted. *Home.* The word echoed through my brain, my heart at the feel of him. *Home.*

"Jesus God, you feel good, Skylar." Brandon's eyes closed in bliss as he rocked into me. They opened, even brighter than before. "Do it again," he ordered.

I eyed him curiously, and after a moment, I reached my hands back again and brought my palm to his cheek weakly.

"Not like that!" he barked. "Come on, Red! I thought you could give as good as you got!"

I frowned, even as he pushed his hips upward in a way that forced me to close my eyes.

"Do it," he ordered again.

His voice was steel, and once again I wanted to fight with him just as much as he wanted to fight with me. I swung my hand back again, and this time I didn't hold back as I brought it hard enough against his cheek that I left another bright red mark on his ruddy skin.

"God!" he cried, in obvious pleasure. He moaned, and slipped his hand again to my clit, where he continued the torture he had started in the beginning. Soon I was moaning right along with him, mirroring that sweet rhythm he maintained with his hips.

His fingers quickened between us, and he thrust into me hard, forcing me to feel his entire length as far as it could go. He continued to drive me higher, his other hand holding my hips tight as I started to lose my ability to focus and sit straight up. Those skillful fingers drove me up to that high all over again, but slowed once more. My head was in a tizzy of all-consuming frustration and desire. I couldn't take much more of this.

The pressure of his thumb increased and he jerked his hips to pound into me. I felt that heat inside me continue to rise until suddenly he reached up and swiftly brought his hand across my cheek, its mild sting sending me off and shattering on top of him as if I myself had split into a million pieces.

"Fuck!" he cried out his own release along with mine, grabbing my hips roughly to prevent me from collapsing and ramming even deeper into me from below. "That's right, take it, baby! God, Skylar, FUUUCK!"

He pulled me down to collapse on his chest, slick with exertion and heaving with deep breaths that matched my own. The world felt hazy and as if it were spinning around me in that way that only comes from an intense orgasm.

"Holy shit," I said through shallow breaths. "That was..."

"Yeah," he agreed, struggling to regain his own breath. He turned his head into my hair and inhaled. "Wicked good," he said as his lips drifted over my forehead, my cheeks, feathering over my lips. "Good girl."

The effect of the two words were instantaneous. My eyes popped open, and my entire body tensed.

"No," I said clearly as I pushed off him and scooted a solid two feet away from him.

He just watched me, completely dumbfounded.

"Brandon," I said, this time careful not to meet his eyes. Frantically I pulled my shirt back up, and the sheets around my lower body. "Please. If you...if you love me, you won't do this again. You won't use me like-like a Band-Aid for whatever it is you're struggling with. You won't manipulate me like that."

He froze. I exhaled, grateful that something I had said had finally broken through, even though the guilt clearly written over his handsome features hurt me too.

He sighed, long and low. "Is that what you think I was doing?"

"Isn't it?"

The seconds fell like rocks between us. But in the end, he nodded.

"Shit," he said as he covered his face with a pillow. "Shit." Then he pulled the pillow away as something occurred to him. "Is that why you're doing this conversion thing?" he asked in a low voice. "Trying to fix yourself for me?"

I waited a beat, then answered. "What else?"

"Skylar...I told you, we're past it. You don't need to change anything for me, baby. Fuck, I don't *want* you to change for me."

"It's fine," I said. "I offered to do it, didn't I? In a manner of speaking, it's one way to atone for the mistakes I've made."

Brandon snorted. "That's a very Catholic thing to say. You sure you actually need to convert?"

I rolled my eyes, even though he couldn't see me well in the dark. Brandon sighed, his breath causing the skin behind my ear to warm. I scooted back toward him, wanting to let him know that he wasn't alone. I wasn't angry. I had made my choice, as much as I didn't really like it. But I needed him to choose us too.

Brandon hugged me close.

"I love you," he murmured into my hair.

I relaxed a bit more into him, although not completely.

"Good," I whispered.

He kissed my shoulder, tightened his arms again and didn't let go.

Twenty-Three

Brandon left early the next week for meetings in Washington and LA. He was getting tired of traveling so much, but as he continued to negotiate selling his shares of Ventures, I knew it was important to him that the company remain stable rather than simply going to the highest bidders. It was a long process, and a time-consuming one.

The day before, we had gone together to a small, early morning Mass at our local parish (it felt very strange to refer to a parish as part mine). Hope had arranged for a few photographers to be present as I received the Rite of Acceptance as a catechumen, with Brandon acting as my smirking sponsor.

It was a brief ceremony, with a few clearly rote phrases welcoming me to the community spoken by Father Garrett, in which I was invited to stand in front of the parishioners and confirm my desire to join the church. That was the most mortifying part. Normally, Father Garrett told me, they would cluster the Inquirers (as we were called) into groups at certain times of the year. But we were a special case and so Brandon and I stood near the altar by ourselves, with a photographer from *The Globe* clicking away as Brandon introduced me to the parish with his trademark charm. Afterward, Father Garrett began the brief script we had gone over in his office.

"What do you ask of God's Church?" he asked.

I took the microphone from Brandon and recited the answer I had been taught: "I ask the Church for baptism and to receive the Word of God."

I was then presented with a copy of the Gospel, toward which I bowed my head. A few more pictures were taken, and after I sat through the Mass, Brandon gave a brief interview with the *Globe* reporter. Then we went home.

It hadn't taken long. Maybe fifteen minutes in all. But I walked out of the Church feeling different, and not in an entirely good way. So by Monday, I was glad to be on my own to process things for a bit.

Brandon had left me early in the golden morning light, giving me a flash of muscle while he covered me with his body, letting me know just how much he would miss me while he was gone. He had also given me another mission: call Margie and find us a new place to live. Considering all of the other things about my life that seemed out of my control, it was a task I was now willing to take on. We were both heartily sick of the cold-edged penthouse and more eager than ever to find a place that felt like us.

So, while I didn't have a lot of time to spend house hunting, I found myself spending my lunch hours paging through real estate sites, although without the slightest idea what I was looking for. Did we want a house or an apartment? In the center of the city or outside of it? Did Brandon want another massive house on the Common or in Back Bay, or would he be okay with something more modest? After a few days of looking, the process was starting to cause more stress than anything else.

"What about this one?" Jane asked through my monitor on Wednesday. She was working from home on her computer, and it was nice to see my friend's face as I scrolled through listings with her.

I clicked on the link and scowled at the modern construction out in Natick. "Ugh, no. That place looks like a refrigerator."

"Well, it's environmentally friendly. Isn't that what you wanted?"

I sighed. "Ideally, yes, but we can always make those changes after we buy. I don't want some place that looks like the inside of a laboratory. That's what we're trying to get away from."

"Well, what *do* you want?" Jane asked for the millionth time. It was a question I hadn't been able to answer very well.

I leaned my head onto my fist. "Like the Cape, I guess."

It was the only answer I could come up with. I wasn't particularly interested in interior design, having never really had a place to decorate in the first place. I had lived in exactly three places my entire adult life: my grandmother's sagging brown house in Brooklyn, the university-issued apartment I'd shared with Jane through law school, and Eric's tiny place in the North End. Only the last had required me to actually furnish it, and even that was minimal and mostly secondhand—a far sight from the essentially unlimited budget I was working with now.

I didn't count the ice palace. The penthouse felt like a hotel, a lavish pit stop, and always would.

I clicked aimlessly through other listings around the Boston area. There were so many unanswered questions that Brandon had laughed off as he left. When I'd asked about our price range, he had given me a look like I was crazy. When I'd asked about size, amenities, neighborhood, he had shrugged every time and said it was up to me. He just wanted a place where the two of us could be happy, he said. A place that felt like home.

Whatever the hell that meant.

"How about this?" Jane said.

I clicked on the link she sent me, which took me to a picture of a sprawling ranch-style home on several acres of property in Newton. I scowled.

"Ugh," I said. "Do I look like a soccer mom? That place is so cookie-cutter."

"I give up!" Jane said. "I have better things to do than get shot down for everything I send you."

"Would *you* want to live in a house like this?" I retorted.

"Of course not! But I'm not the one who's engaged to someone who basically wants to create his own version of *Leave It to Beaver*."

I snorted. "Come on. Just because he wants a family doesn't mean Brandon is a fifties' sitcom character."

"Meh. You say potato..." Jane replied.

As I passed the mouse over a new listing on the map, a thumbnail photo of a house popped up. I froze, knuckle in my mouth.

"Earth to Skylar. Did you get lockjaw? Seriously, chickie, you look like you're about to start drooling on your keyboard."

"Holy shit," I whispered as I clicked on the listing and started to page through the photos.

"Sky?" Jane asked. "Did you hear me?"

"Janey? I gotta go," I said. "I gotta call a realtor."

* * *

219

Five hours later, I was standing with Lucas in front of a gated property in Brookline. It was on the south side of the reservoir, and through the tall iron gates, I could see nothing but green grass and trees that blocked the house I knew was inside.

"Looks like a nice place," Lucas said, although he was inspecting the mostly empty street like a mugger was about to pop out of one of the nicely trimmed hedges bordering the sidewalks. "Looks safe."

I looked at him and smiled. "Yes, it does."

A silver Lexus glided around the corner and pulled into the driveway next to us. The window rolled down, and a woman in a smart red suit popped her head out.

"Are you Miss Chambers?" she asked with a curious glance at Lucas.

I nodded. I'd given my mother's maiden name, thinking it would be better to give an alias to someone I didn't really know. "I am."

She smiled, although I didn't miss the look up and down that clearly wondered about my age. Yes, I'm young. Get over it.

"I'm Shelly from Premier Properties. Well, get in, hon. I'll drive us inside."

I turned to Lucas. "You'll wait here?"

He gave a curt nod. "I'll stay in the car."

After Shelly entered the code for the gates, we drove down a short driveway sheltered in a tunnel of massive oaks. The property wasn't actually as big as it seemed from outside the gates, but it was completely surrounded by a stone wall—not something that I would have looked for otherwise, but which right now felt nicely secure.

"Your...husband didn't want to come inside too?" she asked as she drove.

"Oh no, that's just my bodyguard," I said as I took in the lawn dotted with several more trees. This place was basically a park.

Shelly gave me a look that was even more curious. She started to gesture to the property around us as she steered us down the drive. "So, the house sits on three solid acres. It includes the main house, a tennis court in the back, and a couple of outbuildings that have been converted into two-bedroom cottages.

Dad, I thought. Bubbe. Brandon would be way too excited about the tennis court.

"There a small orchard in the northeast corner with some apple and pear trees, if you like that sort of thing." She looked me up and down again, clearly guessing that I did not. "Four-car garage, and a circular driveway for any, um, social gatherings you might have here."

There was that look again, the one that was clearly doubtful about my ability to enjoy that aspect of a home like this. I rolled my eyes and ignored her. I was going to have to have Margie find me a different realtor.

Shelly parked in the driveway, and we got out to look at the house. It was a gorgeous white colonial with black trim. It had two main stories, a basement, and a white wrap-around porch.

The second she opened the front door, I knew. This wasn't just any house—this was *our* house. Shelly guided me around a downstairs that was big but not too big, covered with dark wood flooring and matching trim that lined the baseboards, windows, and ceilings. The rooms ran into each other fluidly: family room, sitting room, party-size kitchen, office. A solarium sat off the kitchen, looking out onto the aforementioned orchard, which was now heavy with late summer fruit.

We wandered through the upstairs, which had four bedrooms, including a master suite with a large walk-in closet and an en suite bathroom. The house wasn't as big as any of Brandon's properties, although it was still at least three times the size of my family's house in Brooklyn. The rooms were spacious and open, and there was plenty of space for guests or for my family to live or visit.

I lingered in the solarium after I'd gone through the rest of the house, looking out at the trees off the back patio. I could so easily imagine Brandon and me in this space, sipping on morning tea and coffee, reading the news to each other, making love in the early morning light. Where Bubbe could make her famous dinners or just put her feet up herself while Ana cooked. And maybe, I realized with a twinge, a few smaller feet might run around these floors as well one day.

I turned around to Shelly, who was examining her nails at the kitchen counter, clearly ready to go.

"It's beautiful," I said to her, and she nodded, as if it were obvious. "I think we might take it."

At that, Shelly perked up visibly. "We? You and your..."

"Fiancé," I said, surprised by how the word thrilled me just then.

221

Shelly's gaze flickered to the ring on my finger, and she straightened. "I see. And you and your fiancé...you'd be able to put down enough for the property?"

I turned back to the trees and smiled to myself. "Yes," I said. "I believe we would. Excuse me. I need to make a quick phone call before we leave."

I stepped outside on the back porch and sat down on the steps to dial Brandon's cell. It was hot in Boston for late September, enough that I had shucked my suit jacket long ago and was sitting in just my pencil skirt and silk shell. But the lush greenery of the orchard made it feel relatively cool in the shade.

"Hey, beautiful," he answered on the second ring.

I closed my eyes against a breeze and relished the feeling his deep voice sent through me. Although I had wanted a few days to myself, I was more than ready for him to come home.

"Hey," I said. "Sorry to bother you."

"Not possible, Red," Brandon said, and I smiled again. "What's up?"

"I..." I ran a finger over my knee. "I think I found our home."

I was careful about my word choice—he would know what I meant by that.

There was a pause.

"Yeah?" His voice was low, but slightly eager, like a kid who wasn't quite sure whether to believe that Santa Claus had actually shown up.

"Yeah," I said, just as quietly. I glanced around at the beautiful house and property. I wasn't quite sure it was real either. "It's a house, in Brookline. Colonial craftsman-style. Gated on three acres. Four bedrooms, plus an office for you. There are also separate guesthouses where Bubbe and Dad could live or stay. Private, a few blocks away from the reservoir. It would be a great place...a great place to raise kids..."

My voice choked up a little at the end. It was a subject we had barely discussed, although I knew eventually it was something we both wanted. It would be painful for a while yet. But sitting here, I could see that future so clearly. It seemed more immediate than I'd ever thought.

Brandon was quiet for a moment. "It sounds amazing."

"It's more than that," I said. "I don't know how to explain it, but it feels like...home, Brandon, it really does. More than any place I've ever been. More than even my family's house in Brooklyn." The house, I thought with a sinking feeling, I'd never go back to.

"Buy it."

I gawked at the trees. "What? It's not like your other places, Brandon. It's not super big or anything, and it needs some work on the inside. Don't you want to come back and see it for your—"

"Just buy it," he interrupted. "Call Margie today and have her put down an offer. She's done it for me before; she can do it again."

Was he crazy?

"Brandon," I tried again, "you haven't even seen the place. That's a major gamble to take sight unseen—"

"You love it?"

I glanced back at the house, unable to keep myself from smiling. "I do."

"Then just do it. I want to get out of that apartment as soon as possible. Besides," he paused. "I trust you, Red. *You're* home to me. If it feels right to you, I'm going to love it. I already know."

This time I couldn't stifle my grin at all. I turned my face up to the sun, letting it shine down onto me through the trees.

"Red? You there?"

In response, I giggled. For a moment, the world felt light.

"I want you to see it," I said.

Brandon just laughed in response. The feeling was infectious.

"As soon as I get back, Red," he agreed. "I can't wait to see our new   home."

Twenty-Four

The next evening at work, I was watching the clock while I worked a motion for a new case. It wasn't because I was ready to go. Actually, it was the opposite. I was engrossed in work, and time seemed to fly by. I had another "lesson" tonight with Father Garrett, which I was not looking forward to.

I hadn't expected it to happen so quickly, but work had become a place of solace. As the news coverage of me and Brandon picked up, the main entrances to the apartment building and even Kiefer Knightly were hounded by reporters, day after day. Lucas had been joined with a second security guard just to make sure I could enter the building safely, and my assistant had to vet several phone calls a day from reporters, as well as other people calling to tell me just what they thought about my life decisions. After being screamed at by a man in Bristol, Connecticut that I was a no-good whore who was going to burn in hell, I requested that Peter stop putting through calls that weren't scheduled beforehand.

In that way, I newly appreciated being surrounded by lawyers who practiced confidentiality for a living and who quickly saw me as a co-worker, not a spectacle. The stark halls of the firm became a retreat from the trappings of my real life.

A knock on my open office door pulled me out of the paperwork I was immersed in.

"Mail's in."

I looked up and saw Kieran holding an envelope. She sat in one of the chairs facing my desk and handed it to me with a knowing look.

"What happened to Manny? Isn't this a bit of a demotion for you?" I joked as I took the letter, but all humor died as I saw the return address: Board of Bar Examiners, Boston, MA.

My heart gave a giant thump.

"Well, go on. Open it, and then I can congratulate you properly for dealing with all the shit you've been through recently and still managing to pass one of the hardest bar exams in the country."

I reached eagerly for the letter opener on the desk. "But no pressure, right?" I took a deep breath. "Well, let's see if I still have a job tomorrow."

I ripped open the envelope and pulled out the seemingly benign slip of paper.

"Well?" Kieran said. "Do I have to fire you?"

I scanned the paper, then looked up with a cheek-splitting grin. "No. I passed."

"Good. I knew you would."

I set the paper down and folded my hands over my mouth to hide the smile I couldn't quite stifle. This felt good. It felt damn good. It was the cherry on top of the Brookline-house-shaped sundae that was this week. I didn't even care that I still had two hours with Father Garrett ahead of me. Nothing could take away this feeling.

"How are things at home?" Kieran asked frankly. "How's Brandon doing?"

Except that. And just like that, the good feeling melted away, and the room turned a few shades darker.

I sighed. "They're...yeah."

"You look tired," Kieran said bluntly. "The nightmares are still happening, aren't they?"

I leaned back in my chair and folded my hands over my chest. "I—we talked about it. But..."

"But what?"

I tilted my head. "You know Brandon. He's insanely busy, and thinks therapists just make everything worse." I pursed my lips and sighed. "I don't know what to do. He acts like it's no big deal, but it is. Kieran, I don't think he's gotten a decent night of sleep in almost two months. Not since—not since the kidnapping."

Kieran worried her red lip between her teeth a moment, and her otherwise perfectly smooth brow wrinkled slightly.

I sighed. "Okay, it's not just that. He's...it's hard to explain. Rougher somehow."

"Rougher?" Kieran's alarm—and surprise—was clear.

"No, no, no," I said. "Not like that. With me, he's great. We might be better in some ways than we ever were." I crinkled the empty envelope between my hands as I considered how to explain the slight changes I had noticed. "So, last month, you know he got into a few bar fights, and Cory threatened to quit. There's been

225

nothing since, but he's losing weight. He goes on these ten-mile runs in the mornings instead of just five. And yesterday in a sparring session, he gave Harvey a black eye."

I didn't mention the particularly physical sex from last weekend. I shook my head. They were all small changes, relatively speaking. But everything in my gut told me something inside Brandon was getting worse, not better. And I had no idea how to fix it.

"He used to get the nightmares when he was a kid," Kieran said once she had digested my words.

I nodded. "Yeah, Susan and Ray told me something like that."

Kieran nodded. "A social worker diagnosed him with an anxiety disorder, and several of the homes he stayed in drugged him pretty intensely at night to force him to sleep. That allowed some of the kids to torment him there, too. One kid even tried to suffocate him. Did you know that?"

My mouth fell open. "No...I had no idea."

Kieran pressed her lips together. "It's why he's so against any kind of medication or therapy. And if you tell him I told you that, I'll demote you to the mail room."

I held up my hands in mock-surrender, although the news reeled through my head. Brandon's adamancy against "being fixed" now took on new meaning. "My lips are sealed. How did you know?"

She gave me a look, like I should have figured it out. "Whose house do you think he was at when his mom was out on the streets looking for her next fix? I lived right across the hall. Sometimes we could hear him dreaming through the hallway, and we could *definitely* hear it when his dad was home. That fucker..." Kieran trailed off, shaking her head, visibly angry. "Well, anyway. No use thinking about that guy anymore."

I gulped. "Was it...what causes them, do you know? Is it PTSD?" It was the only thing I could think of that matched his symptoms, which I had Googled extensively.

Kieran twisted her mouth, like she knew she wasn't supposed to be telling me any of this, but also knew she had to.

"Look, I'm no psychologist. I think PTSD is probably the closest thing to it, combined with the anxiety disorder. The fact that the nightmares started during the years of trauma probably complicates things a bit, but who knows?" She paused, tapping a finger over the red slash of her mouth. "I know his social worker told my mother it

226

was likely triggered by neglect, which was, of course, the catalyst for all the shit he went through, plus a healthy dollop of survivor's guilt."

"Survivor's guilt?" I asked. "For what?"

"For his mom," Kieran said, as if I should have already pieced that together myself. "After she died. Maybe even before. He found her smashed out of her mind more than once. Probably thought she was dead when she wasn't."

I shook my head, considering. He didn't speak a lot about his birth parents. He'd really only mentioned his mother a few times, episodes of his past he carried with him everywhere. After taking me to meet Ray, he had shared the conditions of his permanent housing with the Petersens when, at age fifteen, the courts had given him the choice between them and his mother, who had tried to regain custody. He had chosen the Petersens, and his mother had died the following week of a drug overdose.

"I killed my mother," he had told me, and my heart broke for him even as I said over and over again that it wasn't true.

I knew that Brandon had gone through extensive counseling after that. It was a condition of being allowed to stay with the Petersens and attend MIT as a sixteen-year-old math whiz. Those years had been difficult, and eventually led to his unhappy marriage, but he'd also been able to reinvent himself as one of Boston's greatest success stories. He didn't need to be fixed, as he told me—he'd already fixed himself.

Except that clearly, he hadn't. Some things had resurfaced, and I wasn't entirely sure why.

"I have a theory," Kieran said casually as she stood up. "I think it's the hospitals that started it again."

I looked up, torn out of my thoughts. "Hospitals?"

Kieran twisted her lips, as if she was meditating on the idea for a moment.

"I think about the worst things that have happened to Brandon," she says. "And he always ended up in a hospital. Riding with his mom in an ambulance one too many times. A social worker finding him after his dad broke his leg."

I cringed. I hadn't known about that either.

"His mother dying there," Kieran continued. She looked pointedly at me. "Your dad. Yeah, he told me about that. And then you, of course."

I stared at her with my mouth open as I followed her epiphany.

"Those days you were out in the hospital, he was...not good," Kieran said. Then she shrugged. "It's just a theory. But one thing's for sure, The nightmares didn't stop until he was out of a stressful environment and seeing a good therapist. Once he was around people he knew weren't going anywhere anytime soon." She looked straight at me, her dark, prickly gaze piercing through me the way only Kieran's could. "Do you remember what I said about him all those months ago?"

I nodded. Kieran had been one of the first people to support me and Brandon, but she was also the first to warn me, too. He's complicated,she'd said, back when we'd first gotten involved. He doesn't need more of that in his life.

Except I'd brought plenty more of that. Between my father's criminal problems, and the fact that up until just recently, I'd technically been an extramarital affair, I had been nothing but one big complication for Brandon. The thought made me wilt.

"Skylar." Kieran's voice was sharp.

I looked up.

"I can see you wallowing," she said. "But what's going on with Brandon right now? Not your fault."

"But—"

"Everyone has complicated lives," she said as she crossed her arms. "I wasn't trying to imply that yours were inordinately bad. The reality is, Brandon has a tendency to make things even *more* complicated than they have to be. No one forced him to run for *mayor*, for Christ's sake, just like no one forced him to own two companies instead of one, stay married to Miranda for fifteen years, or make payments to a weird gangster. He does this to himself. You don't have to blame yourself."

I tapped my pencil on the desktop, but didn't answer. She had a point, although I still thought it was a bit unfair to Brandon.

"Okay," I said, wondering what I was supposed to do with this information. "Sure. I guess so."

"Good," Kieran said. "Maybe the best thing for you two to be thinking about is how to simplify. How to put down roots a bit

228

more." And with that, Kieran clapped her hands on the arms of the chair and stood up. "Get out of here early, will you? Go home and celebrate, but don't get too drunk. Starting tomorrow, you're a real lawyer."

I was left there, still grinning and holding the paper in my hand. I had passed. I knew I would, but I was surprised by just how good the knowledge felt. My life had somehow become a stranger to me in the last several months, full of so many changes, good and bad. This was a reminder of what had been important to me before Brandon, before my life had gotten so swept up in his.

The paper rustled under my fingers, material and real. I smirked. Kieran had said to celebrate, and that was exactly what I was going to do.

* * *

After spending two hours with Father Garrett talking about the concept of absolution, I had desperately needed a drink, and was thrilled to find that Eric, Cherie, and Steve wanted to celebrate their own exam results. It had been way too long since I'd taken a moment to enjoy the fact that I was still only twenty-six—almost twenty-seven. That my life, despite all the recent pressures, was still relatively wide open.

Twenty minutes later, I was sipping on a whiskey soda, flipping through a deposition while I waited for my friends.

"Hey, Cros," Eric said, interrupting my train of thought as he dumped his briefcase into the booth and hung his suit jacket on the hooks mounted next to us.

I watched behind him as Steve and Cherie jostled into the pub, clearly bickering about something while Steve kept reaching behind Cherie to tap her shoulder. Eric followed my gaze.

"Oh, *those* two," he said with a disdainful roll of his eye. "Don't even get me started. They just reported their relationship to HR last week, and it's fucking nauseating."

"Really," I said with interest as they approached. A year ago, Steve had been trying his damnedest to get me on a date with him. I was frankly surprised he could keep something going for more than a few weeks.

"Hey, Crosby," Steve said as he threw a thin arm around Cherie. "How'ya been? You're looking good these days. Even better than when we worked together."

I didn't answer, since Cherie quickly threw an elbow into Steve's gut.

"Drinks," she said shortly as he stood back up, fixing his horn-rimmed glasses. "Now."

"My lady," Steve said, mimicking a bow before he grabbed her around the waist for a sloppy kiss. Then they both hoofed it to the bar.

"See what I mean?" Eric said. "Nauseating."

I chuckled. "Well, not everyone has what you and Jane have," I joked, then cringed at my misspeak. Yeah, I probably shouldn't have brought that up.

"Jane," Eric repeated glumly.

I rubbed his shoulder sympathetically. "Sorry. I shouldn't have said anything."

He shrugged and folded his hands over the table. "I'm guessing she probably told you about the lingerie she found in my room."

"In your bed, I think it was," I corrected him, earning a slightly dirty look.

"Fine," Eric bit out. "It looked bad, I'll admit that. Okay, it *was* bad. But in my defense, we werebroken up until about fifteen minutes after she showed up. And we never said we were going to be exclusive to begin with. I tried to do that, and she dumped me."

"You couldn't have at least changed the sheets before she got in them?"

"I had to work late the night before, and I forgot, all right?" Eric looked up at the ceiling and sighed. "You know what our hours are like, Cros, and so does Jane. It was an honest mistake. Plus, you know Jane. She can be really...insistent."

I blanched, and Eric had the decency to blush.

"You never brought girls back to the apartment before Jane," I pointed out. "What gives there?"

Eric just took a long swig of his beer. "Imiphesser," he mumbled over the rim.

"What?"

He sighed and set the bottle back on the table. "I *miss* her, okay? I was lonely that night, and I miss...Jesus, I can't believe I'm talking about this to you. I miss *holding* someone when I go to sleep. Jane. I miss falling asleep with Jane. So I invited a girl back so I wouldn't be alone. Except she left a pair of microscopic underpants in my sheets, and in my stupidity, I forgot they were there at all, and now I've fucked up the best thing that's ever happened to me. Fuck!"

He fell forward, clasped his head in his hands, and groaned. I reached out and patted him on the back.

"Hey," I said. "It was a dumb mistake, but I bet she'll forgive you. If it's any consolation, I'm pretty sure she misses you too."

Eric peered at me between his fingers. "You think so?"

I shrugged. "I *am* her best friend. I have a pretty good hunch about these things."

He screwed his face up into a knot. "She just makes me *so* fucking crazy, you know that? When she's here, things are great. They're more than great...they're..."

"Perfect?" I suggested.

He nodded hopelessly. "But when she's gone, it's like I don't exist. This was the first time I ever saw that she actually cared about whatever it is we're doing. And now...she won't take my calls, nothing. It's like I don't exist. She's totally ghosting me."

I frowned and took a sip of my drink. "Well, I know for a fact she cares. She wouldn't have been so pissed if she didn't." I perked up. "Hey—she'll be at the engagement party. You can talk to her then."

Eric raised a skeptical brow. "Really? You think that's the best idea? I know we're friends and all, but Jane's your maid of honor. I won't be offended if I'm not invited."

I frowned. "Stop it. Of course you're coming. Plus, the wedding planner rented out a private room at the Martin. Networking central, my friend. Plus, Jane'll have nowhere to run."

"Hmmm," Eric said. "We'll see." Then he changed the subject. "So, things between you and Sterling...they're good now?"

I rolled my eyes at him. "You've seen the guy half-naked, Eric. You can call him Brandon."

"Ah, *no*. He's my boss. He's not Brandon until I make full partner or he's done with the firm."

"Well, we're good," I said. "Considering."

231

Eric grimaced. "Yeah. You guys have had a time. But he's okay with...you know?"

He didn't want to say it, but I knew what he meant. Eric had been present when Brandon had learned about the abortion, and had also watched when he'd pushed me away.

"Yeah," I said. "Mostly. It'll just take time. Luckily, he's got the campaign and divestitures to keep him plenty occupied."

"It's funny," Eric said. "I heard about all that, so I was surprised that he's not selling his shares at Sterling Grove yet."

I frowned. This was news to me. As far as I knew, Brandon had been very busy negotiating his exits from both of his companies so that he could run for office free of any ethical problems.

"Wait, what? Do you think he's having a hard time finding buyers for his stake?"

Eric shook his head adamantly. "It's not that. The senior partners were all pissed about it at the staff meeting. I guess a few of them had their eyes on his stake."

"Huh." It wasn't the first sign I'd seen that Brandon was becoming less and less passionate about his campaign. A part of me was starting to wonder if the stresses associated with public life were getting to him as much as everything else.

"I'm going to tell her again I love her, and that's it," Eric said, pulling me out of my thoughts as he slammed his empty pint glass on the table. "Stubborn woman's got to listen at some point. We're in love. She loves me—I know she does. There's got to be a way to figure this shit out."

I gave him a wry smile. Eric in love was sort of adorable—half-confused, half-determined. It was a far cry from his usually stoic persona.

"*Mazel tov*, friend," I said, and he gave me a weird look.

"Jesus Christ, Cros," he said with an amused shake of the head. "You're going to make the worst damn Catholic."

Filled as I was with two whiskey sodas and no longer thinking about the massive catechism book tucked away in my bag, I just raised my glass and shrugged.

"Hey, we're New Yorkers," I said. "If there's anyone who can make Jewish Catholic work, it's us."

Twenty-Five

I arrived back at the apartment to the sound of the Red Sox game on the flat-screen. Brandon's luggage was still sitting in the foyer, and the remains of a burger and fries were on the table. I grinned. Brandon was home early.

The man himself strode out of the bedrooms, shoes off, tie undone, and his light blue dress shirt untucked and unbuttoned to reveal the stepladder of muscle he and his trainer maintained so exquisitely. He was clearly coming in to check on the score, but the game basically disappeared when he caught sight of me.

"Hey!"

Brandon veered around the couch and made a beeline for me. His immediate grin was contagious, as was his laugh as he hoisted me up in a full-bodied kiss, dangling my feet off the ground.

"You're home early," I mumbled into his lips as he finally stopped for breath.

"I had the plane on standby."

He continued to pepper kisses all over my face. I laughed, and finally, he set me down.

"We finished early," he said, watching curiously as I played with the ends of his tie. One blond brow quirked at the movement. "It's done."

"What's done?" I murmured, transfixed by the play of his tie and the way his stomach muscles tensed at the movement. It had been five days since I'd seen him. It felt more like five months.

"Ventures. I'm out."

I let the silk drop against his torso and looked up. "You mean the Jackson Anderson deal...?"

Brandon sighed and nodded. "Yep. Anderson finally signed the papers. There's going to be a transitional period. The guy micromanages like you wouldn't believe. Seriously, what a control freak. Do you have any idea how annoying it is to be talked to like an idiot by someone ten years younger than me?"

I smirked. "Must have been like looking in the mirror. I've seen photos. You guys could be brothers."

In return, I just got a withering look. I chuckled.

"Anyway," Brandon continued, "he's a decent guy underneath it all. You can tell by the way he looks at his fiancée. Sheesh, babe, you think I'm bad? Lexi has that guy totally whipped." He grinned. "You'd probably like her, come to think of it." Then he sighed again. "Anyway, he won't tear the company up, so there won't be a slaughter when Ventures is absorbed. People will still keep their jobs." He wrapped both of his hands around his neck, looking over my shoulder at the view of the city below us. "It's the end."

There was something in his voice I couldn't quite place. A nostalgia, maybe, but also a relief. Ventures had been Brandon's baby, but in a way, I knew he wasn't as attached to it as Sterling Grove. The investment group had been born out of the firm he'd inherited from his deceased father-in-law, Stan Keith. He'd come to it by way of his marriage to Miranda. He'd dissolved the hedge fund after Stan had passed and willed him the shares, and then used the capital to start his own investment firm, which had become one of the most successful in the Northeast—no small feat when he wasn't in New York.

His accomplishments with Ventures had been consuming and worth his pride. But it was the last connection he had to Miranda and her family, even if only from that history.

"Are you okay?" I asked as I reached up to turn his face back to mine.

The melancholy look transformed again to something sweeter; his blue eyes shined with love, and my insides warmed.

"Yeah," he said as he kissed me again. "I'm good. Now I guess I have no excuses but to give everything I have to the campaign. Cory's going to be thrilled."

At the mention of Cory, the warmth in my chest faded, and I turned back to the kitchen to get some water. But apparently, I didn't turn away fast enough.

"What's that look for?"

I turned around from the other side of the counter, plastering what I hoped to be a pleasant smile on my face. "What look?"

Brandon feigned terror. "Red, you look like a serial killer with that smile. Seriously, baby, why do you even try to fake it with me?"

Immediately, the smile turned genuine, and I followed Brandon to the couch. He flipped off the volume of the Sox game and faced me, taking my hand in his.

"What's going on?" he asked. "Just tell me."

I took a deep breath as I thought over the conversation I'd had with Kieran, and then with Eric.

"Be honest," Eric had said. And he and Jane were both right. Brandon's and my problems really came from not being totally honest with each other.

"Sometimes," I said stiltedly, "sometimes I miss just being me. Just being Skylar. Who studies. Who works. Who goes to the bar with my friends. Who doesn't have to have security or press following her around."

Brandon opened his mouth, but I rushed in, eager to dispel the sudden doubt written so clearly across his face.

"Don't think I want out of this, okay?" I said. "I *don't*. I might miss parts of my old life, Brandon, but I can't *live* without you. And I don't want to stop you from following your dreams. I just..." I stopped, trying to find the best possible way to state what I was thinking. "I need a better balance. I need to find a way to live this life that makes it still mine. Do you...do you understand that?"

He stared at me for a minute and ran a hand back through his hair as he processed my words. But then, to my surprise, he smiled, a slow, sweet smile that told me the one thing my heart was yearning to hear: he understood.

"I get it," he said softly. "Better than you know. Shit, I..." There went that hand again, further rumpling his curls. "I remember what it was like, being swept up into this world. It's just been so long that I had forgotten. I'm sorry for that, Red, I should have known better."

I shrugged, toying with the calloused pads of his fingertips. "It's not your fault. I need to speak up better. Maybe in a way that's not yelling at you in the middle of the night."

"Or threatening to sleep in separate rooms?" Brandon clutched my fingers, and I winced at the memory. "Don't run away. Just tell me. I want you to be happy too, Red."

My heart sang with the simple statement. It was in these moments, not the big gestures, that I felt truly loved, when I was truly happy.

"I want to slow down a little," I said. "I feel like we're hurtling through everything, on a timeline because of the trial, the press, the campaign, even us. I miss those days when we just enjoyed an afternoon together working on the couch or messing around

235

Cambridge. And the idea of being a first lady..." I made a face. The phrase sounded so ridiculous. "I'm not going to lie. It scares me. Brandon, I know you say I won't have to give up anything for it, but babe, I already do. Lucas follows me around everywhere. People take pictures of me in the street."

He didn't say anything for a moment. He knew, I thought, that there wasn't much he could do to make that better. Even after the trial, after there were no more threats coming out of New York, there would still be no more bouncing around neighborhoods or taking weekend drives on a whim—not as long as Brandon was in politics. The craze in Woodstock had shown us both that.

Brandon sighed.

"I'll make it better," he said, but his eyes were sad. "I don't know how, but I'll make it better."

The sadness in his voice immediately had me scooting across the couch and into his arms. I buried my face against his chest, luxuriating in the feel of skin to skin.

Brandon said nothing as he continued to stroke my hair. We stayed like that for several more minutes until eventually, I reached over and turned the volume of the TV back on. The truth was out there, and there was no easy fix to the problem. But in the end, we'd find a solution. I had faith, or so I kept telling myself.

* * *

Much later, closer to morning than night, I woke up in the dark of the room where Brandon was still sleeping beside me. It was the first time in weeks that I had woken on my own, the fury of my thoughts jerking me out of sleep instead of Brandon's thrashing body. The curtains were still open, and the full moon outside was a spotlight on my face.

After several minutes of tossing and turning, I decided to get up, leaving Brandon's sleeping form.

I shut the thick doors of the bedrooms and the hallway entrance, and then wandered over to the baby grand piano that sat in front of the window, the moon shining down over it like a spotlight. I had played it several times in the last month, usually on Brandon's request. It had become one of our favorite pastimes in the evenings when we came home—he would grab a beer and look over campaign materials while I practiced.

I took a seat on the black lacquered seat and pulled up the fallboard, drifting my fingers lazily over the keys. My body was still half asleep, and my hands felt slow. But soon the notes came fluidly.

Chopin had always been one of my favorite composers. He tended to prefer minor keys, and the trills that required a feather-light touch on the keys reminded me of waterfalls, dipping in and out of crescendos and decrescendos. I moved through a few preludes, then a nocturne or two, but there was a piece I was dancing around, a favorite I knew I'd get to eventually.

Brandon asked me once to play a song that reminded me of us. I'd chosen the Waltz in C Minor, a famous piece that moved in between fast and slow cadences, between furious arpeggios and lilting walks. At the time, it reminded me of the way Brandon and I always seemed to stop and start, the way we fought and made up, the way our relationship either seemed to sprint or trip over itself.

And despite the fact that he didn't have any musical training whatsoever, he's understood what I meant. That had been the night he'd first told me he loved me, had asked me to move in with him. The last night before everything in our lives went to hell.

I was halfway through the piece before I knew I'd even started playing it. My hands flew up and down the keys, finding a moment—finally—to let out the angst, the pain, the hurt, the love that I kept so cooped up most of the time. I played as the music spoke for all of those unnamable emotions I'd kept locked inside.

But soon my breathing turned hoarse as the angst of the music filled me. Soon I had to stop as I collapsed over the top of the keys to catch my breath against the lacquered wood. The long, painful breaths shook the cracked rib that still wasn't healed entirely, but I let them come, hoping that afterward, I'd feel just a little bit lighter.

"Why'd you stop?"

The deep voice shook me out of my reverie, and I sat up with a start and another deep, concerted breath.

"Wha-what?" I asked.

Brandon stood a few feet from the piano, clearly having shuffled in after tossing in bed like he normally did. He was in nothing but his black boxer briefs, the moonlight casting shadows over his lean, muscled form. His hair was standing up on one side, but I didn't even notice it. All I saw was the sharp worry in his eyes, even in the dark.

He came to sit next to me on the piano bench and slid his fingers over the keys without making a sound.

"That song," he said. "I remember that song."

I sucked in another breath. "You-you do?"

He looked at me sadly and rubbed his hand over his cheek. "Of course I do, Skylar. You played that song for us. That's *our* song, baby."

His memory made me cry. The stress that continued to build, the worry I always felt, came in a flood, and I broke down against his shoulder.

"Sssshhhh," Brandon's voice crooned as he wrapped an arm around me.

I hadn't realized just how intensely frustrated I was until I'd started to play, allowing the emotion in the music to fill the void I'd created in order to manage the chaos of my life.

"I didn't—I don't—I don't know how—"

I couldn't get a full sentence out as sob after sob wracked through my chest.

Before I could try again, Brandon slipped one arm under my knees and another behind my back, lifting me easily off the piano bench and carrying me over to the couch. He sat down with me cradled on his lap, pressing me close enough so he could bury his face in my neck while his hand threaded into my hair.

"Hush," he said through a cracked voice. "I got you, baby."

The sound of the familiar nickname only made me cry harder, enough that it took me a few moments to realize that Brandon's shoulders were shaking. He was crying too.

"What if—" I hiccupped over my words— "what if we don't—don't know—how to do anything but hurt each other? Hurt ourselves?"

There it was: my greatest fear, spoken aloud. I didn't want to believe it, but as complications continued to mount, a part of me wondered if we'd ever be able to get back to the simplicity that marked our best times together. We both came from dysfunctional families, both children of addicts, of people who didn't know how to love properly. It was like Kieran said: we did this to ourselves. What if we couldn't break that cycle?

Brandon kept stroking my back, refusing to let me move while he kept his face buried in my neck. He was starting to shake slightly in my arms—clearly my fears were not unfounded. As if of their own accord, my hands wove themselves into his hair and started to stroke him back, hoping to calm him.

"That's not us," he murmured finally into my hair.

He hugged me even closer, refusing to let me go. The movement made my sore ribs hurt, but I didn't care. Nothing had ever felt as good as this—having him close again—and I clutched him just as tightly. We were buoys to each other in a storm of our own making.

"I had a dream," he whispered in my hair. "Another nightmare. But I heard the music and it calmed me down."

Slowly, we rocked each other through the darkness that threatened to consume us.

"That's not us," Brandon said again. "That's not us."

Eventually, we fell asleep again, entangled like that on the couch, and didn't wake up until the morning rays of sun blasted through the wide picture windows. I regained some faith that everything would work itself out if we just tried hard enough. But it wasn't until the next day, when I was back in my office, at my *own* job, that I realized I'd forgotten to tell him that I'd passed the bar exam. Not for the first time, another part of my life was being eclipsed by his.

Twenty-Six

Two weeks later, David was driving us to The Martin, one of the fanciest restaurants in Boston. I'd been there once before with Brandon. For years, it had been his restaurant of choice to wine and dine clients, and he'd cultivated loyalty from its staff that all but ensured discretion.

We were there to celebrate our engagement, which had just been announced to the press a few days before. Although I'd just wanted a small family party—if anything at all—Cory and Hope had both insisted it would be the perfect way to continue rolling out my rebranded personality to the public. So, a big fancy affair it was, complete with a hundred of Brandon's closest friends who also happened to be campaign donors.

I wiped my hands, which were damp and clammy, with a handkerchief and used it to blot my carefully made up face.

"How do I look?" I asked for what must have been the tenth time.

Brandon, who was looking indecently good in a black suit and robin's-egg-blue shirt that matched his eyes, looked over the sleek black cocktail dress that fit me like a glove. He growled like a cat, making me giggle.

"Good enough that I should probably avoid looking directly at you when we're talking to donors," he said with a cocky half-smile. "You don't need to be nervous, Red. It's a party for *us*. And I'm the one asking for their money anyway, not you."

I reached back to touch the simple ponytail that Mary, the stylist who had done me up for Brandon's announcement speech and who had since become a standard part of his entourage, had put together. My look was understated, but it was the first time I'd been styled for an event like this and felt like myself.

From where he'd sat in the living room with the rest of Brandon's core team, Cory had taken one look at me when I'd come out of the bedroom and balked.

"She can't wear *black*," he'd protested. "It's too boudoir! Mary, we're tryin' to get *away* from the dirty mistress thing, not shove it in their faces!"

"Cory!" Brandon had shouted from the bedroom, where he was still getting dressed.

Jane, who had flown in for the party and was enjoying an early glass of wine with Hope and Omar, had shaken her head with disgust and muttered something to herself about "this guy." Mary, who had come out to retrieve a few more things to tend to Brandon, had just stared Cory down until he looked away, although his pinched expression remained.

"Get over it," she'd said. "She's Carolyn Bessette, not Jackie Onassis."

"Exactly!" crowed Jane from her spot at the bar. Brandon had surprised me by flying her in for the weekend, sensing I might need some moral support at this thing.

"Ohhhh," Hope had said approvingly from her spot next to Jane. "Yeah, I *definitely* see that. Good eye, Mary. "

Cory had opened and shut his mouth in a firm line, but followed directions. Strangely enough, Mary seemed to be the only person in Brandon's entourage he didn't argue with. As much, anyway.

As the Mercedes was stopped in traffic a few blocks away from the restaurant, I was shocked when I looked over and saw Brandon pulling a pack of cigarettes out of his jacket pocket. He had rolled down his window a bit and was in the process of bringing the lighter to the end of the cigarette when I finally found my voice.

"What the hell are those?"

He pulled the lighter away, looking at the cigarette and the lighter as if they had appeared in his hands by mistake. "What? You don't ever like a cigarette when you're nervous?"

I frowned. "No. And you don't either."

Brandon just quirked a brow. "Maybe I do, and you just don't know it, Red. I have to keep some mystery in our relationship."

I scowled, then glanced up as he was starting to light it again.

"Hey!" I said, once again interrupting his progress. "You're still going to smoke it?"

Brandon turned in surprise, the unlit cigarette still hanging from his lips. I had to admit, it did make him look sexy, in a cartoonish sort of way.

"Don't," I tried. "Please. Look, I'm not judging if you need something to cope with all the stress you're under...but don't do that. Don't shove carcinogenic shit into your body. And besides...well..."

Brandon quirked an eyebrow with a bit of amusement. "Besides what?"

I blushed. "I like kissing you. Like, a lot, as you know. But I won't anymore if you start tasting like an ashtray."

All traces of amusement were immediately wiped from Brandon's face. He looked down at the pack and lighter in his hands, then back at me. "Seriously?"

I nodded. "Seriously. I've been with smokers. My dad's a smoker. It's gross."

Brandon blinked for a second. Then, like lightning, he threw the cigarettes and lighter out the window.

"Done," he said before taking my hand to tug me closer. "Now you better kiss me. I gotta have *some* way to relieve all this stress, Red."

Ten minutes and a lot of "stress relief" later, I followed Brandon out of the car and into a barrage of flash bulbs. Hope had actually called the press to the event, and we'd been carefully prepped for the thirty-second walk between the curb and the restaurant entrance.

"Breathe," Brandon whispered as he took my hand.

I was grateful for the anchor. With all the flashes in my eyes, I couldn't see a thing. I followed him down the red carpet the restaurant kept rolled out to the curb. It was that kind of place.

"Mr. Sterling!" called the reporters. "Miss Crosby! Can you answer some questions for us?"

"I could do a few," Brandon agreed amiably as he steered us over to a cluster of reporters. He couldn't let go of my hand if he'd wanted to. I had it in a death grip.

"You don't have to say anything," Hope had told me as Mary had put on the last touches of my makeup.

"That's right, sweetheart. Just smile and look pretty," Cory had added in his characteristically acerbic way.

I'd frowned at the time, resentful of the idea of being nothing more than a prop, but right now, I was happy to stay silent. I was also happy that Mary had been hired to help me for the duration of the campaign. It was strange, but the mask of make-up and finery *did* help me feel more equipped to take on the press.

"Andrew Davis, *People Magazine*. Congratulations on the announcement, Mr. Sterling. How'd you pop the question?"

Brandon glanced down at me, and I shrugged. We'd talked about it before, and everyone had agreed that the actual story was too much—the song, the fact that I'd made a speech and asked him first. Cory had argued that it made me look desperate. Brandon had looked like he wanted to punch his manager in the face, but in the end, we agreed on a few facts from the night we could share.

"It happened at my birthday party last month," he said with that cool politician's smile I was starting to see more and more. "Spur of the moment. What can I say? When you know, you know."

There was a chorus of hushed awwws.

"Gemma Drake, *Boston Globe*. Will Ms. Crosby be a regular fixture in the campaign now? Can we expect her to have some speaking engagements as well?"

I glanced at Brandon again, but this time he didn't look down to check with me before speaking.

"Probably not too much. Skylar's a first-year associate, and we all know how hard they get worked. I barely see her as it is, so I don't want to share her too much with you guys."

The reporters laughed along with him, and I marveled, not for the first time, at just how good Brandon was with the press after being coached extensively by Hope. Since the mishap in Woodstock, his photo-op schedule had picked up considerably, and he was now a serious media darling. Even stranger was the way that I had become central to that dialogue. More than anything, they seemed to be obsessed with the way he loved *me*.

I had also noticed, however, that the bruising on his knuckles continued as his workouts each morning grew more and more intense. I also knew that Mary was complaining about having to take in his pants because he had lost more weight.

"How are you liking catechism classes, Skylar?" shouted another reporter.

I looked into the flashes and did my best to smile, although I couldn't tell who had actually asked the question. Beside me, Brandon tensed.

"Um, they're progressing well," I answered, saying no more. That was about all I could say without either lying or offending someone.

Hope, it appeared, was a Machiavellian genius. She'd sent out a brief press release last week announcing the engagement and my conversion to Catholicism, and although the abortion had resurfaced somewhat, all of it had been reframed just as she'd said: I was now a sinner atoning for her mistakes, and people were eating it up. Too bad every time I went to another meeting with Father Garrett, I ended up feeling like I should go to confession just for the big lie I was undertaking. Did everyone who converted for love feel this way?

"Last question, guys," Brandon said as he squeezed an arm around my shoulder. He bantered with the press for a few more minutes before guiding me inside the restaurant to where Hope, Cory, and Mary were both waiting for us in the lobby.

"That went *great*," Hope said emphatically as Mary reached around Brandon with a lint roller. "They absolutely ate it up. Don't you think, Cory?"

Mary moved to me with a smile, rearranging my hair slightly and helping me reapply my lipstick and powder my face. The only press inside the party was a photographer and a reporter from *Vanity Fair*, who were running a feature on Brandon's campaign. They had been following him around all week, and tonight our relationship was the focus. I needed to be camera-ready at all times.

"Yeah, yeah, it was fine," Cory said. "Try not to talk about her job so much. You make it sound like she's the one earning all the money. You basically cut off your own balls that way."

I frowned, and Brandon rolled his eyes. Cory had mostly dropped the annoying nicknames after I'd officially become Brandon's fiancée, but he still had a problem referring to me by my name.

"Also, we need to work on this one's smile, Hope," he continued. "She looks like she getting a root canal every time she looks into the camera."

My scowl deepened. "It's really hard to see."

Cory didn't even look at me, busy as he was checking the photos that were already being uploaded to local gossip sites.

"Overall, it's looking good," he said. "They're fuckin' eating it up."

"I'll say. Mary's a genius," Hope said as she looked over his shoulder. "Check that out—'Camelot Returns!'" She slapped her hands together and did a little victory dance. When everyone stared at her like she was crazy, she stopped. "No one else gets that? You

244

two were just compared to the Kennedys. Did I call it, or did I call it? In Massachusetts, you can't do better than that!"

Brandon grinned at the news, and I tried to return his smile. It wasn't too hard—his joy, no matter what, was always contagious. But still, it wasn't something I would normally be that excited about. After all, the Kennedys ended in tragedy, didn't they?

"Well, let's get in there," Cory said. "You've got donors to woo, buddy, and everyone's going to get nice and drunk to help you celebrate the love of the century."

His voice sounded about as sarcastic as it could, but Brandon just took my hand and pressed his lips to my knuckles.

"Come on," he said with a look that finally made me smile for real. "Let's go celebrate."

* * *

Two hours and two glasses of champagne later (Cory was holding us to a strict one-drink-per-hour limit), my cheeks hurt. Brandon and I had completely circled the room and done our best to charm as many of the moneyed residents of New England as possible. It wasn't difficult, for Brandon anyway, since he had already been a part of these circles for a long time. But if I had to hear one more time how "charming" it was that my father was a garbage collector, I was going to scream.

I was able to get a moment alone with the people I actually knew. Bubbe, Dad, Ray and Susan, all entertained by Jane for the first part of the evening, had stayed long enough to give Brandon and me their kisses and congratulations. But once the photographer had started snapping pictures, they made their excuses to get out of dodge—Bubbe, only once I'd promised to let her make dinner for all of us sometime soon.

"We should come together as a family," she said with a kiss to my cheek. "Have a real celebration."

I couldn't agree more.

Now I stood in a room full of strangers, most of whom had finally had enough to drink to stop staring at me like I was a circus animal.

"How're you doing, Cros? You look like you're about to make a break for it."

I turned to find Eric standing next to me with two drinks in his hand. He held out one of the glasses to me.

"Thought you could use this. Looks like they have you on a pretty tight leash."

"Oh, you saint, you," I said as I accepted a whiskey soda and took a hefty drink as I scanned the crowd for Cory. "All I've been allowed are two glasses of champagne. Hope doesn't want my face to turn red from the alcohol."

Eric chuckled and took a sip of his own drink. "You renegade, you. So, I hear conversion classes seem to be going well. It's all over the papers. Your profile in *People* looked particularly angelic."

I gave him a dirty look, and Eric laughed again.

"How's Jane?" I asked sweetly.

Eric's smirk morphed into a frown of his own as we both found my friend across the room, flirting obviously with one of the wait staff. "Really? You had to go there?"

I shrugged. "Eye for an eye, my friend." I nudged him in the shoulder. "Does it matter? I saw you getting cozy with Ana a little bit ago. Now, I thought you didn't do sloppy seconds, even if they were your own."

"Yeah, well..." Eric trailed off on the pretense of taking another long sip of his drink, his eyes immediately searching out my best friend again. "Things change," he finally said. "It's time to grow up."

"That's all, then? You and Jane are done?"

But he didn't answer. We lapsed into silence, watching the crowd. Brandon was cornered by three donors, all vying for his attention while Cory hovered like a gnat. On the other side of the room I could see the only remaining guests who weren't lawyers or invited by the campaign team hovering together in a semi-circle: the members of Brandon's household staff, David, Ana, and Harvey, his trainer.

Ana caught Eric and me watching them, and gave Eric a coquettish little wave. She looked a far sight from the housekeeper I normally saw in jeans and a T-shirt. Dressed in an almost indecently tight red dress, her wild curly hair piled on top of her head, she was the personification of sex. And if the way Eric was shifting uncomfortably beside me was any indication, he thought so too.

Eric smiled that peculiar grin that transformed his face from average and a little grumpy into something that got him more tail than any guy in Boston. Ana suddenly looked like she'd just witnessed a peep show, and I felt like a very uncomfortable voyeur watching them trading glances. Across the room, Jane clearly noticed them too and stiffened visibly, even with her hand on the waiter's shoulder.

"Excuse me," Eric said as he pushed off the wall. He straightened his tie, and strode back into the party with a clear objective in every step.

"Oh well," I murmured to myself after I downed the rest of my drink. "Better get back to it."

* * *

Another hour later, I desperately needed to stop smiling. So, after visiting the bathroom, I decided to take a breather on the balcony that jutted out over the restaurant's patio seating and looked out to the Boston Harbor. Unfortunately, I pushed aside the thick curtains dividing the balcony from the event room to find it was already occupied.

"I'm just saying, you don't have to fucking do it in front of me!" Jane was shouting. "If you want to be a man-whore, that's fine. You're going to do it anyway. But I don't need to see you rubbing your dick on every woman at the party!"

"You're kidding, right?" Eric paced around the balcony, yanking furiously at his shirt collar. "When I had to watch you practically molest one of the caterers? That guy's going to be in therapy for years because of what you did to him behind the drink cart."

"Um, guys?" I ventured, raising a hand and letting the curtains shut behind me, but both of them were too steamed up to even notice my presence.

247

"Don't be jealous just because you lost your fucking mojo, and I still have mine," Jane snapped.

"Is that why you're so jealous, Jane?"

"Well, I don't know why else you'd need to fuck half of Boston unless you were compensating for something."

Jane cast a downward glance toward Eric's crotch, which made him turn bright red. Then he quirked one eyebrow, and gave her a look in response.

"Guys," I started again, but they just kept going.

"I never heard you complain. Unless screaming my name loud enough to make the neighbors call the landlord counts."

"You *would* bring that up," Jane seethed. "Jesus, do you have *any* class at all?"

"It must have disappeared after hanging around you all summer."

"Or from the skanks molting in your bed. The kind who wear poly-blend G-strings like the one I found, maybe? You better be careful, Petri Dish. I hear syphilis is making a comeback in Boston."

"That's rich, coming from the get-around girl of the Eastern seaboard," Eric retorted. "When was the last time *you* got tested, Jane?"

"Get-around girl? Who are you, the fucking Beach Boys? You gonna break into a five-part harmony for us, Eric?"

"It doesn't matter who I sound like. It just matters that it's true," Eric said in an even, nasty tone that made Jane's eyes bulge out of her sleek black frames.

"Fuck you *and* the mountain of your mommy's cash you rode in on, you golf-playing, Brooks-Brothers-wearing, popped-collar *fuckboy*," Jane spat. "You pretend you're nothing like those rich kids you grew up with, but when it really comes down to it, you're just like them. Don't get your way, and you throw a fucking tantrum! You want a pacifier, you big fuckin' *baby*?"

"*I'm* the one throwing a tantrum?!" Eric started to shout, although a glance back toward the party turned the last word into a squeak as he recalled just how many of his senior colleagues were in the room. "*You're* the one who plays hide-and-go-seek every time it gets hard," he gritted out, thrusting a finger toward Jane. "I put my fucking heart on the line, and you stomped all over it with your combat boots. Now I'm moving on and you can't take it, so *you* have to throw a fit like a fucking toddler. *Not me!*"

"Eric—" I started to put in, but he just held a palm up to silence me.

Jane said nothing, just tipped her chin up slightly and clenched her jaw. It might have been the reflection of the moonlight off her glasses, but I swore her eyes were glistening. My jaw dropped—my best friend never cried.

The standoff between the two of them felt interminable, until finally Eric stepped back.

"Whatever," he muttered with a shake of his head. "It's not like it ever mattered anyway. A zebra doesn't change its stripes. I should have known better than to ask the Whore of Babylon to start acting like the Virgin Mary."

With one last black look, he brushed angrily past us both.

"Nice comeback, fuckwad!" Jane called after him, only to receive Eric's middle finger in response before he swept off the balcony. She turned back to me, trying and failing to mask the despair on her face. "If he's going to insult me, it's not *really* going to land if he mixes metaphors. Have the decency to be creative, at least."

"Oh, Janey."

I cocked my head, but didn't say anything more while I reached out to rub her shoulder. Jane took a few deep breaths, then ran her fingers under her glasses to pull moisture away from her eyes, careful not to smear her eyeliner.

"What can I do?" I asked after a few moments.

Jane looked to me and bared her teeth in a smile that looked more like a grimace. "Nothing. It's okay, really."

"Jane..."

She shook her head, took a deep breath, then released it heavily.

"It's fine," she said. "Nothing a hot cater waiter can't help me fix." But when she looked at me, there was pain in her dark brown eyes that made my heart twist. "You mind if I leave a little early? I'd like to make use of that hotel room before I turn into a pumpkin."

"Of course, friend."

I pulled her in for a hug, which she accepted stiffly before relaxing.

"Thanks," she said. "Well, onward. Coffee before my flight tomorrow?"

I nodded. "You got it."

And with that, she left.

Twenty-Seven

After Jane left, I turned back to the harbor, not quite ready to go back in. I leaned over the railing, looking down over the clamor of restaurant patrons and the twinkle of the water beyond them. The night air was cool, but not uncomfortable, especially after the heat of the party. I breathed in, enjoying the briny air.

"You look lonely out here by yourself."

I turned around to find Julius Trout popping his white-blond head through the curtains. I smiled politely. I didn't want company, and certainly not his, but I also didn't want to offend Brandon's biggest donor.

He was the kind of man who had entitlement engrained in every cell of his body: the way he walked, the way he stuck out his lower lip as he perused people like cattle, and brushed his hands over his custom-made suit, fawning over himself with ever touch. His sense of himself was clearly inflated, and substantiated only by his multi-billion-dollar empire.

Trout came to stand next to me at the balcony, and we both looked out at the harbor in silence as he pulled a cigarette out of his pocket and proceeded to light up. My nose twitched, irritated by the way the ash covered the breeze.

"When I was a kid, my family used to live just over there," he said, making smoke scribble through the night as he gestured toward East Boston. "My father owned a housing complex. Used to be all Irish back then; now it's filled with all those other types."

I kept facing the harbor, not wanting to show my distaste for Trout's racism. I had met his kind before—the "good old boys" who couldn't stand a changing, more diverse world. There were a lot of them in Boston.

He smiled at me with a mouth full of capped teeth, and not for the first time that night, I stifled a cringe.

"Bran's a lucky man," he said as he looked me over openly.

I clenched my drink and tried to maintain my placid smile, hoping I didn't look too much like serial killer. It wasn't the first time tonight that I had heard Brandon referred to by his shortened name. It hadn't escaped me that the only people who ever called

Brandon "Bran" were people in this ridiculous, money-drenched world, with the exception of Ray. I wondered if that was something Miranda had adopted from his foster father—a word she thought signified fondness, when, considering Ray, it was likely more associated with his thirst for his charge's potential.

"I can see what he sees in you," Trout continued, his gaze prodding over me. "Even if he was out of his mind choosing that ring. A girl like you should have the biggest rock his money could buy, not these pebbles. A diamond for diamond."

Trout took a long drag of his cigarette, wrapping his thick lips around the tube in a way that strongly made him look like the fish he was named for. His other hand crept down the railing. Like I was somehow divorced from my own body, I watched as he gently stroked his thumb up and down my forearm.

"You know, I just gave Bran's campaign a hundred thousand dollars," he said before taking another pull of his cigarette. "Not a lot of men can do that."

"They certainly can't," I said as I was finally able to make limbs obey my thoughts. I pulled my hand away carefully and gave Trout a thin smile before tipping down the rest of my drink. *Shit. Wrong move*, I thought as the alcohol immediately flew to my head. I really hadn't eaten enough tonight.

"I know Brandon really appreciates it," I tried again.

"Does he?"

Trout took one last drag on his cigarette, then tossed it carelessly to the ground. He stomped it out with his shoe, then kicked it through the rungs in the railing to the patio below. There was no obvious reason for kicking a cigarette butt down to where people were eating other than he just could. It took everything I had not to say anything.

But before I could take another tack, Trout took a step toward me, then another. I found myself being backed up to the railing, caught in the looming shadow of his jowly, leering figure. *What the fuck is happening?* is all I could think. Over and over again.

"You're very beautiful," he said as he reached out to trace a finger around my jaw. I shuddered. "And the truth is, I've never been very good about stopping myself with beautiful women."

As if he'd just confessed a mild weakness for chocolate instead of a penchant for sexual assault, Trout shrugged. Suddenly terrified,

I looked over his shoulder. All I could see was Messina. Trout's thick lips were Messina's thick lips, and his slimy touch echoed Messina's. My limbs froze and my skin crawled. It was like I couldn't move.

Breathe, I could hear my therapist saying. But how?

"I should really get back to the party," I said, finally finding my voice.

But as I tried to shift out of his way, his hand clamped around my wrist like a vise.

"Just a moment, Skylar," he said. "What a beautiful name, really. We were just getting to know each other."

"Mr. Trout—"

"Julius, please."

"Mr. Trout," I said again as I tried to tug my hand away, to no avail. "I really should be getting back—"

I couldn't even finish my sentence before I was pushed up against the wall, and a long, slimy tongue was being shoved down my throat in spite of the way I banged my fists on his shoulders.

"What the *fuck*!"

It happened so quickly, I couldn't even see exactly how. One second, Julius Trout had his hand on my ass; the next, he was shoved up against the brick wall of the balcony, pinned at the neck by six feet, four inches of *very* angry Brandon.

"You want to explain to me why the fuck you just had your hands all over my fiancée, Julius?" Brandon growled with a face like a hurricane.

"I don't know what you're talking about," said the older man calmly, despite the fact that a very big hand was dangerously close to crushing his windpipe. "She made a move on m-me."

The last word came out like a cough as Brandon squeezed harder.

"Brandon, stop," I tried to put in.

"Why," Brandon gritted out, not even looking at me. "Is he telling the truth?"

"Oh my God, of *course* not, but—"

"That's what I thought," Brandon said. He loosened his grip slightly just before slamming Trout back against the wall. "So what does it matter what I do to this piece of shit?"

And before I could respond, he delivered a nasty right undercut straight into Trout's belly, causing the man to double over, his bloated face nearly purple.

"Brandon!"

I yanked on his arm, but Brandon didn't move. Instead, he pulled Trout back up to standing position by his lapels and slammed him back against the wall.

"I think you owe my fiancée a fuckin' apology, Julius, before you get the fuck out," Brandon said with a ticking jaw. "Or am I going to have to beat the manners out of your snide fucking face?"

Trout grimaced, but his glassy eyes slowly refocused in my direction.

"M-my humblest ap-apologies," he croaked to me, but even with his bloated, face, he had nothing but a black look for Brandon.

Again with an arm like lightning, Brandon delivered another punch to Trout's stomach that caused the man to wheeze and collapse to the ground.

"Brandon!"

We whirled around to find Cory poking his head through the curtains. He stared down at Trout, who was just barely propping himself up on one hand.

"Jesus!" Cory raced to the side of the older man and helped him up, shooting a nasty glare in my direction, as if to say, *this is all your fault.*

"What?" I mouthed, but Cory just shook his head.

"Come on, Julius," he said as he helped the old lech to the door. "Let's call your car."

"I'm...*fine*," Trout managed to get out. He stopped at the curtains. "But you can kiss your donation goodbye, Sterling." And with a look over me that still managed to make me want a shower, he allowed Cory to walk him out.

"You didn't have to—my God, Brandon, are you okay?!"

When I turned to interrogate Brandon, he was slumped toward the brick wall, both hands on his chest. I stepped toward him, and the wheezing sounds coming from his throat grew louder and louder.

"Babe," I said as I laid a hand on his back. "Babe, are you okay?"

He didn't answer, just slumped to the ground on his knees and, as if automated, started to rock back and forth, keeping his hands clenched at his chest while he struggled for breath.

"Fuck," he kept muttering to himself in wheezing, strained breaths. "No, no. *No.*"

"What the *fuck* were you thinking?!"

Cory burst back onto the balcony. He stopped short when he saw Brandon crouched on the floor, rocking like a small child. Back and forth, back and forth Brandon moved, one arm wrapped back over his head while he crooned softly to himself. He started to shake violently. Immediately, I fell to my knees beside him and tried to pull him into me, but he shook me off and continued rocking.

"No, no, no," he crooned softly, his eyes squeezed shut, the lines over his forehead in full relief.

"What the fuck did you do?" Cory asked as he stepped toward us. "What's wrong with him?"

"It's a panic attack, you asshole," I snarled as I rubbed Brandon's back. He didn't move away, which I took as a go-ahead to continue.

"Fuck...what should I do? Call an ambulance?" He glanced back toward the party, clearly wanting to do anything but make the phone call.

This time Brandon let me put both of my arms around him. Ray and Susan had already left the party long ago. Who would know how to help?

"Just get Kieran," I ordered. "Now."

Two minutes later, Kieran appeared on the balcony, took one look at Brandon and me, and whipped out her cell phone.

"Hey Push," she said a minute later. "It's happening, just like I said. Can you send in the prescription? I'll have Margie pick it up." She hung up and sent off a quick message, presumably to Brandon's assistant.

"Get a paper bag from the caterers," Kieran called to Cory, who immediately darted out, and returned within about thirty seconds, bag in hand.

"Brandon?" Kieran asked as she squatted eye to eye with her friend. "Take this. Breath into it. You remember how."

255

But it was like Brandon couldn't even hear her, full as he was of shakes and anger. He stared straight through her, with eyes so dark they almost looked black.

"Jesus," I whispered, even as I rubbed his shoulders. I looked at Kieran, terrified. "What do we do?"

"Sing to him," she said, nodding her head toward him. "It's the only thing that ever helped. When he was a kid, I used to find him freaking out, banging his head against the wall. I'd come in there, and I'd sing whatever stupid song I could think of. New Kids. Cher. Whatever. But it helps it stop faster than it would normally."

I pursed my lips, hesitant to treat Brandon like a small child, but at this point I was ready to try anything. So I leaned in and covered his rocking back with my body, wrapped my arms around his shoulders so I could tuck my chin close and sing into his ear.

I started quietly, searching for the words of "Thunder Road," one of Brandon's favorite songs, humming the piano intro here and there under my breath.

"Mary's dress waves," Kieran offered beside me, nodding in approval.

I continued to sing, recalling the words of a song that gave solace to many, even once for the two of us, dancing alone together in my kitchen. Using Springsteen's poetry, the way he described the everyday beauty of a woman dancing on a porch, songs on a radio, the connection between two people that exists beyond just lust, I gradually brought Brandon down from whatever internal ledge he was standing on. With every awkward hum, his shaking started to subside, and eventually, Brandon stilled in my arms, crouched but no longer rocking.

"Shhhh," I crooned as I pulled him closer. I fell back onto my seat, sitting against the wall, and at last, Brandon relaxed long enough to let me pull him closer. He took the paper bag in my hand, and slowly started to blow in and out of it.

I looked up at Cory, who was still standing by the doors, watching the entire scene with clear disgust. "He needs a glass of water, I think," I said.

"He needs a fuckin' therapist," Cory said, but nevertheless darted out to fetch the water.

"I..." Brandon managed to scrape out between shallow breaths, "don't...need...to be..."

"Fixed. Yeah, yeah, we've heard that line before," Kieran said sharply. "But it's bullshit, and you know it."

Brandon said nothing, just continued to breathe out of the paper bag. He still managed, however, to send a formidable glare at his best friend.

Kieran just crossed her arms and glared right back.

"You ready to talk like a big boy?" she asked.

"Shut up, Kieran."

"Look at what you're doing to yourself!" she snapped. "To Skylar, with this anxiety. You couldn't get away with breaking people's faces in high school—you think it's going to work when you're the public face of Boston? You're lucky you have a curtain to cover this shit show!"

Another withering glare. Kieran didn't even blink. Then she crouched back down next to her friend and put a hand on his shoulder. Brandon was able to sit up against the wall by himself, but still continued to breathe through the bag while his other hand grappled for mine.

"I don't know what has got you regressing like this," she said quietly, and when Brandon tried to lower the bag to respond, she held up a hand to stop him. "Skylar told me everything. No, no, you don't get to get mad at her. Who else was she supposed to talk to?"

Brandon flickered a quick blue look at me. I wrapped my arms around my middle, but I didn't look away.

"You can pretend with everyone else out there, my friend," Kieran said. "But you can't pretend with us."

Brandon took a deep breath from the bag, and then blew it out, the crackle of the paper filling the air. After a minute, he turned away from both of us.

Kieran sighed and stood up. She brushed the dust off her sleek black suit and looked out to the harbor.

"You're never going to make it through an entire mayoral campaign like this," she said frankly. When she looked back at Brandon, her eyes were steel. "Margie's on her way here with a valium prescription that Pushpa sent in. As soon as you can get yourself together, you and Skylar should leave. You have some things to figure out without an audience."

She left us on the balcony together, and we sat there quietly while the cool breeze from the harbor washed over us. There was a chill to it; summer was over.

Brandon didn't say anything the entire time, even after he had dropped the bag and began to take normal breaths again. He didn't say a word; didn't even look at me. But when I moved to follow Kieran, thinking he needed some time to himself, his hand snapped out and touched my elbow, wordlessly asking me to stay.

So I did. And for nearly twenty more minutes, we sat together in silence, waiting until Brandon was able to be the cool, charismatic figure everyone on the other side of the curtain had come there to see.

Twenty-Eight

"I don't think I could eat one more bite of food!"

Pushpa Srivinasan sat back in her chair and rubbed her belly like she was a round old man, not the eminent Chief of Surgery at Mass General. Tiny and delicate at about five foot two, she was the opposite of fat, but that didn't stop her from looking at her jeans like she wanted to unbutton them. We all looked about the same: me, Brandon, and Kieran, whom we had finally invited to dinner with her wife.

"Seriously, Skylar," she said with her slight British accent. "That was amazing. Where did you learn to cook like that?"

Beside me at the table, Brandon snorted, earning a smack on the shoulder from me.

"What?" he asked, feigning innocence. "Sorry, it was just the mention of you at the stove."

I rolled my eyes, but turned back to Pushpa. "Unfortunately, he's right. I'm a terrible cook. My grandmother actually made all of this for us."

Pushpa looked around, as if expecting Bubbe to pop out from behind the sofa. "Well, why isn't she eating with us?"

I shrugged. "I tried to invite her, but she had bridge club tonight."

"Sarah's social calendar is busier than my campaign schedule," Brandon joked as he slid a finger over his plate to lick up the rest of the sauce. Bubbe had made roasted chicken with drippings that were to die for.

"So," I said as I sat back in my chair with my glass of wine. "I want to know how you and Kieran met."

Pushpa, Kieran, and Brandon all shared an awkward look and then burst out laughing. I just took a patient sip of wine and waited.

"The short of it is, I met Kieran when I was just an intern and she was in law school," Pushpa said, with a brief glance at Kieran that made me smile.

Kieran wasn't much for public displays of affection—that much had been obvious all night, although that didn't stop Pushpa from occasionally rubbing her knee or casting googly-eyed looks at her wife. A few times I saw Kieran's mouth twitch, which made me wonder if their rapport was more of a cat-and-mouse game they played together.

"Come on, there's more to it than that," Brandon said as he laid his arm over the back of my chair.

"What's the long of it?" I prodded.

Kieran rolled her eyes. "You are both terrible at telling this story. Brandon, you in particular *always* leave out the most important details."

For a moment, Brandon's face darkened, but he said nothing, just drank more of his wine.

Kieran looked at me. "We were in our last semester at Harvard. And Brandon couldn't handle the pressure."

"That's a bald-faced lie," Brandon said. He sounded like he was joking, but the hand draped over the back of my chair gripped my shoulder a little tighter.

Kieran just rolled her eyes and turned back to me. "Graduation was two months away. Brandon had decided that instead of just staying with, you know, his first ridiculously successful company, he needed to start his own firm. Right out of law school. Because that's a totally realistic way of doing things."

I glanced at Brandon, who was suddenly interested in the parsley garnish on his plate.

"And I think we all know just how Brandon responds to stress," Kieran continued.

"Kieran." Brandon looked up, all joking gone from his face.

Another eye roll. "Come off it. We're telling this story to your future wife, not *US Weekly*. And considering how many times Pushpa has stitched you up over the years, it's not like we have any secrets from her either."

"What is it?" I asked, suddenly feeling a bit lost. "What happened?"

Kieran looked straight at me, her nearly-black eyes piercing through all levity. "You've seen it for yourself. When Brandon gets stressed, what does he do to curb anxiety?"

I opened my mouth to say I didn't know, but I realized I did. There had been several mechanisms I'd noticed over the last several months.

"He runs," I said. "Exercises like crazy."

Kieran nodded, as if waiting for me to continue.

"He...smokes," I said with a dirty look at Brandon, who exhaled forcefully out of his nose. Then I looked up, full of sudden epiphany. "He fights."

"I do not *fight*," Brandon put in, removing the arm around my chair so he could set both elbows on the table. "You make me sound like a schoolyard bully."

"You kind of were back then. I believe that night I literally pulled you out of a basketball court in Southie." Kieran turned back to me. "See that scar above his eyebrow? That's from the nasty gash he had that night. Swelled his eye completely shut."

All three of us turned to examine Brandon, whose ears were bright red. I had noticed the scar before, but he'd always blown off my inquiries. "Kid stuff," he'd say. "Just messing around."

"Yeah, well, you should have seen the other guy," Brandon mumbled, clenching his fists on the tabletop.

"Oh, I did," Kieran returned. "Pretty sure you broke Jimmy Calhoun's arm. Ma said he was in a cast for two months after that."

Brandon smirked. But I no longer found the conversation amusing. I was under the impression that his brawling had ended when he met Miranda, but apparently, that was just the heavy stuff. This was news to me.

"You did give Harvey a split lip yesterday," I said quietly.

Brandon looked up with an expression that was half irritation, half concern. The tone of the conversation was still light, but my gut clenched. I had seen a little of what he was capable of at our engagement party two weeks ago, and it was terrifying. He was incredibly lucky that Trout hadn't pressed charges, which I suspected was only because of the fact that I could also counter with sexual assault claims—claims that Trout had apparently dealt with before. Since then, there hadn't been any more outbursts or panic attacks, but something seemed to be simmering just under the surface, and when Brandon let it out during his training sessions, Harvey usually suffered for it.

"That wasn't fighting. We were sparring. It's part of my training regimen."

"Well, it wasn't the first time," I murmured before diving back into my wine glass. "The guy's going to start including plastic surgery as part of his fee."

261

Kieran just smirked. "Your workout regimen is to bust up your trainer's face? Sounds like not much has changed."

This time she was on the receiving end of Brandon's glare, but Kieran just cocked an eyebrow. I grinned and then stood up to clear the dishes. Kieran was better than anyone else at deflecting Brandon's intimidations. Maybe it was because they had grown up in the same rough place. She had that same kind of hardness about her—maybe even more so. After all, she'd had to stay until she was eighteen.

"Anyway," Pushpa said, somewhat eager to dispel the tension. "I was there that night they came in—working the graveyard shift in the pit."

We all turned our attention back to her. Pushpa had been regaling us with stories about her job all evening—listening to her was like listening to someone narrate *Grey's Anatomy*.

"It was about two in the morning when Kieran walked in with an absolutely pissed blond giant wrapped around her," she began. "She was the most impatient thing I'd ever seen. Instead of waiting to be placed in a bed like everyone else, she dumped Brandon in a seat and started walking around the emergency room, looking for doctors to see him right that minute. She practically ran straight into me in the middle of a crowded ER. Very insistent, she was."

I glanced at Kieran, who said nothing. "Then what?"

"I tried to tell her that she needed to wait her turn like everyone else, but, and this may truly surprise, Kieran doesn't listen to the word 'no' very well."

Pushpa smiled with recollection, and Kieran shrugged, as if familiar with the critique.

"Why do you think I made partner by thirty-five?" she said. "You think John Knightly wanted *me* to be the first female partner at Kiefer Knightly?"

Pushpa shook her head fondly, then turned back to me. "Eventually, I did get around to sewing up Brandon's face."

"Hurt like hell," Brandon joked as I returned to the table. "Pushpa is brutal."

"I don't think that's true. You simply have no tolerance for pain," Pushpa returned cheekily. "Anyway, once I was finished, Kieran chased me down the hall. I was still a total mess. Blood from the cut had gotten all over my scrubs, and I needed to change. But she stopped me, and started gabbing on and on—"

"Correction: I do not *gab*," Kieran interrupted.

"Gabbing on," Pushpa replied with another bright smile. "About my skills and how my stitches were very tight indeed, and loads more other things that informed me she didn't know a bloody thing about surgery."

I chuckled at Kieran, whose dark eyes, despite her omnipresent frown, glowed toward her wife. Brandon reached over to grip my hand, clearly thinking the same thing.

"And just when I'm about to ask this strange, mad girl why she is going on and on about some article she read in *Harper's* about the life of a surgeon, she stops talking just long enough to kiss me, right there in the middle of the ER." Pushpa held a hand to her lips, as if the touch could resurrect the memory. "I was so angry."

"You liked it," Kieran said smugly.

"I was *furious*," Pushpa reiterated. "And the only reason I agreed to meet her for dinner the next day was to tell her. Except I enjoyed dinner so much, I decided to wait until the next one. And the next one." She shrugged and reached up to brush a nonexistent hair from Kieran's face. "I don't know, my love. Maybe one day I'll get around to telling you how inappropriate that was and that I never want to see you again. But there never seems to be a good time." She looked back at Brandon and me and grinned. "Thirteen years later, I'm starting to think I'll never get around to it. I'll have to wait until Brandon lands himself in the hospital again."

The return of the conversation to Brandon's brawling brought another cloud over the table. After all, we had all been there two weeks ago when Pushpa had brought the Valium prescription to the apartment herself and examined his knuckles. Nothing had required stitches, but she had still taken one look at him and written down three different referrals for therapists, all of whom specialized in PTSD and child abuse trauma.

"So is that what this was for?" Brandon asked as he set his napkin on the table. "Some sort of bullshit intervention?"

And just like that, all of the levity was gone. Kieran and Pushpa both looked directly at him. Even though I'd invited them here, I had the urge to block their gazes. I hated cornering him like this, but it had to be done. Even though I'd learned the trick of using

Springsteen at two a.m. to soothe Brandon's nightmares, they still came like clockwork, along with other signs of stress. More and more often, I'd noticed cigarette smoke clinging to his clothes when he came home after campaign events. And then there was the damage he was doing to his trainer.

"Have you gotten some help yet?" Kieran asked.

Brandon exhaled heavily through his nose. "I don't need to talk to some shrink I can think circles around in the first place."

"Wrong," Kieran interrupted. "And you're not going to exploit Pushpa's access to prescription drugs so we can enable your denial. Skylar's going to catechism classes just to appease the make-believe problems of your would-be constituents. The least you can do is see a fucking therapist to fix the real problems you actually have."

"I don't need to be fixed!" Brandon exploded, pushing his chair back from the table. He stomped to the kitchen while we watched, suddenly overcome with a need to do dishes.

Cautiously, I followed and set a hand at his waist. "Come on. Please listen to them. I'm worried about you."

Brandon turned the sink off, but stood over the sudsy water while I leaned against his back. The front of his shirt had bubbles sticking to it, which might have been funny if he hadn't been gripping the edge of the counter hard enough to turn his knuckles white.

"They're all quacks," he said once he finally turned around. He looked at me, then at Kieran and Pushpa, who had brought the rest of the dishes into the kitchen and were now sitting at the bar. "I've tried. Red, you *know* I've been trying—I've seen all three of those shrinks in the last two weeks."

I nodded and patted his shoulder. It was true—he had been trying to find someone to help. Unfortunately, he also hadn't seen any of the therapists Pushpa recommended more than once. Meanwhile, the stress of the campaign, press coverage, and the Messina trial continued to mount.

"And what did they say?" Kieran asked pointedly.

Brandon sighed, frustrated. "Nothing I haven't heard my entire life. PTSD. Childhood trauma. Triggers. Fucking anxiety disorder. All of it."

"Prognosis?"

"Also a lot of the same," Brandon snapped. "Exercise. Get more sleep. Talk it out in session. Avoid stress and triggers." He snorted.

"Brilliant, four-hundred-dollars-per-hour answers. Fucking everything in my life is a trigger."

"Brandon," Pushpa started gently as she folded her graceful hands on the countertop. "There are medications you can try too. I'm sure if you broached the topic, a psychiatrist would give you plenty of options that might work well for your situation."

"I don't want to be drugged up," Brandon said bitterly. "You sound just like Miranda, shoving pills down her throat for every little thing. Not to mention literally every social worker I ever had."

I cringed, partly at the mention of his ex-wife, but mostly at the references to medications he was forced to take as a ward of the state. A silence settled over the kitchen. Brandon stared at the floor while the rest of us watched him. Finally, Kieran spoke up again.

"Something needs to change, B," she said matter-of-factly. "You can't go on like you have been. Panic attacks. Night terrors. Fights."

The atmosphere in the room felt heavy. Burdensome. There were no easy answers for the situation we found ourselves in. And I could tell by the stubborn look on Brandon's face that he wasn't about to admit any connection between his regressions and the biggest stressor in his life: his political campaign.

"I'll keep trying," he muttered finally before turning to wash the rest of the dishes.

The plates clattered while Brandon put them in the sink. Pushpa, Kieran, and I all watched wordlessly while he struggled to rinse and load them into the dishwasher. It was a solid five minutes before Brandon finally whirled around, spraying me and half the kitchen with the nozzle as he did so.

"Can you all stop staring at me like I'm a goddamn zoo animal?" he demanded.

Pushpa stifled a giggle, while Kieran just smirked.

"Jesus Christ," Kieran said. "What are you, five? You can't do *dishes* without making a mess?"

Brandon just reached into the sink and splashed water at her. "I might be messy, but now I'm done, no thanks to you jokers." He wiped the soapy water from his hands and draped the dishtowel over the sink. "Now, didn't you guys bring Parcheesi or some stupid game like that? If you're going to teach Skylar and me how to be a lame married couple, we might as well get started. Fair warning: Red and I are going to kick your asses."

And with that, any more mention of Brandon's struggles disappeared. But every so often, my glance would trail back to the kitchen, where the small orange bottle of Valium, with its two or three remaining pills, sat on the table. I couldn't help but wonder when they would be needed again, and what would happen when they   were   gone.

Twenty-Nine

My keys clinked in the tray on the foyer table as I entered the apartment late the next Friday afternoon. I'd actually gotten off early, since Brandon had apparently threatened to pull his account from Kiefer Knightly unless they let me off early for my birthday.

I was twenty-seven. It wasn't a particularly major birthday. But the events of the last year (or at least the last nine months)—dealing with my dad's addiction, graduating from law school, starting a new career, and, of course, the rollercoaster of my life with a certain tycoon—made it feel more consequential than normal.

"Babe?" I called out as I walked in. The apartment was silent, and there was no sign of said tycoon anywhere.

I'd been woken up that morning with a kiss and breakfast in bed that had quickly turned cold when I'd decided, upon seeing Brandon's shirtless form in low-riding joggers, that breakfast could hang while I feasted on him instead. But we'd both had early meetings, and when I kissed him goodbye from the car before Lucas escorted me into my office, I'd been adamant about the fact that I didn't want anything big for my birthday. Just a quiet evening in.

And yet, here I was, well in, while Brandon was clearly out.

My phone buzzed next to my keys.

"Hello?" I answered it.

"Hey Red," came Brandon's voice. "You home yet?"

"Um, yeah. Where are you? Considering you had to blackmail the firm to get me off today, I figured you'd at least be here."

His chuckle vibrated through the line. "I'm waiting in the garage. Get changed and meet me down here."

"Okay," I said as I started back toward the bedrooms. But halfway through the apartment, I stopped.

"Um, Brandon?" I asked.

The chuckle was louder this time. "Yeah?"

I looked around the living room, turning three hundred and sixty degrees before I answered. "Where's our stuff?"

Everything was gone—at least, everything that had belonged to us. The original, hard-edged furniture in the rental remained, but the piano, the random pieces of secondhand furniture from my old apartment, the various knick-knacks and bits of clutter that accumulated just from living—it was all gone.

The chuckle morphed into an outright laugh. "Just get changed and come down," Brandon managed to get out before the line went dead.

Suddenly feeling like a little kid on Christmas morning, I raced into the bedroom only to find my suspicions confirmed—the closet was empty too. Everything had been cleaned out of the room as well, including all of Brandon's things.

Except just a few items: a long black evening gown, a few pieces of my jewelry, and a shoebox, all laid neatly on the bed with a note beside them bearing Brandon's familiar scrawl:

Mary helped me with your first birthday gifts. Put them on and meet me in the car.

Love,

B

With a smile, I picked up the dress that had been laid flat across the bedspread. It was black and strapless, a simple Michael Kors cut midi-length, with a wide panel of ruched silk around the waist to add some detail. Chic, simple, and exactly the kind of thing I would pick out for myself.

I picked up the shoebox and opened it to find something that wasn't new at all: a pair of crimson Manolo Blahnik pumps—the same shoes that Brandon had tried to give me last winter. It was his first awkward attempt at turning our fated meeting into something else. He'd tried to seduce me with shoes and a terrifically misogynistic proposition that was more *Indecent Proposal* than marriage proposal.

My fingers played across my lips as I took in the joke...and the fact that he had kept them all this time, even though I'd told him in no uncertain terms to burn them, along with any way he had of contacting me. Now we were getting married. It was funny how things could change so much in so little time.

Without thinking twice, I pulled off my work clothes and slipped on the dress, which fit like a glove. Mary had exquisite taste and was really starting to understand what I liked. Then I put on the shoes, praying that they'd look terrible just so I wouldn't give Brandon the satisfaction of watching me enjoy them.

"Damn," I whispered as I looked at myself in the mirror. I really hadn't wanted him to win this one, but now that I had the shoes on, there was no way I was going to take them off.

I turned from side to side, smoothing out the dress and looking myself over. The effects of the campaign were clear. I was also a little thinner than usual, probably from the stress I'd been under for the last few months, combined with long work hours that often had me skipping meals.

But I didn't look bad. Being forced to work with a stylist also had its perks. For the first time in my life, I was genuinely well groomed—my eyebrows were threaded, legs were waxed, nails buffed (I refused nail polish, but Mary insisted I at least needed to have my nails manicured). My hair was trimmed and when I shook it out of the twist I'd pulled it into this morning, it fell nicely over my shoulders. I felt pretty, but more importantly, I still felt like me.

My phone buzzed on the bureau with a message from Brandon.

Brandon: u coming?

I rolled my eyes. Impatient as always. I picked up the black clutch that had come with the outfit and put my phone and wallet inside. Then, with another fluff of my hair in the mirror, I was gone.

* * *

"I *knew* you wouldn't be able to resist those," Brandon said once we were on our way.

David and Lucas had tactfully looked away after Brandon had caught sight of me walking through the car garage, and I was glad, since the way he bit his lip made a flush cover my body in about two seconds.

He reached out and touched one red pump, then drifted his finger up my crossed leg, which was now bared to mid-thigh because of a slit in the dress.

"Damn," he murmured, low enough that the men up front wouldn't be able to hear him. "Mary didn't tell me about this part."

With a quick glance toward the front seat, his fingers slid under the fabric of the skirt and nudged my legs apart.

"Brandon!" I hissed, pushing his hand away although I couldn't keep the silly grin off my face.

I gave a vicious nod toward the front of the car, but Brandon just chuckled and gave an impish grin.

"Headphones," he said as his lips dipped to my neck. He grazed his teeth down the soft skin just under my jaw. "You don't even have to be quiet."

I gave him my very best withering glare, but it didn't stand up much to his Cheshire grin. My legs were opening of their own accord by this point, and the mischievous finger slipping between them was already starting to breach the edges of my underwear.

"Oh!" I exclaimed as his finger entered me. I leaned back in my seat and stared up at the ceiling of the car.

"Shh," Brandon said with another nip of my neck.

A second finger joined the first, and his thumb clamped over my clit through my underwear. He squeezed his hand together, pulsing ever-so-slightly from outside and within. It was almost too much bear. In fact, I realized as a familiar thrum started to vibrate through my body, it *was* too much to bear. Especially with two other men— technically our employees—sitting not five feet in front of us.

"What—*oh*—what are y-you doing?" I managed to get out as my head knocked backward against the top of the seat.

"Helping you relax a little, baby," Brandon said as he placed low, gentle kisses up and down my neck. "Birthday present number two."

I grasped at the handle of the door on one side of me, the collar of Brandon's shirt on the other. His fingers and lips continue to work their dual magic, driving me higher and higher until I forgot about the men in the front seats. I forgot about Brandon. As I was finally pushed over the edge, I practically forgot my name.

It was only after Brandon's hand disappeared, my skirt was pulled down, and the door had actually been opened that I was able to open my eyes again. Brandon was standing outside, several sentences into a conversation with Lucas about parking.

Brandon leaned back into the car and offered me a hand with a smirk. "Can I help you out of there, Ms. Crosby?"

I shook my head and gave him a dirty look, although I couldn't stop the silly grin spreading across my face. "That was cruel."

He pulled me out of the car and secured me next to him with a hand around my waist.

"It's your fault," he growled into my ear. "You know what your legs do to me."

I elbowed him lightly in the stomach, even though I couldn't stifle my grin. "*You're* the one who gave me this dress."

Brandon shook his head as he perused me up and down, the action making the longer curls on top shake a bit in the wind. "Mary didn't tell me about the slit. Just about stopped my heart."

"Should I cover up, then? I could change back into pants if it's too much for you." I batted my eyelashes, doing my best impression of Bettie Boop.

"Don't you dare," Brandon growled. And with a brief stamp on my lips, he turned me toward our destination.

It was dark, so much different than the last time I'd been here—and yet, everything was the same. The wrap-around porch. The white paint and black trim. The oak trees that lined the drive, now turned the various hues of orange, yellow, and red of mid-October.

"You look like you belong here," Brandon said as he observed me looking up at the foliage. "With your hair, you look like some kind of wood-nymph."

I smiled. "What are we doing here?"

In response, he pulled a set of keys out of his pocket and pressed them into my hand. "Happy birthday, Red."

I took the keys numbly, staring at them for a moment before I took a shaky step toward the house. "But—how—what did you—how did you—"

Behind me, Brandon chuckled. "After you sent the listing to Margie, I told her to expedite the sale. I went to see the house that week and signed the papers. In both our names, Red. Craig and Lucas set up security in one of the back houses. We're good to go." He stepped closer and wrapped his arms around me, setting his chin on my shoulder so that we could look at the house together. "Welcome home, baby."

I hadn't really known until that moment just how much I had been truly craving a home of our own. Maybe it was the chaos of the last several months. Maybe it was the fact that my family had been uprooted from the house of my childhood. Maybe it was the trauma of being kidnapped from my own abode, but I badly needed a safe

271

haven like this. Looking at the house that I had known in my soul was supposed to be *ours* from the second I'd seen it, holding the keys in my hand—some piece of my heart I hadn't known was gone clicked back into place.

I turned around and launched myself at Brandon. If it was possible, I adored him even more than I already had. Of all the things he could have done to show that he loved me, this topped them all.

"I love it!" I squealed as he whirled me around in a circle.

His laughter bounced around the driveway and into the trees. The whole property was filled with our joy.

"Come on, Red," he said after he set me down. His eyes shined with unfiltered adoration, and he took my hand. "Let's give ourselves the grand tour."

I grinned and nodded, but before I could take a step, I was swept off my feet, princess-style, and carried up the steps of the porch. I whooped in surprise, clutching Brandon's neck.

"I know that technically we're supposed to wait until we're actually married to do this," Brandon said as he squatted down for the doorknob. The door fell open, casting a stream of warm light over us. "But I didn't want to wait to carry you across our threshold."

I pressed my forehead to his. I was too happy to speak. He stepped inside and kicked the door shut behind him, and it was only then that he set me down. Hand in hand, we walked around the house, where I saw my furniture set up in a few different places. The rest of the place was decorated with other unfamiliar pieces.

"Margie found a designer to help," Brandon said anxiously as he followed me through the living room and into the kitchen. "If you don't like anything she picked, we'll change it. I just know you're not really much for decorating..."

I drifted my free hand over the top of a sage green sofa sitting in the atrium. Just like everything Brandon owned (that apparently *I* would own, I realized with a little discomfort, but nothing like I had six months ago), it was exquisite. But as I looked around the house, taking in the blend of modern and comfortable, the dark wood pieces, the warm lighting, that discomfort faded quickly. Everything had its place. Everything felt like it belonged in my life, and in his.

272

Even the fireplace in the living room, which I saw through the hall was already lit.

I looked back at Brandon, unable to keep the silly grin off my face. "I love it. I love *everything*."

Brandon's face-splitting grin was immediate. Who needed lighting if I could make him smile like that?

"I can't believe you did this," I kept saying as I continued to look around. "I can't believe you...the dress, the shoes, *this* house..."

I trailed off as my eyes found him again. We stared at each other, and the air crackled.

And then it was like our interlude in the car hadn't happened. I couldn't think of anything other than being close to him. Suddenly, I was in a frenzy, kicking off my shoes, and reaching behind to unzip my dress, which I barely had the presence of mind to lay on the counter so it wouldn't become a wrinkled mess. It wasn't until I was in the process of shimmying out of my underwear that Brandon, caught in a trance, finally seemed to realize what I was doing. Then he sprang into action, ripping at his tie and hurling his jacket on top of my dress.

Once my clothes were off, I couldn't wait for him anymore. Brandon was shirtless, pants still on but unbuttoned when I hurled myself into his arms. He caught me easily, and our lips crashed together as we toppled backward onto the sofa under the glass panes of our new atrium, through which the stars glowed above.

"Off," I muttered as I tore at his pants under my legs. "I need you."

Obediently, he lifted his hips and pulled off his tuxedo pants, which I was able to toss over the matching ottoman before I straddled his naked body.

It was easy sometimes to forget what a work of art he really was. The last few months of stress and over exercising had turned his already lean, muscle-bound body into something that looked like it should be on the cover of *Sports Illustrated*, not in my new kitchen. He sighed contentedly as I played my fingers over the ridges of muscle, feeling the way each hard edge resisted slightly against my fingertips. Finally, my hands drifted all the way down, and I took him in a solid grip.

His sharp intake of breath revealed that he was more than ready to get on with business, but, as if he understood that I wanted to take

273

control right now, Brandon remained still, staring up at me with wide, fathomless eyes. Our eyes locked. I couldn't have said how long we stayed there like that: him lying back, me sitting on his hips, my hands wrapped around his solid length. It wasn't until my thumb drifted involuntarily up and down him, that he stirred under me.

"I just..." My words faded, as I was still caught up in the moment. My thumb continued to play as I closed my eyes languorously. "Sometimes with you, I feel like I'm caught in a dream. And I never want to wake up."

Brandon watched me intensely, his jaw clenched, insistent desire etched over his strong features. His hands slid over my shoulders, and gently, he pulled me down so that my forehead rested on his.

"Baby," he whispered as we lay there, forehead to forehead, caught in our own cocoon of love. "It's been a dream since I met you. The only dream I ever want to have."

"Even the bad parts?" I wondered as my heart caught in my chest.

Brandon's hands slid down my back as he urged me closer. He caught my mouth and sucked delicately on my lower lip.

"All of it," he said. "Every single moment."

My breath caught in my chest at his tender words.

"I need you," I said again, stumbling over my own voice as I reached between us. I guided him toward my slick entrance, and he slipped in easily, causing him to grunt loudly as I took him all at once.

"Fu-uck, baby," he said, his entire chest arching off the cushions at the sudden joining.

I pushed up and started to move.

"I love you," I tried to get out in between rolls of my hips, but I was already reduced to one-word sentences at the fullness of him. It came out as just "love." That was what Brandon did to me. Words couldn't come close to articulating what we were together.

Brandon's hands settled over my hip bones so that his thumbs came together over the sensitive bundle of nerves at our joining.

"I love you too," he echoed, though his eyes shuttered as I found a more insistent rhythm that matched the light stroke of his fingers. "You are my heart. You are my everything, Skylar."

"Tell me," I murmured as I continued to rock, taking all of him the way he took all of me.

It was too much—it was always too much with Brandon. The hardness of his body, the pressured, yet subtle touch of his fingertips, the growl of his voice, the warmth of his skin. Even his familiar smell of soap and almonds. I was overwhelmed, and it was precisely that overwhelmed feeling that allowed me to experience the kind of release with him I could never attain with anyone else. Brandon filled me up, in every single way possible. That was what we were to each other, and I finally understood that now.

I cupped my breasts, my thumbs tracing over my nipples as I rocked a bit faster. My entire body tightened, and I could feel Brandon throbbing with his own impending release.

"Please," he begged in between haggard breaths. "Please, baby. I'm so fucking close."

His thumbs pressed harder. I pushed faster.

"Just...a few...more...OH!"

Suddenly the wave of pleasure that had been building inside me crashed, each muscle in my body seizing up like a jolt of electricity was shooting through each nerve, each capillary.

"FUCK!" Brandon yelled his own release as his thighs tensed, and the muscles of his torso somehow grew even more rigid, even more defined. His finger dug into my thighs as he pulled me down on top of him, forcing me to take him even deeper as both our bodies shook.

And just as quickly, we came down together. As if he couldn't bear for us to be separated, Brandon gently pulled me into his chest once more. I closed my eyes and listened to the sounds of our new home. The rustle of the tree leaves outside the windows. The mild hum of the refrigerator. The crackle of the fire down the hall. And through all of that, most immediate to me were the sounds of us— our mingled breaths, heartbeats, caresses, and sighs. Through all of the surrounding noise, there was always us.

Thirty

As happy as I would have been to keep breaking in the new house for my birthday, more festivities had been planned. Brandon had tickets for my favorite pastime: visiting the symphony. He also surprised me by inviting Jane and Eric to go along too.

"I still can't believe you came," I said as Jane and I followed the boys to Brandon's box seats. "You know, considering what happened at the..."

We had talked several times since then, but Jane had steadfastly refused to discuss the fight on the balcony, and so had Eric. I didn't know how, but somehow the two of them had reached a sort of detente.

"It's cool," Jane said as she clutched my arm. "I wasn't about to miss out on my best friend's birthday or the luxe private jet Moneybags there sent to get me. Again. That plane is *nice*, chick. Anyway, the Walking Pathogen and I can get along for a night here and there, because I am *not* sharing you."

She had assumed that Eric couldn't hear her, but I knew better as I caught the black look that flashed across his face.

"I don't think you'll be able to keep that peace if you keep referring to him as an infectious disease," I said as we entered the hall.

The four of us filed to our seats, and I was surprised when Jane and Eric took seats together instead of bookending Brandon and me. They both looked at each other as if in surprise, but shrugged all at once as if mutually agreeing that seat choices weren't worth a battle.

The hall filled up, and we all sat back to enjoy a rousing rendition of Mahler's *Fifth*. It was one of my favorites, and the guest conductor was a legend. I recalled the last time Brandon had surprised me with a date to the symphony—Valentine's Day. It was one of the first times I'd really allowed myself to become vulnerable with him, partly because it was one of the first times he'd really shown his true, thoughtful side. Much like tonight, it was an evening filled with signs that he knew me and paid attention to the person he found.

As the strings sounded, I took Brandon's hand and squeezed. Surprised, he smiled and kissed my knuckles lightly. Even in the dim light of the hall, his eyes sparkled with adoration, and my heart was filled with gratitude that this wonderful, complicated, sometimes tortured man was in my life.

* * *

"Good birthday, Red?" he murmured as we exited the hall after the performance. From behind me, he clasped his hands on my bare shoulders and nuzzled my ear.

I smiled, my body feeling warm and light. "The best." When Brandon did gifts himself, he really did them right.

He hummed contentedly, and we followed Jane and Eric down to the main lobby. Jane and I stood to the side while Eric and Brandon went to retrieve our coats from the coat check.

"Thanks for coming out again, Janey," I said again to my friend, who was pounding a glass of wine she'd snagged from the concessions table just as they were packing up. It must have been harder to sit next to Eric than I'd thought.

She tossed back the rest of the wine and gave me a wide, cheesy grin. "Anytime, chickie, anytime." Then her face twisted with displeasure. "Shit."

"What?"

"Two o'clock. Look—very carefully—and then you need to get behind this pillar. Your hair is like a homing beacon for assholes."

"Oh, like your spikes are much better?" I grumbled.

"We don't have time to for this!" Jane hissed. "Even though, for the record, your hair could direct airline traffic in a snowstorm, and you know it. So, I'm pretty sure that Jared Rounsaville is going to notice it in a room full of black tuxedos!"

At that name, every hair—no matter what color—on my body stiffened. My eyes grew wide enough to split my skull as I stared at Jane.

"Tell me you're joking."

She shook her head. "Not even a little."

I gulped. "We have to get Brandon and Eric and go. *Now*."

"Does Brandon know what Junior Khaki Boy Scout did?" Jane asked as we started to worm our way through the crowd. Thank God, Eric and Brandon were next in line, even though that mostly consisted of Eric waiting while Brandon chatted with the numerous people seeking his attention.

"He does," I confirmed. "And considering how tightly wound he's been lately, I really don't know what he'll do if he sees him..."

Jane cut a sharp look back at me. "It's still that bad?"

As I passed one of Brandon's donors, I gave a brief smile and spoke through my teeth. Then I checked over my shoulder and relaxed once I saw that Jared was safely out of sight. Maybe we'd get lucky after all, and he wouldn't see us.

"Yes," I said simply. "It is."

I didn't expand—I didn't need to. Jane just squeezed my hand behind her, and went back to guiding us through the crowd.

"Well, at least you'll be able to confess your sins together after he kills Jared," she joked, earning a dirty look from me. "Oh good, they're close. Let's scram and avoid murder."

Unfortunately, getting out of the hall was tougher than expected. Even before the campaign, Brandon was a magnet as one of the symphony's top donors. His money almost single-handedly funded the youth orchestra, which focused on local outreach in poor neighborhoods around Boston. And now that he was fully in the public eye, everyone wanted a piece of him. We could barely go anywhere anymore without getting mobbed.

"Hey," I said as I finally elbowed my way to where he was deep in conversation with a well-dressed older woman. "Where are Lucas and Craig?"

"Hey beautiful, there you are," he said with a bright grin. "I sent them to get the car. Red, this is Elodie Blake. She's the Chairwoman of the Board of Directors here at the symphony. Elodie, Skylar is my fiancée. She's the reason I've gotten a bit more involved here, since she's an incredible musician herself."

"Oh, really?" Elodie replied in a voice that was a dead ringer for Katherine Hepburn. It was an accent that belonged almost exclusively to the old money in Massachusetts. She looked me over with renewed interest. "What instrument?"

278

"Piano," I said as kindly as I could while subtly scanning the crowd for Jared. I *really* wished Brandon hadn't left our security outside. It seemed like a bad idea in a crowd like this.

Behind Brandon, Jane was making bug eyes at me through her oversized glasses.

"She studied at NYU," Brandon continued as he wrapped a proprietary arm around my waist. Under normal circumstances, the pride in his voice would have made my belly flip, but right now, I just wanted to get out. As if he could feel my nerves, Brandon frowned.

"Um, babe?" I interrupted Elodie's rattling on about NYU's music program. "Sorry, Elodie. I'm actually not feeling that well. Could we make an early exit?"

Brandon's handsome face transformed with concern. "Yeah, of course. You okay?"

I grimaced to Elodie, who was watching curiously. "I'm fine. Just a nasty headache."

"Oh, yes. I get migraines sometimes. Absolutely horrid," Elodie joined in. "You should get her home, Brandon, and give her a shot of whiskey in a dark room. Only thing for it, truly."

Brandon draped my coat over my shoulders. "I'll have David pull the car around back instead. They'll move quicker."

"Sounds good," I said with a grateful smile. "It was lovely to meet you, Elodie."

We were stopped by at least five more people before I was able to tow Brandon out of the main hall and to the service entrance in the back where Jane and Eric were waiting.

"I'm coming, I'm coming," Brandon laughed as I practically yanked his arm off. "Jeez, you really weren't in the mood to mingle." He smirked. "Headache. Right."

I blinked as innocently as I could. "My head is absolutely pounding. I'm telling you."

Brandon just snorted. "You are the worst liar, Red. And if Elodie wasn't blind as a bat, she would have known you were full of shit too."

We all popped out into the alley laughing, until we turned to find Jared standing in his tuxedo shirt, arm propped over a girl against the brick wall. They both looked like scared deer at the sight of us, and time froze.

"Fuck," Jane muttered behind me.

"Go inside." Jared shuttled his—date? conquest? Who knew?—to the door. "Well, I guess this was inevitable," he said as the door shut behind her. "Jane. Eric. And Skylar, how are *you* doing?"

He couldn't hide the sneer on his face, and I wondered now how I had ever thought this cocky little shit was my friend. Everything about him screamed entitled, spoiled brat.

"Fucking terrific," I said, stepping in front of Brandon, whose body had instantly pulled tight as a drum at the sight of Jared. "I'm engaged, no thanks to you."

Jared's eyes flickered down to my ring. "So I heard. No surprise, really. I guess trash attracts trash, after all.

Brandon growled, and I gripped his wrist tightly, willing him to stay put.

"That's probably why Skylar never went for *you*, you arrogant bag of half-composted chicken shit," Jane retorted.

Jared crossed his arms in her direction, but looked to Eric instead of even acknowledging Jane's existence. "Her, Eric? Really? I'm surprised you're still tagging that. Seems a bit beneath us, don't you think?"

No one missed the way he grouped Eric with himself—part of the same social set—old money in the Northeast. Jane opened her mouth to issue another sharp reply, but Eric pulled her back behind him.

"What do you want, Jared?" he asked directly, with a calm that no one else in the alley seemed to have. "You're standing in an alley picking a fight with four people who despise you. So, what do you want?"

I watched curiously, keeping my hand on Brandon's wrist. He was strangely silent, but if the ticking pulse under my fingers was any indication, my man was a bomb ready to detonate. I needed to find a way to diffuse the situation immediately.Goddammit it, where the fuck was David? Where was the gorilla-shaped security team when we needed them?

Jared stepped forward, now walking dangerously close to both Brandon and Eric. Pride makes people do stupid things. This guy was either incredibly naive about his power, or he had a death wish.

"Maybe I just wanted to offer my *friend* congratulations on her engagement," he said nastily. Purposefully, he turned to Brandon

280

and smirked. "You okay, there, Sterling? You look like you've having trouble breathing. You need someone to rock you to sleep? Sing you a little song?"

The pulse under my fingers ticked up again. So, the scene at our engagement party hadn't been kept totally under wraps. Shit.

"He's just allergic to your bullshit, Jared," Jane put in. "Why don't you go wank off somewhere else, since we all know that's the only way you get any."

"Well, it's better than whoring around all of Boston every night of the week, Jane," Jared snapped. "Why anyone would touch a fucked-up freak like you, I'll never guess. I'm surprised *you* weren't the one knocked up, considering how much you get around. Tell me, what's the going rate?"

The words barely got out of his mouth before Eric's fist met Jared's razor-straight nose. Well, what used to be his straight nose, since when he was finally able to stand back up after a few minutes of squealing like a pig, there was blood flowing down his face. It was definitely broken.

"Fuck!" Jared cried out in a voice that was clogged with blood and tears. "You bwoke by dose!"

"Talk about Jane like that again, and I'll break more than that," Eric replied with supernatural poise. The only signs that he was remotely upset were the way the tip of his nose had turned red and the way he was shaking out his palm.

"We should get you some ice for that," Brandon said as he moved past me to tower down over Jared, forcing the younger man to look up at him with blood pouring down his face, staining the snow white of his shirt.

"What?" Jared asked snottily as he clutched the bridge of his nose. "You want a cheap shot too, Sterling?"

For a minute, I thought he really might punch him, just like he had done to Trout. But very slowly, despite the fact that his shoulders were vibrating with anger, Brandon bent down so that he was eye-to-eye with Jared. When he spoke, his words, tangled in his thick South-Boston cadence, were low enough that I almost couldn't hear him. Almost.

"If I wanted to hurt you, motherfucker, you'd already be dead."

281

Brandon's voice balanced on a knife-edge, and the menace in it was unmistakable. Jared blinked, having gone stock still while the hairs on the back of his arms clearly stood up.

Brandon stood up and dusted his hands off, like just being in Jared's proximity had gotten him dirty.

"But you're not worth it, you piece of shit," he said, a little more loudly. "You think I don't know your grandfather's part in the whole thing? You think I don't know about how *he* convinced Miranda to hire an investigator to watch me? You think I don't know about the oppo research he's done on me so your brother has a nice, easy mayoral run? He hasn't announced, but you think I didn't know about that?"

I gaped, and I didn't have to look back at Jane or Eric to know they wore the same incredulous expressions. This was completely new information—both the insidious actions of Jared's family as well as the fact that Brandon had secretly been researching them.

Jared didn't answer, just glanced back and forth between me and Brandon with angry, frightened eyes. But it was truly Brandon's face that I found more alarming. A different kind of grin, one I'd never seen before, something almost sinister, spread across his features. He was no less handsome than before, but you couldn't look at that face and not be scared. I was terrified.

Then he reached down and grabbed Jared by the shirt front, yanking him up with one clean movement and slamming him against the brick wall.

"Do you have any fuckin' clue who you're dealing with?" Brandon said into Jared's tight face. He shook his collar, slamming him against the wall again. "Do you?"

Jared gritted his teeth. "I'm not scared of you. You're pussy-whipped. Everyone knows it. You're a joke."

Another slam, and this time, Jared's head hit the bricks with an audible crack. Jane, Eric, and I all winced.

"This is *my town*. I know everything that happens here. And when I'm done with you and your family, you won't have a political foot left to stand on," Brandon said in a voice that was practically a growl. "Who do you think has been quietly buying up stake in your father's tax firm? I fucking *own you*. And you don't even know it."

Jared had carefully trained his bleeding features still, but I could see the whites of his eyes showing. Then Brandon slammed him against the wall one last time and let him slump to the ground.

"Get the fuck out of here," he said as he stepped over Jared's splayed legs as if he were nothing but street trash.

We all watched in silence as Jared scrambled to the door and disappeared with one last terrified look at Brandon. The door closed with a bang, and a cloud of silence settled over the alley as we stared at the place where Jared used to be.

Brandon turned, and when he met my face, his fury melted.

"Baby," he said as he took several steps toward me.

I shook my head, holding a hand out as I stepped back. "I–I need a minute."

"Skylar, he's not going to do anything again. That's why I have the research on his family. That's why I bought stake in his father's firm."

"It's not about that!" I shouted, the sound of my voice echoing down the brick alley.

I looked around wildly, suddenly eager to be out of this space. Who knew how many people had had their noses broken or their eyes punched in this exact spot. Eric and Jane stood close together, watching with concern.

Brandon's brows furrowed. "Then what? He's not going to bother us anymore, Skylar. I made sure of it!"

"You really don't get it, do you? That was some scary shit you just did there, Brandon."

"Skylar, I was just giving the little shit exactly what he deserved," Brandon tried to argue, but I cut him off.

"I need to walk home," I said. "I'll be there in a bit. But this...I just need a bit of time to think."

As if on cue, David rumbled up with the Mercedes, while the Escalade carrying Lucas and Craig pulled up behind him, and they jumped out. Craig took one look at the blood on his boss's hands and frowned.

"What happened?" he demanded.

Brandon sighed.

"Lucas, I need an escort home," I said to my bodyguard.

I turned to walk away, not even waiting for Lucas to follow me down the street. But I only made it a few steps before my arm was grabbed and I was whirled around.

"Skylar," Brandon started, but I jerked my arm away.

"Brandon," I said as calmly as I could muster. I was past the point of anger. I was scared of the man who was supposed to become my husband, and I really wasn't sure what I was supposed to do with that. "I love you, and I'm not running away. But I need some air right now. I need some space to think."

And before the forlorn look in his deep blue eyes could keep me from leaving, I turned around and walked out of the alley. Each step that took me away from the nasty events somehow only added more to   my   confusion.

Thirty-One

With Lucas just behind me, I stormed through Back Bay and through the heart of the city, eager to find some clarity in the thoughts swirling through my head. I was so distracted I couldn't feel the blisters developing on my heels until I reached the Common.

"Goddammit," I muttered as I stepped onto the grass and slipped off the new red shoes.

"You okay, Ms. Crosby?"

Lucas jogged up next to me, and I smiled grimly.

"I'm fine. I shouldn't have taken them off. You don't have a Band-Aid on you, do you?"

Lucas shook his head. "We could run over to the CVS on the corner. Or we could just go back to the house."

He couldn't quite mask the eagerness in the last statement. I sighed and held my shoes in one hand.

"I just need a few more minutes," I said. "Then you can have David or whoever pull a car around."

I didn't have to ask whether or not there was a car close by. Another perk of security, I supposed. I'd never be stranded in bad weather again.

With Lucas trailing, I wandered into the Public Garden for a bit. It was still a bit warm for October—Boston was experiencing an Indian summer, and although I was happy to have my light wool coat draped over my shoulders, my feet weren't uncomfortable in the grass.

Eventually I found myself on to the short suspension bridge that crossed the pond. I stopped in the middle and leaned out over the water to watch the flickering yellows and oranges of the fall foliage reflecting in the pond's smooth surface. The peaceful mood of the park went a long way to undo the tension clawing through me. In here, with the whispering of the trees and the way the willows drooped over the grass in the moonlight, it didn't feel like I had just watched my fiancé announce his intention to ruin an entire family's fortunes.

"Barefoot in the middle of the Boston Common? That's gross, Red. Even for me."

Startled, I looked up to find Brandon standing next to me. He looked a little worse for wear—like he'd spent a good amount of time walking around the city himself. He'd lost his tuxedo jacket and bowtie, and his sleeves, now slightly grubby and stained with the remnants of Jared's broken nose, were rolled up to his elbows. His hair was no longer combed, looking more like he'd been running his hands through it for the past hour.

"The problem with the security is that now you can always find me," I muttered as I continued to stare at the water. "I did ask for space."

I found, however, that I wasn't mad that he was there.

"I gave you some. And then I came to find you. I don't like the idea of you wandering around by yourself at night."

He edged closer so that we were no more than a few inches apart, and looked down into the water with me. I could see both of our hair gleaming in its surface: two bright spots of red and gold, almost the same colors as the leaves on the changing trees.

I turned, still leaning on the stone wall.

"Did you...are you okay?"

I hadn't considered it until now, but there was a very real possibility that he had had another panic attack once I'd left. I thought back to the night of our engagement party, and a wave of guilt swept through me. I shouldn't have gone anywhere until I knew he was calm again.

But Brandon shook his head. "I'm okay. I..." He took a breath and pushed it out slowly. "Eric and Jane were there. And I...I felt more in control. Not like last time." He looked at me with a particularly sweet gaze. "The singing helps, you know. I feel like a little kid. When I get upset, I think about your voice...and it helps."

I gulped, but let him shuffle close enough that our shoulders touched. As if by instinct, I leaned my head on his shoulder and closed my eyes. And immediately smelled something I didn't want to.

I sat straight up again and looked at him accusingly. "You smoked!"

Brandon stood up from the bridge and twisted his lips together guiltily. "Ah..."

"Again!"

He still didn't say anything, just stared at the ground.

"Brandon!"

Finally, he looked up. "What? What do you want me to say? Yes, I had a cigarette or two while I walked. And it's better than..."

"Than what? Getting into random fights?"

"Well, *yeah*!"

We stood there, glaring at each other, until finally Brandon reached up and tugged at his hair, causing it to stand up for a moment before it flopped back down.

"Where are they?" I asked.

He didn't say anything. I stomped my foot.

"I know you have them. Where are they?"

Like a guilty teenager, he pulled the flimsy box out of his pocket and held it up. I bit my lip, willing myself not to yell when I found that the box was almost empty.

"This isn't healthy," I said.

"Skylar, it's just a way to deal—"

"That will eventually kill you," I cut him off. "I'd like to be your wife without having to cart you to chemotherapy every other day, thanks. Not to mention I'd like you to stick around to see our kids have kids. Cut it out."

Brandon opened his mouth, then closed it again.

"You need to cope?" I said as I stepped closer, back into the space where our bodies naturally seemed to draw toward one another. "Call a therapist. You call me. I'll sing Springsteen to you over the phone during a staff meeting if I have to. But you have *got* to stop finding coping mechanisms that hurt you or other people. Kieran...the therapists...even Cory! We're all telling you the same thing: something has to change. And you're not listening."

We stood there for a moment, still not touching, blue eyes meeting my green while Brandon clenched his jaw. He knew I was right. But the decisions he had to make weren't ones I could make for him.

He leaned in, sensing my resolve breaking. But the scent of nicotine wafting off him made me think of something else.

"Besides," I said as I stepped back. "I told you before. I can't kiss a smoker."

At that, Brandon's eyes genuinely bugged out. "You were serious?"

I crossed my arms. "As a heart attack. Or, you know, emphysema."

It took him exactly two seconds to stride to the trash bin a few yards away and toss the cigarettes and his lighter into it. He came back with a satisfied look.

"Done."

"Yeah, I've seen you do that before."

He took a pack of gum from his pocket and put a stick in his mouth.

I just shook my head. "And that doesn't do anything to hide it, just so you know. I could taste it when you came to bed two nights ago, and last Friday too."

Brandon frowned as he chewed. "I thought I did a good job of hiding it."

"Brandon, how much time have you spent with your tongue down my throat?"

In response, all I got was a very self-satisfied leer. I rolled my eyes, but couldn't quite stop myself from smiling.

"Fine. I'll get the patch," he conceded as we turned back to the river.

The lightness faded as the events of the evening washed over both of us again. The sounds of the city were slightly muted by the wind filtering through the trees, and here and there I could hear squirrels chirping at each other as they went to sleep.

"I don't want you to attack Jared's family," I said quietly.

"No."

Brandon's response was immediate, without the usual room for negotiation he generally showed me. I opened my mouth to argue back, but he shook his head, the motion causing a few errant curls to fall over his forehead.

"This isn't about vengeance, Red. If it were, I'd have already torn apart George Rounsaville's firm. Shit, I could do a lot more than that, and you know it."

He sighed, rubbing a finger over his lips. He wanted a cigarette, I could tell. I was definitely going to have to make sure he got that patch like he said.

"It's about leverage," he continued. "Jared and his family won't think again about messing with me or mine. Not as long as I own them." He shrugged. "In the end, it's about business and family. And he's not allowed to fuck with either."

I gazed at him with a bit of shock. This ruthless side of Brandon wasn't one I'd seen often, even if the rational side of me had known he couldn't have achieved everything he had without some cutthroat instincts. It just wasn't a side of him he usually showed to me. Until now.

He turned his gaze toward the path beyond us.

"Do you remember the first time I followed you in here?"

As if I could ever forget. I had been so awestruck by the man I'd done everything that, as a child of the most urban of urban environments, I knew *not* to do: run alone into a city park in the middle of the night. Oh yeah, and during a freaking blizzard.

But even then, with a snowstorm whirling around us, I barely remembered anything other than his kind, curious face, the way his blue eyes had sparkled through the storm. The desire and intensity that had emanated through the gusts. I hadn't even known his name, but I'd known I wanted him. More than anything.

And he had wanted me. The truth of that hit me—he had never been someone who would let others stand in the way of what he thought was right. And from the beginning, he had known we were right, even when I didn't.

"I couldn't see anything but you," he said quietly as he slid his hand down the railing of the bridge so that our pinky fingers just barely touched.

Suddenly it was like we were the only people in the park.

"Skylar," he spoke slowly, searching for words. "What these people—Jared, Messina, your mom, Miranda—what they all did to us...there's a part of me that wants to...serve them all the same kind of justice."

His eyes sparked, with a strange mix of love and the same danger I had seen in the alley. But I didn't pull away.

"And if it had been twenty years ago, Skylar, maybe even just ten...I wouldn't have thought twice about it. Now..." He raised a hand and pushed a few strands of hair out of my face. "I want to be a better man. For you. For us. But baby, you can't just expect me to sit like an idiot while people attack me and mine. You have to let me use the weapons I have."

289

I exhaled a breath I hadn't known I'd been holding. Brandon was such a loose cannon right now, but I knew in part it was because of the lack of control he felt over our lives. And if I was being honest, I didn't want to be a victim either. And there was a part of me that took satisfaction in knowing that he could and would do what needed to be done to protect us.

"Okay," I breathed

He was casual, leaning against the rail. The only thing touching was our fingertips, but his face was like fire. Involuntarily, I brought my other hand to my mouth.

"Don't do that," Brandon said softly, pulling my hand down. "If I can't kiss those beautiful lips, at least you can let me look at them."

"Brandon..." I said, my breath drawing close. He was playing with fire.

He turned my palm over and started to trace circles over the lines on it. Over the soft pads of my fingers, down over the sensitive interior, over the mound of Venus at the base of my thumb.

"I want to so badly right now," he said as he traced the lines, over and over again, causing goose bumps to rise up my arm. "But you said...plus, you know, there's them."

He nodded toward a row of bushes, and it was then I caught the glint of light bouncing off camera lenses. I sighed and looked back at him.

"Politicians aren't supposed to get wrapped up in bouts of passion," I murmured, utterly mesmerized by the movements of his fingers as they stroked over my palms.

Every cell of my body stood to attention, and Brandon could sense it. A month ago, I would have already been cornered under the shelter of a nearby tree, or dragged off to the nearest alleyway. Would we ever be able to act on that again?

Brandon lifted his blue gaze up to meet mine, then dropped it again to my lips and briefly to my chest before he took another sharp inhale.

"Fuck," he muttered. "I don't know if it's because now I'm not supposed to, but I swear to God, Skylar, I'm about ten seconds from bending you over this railing."

I adjusted my stance, arching my back slightly to relieve the sudden ache between my legs. Brandon caught the movement, and his eyes dilated.

"*Fuck*," he muttered again.

And yet neither of us made any move away from the bridge or from each other. It gave me a moment to take him in and all the indications of the struggle that mirrored mine. The way his tensed forearms tested the limits of his rolled-up shirtsleeves. The way the muscles of his neck pressed against his collar. The way his broad chest rose and fell with heavy breaths.

He wasn't kidding when he said he wanted me, and as his searing blue eyes scanned my body too, I was pretty sure he could see the same in me.

Brandon darted a quick glance around the park.

"Fuck it," he growled.

He snaked his hand around the back of my head and yanked me to him so he could curve our lips together in a kiss that consumed us both, cigarettes or not. For one, two, three seconds, he devoured my mouth, sucking on my lower lips, twisting his tongue around mine, grunting into the nonexistent space between us until, just as quickly, he released me, and we both stepped backward, like suddenly split magnets.

Both of our chest heaved, and Brandon pulled at his collar.

"Can we go home now?" he asked in a voice that made it clear that despite being a question, it wasn't a request.

I bit my now-swollen lower lip. His eyes practically turned black.

"Let's go."

He grabbed my hand, and without waiting for my response, started towing me out of the park. I was still speechless. That was what the man did to me.

* * *

Once we were back at the new house, it was like we hadn't already found each other's bodies twice that night. Brandon's hands were all over me as he unzipped my dress, pulled my legs around his waist, and carried me up to our new bedroom, where he set me down on the ground.

291

"Damn," he said as he looked me over while undoing his shirt.

I wore nothing but my lingerie—plus the blush all over my body from the way he was looking at me.

"Skylar," he said slowly as he pulled open his shirt.

My mouth dropped. It really didn't matter how many times I'd seen him like that

"Wha-what?" I stuttered, completely transfixed by his casual striptease.

Brandon smirked. "Baby, I—" he paused after tossing his shirt onto the armchair in the corner. His pants were unbuttoned and unzipped, revealing the deep V of his lower abdominal muscles before they sank below the waistband of his boxer briefs.

Finally, I was able to drag my eyes upward, and I was stilled by the fire in his eyes. The aggression of the evening wasn't completely gone, then, and he was clearly in need of some way to purge it.

"Do you trust me, baby?" he asked slowly, one eyebrow quirking upward.

I nodded. "Of course."

He smiled, slow and mischievous. "Good. Go into the closet and grab a tie."

I frowned. "What—"

"Just do it," he said in a tone that brooked no reply.

Normally I might have argued back, but my curiosity was piqued. I went into the large walk-in closet that now housed all of our clothes and, once I finally found them, started flipping through the ties neatly arranged in one of the drawers.

Unfortunately, right when I lifted up the red paisley one I liked, I saw something else that made my blood run cold.

"Christ, Red, it doesn't matter which one. I'm tying you up, not wearing it," Brandon called good-naturedly from the bedroom, where I knew I'd find him undressed.

And for once, I couldn't have cared less.

Gingerly, I reached into the drawer and pulled out the gun lying underneath the rows and rows of brightly colored fabric. I didn't know much about guns, but this one looked like the kind that police officers carried in their belts. It was heavier than I'd imagined, and the metal edges were cold.

Carrying the gun like a piece of dirty laundry, I reentered the bedroom. It wasn't until I walked to the bed that I realized I was still clutching the red paisley tie. I dropped it to the ground, where it lay like blood spilled across the white carpet.

"Took you long enough," Brandon said from where he stood in just his briefs at one of the windows overlooking the orchard. He turned around with a grin that disappeared as soon as he caught sight of me. "Shit."

"What. The fuck. Is *this*?"

I swallowed hard, unsure if I could even get the words out again if I wanted. It felt like all the blood had stopped running through my body.

Brandon crossed to me quickly to grab the gun, then released the magazine, and checked the chamber.

"Jesus Christ, it's *loaded*!" I practically detonated when I saw him push the magazine back into place.

He just frowned. "Um, *no*. It's not loaded unless I actually chamber a round."

I just stared at him like he was speaking a foreign language. "But there are bullets. Inside it."

Brandon smirked. "It wouldn't really serve its purpose without them, Red."

At the sound of my nickname, something inside me snapped. Humor? *Now*?

"This is not the time for jokes," I said. "You have a gun in your tie drawer. A gun filled with bullets that could actually kill people. What happened to 'using the weapons you have'?" I blinked as a thought occurred to me. "Have you *always* had a gun in your house?"

Brandon shrugged, but had the decency to look uneasy. "Not for a long time. But now seemed like a good time to pick up the skill again. What? It's perfectly legal. I have a license."

"Pick up the skill?" I stared at the loaded pistol as I sat on the bed. "This isn't a hobby. Guns are not bicycles or knitting."

I grabbed a throw blanket and pulled it over my mostly-naked body. I couldn't have said what color it was. I couldn't register anything about my new bedroom. Suddenly I felt very cold.

"Red."

Brandon sat down next to me and put an arm around my shoulder, but I shrugged it off. Then suddenly, I had to move. I couldn't be in the same space as him and think. I stood up, and with the blanket flying behind me like a cape, I paced about the large bedroom.

"This—what—I—" I sputtered, stumbling over my words, as I couldn't even decide exactly what I wanted to say. I stared at Brandon, who finally looked genuinely worried.

"Why?" I asked.

His brows furrowed, and he looked down at the weapon cradled in his hands. "Why not?"

I balked. "Why *not*?"

Brandon swallowed, and then shrugged. "Okay, fine. I just mean, what have we been talking about tonight? I want to be able to protect us. Protect *you*, of course." He looked up at me again, his blue eyes scared and angry all at once. "Skylar, what happened to you...fuck. That was my fault."

"It was *not* your fault," I said immediately. "That's ridiculous, and you know it."

"It *was* my fault," he argued. "I brought that guy down on you and your family because of who I am, and I didn't anticipate it. You even said so. I brought *all* of them onto you."

I looked at the gun again, then back at him. "This wouldn't have stopped Messina. You have to know that." Then a thought occurred to me. "Brandon, do you carry this around with you?"

He opened his mouth, then closed it again. "I—no. Lucas said that was a really bad idea, and Cory said if I was every photographed with it, it would be the end of the campaign. Done. Boston is really not the kind of place where being pro-gun goes over well."

I rubbed my lips together, considering. "Are you pro-gun? That's not what your platform says."

Brandon sighed again, turning the gun over in his hands. "I'm pro-control; that's not a lie. But that doesn't mean I think people shouldn't be able to own them." He looked up at me, full of determination. "A man should be able to protect what's his, Skylar. Like I said, with the weapons I have."

I cocked an eyebrow and stood up. "Okay, Daniel Boone."

Brandon rolled his eyes. "Seriously."

"Okay, seriously."

I paced back and forth across the room a few times, but in the end, there was only one thing I could say. "You're not doing this to protect us. You're doing it for peace of mind."

Brandon tossed a hand into the air. "Is there a difference?"

"I think so. Just because a gun is in the house doesn't mean you would be able to keep me safe in the event something awful happens. Craig's team is better equipped to deal with that, and you know it."

He made no reply, just kept holding the gun. The way he handled it, with such obvious ease and familiarity, made me nervous. At some point in his life, Brandon had used a gun like this before. A lot. He hadn't killed anyone—I believed him when he told me that—but that didn't take away from the fact that his adolescence and early adult years were filled with violence, from inside and outside his home. Self-protection was a premium he clearly still had a hard time entrusting to others.

But that wasn't a life I wanted. Not for me or—I realized with a gulp—the family we would have one day. With a deep breath, I told him as much.

"I'm sorry," I said as I sat down on the couch. "We—maybe we should have talked about this before you bought this place. Before we agreed to get married. There's still so much we don't know about each other. I could—if you want—I could, um..."

I couldn't quite bring myself to say I'd leave if we thought differently on the matter. But it must have shown on my face.

"Whoa, whoa, whoa," Brandon said as he sat up completely. "Are you trying to break this off?"

"What? No!" I blinked, my eyes suddenly wet. "I'm just...you don't have to change what you are for me. But Brandon, I don't want guns in my house! I don't want them around my kids!"

Brandon set the gun on the bedspread, reached out to take my hand, and pulled me so I stood between his legs.

"Skylar," he said quietly. "I would never put our kids in danger. But I can't live like a sitting duck. *I* can't."

"But—"

"I'll get a safe, tomorrow. You're right—a tie drawer is a stupid fucking place to keep a deadly weapon. But Red...people like us...we're targets. We might be able to live our lives without any protections if we were like everyone else...but we're not, baby. We're just not."

I glanced around our new home, with its comfortable, yet plush surroundings, through a totally different lens. I had never lived in luxury—not in my family's house in Brooklyn, and not in any of the tiny apartments I'd called home. I'd been a regular person my whole life, someone who blended in with the crowd, who didn't need to worry about being singled out.

No more.

"I don't like it," I whispered, even as I allowed Brandon to weave his fingers through mine and drop light kisses over my knuckles.

"Me neither," he said. "But that's where we are." Then he looked up, his eyes bright and earnest. "I won't let anything happen to you again, Skylar. I *won't*."

His voice shook at the end, and I saw just how much my safety meant to him. I cupped his face and stroked my thumbs over the chiseled lines of his cheeks, feeling the stubble that had grown through the day. My fingers found his lips, drifted over the soft edges, and pulled slightly on the lower one, until Brandon bit the edge of my finger.

I considered that night—was it more than two months ago now?—that I'd been taken against my will. Messina's face and touch was still imprinted on my mind, but I'd been diligent about working through it with a therapist and at home. Would it have ended differently if I'd been armed? I didn't think so. I felt safer with people, not weapons.

But that was me.

I looked at the gun on the bed, then back at Brandon, who was waiting patiently—and nervously—for my answer. I draped my arms over his shoulder, then straddled him on the bed. His hands found my waist.

"I meant what I said." I nuzzled his nose. "I'm not going anywhere."

Brandon's chest caved slightly as he exhaled with relief, and he nosed into me, looking for a kiss.

"Get a safe," I said as I dropped one, then another onto his searching lips. "And a therapist."

He lay back onto the mattress, taking me with him as he pulled me down for another kiss that took my breath away.

"Brandon," I breathed once I was able to get a word in edgewise. "I mean it."

I looked to the side of the bed, where the gun still lay, looking harmless on the comforter.

Brandon followed my glance, then looked back at me, his hands tensing slightly as he pulled me even closer.

"Tomorrow," he said. "That's a promise."

And then he kissed me again, and didn't let go. And tomorrow ceased to have any meaning, since when he kissed me like that, time seemed   to   stop   completely.

Thirty-Two

Several weeks flew by, and things seemed to get better. We moved fully into the new house and began to settle into a different routine there, one that often included strolling around the property or the quiet Brookline neighborhood each evening when we both got home from work.

Brandon made good on his promises and actually started seeing a therapist regularly, despite the fact that he grumbled about it every time he came home. A safe was installed in the back of our closet, and I stopped smelling whiffs of cigarette smoke after particularly stressful events. His trainer stopped accruing bruises and cuts every time they worked out. Brandon even had a few nights here and there without his nightmares.

But his campaign schedule picked up too, and there were several weeks when I barely saw him. When he crept into bed around one or two in the morning smelling of gin and the cigars powerful men smoked in their studies and the backrooms of the men-only clubs that still existed in Boston.

I frequently wouldn't get home before eight or nine myself after continuing my twice-weekly catechism classes with Father Garrett, who had managed to invite a reporter along to listen to one full session last week, much to Cory's horror. I couldn't claim to be any more of a believer than I used to be, and I certainly wasn't as excited as I should have been about my baptism in the spring or the huge church wedding that Gloria continued to plan, but at least neither thought made me feel faint anymore. So that was something. Although we had taken some steps toward normalizing our lives, both of us were running ragged, and I for one couldn't wait for the next year to pass so this stage could be over.

On an early morning in November, we went to New York for the days of the trial on which we were scheduled to testify. The trial itself had begun a week prior, and because Messina was small-time enough that he couldn't afford an expensive attorney, the trial was relatively quick for the number of charges levied against him.

Dad had given his testimony the day before, at the end of a list of other men like him who had been swindled and beaten at the hands of the loan shark. Zola hadn't given us much information—he couldn't ethically do so—but we all knew the long list of charges from the arraignment.

Brandon and I were scheduled on the last day of the prosecution's case. The defense had few witnesses scheduled, and all of them would testify within a few more days, so we were planning to stay through the following week for the verdict. With any luck, the jury would deliberate quickly and announce soon.

"The prosecution calls Skylar Crosby to the stand, your honor."

The judge asked me to raise my right hand and swore me in with the Bible. It was a curious experience, considering how much more familiar I was with the text these days. In the crowd, I could see Brandon smirking—he was thinking the same thing.

Zola approached the bench, and we launched into the routine that we had practiced more than once over the phone in the weeks approaching the testimony.

"Ms. Crosby," he began. "Can you explain to the jury what happened on the night of August fourteenth?"

I nodded. "Yes."

On it went. Prodded by Zola's gentle questions and mild meta-commentary—mild enough that he raised minimal objections from the defense—I told the story of my abduction. I avoided Messina's cruel gaze throughout, certain that if I looked at him even once, I wouldn't be able to keep my face straight or avoid breaking down. My palms were slick with sweat as I spoke, and my skin pulled tight like the shell of an egg. One slip, one misstep, and I felt like I could crack in half.

And yet, for all that, the testimony went rather smoothly, with only a few missteps when Messina's lawyers tried to cross-examine me. I was an ideal witness, Zola said—a straight history, photographic evidence, and not easily intimidated on the stand. My challenge instead would be *not* to take the defense attorney's bait.

"They'll try to gaslight you," Zola had said over the phone. "You know it, and I know it. They won't be able to ignore the fact that you were at the Navy Yard, or that you were assaulted, because we have the hospital and police reports. But they'll do everything they can to make it seem like you wanted to be there, that it wasn't actually a kidnapping. They'll make it sound like you did it to yourself."

"What were you wearing the night of your alleged 'abduction' by Mr. Messina?" Primo Cipolla, the defense attorney, began.

"Objection." Zola shot up from his seat at the first question. "Immaterial. Ms. Crosby's clothing has no relevance to whether or not she was abducted by Mr. Messina."

"It does to whether or not she was inviting the attentions she claims my client offered her," Cipolla argued back.

The judge tapped his mouth with a pen. "Perhaps. I'll allow it. Proceed, Mr. Cipolla."

Shit. That wasn't a good sign if the judge already appeared predisposed to think a woman's clothing made her more susceptible to rape.

Cipolla turned back toward me with a slight smirk. "What were you wearing that night, Ms. Crosby?"

And for once, I was incredibly happy that I had absolutely no sense for fashion.

"A pair of old jeans that used to belong to my dad," I said flatly. "And a T-shirt I bought at a thrift shop."

There was a titter around the courtroom, and Cipolla's face turned red. "After a major political event? You were seen that evening in this, were you not?"

He held up the blue column dress I'd worn to the benefit. In the picture, I was sitting down with my legs crossed, the slit in the column dress riding a bit higher than it should to reveal most of my thigh.

I just looked up. "Then you also know I was seen leaving before Mr. Sterling made his announcement to enter the race. I went home and changed, Mr. Cipolla. I was upset and wanted to go for a walk. Don't you like to change into comfortable clothes after a night when you've been eating too much?"

Again, the courtroom tittered, and Cipolla's face turned red as I glanced down at his rotund belly, which pressed at the button holes of his suit jacket. At the other table, Zola tightened his jaw and shook his head infinitesimally, and I closed my mouth. I wasn't being a good witness right now—Cipolla was already getting to me, and now I was goading him back.

"Fine, fine," he said as he walked back to his desk and dropped another picture on the ledge of the stand.

"Where are you in this picture, Ms. Crosby?" Cipolla asked.

300

I examined the grainy black and white photograph. "I'm...I'm in the Navy Yard." The same place, I realized with a dropping stomach, where I'd been taken. How could I not have recognized it?

"And when was this taken?"

I pressed my lips together and stared at Cipolla. "Five years ago."

"And what were you doing there, Ms. Crosby?"

"I was paying off my father's debt to Mr. Messina."

"Debt, debt. That's a funny word. For how much, did you say?"

"That time it was forty thousand dollars," I said through gritted teeth.

"Did your father sign any papers documenting this loan?"

"No, but—"

"And can you prove that you delivered forty thousand dollars to my client?"

"You know very well that your client only accepts cash. Just like every other criminal extortionist in New York."

"Those are some very nice shoes you're wearing, Ms. Crosby," Cipolla remarked.

"Objection," called Zola. "Immaterial."

"Ms. Crosby is a recent law student from one of the most expensive schools in the country," Cipolla said to the judge. "I'm simply trying to ascertain if all of the money she demonstrated was taken out of her account really went where she said it did, or if perhaps she spent some or all of it on herself."

The judge looked over his spectacles at Cipolla like he was a very small rodent. "Overruled, Mr. Zola. Continue, Counsel."

Cipolla looked back at me. I blinked, knowing not to say anything unless I was asked.

"How much does Harvard Law School cost?" he asked, batting his stubby eyelashes in a strange parody of a coquette.

I pressed my lips together. "It's expensive."

"Answer the question, Ms. Crosby," barked the judge.

I sighed. "Approximately sixty-thousand a year."

"And is that with room and board?"

Again, I sighed. "No."

"And approximately how much does housing cost in Boston?"

I glanced up at Brandon, who was glaring bullets at Cipolla. Then I looked back to Cipolla. "Student housing at Harvard Law costs approximately fifteen thousand a year."

"Do you have any student loans, Ms. Crosby?"

I clasped my hands together. "I—no."

There was a slight intake of breath around the room, and immediately I heard a few murmurs arise in the gallery above.

"But that's just because I had a trust from my mother with enough to pay for—"

"You had a trust with enough to pay for my client's alleged loans to your father, along with tuition and fees, at one of the most expensive schools in the world?"

"Well, no, but that's because—"

"Can you tell me what this is, Ms. Crosby?"

Cipolla darted into another line of questioning before I could finish explaining that Brandon helped me pay off Messina. He held up a copy of the brain scan that had been included in the evidence compiled from my hospital visit.

I frowned. "Yes. It's my CT scan from when I arrived at the hospital after Mr. Messina kidnapped me."

Cipolla nodded and stared at the scan as if he were studying a work of art. "That's very interesting, Ms. Crosby," he said. "Can you tell us what the scan revealed?"

I glared at Messina, who was watching the interactions between us with more than a bit of glee.

"Objection. Ms. Crosby is not a doctor. ER 701, your honor."

"Sustained."

Cipolla looked a bit flustered, but reframed where he wanted to go: "Ms. Crosby, what is your understanding of your medical condition on the night of the incident?"

"I had a slight brain bleed from head trauma. A severe concussion from having my head bashed in by Mr. Messina."

Cipolla turned to me. "Now, isn't one of the side effects of a brain bleed potential memory loss?"

"Objection. Compound. Calls for ER 701 expert testimony from a lay witness. Move to strike counsel's testimony on the effects of her conditions."

Before the judge had a chance to speak, I answered. "I'm not a doctor," I said sweetly. "I don't know."

302

Behind Cipolla, Zola made a clearly irritated face. I wasn't being a very good witness—I knew better than to answer that question. Cipolla was getting on my nerves.

"You don't know..." Cipolla trailed off, and I had to grip the edge of my seat not to attack him for the innuendo.

"What about hallucinations?" Cipolla argued. "Or perhaps lucid dreams?"

I gritted my teeth. "Like I said, I'm not a doctor."

"Did you speak with any doctors about these possibilities?"

I waited a beat. "They did mention them. But I never—"

"And did you go to your follow-up appointments with your doctor after the alleged accident?"

I stopped, then looked at Brandon in the gallery, who was watching the scene unfold with obvious alarm.

"Ms. Crosby?" Cipolla looked at me with a look of faux concern. "I'm sorry, Ms. Crosby, did you forget the question?"

At that I glared. "Of course not, you *just* said it!"

Cipolla glanced around the courtroom, toward the jury and the gallery, as if to say, "this poor girl." It only infuriated me more.

"Let's try this again, Ms. Crosby," he said as he turned all the way back around. "Did you go to your follow-up appointment with the neurologist following your hospital stay?"

"I..." I trailed off as I realized just what he was doing. And there was nothing I could do to stop it. "No."

Cipolla smiled like a cat about to catch its prey. "And why was that?"

"I-I forgot," I admitted, as much as I hated to say it.

He cocked his head in sympathy. "And isn't it possible, that in an even shorter timeframe after your accident, in which symptoms for a head injury are that much more acute, you may have forgotten the actual events that led to the injury?"

"I-of course not! I know what happened to me!"

"How long after your abortion last May did you tell your fiancé about it?" Cipolla broke off onto a completely different line of inquiry.

My jaw dropped, and Brandon's eyes practically bugged out of his head.

"Objection!" called Zola.

"Counsel?" asked the judge, who no longer looked quite as bored.

"It's relevant, your honor, to the witness's credibility."

"Counsel, this is clearly character evidence in violation of ER 404. Move on, and you are on thin ice."

But the cat was out of the bag. This could hurt Brandon regardless of whether this asshole was allowed to continue.

"In your testimony, you alleged that Mr. Messina tried to rape you," Cipolla switched gears again, suddenly. "Was there a rape kit done?"

"No, but that's because he didn't actually do that—"

"He didn't actually rape you?" Cipolla reiterated with faux-surprise. "Just like he didn't actually kidnap you against your will or beat you senseless? Just like he didn't actually extort your family or harm your father? Isn't it possible that you may have just made the entire thing up to cover the negligence of your own health in order to win back your fiancé, whom you had just betrayed in a very public manner?"

"Objection!" shouted Zola. "Argumentative. Move to strike counsel's testimony."

"Skylar Crosby has a well-known history of misleading the public and her fiancé," announced Cipolla.

"This is well outside the bounds of impeachment and his allegations are not relevant under ER 609," Zola broke in once more.

"Agreed. Sustained," the judge announced. "Mr. Cipolla, you will stop badgering the witness. If this happens again, we will be having a conference in my chambers."

But Cipolla just turned to smirk at me as he walked backward toward his seat. "No further questions, your honor," he said.

The judge looked at me with something approximating pity. "You may step down, Ms. Crosby."

* * *

There was a short recess for lunch, and then we were called back while the prosecution continued its case, starting with Brandon's testimony. I had felt like I was going to be sick for the last hour, even though Brandon had tried to assure me that I didn't sound as terrible as Cipolla made me out to be. I wasn't so sure. Juries were fickle, and right now, I looked like the bitch who killed my lover's baby and tried to cover it up.

A general murmur sounded through the court as Brandon stepped up to the witness stand. Against the drab surroundings of the courtroom, where most people were dressed in varying colors of gray, black, and tan, Brandon's bright blond head, ruddy coloring, and his tailored, deep navy suit stood out. He looked every inch of his net worth, not to mention worthy of his current "it-boy" status in Northeast politics.

I watched as he answered the questions that he had rehearsed with Zola (and his own attorneys), detailing the moments of his exchanges with Messina. The debts he had repaid to secure my family's safety. The continued harassment he'd witnessed of my father, including our visit to the salon-front run by the man and the now-missing Katie Corleone, my father's ex-girlfriend. And, of course, the moments leading up to his final rescue of me from the abandoned building in the Navy Yard.

"And when you entered the basement, what did you find?" Zola was asking.

I tensed up. This was potentially the worst part of Brandon's testimony—the part where he had to admit out loud that he had assaulted Messina and his cronies in order to save me.

"I found my fiancée duct-taped to a chair, her face beaten black and blue," Brandon said in a voice that shook slightly. "She had a nasty gash over one eye, which was nearly swelled shut, and her neck, shoulders, and face were all badly bruised."

"Oh my," a woman sitting next to me in the gallery whispered, covering her mouth with her hand.

Brandon's eyes zeroed in on me, and I nodded slightly, hoping to communicate with everything I could my gratitude for what he was doing. For the fact that he had been able to find me at all.

Zola asked a few more questions before dramatically turning back to the courtroom, which had gone silent with Brandon's straightforward testimony.

"No further questions," he said before turning to Cipolla with a smirk. "Your witness."

305

Cipolla shuffled a few papers together, then wiped a bit of sweat off his forehead before he stood up to cross-examine Brandon.

"Mr. Sterling," he started. "You're from Dorchester originally, are you not?"

Brandon nodded. "I am." He grinned at the jury, where I had noticed more than one female juror staring at him with a lustful expression. "Same as Mark Wahlberg."

"And were you associated with men by the names of Douglas Murphy and Michael Larsen?"

At the mention of his friends' names, Brandon's expression lost all signs of humor. Behind his lawyer, Messina grinned. My heart fell into my stomach as I recalled the first conversation Brandon had ever had with the man. He hadn't revealed his own name, but he'd mentioned his friends' names as a way of establishing street credibility with Messina. These were friends who were still in jail serving time for a crime they had all committed together. Apparently, Messina had a longer memory than we'd given him credit for.

"Answer the question, Mr. Sterling," the judge prodded.

"Yes," Brandon said. "I was."

"And where are they now?" Cipolla asked, unable to keep the glee completely out of his voice.

"Objection your honor. Relevance," Zola said from his seat.

"Counsel, where are you going with this?" asked the judge in an increasingly irritable voice.

Brandon frowned. "They are incarcerated. At Suffolk County prison."

"For what crime?"

Brandon down at his lap, then up at me, looking incredibly sorry. "Murder."

There was a bit of an uproar around the courtroom, prompting the judge to bang his gavel again.

"I have here," Cipolla said, "original court documents pertaining to the jury. It says that Mr. Sterling was originally represented by a state defense, but gained new representation with a lawyer paid for by his future father-in-law, Stan Keith. Is that correct, Mr. Sterling?"

Brandon frowned, clearly annoyed. "Yes."

"And it also says here that soon after that, your attorney entered a statement from Miranda Keith into the record as an alibi for you. Is that also true?"

Brandon blinked. "I really don't know about the exact timing of all of it. I was a twenty-one-year-old kid. It's been a while."

It was a good diversion—not untrue, but also not a complete answer. The room tittered a little, showing it was still a bit more on his side than Cipolla's. But Cipolla kept chipping away.

"Seems a bit funny," he remarked casually. "You get a new fancy attorney, a girlfriend, and a new alibi all in one week."

"Objection. Speculation. Move to strike counsel's testimony," Zola said.

"Sustained," said the judge. "Mr. Cipolla, you will refrain from making conjectures about the witness."

Cipolla held up his stubby hands in mock surrender. "Sorry, your honor. I'm just curious. Because really, Mr. Sterling, how do we know that you're telling the truth? Particularly when you've had a history of tampering with the court system before this—"

"Objection!" yelped Zola, hopping out of his seat. "Speculation! Misconstrues prior testimony. In addition, your honor, this is outright slander. We will reserve a motion for sanctions."

"Fine," said Cipolla. "But if your fiancée was half-unconscious and barely able to remember anything that happened to her—"

"Objection!"

"I'll rephrase. Suffering from a head injury," Cipolla said before the judge could even correct him. "And you were the only one in the room at the time? How do we know? It's really just your word as a man who has changed his story once before in a court of law, against my client's, isn't it Mr. Sterling? How are we to believe anything you say?"

"Objection! Compound. Move to strike counsel's argument and his testimony!"

"Sustained."

Brandon didn't look angry. He wasn't smiling. He looked down, then looked up at Cipolla, pulling his phone out of his pocket. He looked like the cat who had caught the canary. I was utterly confused. How could he look almost...impish...when his testimony was being refuted completely?

"You don't have to believe it," he said. "My phone was on the entire time. My entire security team heard everything, as they said in their depositions, and as they will tell you when they take the stand after me."

The courtroom erupted.

"Order!" shouted the judge as he banged the gavel. "Quiet down, everyone now!"

But the damage was done. Quickly, Cipolla dismissed Brandon with no further questions, clearly frustrated by the way his cross-examination had panned out, and I was left wondering how Messina's shitty defense attorney had missed the fact that three different men had witnessed the entire exchange.

As Brandon stepped off the stand and walked down the length of the court room, he just looked at me, the slight ticking in his jaw the only sign that he was feeling any sort of stress. I raised my left hand to my lips, showing the smattering of diamonds around my ring finger as I tapped my mouth to blow him the subtlest of kisses through the chaos. His fierce expression didn't change, but the glimmer in his eyes told me he understood. He knew that I loved him. He understood how thankful I was that he had come.

Thirty-Three

A week later, on Thanksgiving, I stood in my new kitchen with Bubbe, Jane, Susan, and Ana while Eric, Dad, Ray, Pushpa, and Kieran all watched football in the living room. We had all agreed on a late dinner to accommodate Brandon's busy schedule, which had required him to be at a VA breakfast that morning, before jumping around to three separate photo-ops through the day. I had expected him home two hours ago, and everyone was getting very hungry, especially since the turkey was done.

"He'll be here soon," I said for the millionth time as I evaluated whether or not the dish holding the cranberry sauce was really appropriate. Frustrated, I pushed it aside. I knew absolutely nothing about being a hostess—every one of the dishes in this kitchen had been picked out by Kathy, the designer.

"Skylar, stop," Bubbe said as she opened the oven to check on the turkey, baster poised like a weapon. "He's a busy man. He'll get here when he gets here. Everyone is having a lovely time and enjoying my dip, so you don't need to worry."

"Really, honey, don't worry," Susan said kindly as she patted me on the back.

I sighed and slumped onto a stool at the counter. "I know. I just...I haven't heard from him all day. I'm worried."

What if he was crippled from something someone had said? What if he was freaking out in at a strange hall, crouched on the floor, literally rocking under the pressure. I checked my phone. No calls, no texts. Nothing.

"Let's focus on the good stuff," Jane said as she slid into a seat beside me. "Like the fact that I managed to come here instead of listening to my mother criticize my hair again for three days straight."

I shook my head. "I still can't believe you managed to convince her to let you go for a holiday. What was it you told her? A national conference for state's attorneys?" I snorted. "Don't you feel bad about lying to your mother on Thanksgiving?"

"Skylar, if you had been spending as much time with her as I have since moving back home, you would have told her you were becoming an astronaut if it meant getting a few days off without her nosing around." Jane reached across me and took a handful of the Chex mix that Bubbe had provided along with her dip. "Besides, you can just confess my sins for me now that you're a Catholic."

Ignoring the sharp look from Bubbe at the mention of my ongoing conversion, I just shook my head. "I'm not Catholic yet."

It was a work in progress. I continued to meet with Father Garrett every Tuesday and Thursday, and Brandon had even come with me a few times to satisfy the church's premarital counseling requirements. Brandon, of course, had managed to charm the pants off the priest, but Father Garrett still seemed less-than-satisfied with the level of piety and obedience I demonstrated. Apparently I asked too many questions. I, for one, was getting tired of being told to quiet my brain every time I stepped inside the church.

"What about wedding planning?" Jane asked. "Any more you need your maid of honor to do for that?"

"Or your grandmother?" Bubbe added meaningfully.

"Or your future mother-in-law!" Susan added with a tinkling laugh.

I shook my head. "Gloria is a force of nature. I have literally had to do nothing but give her a guest list. She's got it covered." I sighed.

It seemed impossible, but the one impending event that wasn't causing me or Brandon any stress was our big fancy wedding at Boston's biggest cathedral. Yet I scowled just thinking about it. No doubt the stress would come once we were closer to the big day next spring, expertly timed to coincide with the Suffolk County primaries. We'd be primped and posted all over the style section of the paper just in time for voters to check off Brandon's name for the election next fall.

Through the hall, we heard a few casual notes sounding off the big piano in the living room—a dark brown Steinway I'd chosen after Kathy had informed Brandon in no uncertain terms that the one he'd bought me did not go with the new house at all. I'd argued that it was silly to ask Brandon to purchase yet another expensive instrument (this was the third one he'd purchased for me), but he had just shaken his head and told Kathy to use the card he had on file for whatever piano I wanted.

Ridiculous man.

310

Bubbe turned her head as she tossed a salad, a smile lingering on her face as she listened to her son play. To my surprise, both she and Dad had refused the offer to live in the house or even the other guesthouse on the property, deciding instead to use the money from the sale of the Brooklyn house to purchase a place in Coolidge Corner, much closer to the T-line and only a few blocks from the synagogue that Bubbe had adopted.

As I sat there, the realization finally swept over me that things were really getting better. They weren't perfect, but for the first time in a long time, my life was starting to settle. This felt good.

Except for the one person who was missing.

As if drawn by my thoughts, the front door opened and shut with a jangle of keys. I hopped off my stool and skipped into the front entry to find Brandon shaking rain off his trench coat, looking weathered and tired in a creased suit after a day of campaign events. Cory and Hope stood behind him, also removing their coats.

Brandon looked up, and when he found me, his face lit up.

"Hey," he said softly as I popped up onto my tiptoes to greet him with a kiss. He wrapped his hand around my waist and pressed his forehead into mine.

"Long day?" I asked.

"You have no idea," he said. Then his head popped up as he took in the sounds and smells that permeated the house. "What's going on?"

I stepped back, clasping my hands in front of me. "We, um...we talked about it last week. Inviting everyone for Thanksgiving?"

Behind him, Cory and Hope looked curiously around the house––they hadn't yet been invited here now that the campaign's headquarters wasn't within walking distance of their boss's home address. Hope gave me a brief wave.

"Hi, guys," I said. "There's plenty of food if you're staying. Drinks in the kitchen, just that way."

I pointed toward the kitchen, and with curious looks at their boss, Cory and Hope both filed in that direction, presumably to get the glasses of wine they all looked like they needed.

"I, um...I'm just going to go change," Brandon said dazedly, and without another word, tromped up the stairs, pulling off his tie as he went.

I stood at the bottom, watching him go and wondering what had just happened. Then I snapped out of it and followed.

I found him in our bedroom, sitting on the bed, hands on his knees with his eyes closed.

"Hey," I said as I entered. "You okay?"

Brandon blinked his weary eyes open and smiled.

"Yeah," he said as he stood up. He turned to the bureau and started undressing. "It's just been a really long day, Red."

"Is this okay?" I asked. Brandon's back was to me while he stripped off his jacket and dress shirt. I tried not to be distracted by the bulging muscles of his strong shoulders. "That everyone is here? I should have mentioned it this morning. Or yesterday."

Brandon turned around, and I was shocked to find an unbearably sweet expression on his handsome face.

"Why should you be sorry?" he wondered. "I was surprised, that's all. I'm the asshole—I had forgotten about Thanksgiving. Anyway, I'm glad everyone is here. It's...nice."

Quickly, I crossed the room and put my arms around his waist. Brandon set his chin atop my head and played his big hands up and down my back.

"I'm glad you think so," I said before I pressed a kiss into the divot between his pecs. "My family is your family too."

My chin was tipped up by one hand, and Brandon looked down at me thoughtfully.

"Is that so?" he asked softly before covering my mouth with his. His tongue twisted delicately around mine. "You taste like red wine," he said as his hands slid down my waist, past the elastic waistband of my leggings. "And fuck me, you're not wearing any underwear."

His mouth found my neck, and his tongue twirled around the sensitive spot just below my ear. A finger slipped between my legs and into the warmth there.

"Jesus, you're wet too," Brandon said with a brief nip to my earlobe.

His finger continued its sweet torture while the other hand at my hip kept me stilled against his efforts. I tipped my head back up to the ceiling while his lips worked some magical voodoo at my neck.

"You think *our* family can wait while I screw my gorgeous fiancée?" Brandon murmured as a second finger joined the first. His thumb brushed over my clit, and my hips jerked in response. "Because *that* is what I need after this shitty day."

"Ummmmm," I muttered, too caught up in his deft touch to answer.

Suddenly, within a few seconds, his fingers withdrew, my leggings were yanked down to my ankles, and I was hoisted up onto a dresser. My bare legs dangled on either side of Brandon's waist as he quickly stripped off the rest of his clothes. His erection bobbed between us, rubbing between my legs over the sensitive spot that had me arching into his tall form while he wrapped a hand around the back of my neck and kissed me senseless.

"Shhhh," he said as I started to whimper. He finally found my entrance, just enough to make me moan again. "Hush," he said, and covered my lips with his as he pushed all the way in.

"Uh!" I garbled against his mouth, squirming against the sudden intrusion.

Brandon just continued to rock into me, one hand clenched onto my thigh, the other at the nape of my neck as he moved, twisting slightly to find the friction between his hip bone and my most sensitive spot. It didn't take long before I was already starting to clench around him—for whatever reason, we were both clearly dying for this.

"Not a sound, Red," he gritted out as he started to move faster.

The dresser bumped slightly against the wall, and I held onto his shoulders for dear life.

"Fuck," Brandon said in between several more torrid kisses. He drew back, and rammed into me again and again, going deeper with every thrust. "Not. One. Word. You want to scream? You do it in my mouth."

His tongue turned over mine mercilessly while he pounded into me. My fingers sought purchase on any part of him I could—his hair, his fingernails scratching into his back in a way that only made him arch and thrust into me even harder.

"Ch-christ," Brandon stuttered into my mouth. The hand at my thigh squeezed harder, and his movements increased. "I'm s-so close, babe. Are you—can you—com—oh, *shit!*"

A torrent of profanity escaped Brandon's mouth as my body suddenly squeezed around him. I squealed and bit into his shoulder as I came, and then he covered my mouth with his to shutter my cries, his hips working once, twice, three more times until he was able to bite my lower lip and groan as he emptied himself into me.

"Jesus," he whispered as he came back to himself.

It took me a solid ten seconds before I stopped seeing stars. "Yeah."

Brandon pressed a slow kiss to my forehead before he pulled away with a sheepish smile. We could hear noises of the gathering downstairs filtering up the stairwell—the clang of spoons on dishes, the occasional jeer at the television. I flushed.

"Thank you," Brandon said as he buried his face into my hair. "That was exactly what I needed."

I didn't say anything, just held the arms wrapped so tightly around my waist. There was a part of me now that just wanted to say screw dinner and kick everyone out for the night.

"Come on, Red," Brandon said as he pulled away, although he captured one of my hands and tugged me off the bureau. "Better get back downstairs. The natives are restless."

Thirty-Four

We came back downstairs to find almost everyone assembling around the large farmhouse table in the kitchen as Dad helped Bubbe carve the turkey.

"I tried to get them into the dining room, but your friends are very stubborn, Skylar," Bubbe said with an evil eye at Kieran and Pushpa.

Kieran just took a sip of her wine and shrugged. "Dining rooms always feel like mausoleums."

I glanced at Brandon. Did I want to know what that was about? He shook his head slightly and went to help set the table.

It wasn't until everyone was seated—Brandon, Bubbe, Dad, Kieran, Pushpa, Cory, and Hope—that I realized we were still missing two.

"Where are Eric and Jane?" I asked.

"They went for a walk around the property about fifteen minutes ago," said Dad as he eagerly helped himself to a giant spoonful of mashed potatoes. "Ma, this looks like heaven."

I pushed back from the table. "I'm just going to tell them that everything is ready."

It didn't take me long to find them. As soon as I stepped out the back door, I could hear them arguing. I sighed. This was really getting old.

"I told you, I'm *not* moving back from Chicago!"

"Jesus Christ, I know that, Jane. But if you're not, I don't see what the big deal is if I'm seeing someone else."

"Excuse me for having fucking feelings, Eric. I'm not a robot. It doesn't exactly feel great to walk in on you making out with your ex-girlfriend. At Thanksgiving, no less."

Oh. No wonder Ana had disappeared by the time I'd come back downstairs.

"Ahem." I cleared my throat and stepped further down the porch.

Jane and Eric stopped when they turned and saw me. They were about two inches apart, stiff with anger, although the way Eric was staring at Jane's lips told me he wasn't just thinking about their fight.

"Ah, hey Sky," Jane said as she took a few steps back, although she didn't stop glaring at Eric.

Eric, for his part, just cleared his throat and turned toward the lawn for a second to adjust his pants. I rolled my eyes. Men always thought they were being discreet when they did that, but it was so obvious.

"Everything all right out here?" I wondered. "Dinner's on the table, in case you were wondering."

Eric turned back around and leaned casually against the deck railing. He folded his arms across his chest. "I don't know. Is it, Jane?"

Jane crossed her arms around her middle and just stared at the ground.

"Right then." Eric turned to me, looking sorry. "I should probably go. Thanks for the invite, Skylar. And give Brandon my apologies."

I frowned at both of them, and then, with a glance behind me to make sure we weren't attracting attention from the party, I stepped out in front of Eric as he turned, blocking his path to the driveway.

"All right," I said with my hands on my hips. "I don't know what the hell is going on with you two, but this back and forth, will-they-won't-they bullshit has to stop."

"Sky," Jane started. "You really don't have to—"

"We got this handled," Eric broke in. "I'm going to go."

I pointed a finger and glared at him. "Do you? Because for the last few months, all I've been hearing from you is how in love you are with my best friend. But she comes back to another woman's underwear in your fucking sheets, and now you're parading in front of her with your newest conquest, who *also* happens to be my housekeeper. In my house. On Thanksgiving! Is that *handling* it, Eric?"

Eric gave me a dark look, but shoved his hands in his pockets and sighed. From where she was now seated on the railing, Jane snorted, and I turned to her with an equally withering glare.

"And *you*! What the hell is wrong with you? Do you know how hard it was for Eric to ask you to meet his parents? To fly to Chicago to tell you he loves you? The man has literally been wracking his brains trying to get through to you, which I *know* is what you want because I know you better than anyone else! You didn't fly out here

316

to spend Thanksgiving with me instead of your family because I'm such a fantastic cook!"

Jane opened her mouth to argue, but I kept charging on.

"Look at this," I said, gesturing toward the house, toward the people in it, particularly Brandon. "Look at me and Brandon. Don't you think that if *we* can make things work after everything we've been through, you guys can handle a few hundred miles for a while?"

"Not everyone is like you and Brandon," Jane said quietly. "As much as Eric and I like each other, Sky, it was never going to work. We both knew that from the start."

I found her watching me with something approximating envy. Eric's eyes were on her, but at her words, they dropped to the floor. He rubbed a hand across his mouth and then kicked at a nonexistent rock on the porch.

I opened my mouth to argue—I didn't believe her. Just like she had seen before I had that Brandon and I were right together, I could see the truth too—that she and Eric did work, better than they did with anyone else. Better than most people did.

But before I could say as much, Eric stepped forward.

"Jane's right, Cros," he said, though he couldn't quite meet my eyes as he spoke. "As much as we might want to, we're not going to be able to do the long-distance thing. I'm not going to move to Chicago, and she's not coming back to Boston. What are we going to do, see each other every other weekend for the rest of our lives? Even if we actually had that kind of time as new associates, it wouldn't work. It's just not realistic."

I wanted to argue that they *could* make it work. That if they loved each other like I knew they did, they could find some way to be together eventually. But as I saw them look at each other with mutual recognition and sadness, I realized that they were both resigned to the realities of their lives. Sometimes things just didn't work out.

"I'm sorry," Eric said as he took a step toward Jane. "About the...underwear." His mouth quirked on one side, and Jane's lips twitched. "And about Ana. I don't need to be hooking up in front of you. Crosby's right about that—I'm being a dick."

I cocked my head as Jane took another step toward him and wrapped her thin arms around his shoulders for a tight, brief hug.

317

"I'm sorry too," she said, just loud enough so I could hear her. She stepped back and took his hand. "I shouldn't have ghosted you the way I did, and I really don't have any right to be jealous now. It was immature and super lame."

Eric gave a sad smile, squeezed her hand, then let go.

"And don't worry about going home with Ana," Jane said as she stepped toward me. Automatically, I wrapped an arm around her waist, and she laid her head on my shoulder. "She seems really nice, and she obviously likes you. Plus, since she's Sky's employee, you really can't fuck with her—otherwise your boss will hate you and Sky will probably fry you for dinner."

Eric blanched, clearly considering that prospect for the first time.

"Just keep a rubber on it," Jane added. "It would be *really* poor form to give your boss's housekeeper crabs, okay, Petri Dish?"

The sadness on Eric's face disappeared, replaced with a droll smirk. "You trying to tell me something, Jane?"

"Me? Of course not," Jane retorted. "But I don't know where those panties have been. And since we know you don't change your sheets..."

"And...they're back," I said as Eric cracked a smile.

"I'm going to get a drink," he said. With one last glance at Jane, he stopped before he went back inside. "I'll see you in there," he said, and then walked away.

"You okay?" I asked my friend softly once Eric was out of earshot.

Jane laid her head back on my shoulder and sighed.

"Give me a day or two," she said honestly. "I will be." Then she stood up straight and adjusted her hair. "Okay, now I *really* need another drink. And if Eric's going to start dating the Brazilian version of Scarlett Johanssen, then I'm going to need more than water to get through the rest of dinner."

* * *

Some three hours later, after I had said good night to Dad, Bubbe, and Eric, I wandered back into the kitchen to find Pushpa, Kieran,

318

and Jane sitting in the atrium sipping on brandy with frowns on their faces.

"What's going on?" I asked as I sat on one of the window benches. Brandon, Hope, and Cory were missing—adjourned, it seemed, to Brandon's study down the hall. No rest for the wicked.

"Does he always talk to Brandon like that?" Pushpa asked with a cock of her head in that direction.

I glanced toward the hallway and back at her. "Who, Cory?"

All three women looked at me like I was stupid for even asking.

"Yeah," I said. "He does. What did he say this time?"

Kieran glared at no one in particular—if Cory had been standing there, the guy would have turned to ice.

"That town hall debate Brandon did last week," she said. "Apparently he didn't do so well."

I frowned. This was news to me. I hadn't been able to attend the event—a case of mine had gone to trial the following day, and I was stuck at the office. By the time I had gotten home, Brandon had been asleep, and as usual, he'd gotten up for his workout the next morning before I was awake.

"What happened?" I asked as I accepted a glass of whiskey from Jane.

"Does it matter?"

"Well, I think it might," Pushpa said in a much more measured tone of voice. "Maybe something happened that really upset the team. The truth is, we really don't know."

"Let's not defend that horse's ass, Push," Kieran said. "I've never seen him do anything but order Brandon—his *boss*—around like a little kid."

"Sort of like you do?" Pushpa chided.

From her perch on a kitchen stool, Jane snorted. I glanced at her, but she held up her hands.

"Hey, don't look at me. Cory didn't act like any more or less of a total asshole from the other times I've met him."

I looked back at Kieran. "What exactly did he say?"

Kieran glanced at Jane and Pushpa. "I'm terrible at impressions. Who wants to do the honors?"

Pushpa just snickered into her drink, but Jane got up and started pacing the room, shoving her hands deep into her pockets over and over again in the exact way Cory tended to do.

"What the *fuck*, man?" she jeered in an excellent imitation of Cory's slight New England cadence. "It should have been *cake*, man, but you *fucked* it up, just like you've been doing all the time, recently. You're even *more* of a fuckin' *moron* than I am, and that's really saying somethin'. But I know *fuckin'* morons, and you, man, are the biggest *fuckin' moron* of them all!"

It was a good enough impression, italics and all, that Pushpa was bent over laughing silently in her chair when Jane finished, and even Kieran was smiling into her drink. But as much as I also liked the impression, something stuck out.

"Did he really say all that, or were you just making it up?" I asked, thinking about the part where fake-Cory said Brandon was screwing up regularly, not just once.

"I added a bit, but the beginning was pretty much what he said. It sounds like he's been riding Brandon a lot these days, huh?" Jane hopped back onto her stool.

I frowned. I personally couldn't stand Cory—it was a big reason why I tended not to attend campaign events unless I absolutely had to. The guy was an asshole, and I frequently wondered if he exacerbated some of the issues Brandon had been having. But every time I brought it up, I was told in no uncertain terms that he was essential to the campaign.

"Brandon says he's the best," I said with a shrug. "And he is dedicated to his job—I'll give him that. It's just that he doesn't have a lot of patience with the other elements of Brandon's life. He wasn't too happy when the press caught wind of the trial, and he's even more pissed that we are taking the next week to go back down for the verdict."

"Gimme a break, Sky. Since when are you so forgiving of assholes?" Jane put in while Pushpa and Kieran just sent skeptical looks over their drinks. "You smacked Brandon for giving you too many gifts, and now you're letting this shithead walk all over him? No wonder Brandon's feeling the pressure."

I rubbed my arm, but didn't meet my friend's acute gaze. Jane pulled her glasses down and stared at me over the thick, tortoise-shell rims.

"What!" I cried finally. "Brandon's a big boy, and I'm not his mother, for Christ's sake. He doesn't want to stop the campaign, and he wants to keep working with Cory. What am I supposed to do?"

"Would he be okay with your boss talking to you like an idiot? If I know Brandon, he'd probably want to deck him?"

I glanced at Kieran with a smile. "I doubt it. *She* talks the same way to him."

"Not the same, and you know it," Kieran said shortly. "Brandon's basically my brother. I'm the only one allowed to talk to him like that. Period."

Pushpa smiled and rubbed her wife's shoulder. Surprisingly, Kieran softened slightly under her touch.

The sound of muffled shouts filtered down the hallway, and I cringed. I couldn't make out the words, but Jane was right—the way Brandon's campaign manager shouted at him amounted to verbal abuse. And for all of Brandon's veneer of confidence, all the people in this room knew the truth: that underneath it all, he was still very much a man who craved the approval of those he cared about. And he wouldn't have hired Cory if, on some level, he didn't care what he thought.

I pressed my head in my hands and groaned. Some Thanksgiving. Down the hall, a door slammed.

"And if that speech isn't fuckin' tattooed in your brain by the time you're back next week, I fuckin' *quit*!" Cory's voice shouted. "I've *had it* with this amateur bullshit!"

A few seconds later, Cory came storming out, with Hope on his heels. He gave all of us a black look, landing on me for a split-second longer.

"Thanks for dinner," he spat, sounding anything but grateful.

Without waiting for a reply, he slammed out of the house. Hope mumbled her thanks in an apologetic tone, and followed him.

Pushpa and Kieran stood up as if one.

"We should probably get going too," Kieran said. "Sounds like you've got some cleanup. Unless you need help?" She gave me one of her trademark, pointed looks.

I just shook my head. "I got it," I said as I stood up too.

Jane moved to collect our glasses and bring them to the sink.

"I'm heading to bed too," she said after giving me a quick hug. She was staying in the guesthouse so that she wouldn't wake us when she got up early for her flight back to Chicago.

After everyone had left, I stood for a moment in the kitchen, tapping my fingernails on the new marble countertop. The evening had started out so promising.

When I went into the office, I found Brandon sitting in his chair, staring moodily out the window that faced the lawn. Most of the leaves had fallen from the trees, and outside the rain was starting to come down heavily—a typical late November night.

"Hey," I said. "Everything all right?"

Without a word, Brandon raised his arm, beckoning me to him silently. When I came, he positioned me between his knees and against the desk, placed his hands on my hips while he laid his head against my stomach. Reflexively, I started to comb my fingers through his thick hair, and he sighed.

"Sometimes," he said quietly. "I'm not sure if it's all worth it."

My fingers stilled in his hair, but I just waited for him to explain. My heart thumped a few extra beats. I didn't think he meant me or my family, but a part of me still wondered. He just turned and buried his face into my skin.

"God, I love you," he murmured into me. He nosed up the hem of my shirt and kissed the bare skin underneath.

"Don't," I said gently as his fingers started to creep under the hem of my pants. As much as I would have normally let him have his way with me on top of his desk, this wasn't the time. "It's not going to help you solve your problems."

"But it might help me forget them for a while."

"That's called denial, babe."

I tipped his face up, brushed my hands over his hair. It was immaculately trimmed—Mary made sure it never outgrew anymore, always camera-ready. I twirled a short strand between my fingers. I missed his overgrown curls.

But his eyes were still wide, with that earnest vulnerability he never showed anyone else. It made me want to shelter him with my arms, protect him from the storm that continued to rage outside. And it really made me want to rip Cory a new one.

"Sometimes," he said, so quietly I almost couldn't hear him, "I think about what it would be like to quit. To stay here. Start a family. Tinker around in a lab. Just...be for a while."

I kept stroking his hair. "Can I ask you something?"

"Shoot."

322

I didn't say it right away, but the question had been bothering me for some time.

"Do you...do you even want to be mayor?"

Underneath my arms, the muscles in Brandon's back tensed. The hand at my waist curved around me, to hold me close. Maybe to prevent me from looking at him while he spoke.

"I..." I could hear him swallow, and the fingers at my back clenched slightly. "I don't know."

And then his chest caved a little, as if the admission relieved some great pressure on his body. Shaking off his hand, I tipped his head up so I could look directly at him. His eyes were as blue and deep as ever, but a small crease between his brows was furrowed deeply. He was worried, but I wasn't sure why.

"Then why do it?" I asked. "Just because they asked you to?"

At that, Brandon shrugged a little. His hand hadn't left me completely, just drifted back so he could toy with the ends of my hair. He followed the waves drifting over my shoulders.

"God, you're beautiful," he said.

I smirked, even though the words warmed me inside. "Nice try."

In return, I got a lop-sided smile. "I had to try, you know."

I didn't say anything, just continued to push my hands through his hair and over his shoulders, not willing to relinquish our eye contact.

"Do you know that your gaze is particularly penetrating?" Brandon asked, although his irritation was mostly a joke. He continued to play with my hair, and now I could see love intermixed with the fear in his expression.

"I'm here for you," I said quietly.

He sighed. "I know, Red."

"Then why do it? Why put yourself through all of this stress if it's not something you *really* want to do?"

"Are you saying I should quit just because it's getting hard?" Brandon scoffed. He released his hold on me and sat back in his chair, folding his hands behind his neck. "I'm not a quitter, Red."

"No one is saying that. No one would."

"That's exactly what they would say."

"And since when do you care what other people say about you?"

But then Brandon looked down, and I remembered that he cared very much what other people thought of him. Maybe not the random people in the city he didn't know—even though I also knew that he was as Boston-bred as could be, and to have his hometown turn on him for any reason would be incredibly painful. But really, he cared about his friends. He cared about Ray and Susan. He cared about me.

Slowly, I crawled on top of him so that I straddled his waist in the chair, then cupped his face to force him to look at me.

"Where do you see us in five years? Ten?" I asked as I stroked my fingers over the soft hair of his eyebrows.

He closed his eyes under the caress, leaning slightly into one of my hands.

"The governor's mansion?" I prodded more as I pushed back some of his hair. "The White House?"

Under my hands, Brandon shuddered, and suddenly I could feel his pulse through his temple.

"The truth?" he said. "The idea of campaigning like that practically gives me another panic attack right now." He sighed. "The debate didn't go so well last week."

"I heard."

He closed his eyes. "I kind of freaked out. I...honestly, I don't know if I'm really cut out for this."

I let my hands drop to his shoulders, and he leaned back, now searching my face for a response. I was trying really, really hard not to smile with relief.

"So...you don't want to be a career politician?" I asked.

Brandon cleared his throat. "God, no. But I made a commitment, Red."

"Brandon, there are four other primary candidates for your party alone. Don't you like any of them?"

He weighed his head from side to side. "I like Joe Ferris. He's a stand-up guy—from Roxbury, actually. But he has no money, just a few of the unions backing him."

"Brandon, *you* could help him." I bit my lip, trying to swallow the excitement I felt at even the possibility of getting out of politics. "I mean, if that's what you want."

Brandon smirked up at me. "Is that what *you* want?"

I softened and leaned down to kiss him lightly. His hands clasped my face, holding the kiss a few beats longer. Then I sat back up.

"I want to support what *you* want," I said. "I want you to be as happy as you make me."

"Come on, Red. You have to tell me what you want too."

But I stayed silent, just watching him, letting my previous words hang in the air.

Brandon rolled his eyes, but the tips of his ears turned pink with pleasure from my comment. "I don't want to be that rich guy who plays with politics. A fucking cliché."

"Who can also do just as much—maybe more—good with his money than any of the other schmucks," I insisted, pushing him lightly against his chest. "You and I both know that politics in this country is basically bought and sold. You can be the buyer."

He sighed, wove his fingers with mine, and then pulled me back down so I was lying on his shoulder. Under my ear, his heart beat robust and true, and his arms wrapped around my back, engulfing me with their strength.

Underneath that facade of strength, I knew Brandon was an intensely vulnerable person. But in the end, I couldn't make this decision for him—I could only be there to support the choices he needed to make.

He grunted, pressed his face into my shirt again, then sat back in his chair so I could see his face.

"First thing's first," he said with a lopsided smile. "Let's get through the rest of the trial, and then we'll see what happens after the campaign is finished. Who knows? Maybe I'll really like being mayor. Maybe it will all be worth it."

I gave him a small smile back, but I wasn't so sure anymore that the campaign itself wasn't the main source of his anxiety. More and more, it looked that way. Still, I didn't say anything. I figured he needed to make the decision on his own.

Thirty-Five

"It's true, what they say," I murmured as we sat in a diner with Bubbe and Dad the following Tuesday. "Attorneys really do make the worst witnesses."

Zola had called to tell us when the trial's final witnesses were taking the stand, and we had been in New York for the last two days, waiting for the jury to deliberate. The defense had finished making its case about my supposed mental breakdown and varying points of Messina's character. All of their witnesses had likely been paid off––the question was whether or not the jury could see that while they deliberated.

Now we waited for the jury to reconvene, which they had been doing for the last two days. Zola said he thought it had to do with the number of counts that Messina was charged with. The only question was really if their verdict would be unanimous. I hoped to God it would be—anything less would be grounds for a mistrial.

"God, I'm gonna miss this," Dad grumbled as he shoveled a forkful of home fries into his mouth. He pointed his fork at Brandon. "I'm comin' around on Boston, but there ain't any decent diners up there."

"Danny, keep your mouth closed," Bubbe snapped.

"That's what we got the bars for, Danny," Brandon said with a smile, letting his accent out a little with "bar" sounding like "bah."

I noticed he did that more around Dad, as if my father's thick Brooklyn slurs rubbed the sheen off Brandon's carefully practiced diction. In a way, I thought, it was nice. It meant that Brandon felt he could be himself around my family.

Dad just shook his head and took a long drink of the cheap coffee that had come with the six-dollar breakfast. Over the last day and a half, we'd been doing nothing but eating out at all of Dad and Bubbe's favorite restaurants while Brandon sat in the car going over campaign stuff with Cory via teleconference. Too worried to let Dad and Bubbe go off on their own without proper security (or even with it), Brandon and I had tagged along to all the spots in Brooklyn, Manhattan, even Queens to enjoy diner eggs, pastrami sandwiches at Katz's, cheesecake at Junior's, and kosher baked goods.

We had even ducked into Nick's the night before to hear Dad's old quartet play. They had picked up another keyboardist since Dad had left, and while I knew it hurt him to see someone else in his place on the stage, I also caught the way his fingers fluttered on the table when they played songs he recognized. His therapy was continuing to progress, and the doctors were now optimistic that Dad would regain his ability to play like he once could. Bubbe had mentioned a song he had written the week before when he thought she wasn't home. The thought made my own heart sing.

So, despite the reason that we were here, it really hadn't been a terrible trip overall. The New York press couldn't have been less interested in a Boston mayoral candidate. Although there had been considerable press on the day that Brandon testified, it had petered out since the Massachusetts governor had announced his intention to run for a third term. For the first time in weeks, we found ourselves without any kind of paparazzi tagalongs.

"Well, I for one cannot wait to get home," Bubbe said as she forked through her plate. "Look at these eggs. Like rubber! Nowhere near as fluffy as Zaftig's."

I had to smile. Bubbe had settled into Brookline, a largely Jewish neighborhood, like a bird in its nest. In less than a month, she had met everyone at her new temple and learned the names of every walkable kosher vendor around Coolidge Corner. It was funny—I had thought that transplanting to Boston would be harder on her than any of us, but in fact, it was the exact opposite. With a new house in a beautiful neighborhood, Bubbe was happy as a freaking clam.

Brandon stifled a smile while he drank his orange juice and squeezed my hand. No doubt he could see the pleasure all over my face, just like I could see it on his. It didn't escape me how much Brandon seemed to enjoy spending time with my family, even if it meant letting Bubbe pick at his clothes or sitting silently with Dad while they watched the Giants games (Dad would never give up his beloved New York sports teams).

But the jocular conversation was short-lived. My phone buzzed loudly on the Formica tabletop, and we all froze, staring at the familiar number on the screen.

I picked it up.

"It's time," Zola said in a hurried, hushed voice. "Thirty minutes."

A few seconds later, I set down the phone and looked to the other three people at the table, who were staring at me, forks held in mid-air.

"Jury's out," I said softly. "Time to go."

* * *

We arrived back at the courthouse in Brooklyn at eleven-thirty. I tried not to notice the weather, which had been threatening a thundershower all morning long. The scant trees lining the sidewalk in front of the courthouse had all lost their leaves, stark and naked limbs against the building. Wind, and cold splats of rain shook down from time to time out of the dark gray sky.

We weren't required to be here. We could have waited for Zola to call us with the verdict. Could have gone back to work and allowed life to keep going as if we weren't waiting on pins and needles to see if the man who had been trying to ruin our lives for the better part of a year was going to have to take the consequences for his actions.

But both Dad's and my therapists had continued to suggest it would be good for us to face our attacker one last time, and Father Garrett had encouraged me to do the same. I'd never thought I'd be taking life advice from a priest, but it seemed to make sense.

"You think they'll convict?" Dad asked when we approached the courtroom.

Zola nodded. "There's always the possibility of a surprise," he said. "A hung jury or maybe a mistrial. But I think the real question now is, what will the sentence be?"

We all glanced at each other, but no one had any answers—no pithy replies or confident statements. Because really, what else was there to say?

We took our seats in one of the pew-like rows of the gallery and stood as the jury entered, followed by the judge. Court was announced in session, and everyone sat down.

The judge shuffled through the papers in front of him for what seemed like an eternity. Then, slowly, he turned to the jury.

328

"Madam Foreperson, please step forward," he said.

The primary juror who had been elected to speak on behalf of the jury's decision stood up in her seat holding a piece of paper.

"Madam Foreperson," said the judge. "The defendant, Victor Salvaturi Messina, has been charged with five counts of racketeering, one count of kidnapping, two counts of aggravated assault, two counts of attempted murder, one count of murder in the first degree, one count of obstruction of justice, and one count of tax fraud."

He paused a moment, either to collect his breath or let the charges sink into the court. I looked around. During the trial, the room had generally only contained us, a few members of the press, and the other participants of the court. Today, however, it was packed with families and other witnesses—all of the people who had been affected by Messina's heinous actions.

"Madame Foreperson," the judge continued. "How do you find the defendant on the charge of murder in the first degree? Guilty or not guilty?"

There was a general intake of breath throughout the room, and all that could be heard were the hum of rolling cameras and the typing of the stenographer.

"Guilty," said the juror, loudly and clearly.

Behind the defense table, I saw Messina drop his head into his hands as the judge continued to read off the counts, and one by one, the juror continued to announce the verdict: guilty, guilty, guilty.

At last, he came to the counts that included my family. "And on one count of kidnapping," asked the judge, "how do you find the defendant?"

The juror blinked. "Guilty."

"And on counts one and two of aggravated assault?"

"Guilty."

From somewhere inside me, a knot was pulled, and a tight coil of stress sprang free. My chest shuddered as a harsh, noiseless sob pushed out. Immediately, I felt Brandon's arm pull me close as Dad grasped for my other hand, and on his other side, I saw him do the same to Bubbe.

We sat there, the four of us linked, as one by one, each of the other jurors confirmed the verdict as delivered. Around us, I noticed several other people hugging each other and blotting tears from their eyes. One woman collapsed completely into the man who had accompanied her. It was her brother, I gathered, who was the murder victim.

But it wasn't until the final juror confirmed the verdict, that the truth of it finally hit me.

He was guilty. They had found him guilty. No hung jury. No mistrial. It was entirely possible that the defense would still mount an appeal, but in all likelihood, it would be denied, and in a few weeks, Victor Messina would be sentenced to something in the neighborhood of life in prison.

On the other side of Dad, Bubbe wiped tears from her cheeks, and Dad just stared stony-faced at the back of the bench in front of us. After months—years, really—of enduring the stress of this man in our lives, it was so strange to realize that justice had actually been served. And maybe, just maybe, we would be free of him.

Soon the bailiff announced the jury's discharge and asked everyone to rise. We did, and Messina stood as well, his head bowed as he slowly, deliberately removed the tie from around his neck. He remained standing after everyone in the courtroom took their seats again. Then he set the tie on the table.

The judge flipped through the schedule in front of him for a moment, then gave Messina a hard look.

"Mr. Messina. Sentencing will take place on Thursday, December twenty-second, at two p.m. Bailiffs, please escort Mr. Messina to his cell to await his sentence."

We watched as two bailiffs immediately approached Messina, who in that moment, finally seemed to recognize that he was going to jail, and potentially for good.

"No," he yelped, as he shook off their arms. "No, I ain't goin'!"

"Mr. Messina!" cried the judge as he banged his gavel. "You will allow the bailiffs to escort you to your cell, else you risk being held in contempt of the court."

"I'm already in contempt!" he yelled, despite the way his lawyer continued to draw a finger across his neck, indicating clearly that his client needed to shut the hell up.

"I'm innocent!" yelled Messina, even as the bailiffs, with the help of two other officers who had hurried in from the jail, managed to encircle his suited waist again with the heavy, padlocked chain used for felons. Quickly, they cuffed each of his hands to the side of

330

the chain, forcing him to hold them awkwardly out from his waist like an angry penguin.

As they escorted him away from the defense table, they passed our seats, no longer blocked from view by the front row of reporters.

"You," Messina growled as he caught sight of us.

He pointed a sausage-like finger menacingly at me, even though his arm was inhibited by its chains. They clinked loudly with each movement. The courtroom had once again stilled as everyone watched his performance.

"This ain't the last you'll be seeing of me, Red!" Messina cried, even as the bailiffs continued to drag him out of the courtroom. "Danny! Brandon *Sterling*! You can believe that!"

Above us, the photographers were clicking away. I huddled into Brandon's side as the fingers on my shoulder tightened.

"Yeah, yeah, yeah," said the bailiff. "Let's go."

"It ain't the last!" Messina shrieked as he was yanked out of the room.

We watched until the heavy door was shut and locked behind him. It wasn't until I felt Brandon turn me fully toward his body so that he could wrap both arms around me that I realized I was shaking. Dad and Bubbe both looked positively white.

"Court is adjourned," called the judge.

"Come on, Red," Brandon said as he edged me toward the exit. "It's over."

Thirty-Six

Two hours later, I was back in the hotel room, packing up my things. Although neither of us said it, following the trial, Brandon and I were both acutely feeling the need to get back to Boston. I had gone straight to the shower and started packing. Brandon had left to run a few last-minute errands around the city before picking me up to leave—to go home, I realized. Something New York would never really be again.

I shoved the last of my clothes into my small suitcase and sat on top of it to close it. Just as I'd managed to get the zipper around the edge, the door to the room unlocked, and Brandon walked in.

"Hey," he said.

"Hey," I answered as I pulled my suitcase over next to his. "How did your errands go?"

"Good," he said. "And I managed to pick up a goodbye party."

He stepped aside to reveal two small children: Annabelle and Christoph.

"Skylar!" they both cried as they ran toward me, knocking me back onto the bed with the force of their hugs.

"Hi!" I squealed as I let them tackle me with kisses. "What are you guys doing here?!"

Brandon leaned against the wall, watching the scene with a wide smile. Then he walked in and sat on the bed next to us.

"I managed to sneak over to Eighty-Ninth Street after my meetings," he said as he wrestled Christoph into a half nelson and let go, much to the little boy's delight. "Janette said I could kidnap them for dinner. What do you say? Should we stay one more night?"

"I say..."

I glanced between the kids. We had planned to go immediately, and I had visions of flopping on the couch in our living room and watching *Amadeus*. I knew Brandon was supposed to be back for a breakfast event the next day, which meant we would have to leave at some God-awful hour. But one look at my two siblings, who looked simultaneously eager and terrified, changed my mind.

I smiled. "Madame Tussaud's and Gray's Papaya?"

Although they clearly had no idea what I was talking about, both kids threw their hands in the air and cheered loudly at the proposal.

"Are you going to stay in New York now, Skylar?" Christoph asked.

I smarted. His English had already improved a lot since the last time I'd seen him in July.

"No," I said. "I don't live here anymore. Brandon and I live in Boston."

"So, you're leaving?" Annabelle asked. When I nodded, she mimicked the motion to herself. "That's okay. People leave sometimes. Even us."

I frowned. "What do you mean, honey?"

"Daddy went back to France," she said wistfully. "*Maman* said we will not see him for a long time. And she says after Christmas, we are going away too, to a school a long train ride from New York."

I nodded. This was the same story I had heard from Janette. The little girl shrugged, but underneath her veneer of nonchalance, I could sense a sadness, one that that was clearer on Christoph's face. Their father was gone, a criminal, and they weren't sure if he would ever be back. On top of that, their own mother couldn't bear to be around them and was shipping them off to school out of state instead of keeping them with her.

In some ways, I understood why Janette was doing what she was doing. She understood her failures as a mother, and felt her children would be better away from her cold family. But I also knew what it felt like to pushed away by her. The kids and I would always share that unique pain.

My heart squeezed, and I looked up at Brandon. As if he could read my mind, he shrugged. It was my choice, he seemed to say. Whatever I wanted to do would be fine with him.

I turned back to my half-siblings. "I want to show you something," I said.

We sat down on the couch, and I pulled out my computer. I opened a screen with Google maps, pinpointing the location of their new school.

"This is Andover Prep," I said, pointing at the green spot on the map. "Your new school, where you'll start after the holidays."

Annabelle nodded sadly. "Yes, I know. Maman showed us this same map last week. She says she is only five hours from us." She shrugged again, an incredibly Gallic gesture I recognized from when I had lived in France myself. "Our last school we had to take a plane. This is better."

"Much better," I agreed. "Did she show you this?"

I typed in the new address of the house, and connected the two locations with driving directions. I traced the thick blue line as I spoke.

"This is where Brandon and I live now," I said. "And this is where you'll be at school. We're only thirty minutes apart, see?" I squeezed both kids, who were suddenly enraptured by the screen. "That's only the length of one episode of *Ninjago*," I told Christoph, who immediately lit up. "So, we'll be able to see you all the time."

"Looks like we're going to have some Little League games to go to in the spring," Brandon said as he smacked his hands together eagerly. "These guys are going to need to get into some sports and stuff."

"*Qu'est que c'est* Little League?" Christoph asked his sister, who just shook her head.

"*Je ne sais pas*," she said in her quick, snippy way.

"Oh, man," said Brandon as he picked the little boy up and swung him onto his back, provoking a barrage of giggles. "Do I have some stuff to show you."

"You'll spend Christmas with us," I told Annabelle. "And lots of weekends, okay?"

The child glowed when, after a moment, she nodded her head.

"*Oui*," she said. "Okay."

I nodded. "Now let's go get some hot dogs and stare at some wax people."

"Wax?" Christoph yelped from his place on Brandon's shoulder. "What is wax people?"

We all erupted in laughter, and Annabelle and I followed the boys out the door so we could show him just what I meant.

* * *

Later that night, after the kids had gone back to Janette's family on the Upper East Side, and Brandon and I were alone, I turned to him in the darkness. The hotel blinds were open, and the glow of the city shone through the window, an eerie reminder that in a city like New York, we were never really alone. Already I yearned for the peace of our property in Brookline. I missed hearing the wind in the trees outside our bedroom.

"I keep thinking about them at that school, by themselves," I said.

Brandon was turned away, looking toward the Central Park view. He waited a few moments, then turned to face me.

"Me too," he said. "They're so young."

I knew without asking that he was remembering essentially being abandoned by his parents—multiple times—by that age. One day I thought we might be able to take them in permanently, and I had a feeling that Brandon felt the same way. But that didn't need to happen right away. There was this feeling that for the first time in a while, maybe we could take things a bit more gradually. Maybe things didn't have to be such a rush.

"How did it feel today," he asked quietly. "Facing Messina like that?"

I lay back on my pillow and looked up at the ceiling. The events of the trial had been on repeat over and over again in my mind, always ending with Messina's nasty threat at the end. But he was guilty. He was being held, and then he would be sentenced in another two weeks. And considering the way he had looked at him at the end, I doubted the judge would be lenient.

"It feels good," I said finally. "I feel...lighter."

My therapist had been right. There was some closure in being here. I wouldn't feel completely at ease until I knew the man was locked away for good, but this was a start. A really, really good one.

"I thought so," Brandon said.

We lay side by side, looking up at the ceiling, breathing silently for a bit.

"Dr. Jefferson thinks I need to do the same thing," he said quietly.

I said nothing, just listened curiously. Brandon didn't talk much about his ongoing therapy sessions other than to grumble when his weekly appointment came around. But they did seem to be helping.

"He thinks I need to visit my father."

It was clear from the way Brandon said it that he didn't mean Ray. I turned again on my side. The moonlight cast a bluish glow over his bare chest, and made his eyes look almost alien in the dark. Alien and incredibly beautiful.

"I've never seen him," Brandon said softly. "Not since he went in again when I was a teenager. He's supposed to get out in two years. Did you know that?"

Wordlessly, I nodded. Brandon had told me about John Sterling on our first real date. I remembered everything.

"Why do you want to see him?" I asked.

Brandon sighed, then turned onto his side.

"I realized something this week," he said quietly as his hand pushed the covers down to my waist.

He brushed his hand over my belly, and up to rest in between my breasts, covered only by the thin nightgown. It was a move that was more sweet than erotic, resting his hand over my heart. He kept it there and looked back at me.

"What's that?" I asked.

"This trial...I saw how you felt. Free, right?"

I nodded again, but didn't say anything.

Brandon sighed, and his hand pulled lower, down to rest over my stomach.

"I felt it too," he said. "A little." Then he closed his eyes. "I want more."

"You think seeing your dad is going to give you that?" I had other thoughts about what might give that to him, but that needed to be his decision.

"Dr. Jefferson seems to think so." He opened one eye. "You can say it. I know you want to."

I took a deep breath and grinned. "I told you s—oh!"

A second later, I found myself tackled back into the bed while Brandon went to town tickling every part of my bare skin he could find.

"Ahh!" I screeched as his fingers dug into my side. "Uncle! I give up! Uncle!"

"Ha!" He collapsed back down on the pillow, satisfied with his victory, and used one arm to pull me close again.

The quiet of the room descended, and we both closed our eyes.

"I don't want to be mayor, Red."

At first, I wasn't sure he had actually said it. The silence between us was so complete, and he looked asleep. Had I imagined it?

But then, Brandon opened his eyes again and looked at me, an arrow-straight gaze of dark blue.

"Say something," he whispered. "Are you...are you disappointed in me?"

Immediately my mouth dropped. "What?"

Brandon shrugged, his gaze fearful. "I–you know–I've already put you through enough with this, and—"

"Brandon, I don't want to be the mayor's wife!"

The words jumped out before I had enough time to formulate them completely, and I clapped my hands over my mouth. In response, Brandon laughed.

"It was that bad, huh?" he asked with a wide, white grin.

I dropped my hands, then shrugged a little. "Well...I didn't want to say anything..."

"And I'm guessing you don't want a big Catholic wedding either?" Brandon said. "You, um, probably don't have to keep up with Catholic school if you don't want to..."

At that, my eyes bugged out, and his laughter filled the room.

"Holy shit!" he crowed as he rolled onto his back and clapped his hands. "Oh shit, baby, if you could see your face right now!"

"It's not funny!" I yelped even as I laughed myself. I sat up in the bed and proceeded to wallop him with a pillow, which only made him laugh even harder.

"Was it really that bad?" he asked between chuckles.

I rolled my eyes. "No. Mostly it's just...I don't know. It's a little fake, you know?"

"Red, why didn't you say something?"

I shrugged. "I was just trying to do the right thing." Then something occurred to me. "Do you still want to get married in the church? Or raise our kids Catholic? Because if that's important to you...I'll finish it. I was only ever doing it for you, anyway."

Brandon sighed, but still didn't wipe the smile off his face as he sat up completely. "Skylar, I don't give a shit what religion you are or aren't. You could be a Wiccan with a pentagram tattooed across your forehead, and I'd still want to marry you tomorrow," he said.

I rolled my eyes, but grinned anyway.

337

"Seriously," he said. "I'll have Margie call Father Garrett and tell him that you've had a change of heart. I'll tell him I'd rather marry an agnostic sort-of-not-really Jewish woman. I'm sure with the generous donation I made to the church, he really won't care whether or not you finish catechism."

I snorted. "*I'll* call him," I said. "It's the least I can do after making the man sit for hours with me in his office every week."

"I doubt it was a hardship," Brandon said as he leaned back in the pillows, pulling me down with him. "I doubt he gets many excuses to look at beautiful women."

I snorted, but let the joke fall between us.

"So, what do you want, Red?" Brandon asked before he pressed a quick, sweet kiss to my forehead. "No campaign. No conversion. We found our house. We're going to get married like the heathens we are. What happens after that?"

I closed my eyes, inhaling his warm, sweet smell.

"I don't know," I said finally, after he'd kissed both cheeks and my mouth again. "I think I just want to...be for a while. Is that okay?"

Brandon leaned in and kissed me full on the mouth, a long, tender kiss that meandered and wove a spell with lips and tongue. When he finally pulled away, I felt like I was floating a foot off the bed, even though I was still trapped in his arms.

"Being with you," he mumbled, "sounds fucking perfect."

He was just starting to kiss me again when suddenly there was a loud rap on the hotel room door.

Brandon jerked up. "What the..."

"Brandon! Open the fucking door, man!"

"Is that *Cory*?" I asked with disbelief. "What, does that guy have super-human radar? You literally *just* decided you were going to bow out."

Brandon shrugged, his big shoulders rippling. He pushed himself off the bed and threw on a t-shirt over his boxer-briefs before answering the door.

Cory blasted into the room with the turmoil of a hurricane.

"When I tell you to keep your phone on, that doesn't mean turn it off at five o-fucking-clock, man!" he yelled as he walked in.

I pulled Brandon's white button-down over my chemise while I got up from the bed. My nightgown was modest, but the thin material didn't leave much to the imagination. I wasn't interested in watching Cory's eyes drift while I told him where to shove it.

Brandon just watched his campaign manager pace the room with an exhausted expression "We were a little busy. I told you I would call you when we got back to Boston tomorrow morning."

"Yeah, well. That's not fuckin' up to you, is it?" Cory retorted as he whirled around, causing his tie to smack him in the face.

I frowned at him with disgust. It was eleven o'clock at night. Did this guy ever go anywhere without being dressed in a full suit?

"What are you doing here, Cory?" Brandon asked. I glanced at him, but he shook his head slightly. I understood—he didn't want to break the news of his defection tonight.

I bit my lip and looked down, knowing everything I thought generally showed on my face.

"What am I *doing* here?" Cory repeated, spittle flying. "Tracking down my rogue fuckin' candidate for one. You'll 'call tomorrow,' huh? After you've already taken three more days off during primary season? A day before you're giving the most important speech of the campaign?"

"You say that about every speech, Cory," Brandon said irritably. "Tomorrow is just a photo-op at the Children's hospital, not a televised debate."

"Goddammit, Brandon, that's just it! *Every* event is important. And I've *had* it, man! I'm tired of being your babysitter, tracking you down for every goddamn thing when you get distracted by your little sidepiece! It's fuckin' ridiculous! You two are *fuckin' ridiculous*!"

"Cory!" Brandon thundered. "Stop!"

"Whatever." Cory spun around, checking his phone. "You've got a breakfast in the morning. If we leave now, we can still get to Boston by three. And don't even try to argue with me. You're getting in the fuckin' car."

I pulled my arms across my chest, working somewhat unsuccessfully to trap the anger I felt bubbling up. It wasn't just that Cory had insulted me yet *again*—it was this, the way he always talked down to Brandon. And now I knew he didn't have to take it anymore. Neither of us did.

I looked to Brandon, who was close to seething himself. He caught my eye, and then I saw a glimmer that hadn't been there before.

"Can I?" I asked.

At that, Brandon smiled fully. "Have at it, baby."

"Cory?" I asked sweetly, disarming the man in his tracks.

"*What*?" he practically spat at me.

"You're fired."

Cory's rat face screwed up in confusion. He looked to Brandon. "Is she high? What does she think she's doing?" He looked back at me with disgust. "You're not my boss, lady."

"She's the boss of me. So I guess that makes her the boss of you, too." Brandon said in a genial voice. But then his expression turned hard. "Really, though. You're fired."

Cory's face turned white. "You can't be serious."

"I'm dropping out of the campaign, Cory. It was a mistake to enter from the start. Look, I appreciate everything you've done—I really do. But if politics means anxiety attacks every time I give a speech, and being constantly berated by someone who is *supposed* to be working for *me*, well, then...you and the campaign can both fuck off. I don't need this."

Cory looked back and forth between Brandon and me like he was watching a ping-pong match. "Are you...are you fuckin' *kidding* me?" he sputtered like a teapot about to boil. "You're going to turn down the political career of a lifetime to what...play house with Jessica Rabbit?"

"My name is Skylar!" I practically shouted.

Cory whirled around to Brandon. "You could have everything! I don't attach myself to losers, Brandon, and if you just got your head in the game, we could go all the way! The governor's mansion. The fuckin' White House! Seriously, how are you going to throw that away for a *garbage collector*'s daughter?"

And at that, Brandon finally appeared to lose his cool. In three swift steps, he had grasped the rodent-like man by the collar and had him pushed against the back of the hotel door.

"I'm only going to say this once more," he said in a voice that was much calmer than he looked.

For once, Cory kept his mouth shut. His toes, I noticed barely touched the ground.

"I'm done," Brandon said. "That's it. The campaign is over, and if you're smart, you'll take my reference and look for work elsewhere. In the meantime, if I *ever* hear you say one more fucking word against the love of my life, you're going to wish you'd never heard the name Brandon Sterling. You got that?"

Under his grasp, Cory gasped, but managed to nod with one last dirty look in my direction.

"Good," Brandon said. Then he reached behind him and opened the door. "Now get out."

And with that, he tossed the petty little man out and slammed the heavy door after him. When he turned to me, his shoulders were heaving, like he'd just completed a long run.

I stepped close enough to reach out and touch his chest. His heart beat wildly.

"Are you...okay? Are you upset?" I asked. His face was so stoic, I really couldn't tell.

Brandon just looked at me, and a half-second later, he smiled with sudden happiness so pure and clear, it was blinding. Then he tipped his head back and laughed, loud and long.

"Hell fuckin' *no!*" he shouted as he picked me up and hugged me. "I feel..." he dropped me on the ground and kissed me. "I feel free. Well, not totally. But on my way. And Red?"

I looked up at him, and he cupped my face, brushing his thumb over my cheek.

"Free," he repeated as he pressed his forehead to mine. "And it feels   great."

Thirty-Seven

A week later, we found ourselves sitting at a table at the Cedar Junction Massachusetts Correctional Institution, waiting for inmates to be called in for visiting hours. It was a dank, cement block of a room, with scattered tables and chairs that had been anchored to the floor. Anything in prison could be used as a weapon.

A few minutes later, the inmates who had visitors were led in. Most of them recognized their visitors and headed to their tables, where they were allowed to sit opposite each other without touching while the prison guards stood at the periphery of the room, heavily armed.

An older man hovered at the entrance, looking around with some confusion. But when his eyes locked on Brandon, sudden recognition flooded his leathery features, and he moved with sudden speed.

"That's him," Brandon said.

We both stood up as the man approached the table.

Even if I hadn't been told as much, I still would have known that John Sterling was Brandon's father. Somewhere close to seventy, with wrinkled skin from too many years of alcohol and drug abuse, his tall, lean form was still built like an ox. He had broad shoulders, muscular forearms, and a strong jaw line that persisted in a way most men's don't after a certain age—basically a carbon copy of his son's distinguishing physical traits, but even bigger. I could easily see how he would have scared the living daylights out of most people when he was in his prime. His gray hair was cropped short, but only thinned slightly at the crown, and he had a pair of bright blue eyes that might have pierced if they weren't so dulled from living such a hard life.

But that was where the similarities stopped.

"Well, well, well," he croaked, and then proceeded to hack for at least thirty seconds all over the table. He had a scratchy voice that spoke of years of tobacco usage. When he smiled, I had to fight not to recoil. The man's teeth were a wreck, stained and decayed visibly in several places, likely from years of extreme drug and alcohol abuse.

"Never thought I'd see the day," he said, as he looked Brandon over. "The boys in here don't believe me when I tell 'em you're my son. But here you are, lookin' like a million fuckin' dollars of dirty money. Or is it a billion? Eh, who the fuck cares? You're here, and it only took you twenty fuckin' years."

Twenty years of imprisonment had not done good things for John Sterling. But his voice was rolled thick with the same tones of Dorchester I had heard in Brandon's speech from time to time— flattened a's and open r's.

Brandon was a statue beside me, staring at the man who was responsible for half his genes. I had never seen a clearer argument for nurture over nature in my entire life. In just a few sentences, John Sterling had demonstrated that he was everything his son wasn't: petty, nasty, and above all, weak.

"How you been, Pop?" Brandon said in a voice so quiet I almost couldn't hear it above the din.

Sterling looked his son over with one eye squinted, as if testing to see if the benign question carried some kind of bomb detonator.

"How've I been? I been locked up for two fuckin' decades, and now them pigs just gave me another twenty on Monday."

"Yeah, I heard about that," Brandon said more calmly than I was sure he felt. "I'm sorry."

No one actually said out loud that Sterling had just been convicted for a brutal stabbing of one of his cellmates. There had been no trial, only a plea deal, since the man couldn't afford a lawyer. Brandon had informed me of it a few days ago, telling me I didn't have to come if I didn't want to.

"The man's a murderer, Red," he had said as we sat on the couch at home. "He's rotten, right down to it."

But there wasn't a chance in hell I was going to let Brandon face his worst demon without me there with him. Not when he'd stood by me as I'd faced so many of my own.

"It was self-defense," Sterling said. "You got no idea what kind of crazies are in here with me. He attacked me first. What was I supposed to do?" Then, as if the interrogation was over, Sterling turned his blazing blue eyes on me. The way they echoed his son's was more than a little unnerving. "And who's this foxy little thing you brought home to meet Daddy?"

343

In my peripheral vision, I saw Brandon's jaw tighten, but I didn't dare break eye contact with Sterling.

"I'm Skylar," I said.

"My fiancée," Brandon said tightly. "So you can show some goddamn respect."

"There he is, there's my boy," Sterling crowed, leaning back in his seat. "I knew there was some asshole in there somewhere." He winked at me, and I immediately felt dirty. "I bet you like that part, don't ya, sweetheart?" Before I could answer, he looked back at Brandon. "You gonna be a man? Make her take our name?"

Brandon didn't even bother to conceal his disdain. "She's a grown woman. Pretty sure I can't 'make' her do anything."

Sterling just snorted, sounding like a ball of phlegm was lodged in the back of his throat. "Seems to me a real man wouldn't let his woman chop off his balls like that. You gonna become Mr. Skylar, Teapot?"

I frowned. *Teapot?*

Brandon just gritted his teeth, though I saw his hand clench under the table. "Not that it's any of your business, but we'll both keep our own goddamn names, thanks."

"I'm surprised you're still Sterling anyway," Sterling said, without a trace of irony. "After forsakin' your ma the way you did for them kikes up in Somerville."

Brandon's knuckles turned white. Twenty-five years since he'd last seen him or not—John Sterling still knew exactly how to punch his son in the gut.

"Jesus Christ," Brandon muttered. "Their name is Petersen. They're not even Jewish."

"Ain't he a college-type? Same fuckin' difference," said Sterling bitterly as he pushed a big, calloused hand through his short hair as if feeling for a mane that wasn't there anymore.

Brandon sighed and mirrored his father's action. I shivered. It was clear that some things were bred in the bone.

"You want to know why I keep it? To remind me of where I came from," Brandon said. "And of how far I've come. That kid from the shittiest fuckin' home in the worst neighborhood in Boston can still make something of himself."

Something precious, I thought with approval. Something sterling. And it fit, too. I couldn't imagine him any different.

344

"Yeah. Well." The old man shrugged and scratched at a nick in the top of the table. "It's a nasty little trick, you ask me." His blue eyes squinted at his son. "I heard you pussied out of bein' mayor."

Brandon frowned. "You knew about that?"

Sterling cackled, low and cynical. "Of course I knew. You think I ain't been followin' my own son over the last twenty-five years?" He sat back, surveying Brandon like he was looking in the mirror. "You look just like me at your age. You got the blond hair like your ma, of course, but otherwise it's like seein' myself take over the world." He snorted again. "Another fuckin' life, huh?"

"Yeah," Brandon said. "I guess."

"So why're you here?" Sterling asked suddenly. "You ain't been to see me in over two decades. Why now?"

Brandon took a few breaths, reviewing the words I knew he had practiced with Dr. Jefferson all week. I kept my hand on his thigh, there if he wanted to take it.

"For a long time, I couldn't...I didn't..."

Sterling said nothing, just watched with something close to glee as his son stumbled over his words. I narrowed my eyes. What a horrible person this man was.

"I came here to tell you..." Brandon started again, trailing off once more.

"Spit it out, Teapot," Sterling said again, the teasing tone of his voice bordering on cruel. He looked at me with gleaming eyes—the brightest I'd seen them since we'd met. "You wanna know why we called him Teapot, cutie?"

I didn't say anything, which Sterling took as an invitation to continue.

"Brandon here used to have a speech impediment. When he was three, four, five, six. Any time he'd get worked up, he'd start sputterin' like a damn teapot, whistlin' and spoutin'." Sterling started to toot like a teapot himself. "Woo!" he cried out even as his muscular frame started to shake with laughter. "God, it was annoyin'. Cute sometimes, but fuckin' annoyin'."

"Yeah, well," Brandon muttered. "You'd be scared shitless too, if you were me, waiting for your dad to come home after the Sox lost. I was too busy wondering if it was going to be the belt or of the yardstick to be thinkin' about my fuckin' speech patterns."

By this point, those speech patterns had basically all but abandoned the r's in his diction. "Bar" was "bah," "yardstick" was "yahd-stick." It had taken Brandon exactly ten minutes of sitting with his birth father to regress almost completely back to his adolescence. Suddenly he grabbed my hand so hard my knuckles cracked.

Sterling stared at his son with a gaze like cold steel. All signs of levity, however crass, were gone. The standoff lasted several minutes, and I glanced at the clock, noting that already, half the hour had passed.

"Yeah, well," Sterling said, finally breaking first. "Someone had to toughen you up. I knew what kind of life you was headed for."

"Yeah, but that wasn't the kind of life I ended up having, Pop," Brandon said bitterly.

Sterling just raised an eyebrow. "You think I don't know you were runnin' around with them Westies? You think I don't hear news from the old neighborhood in here? Boy, I know *everything* about you—always have, always will."

"Not everything."

Sterling narrowed one eye, looking remarkably like a pirate. "Come again?"

Brandon sighed and ran both hands through his hair again. "Goddammit. I didn't come here to fight with you."

"Then what did you come here for, Teapot?"

Brandon closed his eyes, exhaled strongly, then opened them again, full of renewed determination.

"I came here to say that what you did to me and Ma was wrong," he said clearly. "You beat us and abused and abandoned us, over and over again. If you hadn't, maybe she wouldn't have needed drugs the way she did. I wouldn't have had to leave and find new parents, wouldn't have been as fucked up as I was. Ma might still be alive if it weren't for you."

John Sterling shook his head and grumbled something unintelligible under his breath. But surprisingly, he didn't argue. The creases in his forehead deepened as he took the words like lashings, and his jaw tightened, but he didn't say anything against a single one.

"But I also came here to say that I forgive you."

And at that, John Sterling's unyielding blue eyes lifted. At one point, I was sure that he had had a similar sparkle, a similar charisma as Brandon. Before years of violence, drugs, incarceration, and personal deterioration had taken their toll.

"You forgive me," he repeated, with an accent so thick it almost sounded fake.

Brandon nodded, and squeezed my hand again. I squeezed back. He wasn't in this alone.

"I can't forget," he said. "This isn't an invitation into our lives. You've done too much, damaged too much. But I can forgive you for the past. Life's too short to hold onto that anger, and I've got too much good in mine—" he glanced at me warmly—"to risk messing it up with things I can't let go."

Sterling looked between us like he was trying to decide something. He opened his mouth revealing stained molars with large black fillings. Then he closed it and nodded his head.

"Okay," he said.

Brandon frowned. "Okay?"

Sterling rolled his eyes. "What are you, a fuckin' parrot? Yeah, okay."

He reached back with one hand and gripped his neck, the action emphasizing biceps that still bulged, even after years in prison.

"I ain't stupid. I know what I did, and I'm payin' for it now, one way or another. I don't think just because you came in here, we're gonna have a relationship all of a sudden. Honest, I don't even know how we'd even start doin' somethin' like that. So I wasn't expectin' your forgiveness, but if you wanna give it..." Sterling trailed off with a shrug that somehow seemed anything but nonchalant. "Sure. I'll take it and welcome."

Before Brandon could answer, a short alarm bell rang out, and one of the guards announced that visiting hours were over.

"I'll try...um..." Brandon grasped again for the back of his jacket, clearly unsure of what to say.

I didn't even know what to say myself. "Nice to meet you" seemed completely inappropriate.

"Don't worry about it," said Sterling.

He reached out as if to touch Brandon, who flinched visibly. In response, the older man recoiled, and I wondered if maybe he really did understand just what he had done.

"See you around, kid," Sterling said as he stood to leave. He glanced back at me, all leering gone. "You too, Red. Go make me some cute grandbabies."

And then he shuffled out of the room in a line behind several other prisoners. We watched as he disappeared behind the thick gray doors. He didn't look back once.

* * *

Outside the prison, while Brandon and I waited for David to pull the car around, I stayed close, watching and completely unable to decipher what was on Brandon's face as he looked at the prison gates behind us.

"Are you okay?" I asked as I tucked my hand into the crook of his elbow.

He glanced at me with a queer smile. "Yeah, I think so. I was just thinking..."

"About what?"

"About...how close I came to being here." Brandon chewed for a moment on his lower lip. "Slip of fate. That I met Ray and Susan. Stan. Miranda." He paused. "You."

"You would have never ended up in there," I said as we looked back at the nondescript building together.

"'Murder...just a shot away'," Brandon quoted.

"The Rolling Stones?" I cited, unbelieving. "Are you actually listening to something else besides Springsteen, Mr. Sterling?"

Brandon just grinned, a thousand-watt smile that lit up the otherwise cold gray day. He tossed a heavy arm over my shoulder and pulled me tight into his side so he could kiss the top of my head.

"Gotta start somewhere, Red," he said, and proceeded to hum— in a very off-key pitch—the refrain to "Beasts of Burden."

The song transported me back to a night almost a year ago now––a freezing, stormy night when the city had been covered with snow. When I'd fled a bar full of entitled, egotistical young men and found myself trapped in the home of a lonely, isolated, soulful tycoon. Never in my life could I have predicted where we'd have ended up.

348

"You know, the more I think about it, the more it doesn't matter," Brandon said with one last look at the prison before we got into the car. Then he turned back to me, his eyes practically glowing with happiness. "Any path I take leads to you, Red."

Oh, how he was right. Any direction we went did lead back to each other. There was nowhere else to go.

I pulled him down for a brief kiss, relishing the way his lips lingered on mine for a minute, warm against the chilly December air.

"One more stop," Brandon said. "And then we can go home."

Thirty-Eight

It ended up being a day for more than just one catharsis. Maybe it was because Christmas was just around the corner, or maybe it was because, as of the new year, Brandon would officially have nothing else to do but serve as a name partner at a firm at which he no longer had any clients. But the day of personal cleansing continued when he asked David to drop us in Cambridge instead of driving all the way into Brookline.

"What are we doing?" I asked after David drove off, leaving Brandon to lead me to the nearest T-station, the red line stop off Kendall Square.

I had to smile a little—it was the same station where I'd insisted on going on our first real date, the one he said made him feel like he was himself again. This was also the first time in months we hadn't been accompanied by a bodyguard. Another weight lifted. Freedom.

Brandon said nothing, just swiped his Charlie card—the one I knew he'd bought that very night—with a half-smile, and waited patiently as I swiped mine. Then he took my hand and led me down into the depths of the station.

"I want to show you something," he said. "I want a fresh start with you. New house. New life. Dr. Jefferson says I never said goodbye to the old. Will you come with me?"

I didn't need to think twice.

For once, the train was quick to arrive. It was a Friday evening, so we were quickly swallowed by students heading to parties at Northeastern and UMB, or commuters from the MIT campus on their way to the other side of the city.

Brandon was quiet the entire ride as we stood in the slowly dispersing crowd. He held the bar over the seats with one hand, the other wrapped firmly around my waist, protecting me with his big body. I didn't fight it or insist on conversation. The hum of the train, the clamor of the people; it was enough for now, while I knew he was still processing the visit with his father.

Slowly, more and more people filtered off until all that was left were the stragglers—the construction workers, the waitresses, the people who were really the salt of Boston's earth.

The train continued to rumble out of the underground tracks and on to later stops. UMass. Savin. When the conductor announced our arrival at Field's Corner, Brandon squeezed my hand, and I finally realized just what we were doing. This was his old neighborhood, the one he hadn't returned to in over fifteen years. Why we were here, I had no idea, but I followed him off the train without a word.

He led me onto the platform, pausing for a moment to look around.

"Well, this is new," he murmured as he took in the gleaming new station, with its steel beams and relatively clean floors. But it didn't take long for him to regain his bearings, particularly once we were outside.

I had been close to Dorchester a few times before, mostly to visit friends who lived in the neighborhood or somewhere close. But they lived on the side by the harbor, by UMB; I hadn't ever ventured this deeply into South Boston, the part that was still economically depressed and fairly rife with crime.

Brandon kept me pinned to his side as he strode down Dorchester Avenue. It wasn't the stereotypical Irish, working-class neighborhood you would see in Ben Affleck films. There were shades of that, but Fields Corner was actually incredibly diverse—I saw almost as many Vietnamese restaurants scattered around as Irish pubs.

"Was it always like this?" I asked as I pointed at a pho restaurant that looked like it had been there a while. Somehow, I couldn't really imagine John Sterling enjoying bowls of vermicelli.

"What?" Brandon followed my finger. "Oh, you mean the Vietnamese places? It started when I was kid. My dad didn't like them much, when they were first popping up."

He then turned down a residential street, and then another. I trotted beside him, taking in the neighborhood that bore a lot of signs of gentrification, but was still mostly comprised of dilapidated row houses, colonials and walk-up apartment buildings with peeling paint and chain-link fences. The pastel colors of most of the buildings seemed to be a joke, tagged with graffiti or just peeling completely off.

The street steadily became emptier and emptier, and I noticed more than once Brandon keeping his head low any time we passed others. Was he afraid of running into someone he knew? Was it because he thought they would recognize him? In his jeans and parka, Red Sox hat pulled low over his face, he looked exactly like most of the other people pacing through the streets.

Then, at last, we stopped, so quickly that I walked straight into Brandon's shoulder. He cracked another half-smile as I rubbed my nose.

"You could give a girl a little warning there, Sterling."

"Sorry," he said guiltily. "We're here."

It was a townhouse, probably about four or five stories high, although it had clearly been split into multiple apartments. There wasn't a surface on it without peeling paint, and at the edges of the plain, sturdy trim and gutters, I could see evidence of mold and moss growing. Dilapidated satellite dishes hung crookedly off several balconies. The chimney that ran up the left side of the building was crumbling, and the chain-linked fence out front was half-smashed to the pavement in one spot.

"Is this where..."

Brandon nodded. "This is where I grew up, Red."

We stared at the old place in silence. It was one thing to know that Brandon was born into abject poverty, that he had experienced extreme neglect and abuse at the hands of his parents. It was another to actually meet the man who had done the abusing, and then see the place where it had happened.

Fury started to mount inside me like lava in a volcano. Suddenly, I was shaking and red, my hands clenching and unclenching at my sides. I knew no one related to Brandon lived in this building anymore—more likely it was full of hip college students looking to be adventurous on the cheap. But behind the crooked fence, I could see so clearly a beaten little boy. Behind those doors, I could see the child who was locked in his room for hours, even days at a time, left to rock himself to sleep.

It wasn't until Brandon wiped my tears off my cheeks that I even realized I was crying. I hurled my arms around his neck, and he caught me easily, holding me flush against his body so that my feet dangled off the ground.

"You're safe now," I murmured into his ear. I couldn't seem to hold him tight enough. "You're safe with me."

He sighed, squeezed me just a little tighter, then slowly set me down.

"I know, Red," he said with a small smile and eyes that shined, even as pain touched their edges. "I know I am."

And when he looked at me, I realized he really spoke the truth. For the first time in months—maybe during the entire time I'd known him—Brandon finally felt safe in his life. My heart swelled. I couldn't have wanted anything more.

Brandon pulled my palm up and kissed the top, then looked back at the house. "Time to say goodbye, like Dr. Jefferson said."

And so, we let the house's presence seep into both of us while a few people walked by, looking on curiously. The sounds of car horns and a rumbling train faded into the background. We stood while Brandon absorbed the place of his youth, a catalyst for so much pain and suffering, then and now. He closed his eyes and took a deep breath. And then he turned to me.

Suddenly I was embraced again, so tight I could hardly breathe. Brandon buried his nose in my hair and inhaled.

"Ah, baby," he kept saying, over and over again, his native Boston accent coming out maybe the thickest I'd ever heard it. "Skylar. Baby. I love you, Red. I love you so fucking much, you beautiful, crazy, stubborn, incredible woman."

It was only when his arms loosened slightly that I was able to look up and see the utter happiness emanating through his incredibly blue eyes. When Brandon was happy, he could outshine the sun. He pressed a kiss on my lips, then another, then another, again and again until I was laughing almost hysterically against the onslaught.

"Ah!" I cried. "Wait! Stop!"

"No," Brandon said in between another several rounds of kisses, landing them all over my face, my eyebrows, my cheeks, even my chin. Finally, he landed one more on my mouth, which turned into something slower, and just a little bit wicked.

"You," he said when he released me again. "Thank you."

"For what?"

"For everything." Brandon chewed on his lower lip, recalling some unseen memory. "You gave me a family again, Red," he said softly. "You. Bubbe. Danny. Annabelle. Christoph. Ray. Susan." He pulled my hands to his lips and kissed them, long, but soft. "I'll never be able to repay you for it, Skylar. But I'll never stop trying." Then a few beats softer: "I sold my stake at the firm."

353

For a second I thought I was hearing things. I hadn't said a word to him about it—had been mentally preparing myself for years of battling Brandon's anxiety with a cadre of doctors, therapists, possibly even medication as he dove back into the high-stress life of a litigator. That had been his plan—to start working more at the family law clinic he funded through Harvard and take on more defense cases at the firm. I still wasn't sure it was what he wanted, but I was determined to support it, no matter what the cost. He had given me and my family everything. The least I could do was give him all of myself.

But now...

Brandon took both of my hands in his and swung them lightly between us. "It's killing me, Red. It's killing us."

I gulped. "But the firm was your dream..."

Brandon shrugged and looked at the townhouse. "It was...maybe like everything else I've done...an opportunity. When you come from nothing, you're conditioned to think you can't turn down opportunities when they show up, because you think it'll never happen again." He looked back to me. "But I think I was looking for something, Red. Something I've been looking for my whole life and never had until I met you." He gave a shy smile. "I don't have to chase anymore, Skylar, because I have everything I'll ever need. Because of you."

He gave another adorable half-smile that brought out his dimples. My heart squeezed.

"But...you don't think...Brandon, you were made to lead. Anyone can see that," I protested. I had only just gotten my head wrapped around it—how could he let his entire life go so easily?

He just shook his head good-naturedly. "I was made for one thing, Red," he said as he pulled me close. "To love you." He pressed a gentle kiss on the top of my head. "I signed the papers last night. The press release went out today. It's done."

Then I realized something else: there had been no nightmares for the last week. None since we got back from New York, since he had told Cory where he could put it. No nightmares. It couldn't be a coincidence.

But another thought occurred to me.

"What will you *do*?" I wondered. "You're like the Energizer Bunny with an enormous brain. Brandon, you're going to be bored to tears if you don't work."

Brandon shrugged. "I'll set up a new lab at the house. Who knows, maybe I'll even take some classes again. But you want to know the truth? I'm kind of excited to take a break. Think about what I really want to do next." His blue eyes twinkled. "I'm excited to see my wife soar instead."

His words caused my skin to tingle all over. We stayed like that for what seemed like hours, wrapped up in each other's arms, nose to nose, blue eyes staring into green. Tears welled up in my eyes; I hadn't known just how badly I'd wanted him to say the words until I heard them come out of his mouth.

"Thank you," I whispered. "Thank you so much."

His lips touched mine softly at first, then a bit more insistently. For the first time, it didn't feel like we were chasing something away, it felt like we were uniting as one front in this crazy life. His tongue touched mine, and I opened willingly. If he wanted me, he could have all of me.

Unfortunately, we were suddenly interrupted by the loud buzzing of Brandon's phone.

"Shouldn't that thing ring less if you're unemployed?" I joked as Brandon pulled it out.

He smirked, but swiped right anyway. "Sterling."

Almost immediately after the person on the other end started talking, Brandon's smiling face dropped to a frown. "*What?*" He grabbed for my hand as he spoke, pulling me close so I could hear the conversation.

"Victor Messina." The clear voice of Matthew Zola rang through the tinny speakers. "I'm so sorry. He was sentenced this morning. Thirty years, but right now, it doesn't matter. He's gone."

I reared back in alarm, but Brandon gestured I should stay quiet while he spoke.

"How does something like that happen?" he demanded. "How does a convicted criminal break out of a prison transport?"

"We're looking into it," was all Zola said. "Most likely one of the guards was on the take, but he killed both of them before we could find out. Look...I don't know where you guys are—"

"Dorchester," Brandon said, now looking around like he expected Messina to pop out of one of the trashcans.

"Is your security with you?"

My eyes widened, and Brandon gripped my shoulder, practically telegraphing with his touch that it was going to be okay.

"No," Brandon said, "but they're on their way."

"Get to your house and stay there," Zola replied. "I'll let you know when he's found. There's only so far you can go with a giant chain around your waist."

Brandon hung up and immediately tucked me closer.

"H-he escaped?" I stuttered, suddenly feeling as if my heart was going to pound out of my chest.

"It's going to be all right," Brandon said as he punched a message into his phone. "Craig's on his way. We'll be home, and they'll get this sorted out. I promise, Red."

"Well, ain't that touching."

It might have been the scent of rotting garbage that only exists in the city in late summer, but I swear I could smell him before I saw his blubbery, greasy face. My entire body seized in fear, and in a split-second, all of the warmth and love of the day was gone. I'd know that nasty voice anywhere.

The voice of Victor Messina.

Thirty-Nine

"Skylar," Brandon barely breathed in a low voice. "Get behind me. Now."

Instead, I turned around in his arms to face the owner of that voice. He was the man who still crept into my dreams from time to time, the man who had violated, in some way, nearly everyone who was important to me. Even though I knew he'd be standing there, my heart still lodged in my throat when I saw Victor Messina's rotund, sweaty shape leaning on the chain link fence across the street. In the mid-December air, his nose was red, and his knuckles were chapped. He was alone and looked a little worse for wear in a pair of ill-fitting brown pants that had stains on the thighs and a t-shirt that was yellowed under the arms and too tight. Stolen clothes for a man on the run.

His wrists still bore the marks of handcuffs, and there were scrapes up and down his forearms. Zola had said he had escaped in transit—had he actually thrown himself from a moving vehicle?

"It's too late, Victor," Brandon said as he pulled my frozen form roughly behind him and started to back us down the sidewalk. I began to shake. "They're going to find you—you know that. I don't know what you're doing here, but I can help. Get you a new lawyer. Get you out of the country if that's what you want."

Messina scoffed, his doughy face practically turning itself inside out with the motion.

"Whadda you take me for?" he asked. His voice was slurred, like he'd been drinking. "Some kinda idiot? Think I'm gonna believe the same people who been tryin' to lock me up are gonna get me off?"

He smirked down at the pavement, like he had a sidekick with whom he was sharing a private joke.

"You believe this guy?" he asked the nonexistent person.

I gripped Brandon's shoulder and fumbled in my pocket for my phone. It was on silent, but I was able to call 911 and stick it back in.

"I was just in the neighborhood, catchin' up with some old friends," Messina was saying. "You know, some'a them remember you, rich boy. They remember when you was one'a them. But you ain't one no more, are ya?"

"I'm just like you, brother," Brandon started to say, pulling out his accent, which wasn't hard since he'd slipped into it pretty easily since we'd stepped off the train anyway.

"I AIN'T YOUR BROTHER!" Messina shouted, suddenly whipping a gun from behind his back.

Brandon and I both froze, his hands still holding me behind him by the waist.

"You think I don't see you back there, Red?" Messina asked. "Come on out, sweetheart. I don't mind shooting pretty boy here to get to you, doll face."

"Don't," Brandon hissed over his shoulder. His face was calm, but the fingers on my hipbones were gripping hard enough to bruise.

There was no way I was going to stand behind Brandon while there was a gun pointed at us. At him. Forcefully, I pushed his hands off me and slipped around to face my accuser.

"What do you want?" I asked, willing my voice not to shake. I failed miserably.

Messina pointed the gun at me as he walked across the street and stood in the middle of the road.

"What do I want?" Messina repeated. "What do I *want*? Well, I'll tell ya, Red. I wanna go back to my own life. I wanna go back to when I didn't have no cops sniffin' around every little deal I made, thanks to you and your fuckin' family." He turned his head and spat profusely. "Danny ain't never been worth the trouble he is. I shoulda just finished him off like they did his dad."

The mention of my grandfather sent a cold shiver through my spine. His death had been ruled a suicide, but we had always known something had been off about it. His own gambling addiction, and his involvement with the Messina crime family to pay his debts, had been suspect.

"I was there, you know, when they did your grandpa," Messina said as he took another few steps closer. "Just a kid myself, but not so young I couldn't help out." He smiled, a wicked, nasty leer as he looked through me toward some distant scene. "He cried like a baby, at the end, you know that?" He clicked his tongue and shook his head. "It's always the fingernails that do 'em. He held out like a man through all the punches, all the heavy blows. But once we started yankin' out them fingernails, he was cryin' like a little girl."

Then Messina looked back at me.

"Wonder what kinda sound you'd make if I pulled out them pretty manicured nails, Red," he said with a nod at my hands.

I clenched at the pockets of my coat, praying that the 911 operators were hearing all of this through the wool fabric.

"I don't know," I said as I stepped to the side. "You almost had me at one point."

In his daze, Messina rotated with me as he kept the barrel of the gun trained right on my face. "So I did, so I did. In more ways than one, didn't I, green eyes?"

He took another step forward, and I had to steel myself not to move. A few steps away, Brandon's entire body tensed, poised for attack. I just needed to rotate Messina a little more...

"Katie seemed to like you," I said, biting back the retorts lodged in my throat as I shuffled a few more inches to the right. I couldn't afford to enrage the man unless I wanted a bullet in my skull. "Maybe I would have too."

Brandon looked like his head was about to burst off, but he still made no sound. Messina just cocked his head to the right, examining me with eyes that were thin slits.

"You're full of shit, Red," he finally pronounced.

Damn me and my glass face.

"I don't know..." I tried again, shuffling further. "Haven't you ever heard of Stockholm Syndrome?"

Messina laughed, a long low creak that seemed to echo around the neighborhood. I glanced around. Were there seriously *no* people around who were hearing this?

"You got jokes," Messina pronounced with a slow nod. "You think you're funny? Well, Raggedy Ann, let's see how funny you are when you're dead. First you, then him. Then I'll go after your precious grandma and your daddy. *Then* we'll see just how *fuckin'* funny you are!"

At that, I heard the telltale click of the loading chamber echoing down the block.

"No!" As if the gun set off the start of a race, Brandon sprang forward with a roar, tackling Messina to the ground and sending the weapon skidding across the pavement.

"Brandon!" I yelped.

"What the fuck!" Messina yowled as Brandon tried to wrestle him down to the ground.

359

But despite the fact that Brandon had several inches and much more muscle on him, Messina was scrappy and desperate, a dangerous combination in this kind of fight. I watched in horror as they rolled across the pavement, a mass of elbows, knees, grunts, and punches.

"Help!" I shouted, finally finding the presence of mind to pull out my phone and shout my location to the operator. "Hi—Hello? Oh, thank God you're there...We're in Field's Corner...on..." I looked around frantically toward the street signs at the end of the block. "Leonard. Off... Clayton—Hey!"

My phone was knocked out of my hand when I was knocked over by the writhing mass of limbs. Both Messina and Brandon were going at each other with everything they had. My heart skipped a few beats as Brandon endured a nasty punch to his kidney, but he managed to roll Messina over with just enough time to land a right jab to his swollen neck.

I scrambled around, looking for my phone, but in the distance, I could already hear sirens. That was the good thing about being in a shitty neighborhood—there were always cops nearby.

"Give it up, you piece of shit! It's...*over*!" Brandon shouted as he toppled over Messina one last time only to be tripped once more.

"Fuck...*you*!" Messina heaved, as he twisted over Brandon and threw his entire body around him. He was weak and tired, but desperation will make men strong.

"The gun, Skylar!" Brandon shouted as he fought off Messina. "Get the gu—AH!"

I watched in horror as Messina rolled off a suddenly limp Brandon, his dank shirt dark with sweat and blood. And not his blood, I realized in horror as I saw Brandon curled onto the pavement, clutching his side. His coat lay open to reveal a bright red stain seeping into the white of his T-shirt.

Brandon looked up, his bright blue eyes clouded with pain. His face looked gray.

"Brandon!" I cried as I crouched down to him. "Oh shit, oh my God!" The words came out like whimpers as I hovered over him. "What do I do? What do I do? Pressure, right? We need to put pressure on the wound."

I continued to babble while I tried to staunch the blood. But Brandon managed to shake his head, even as he pushed his own hands tightly over the bloody spot.

"Knife," he managed to choke out. "Still. Has it."

I twisted to where Messina lay on the ground, cradling his own arm. Torqued in an unnatural position, I guessed it was dislocated, and his face bore the marks of the fight with a gash on his forehead and a nasty scrape across one cheek. But there was no blood pooling from his side. A knife was in his hand, the fresh blood on the silvery edge already darkening.

A police siren sounded from a few blocks away, partially blocked by the din of the street just beyond us.

"Skylar." Brandon breathed hoarsely as he struggled to retain consciousness. "Get the gun."

Heaving a few feet away, Messina stilled at the words. Brandon gripped my hand.

"Get it," he whispered. "Before he does."

The siren in the distance grew closer, over the cars that rushed down Dorchester Avenue. Messina's and my eyes locked on the gun, only a few feet away, and all at once we were both lurching over the pavement.

Messina was bigger, had the adrenaline of someone with the instincts to fight or flee at the same time. But I was smaller, faster. I wasn't hurt. And I needed to save the love of my life.

I lunged over Brandon's fallen form and grabbed for the gun at the same time Messina tumbled over me.

"I don't think so, Red!" he yelled as he pushed me over.

"NO!" I screamed, keeping a death grip on the weapon I quickly realized I didn't even know how to use. I hunched over it, curled up into the pavement, willing the police to get through the maze of streets to where we were.

Messina clawed at my arms, twisting my body around. His hands were ruthless as he worked to pry the gun away from me, forcing me open to him, as he leveraged his body weight over mine in a parody of the rape he'd tried to perpetrate the last time we had met.

"Get OFF ME!" I shrieked at the top of my lungs, causing Messina to grimace. "HELP!"

"Fuckin' bitch!" he screamed.

He reached his fist back, and I knew without a doubt that against the concrete, he was aiming for death, not just a knock-out. I twisted. He lunged. And somewhere in the fray, the gun went off.

With a wheezing gulp of air, Messina collapsed on top of me, holding his stomach while blood almost immediately slithered out of his open mouth.

The rest was a torrent of sound, touch, and smell. My vision blurred from tears, fear, rage, and everything else. So I could only hear the blaring sirens when the squad cars pulled up, the sharp slams of their doors as the officers raced to the scene. I could only feel the sudden rush of fresh air over my body when Messina's body was lifted from on top of me, particularly over the wet spot left by his blood. I could only smell the starchy scent of the officer's uniform.

It was only as I was led to a seat in the back of an open squad car that I could see one thing clearly: the sight of Brandon's immobilized body, strapped to a gurney, being lifted into the back of an ambulance. The doors shut behind him. I couldn't breathe.

Forty

Have you ever had that feeling of déja vu? When you open your eyes and feel like you've been in the exact same situation before? Maybe even before that?

At first, it was the smell that did it: the combination of ammonia, cheap ice cream, and sick people. Then it was the harsh fluorescent lighting, the dingy tiled floors. And the echoing beeps that filtered through the halls from room to room, the hushed tones of doctors as they spoke to patients and their families.

It was the third time I had been to the hospital because of Victor Messina. Three people he had put into the ICU. Three people who had had their lives threatened because of him. First my father, then me. And now, once again, I was the one in the bedside chair, slumped over the small twin mattress, dozing on the scratchy sheets that clothed the body of the person I loved more than anyone.

Just a few months ago, Brandon had been the one forcing his body to sleep in these ridiculously uncomfortable chairs. Who had waited to see if I would ever wake up. Who had wrestled with the uncertainty, the fear, the guilt of the entire situation. And now this time I was the one waiting for him to come back to me.

Blearily, I pushed myself up from the chair and ran a hand through my bedraggled hair. It was still dark outside, and the hospital wing was closed to visitors. I was only allowed in because of the ring on my finger, the one that now marked me as family, or at least, family to be. I wasn't allowed to make any decisions for him while he was unconscious—Ray and Susan had rushed to the hospital to do just that. The fact that I was left out of it all killed me.

"Red."

The deep voice, slightly raspy, but familiar and kind, pulled me the rest of the way out of my sleep. Relief flooded my whole being as the events of the night came back to me all over again. Victor Messina. Brandon being stabbed in the side. The scramble that ended with me shooting Messina through the chest. The arrival of cop cars, an ambulance.

I had been held at the station for what had seemed like hours, released only when Kieran had stormed in and demanded that the

363

cops either file charges or release me. As if I hadn't said that myself. As if I wasn't already a lawyer who was making the same damn arguments on my own behalf.

Bubbe, who had called Kieran, *really* had a big mouth, and thank God for it, since even if I did possess the knowledge to practice law on my own behalf, I did not have the presence of mind to do so. Around one a.m., I was released, once they'd finally taken my statement and witnesses who had been watching from the windows around the neighborhood had come forward to give theirs. I couldn't help being a little angry at them. Where were they when Brandon was getting stabbed?

But there would be no charges filed against me, they said. Messina was a dangerous, escaped convict. Self-defense.

I couldn't have cared less. I just wanted to know Brandon was going to be okay.

His normally ruddy skin was haggard and pale, and his voice croaked a little from having a tube shoved down it during the surgery. Pushpa had rushed into the waiting room upon my arrival to tell me that he'd needed two transfusions, but the procedure to repair his spleen had been relatively minor and had gone well. By some miracle, the knife had slipped through his ribs and missed his stomach completely. He was hurt, and would be in some pain for a while, but would be just fine.

In the early morning hours, with the winter moonlight still peeking through the window, I had never seen anyone so beautiful. His eyes were bright blue, even in the dim light. And his smile still lit up the room like the sun. Brandon was awake. He was okay. We were going to be fine.

"Come here," he said.

Wordlessly, I scooted my chair closer.

"No," he said, shifting in the bed to make room for me, wincing slightly at the movement. "Come *here*."

I stood up, but looked doubtfully at the narrow hospital bed, and then toward the nurses' station in the hall. "I don't know...I doubt they'd want me to..."

"Skylar, I swear to God. If I don't hold you right now, I'm going to bust a damn stitch, so get your ass in the bed."

I couldn't help but smile. If he was ordering me around, he was definitely feeling better. I slipped off my shoes and climbed carefully next to him, allowed him to pull me into his hospital-gown-covered chest, cradling me in the nook of his good side. Brandon released a contented sigh, which I echoed.

Then, the scent of him, that familiar mix of almonds and soap that couldn't quite be masked by the astringent hospital, started to sink in. The events of the past twenty-four hours—hell, the past *year*—came rushing back. And my body couldn't take it anymore. First my toes, then my knees, then my legs, chest, shoulders, arms—everything started to shake.

"Skylar?" Brandon murmured as his arms circled around me, holding me close. "Are you okay?"

His kindness only made me start to shake that much harder. Tears began to well up as I buried my head further into his shoulder.

"Skylar?" Brandon asked again, this time with more concern. "Baby, please."

"Mmmphmamommooo!"

A low chuckle vibrated under my ear, but I only cried harder. It was like a faucet had broken, and there was no way to stop the burst of water.

"Babe," Brandon said gently, although with a lilt of humor. "I can't understand you when you talk like a mouse."

Somehow, I managed to sit up and look at him. "I–almost–lost you!" I managed to choke out in between sobs.

With a half-smile that only made me cry harder, Brandon stroked my cheek. As if by some kind of magic, his warm touch calmed the sobs wracking through my body as his fingers grazed my skin.

"Shh," he crooned, although the smile didn't leave his lips. He was enjoying the fact that I cared so much, the bastard. "I'm here, Red. I'm going to be fine."

He pulled me back into his chest and continued to stroke my hair until at last, the shakes subsided, and we just lay together, calming in the sounds of each other's breaths.

"I love you," I murmured into his chest. "So much. The thought of losing you...Brandon, I just couldn't bear it."

The hand in my hair paused, and I felt the pressure of his kiss at the crown of my head.

"Right back at you, Red," he said. "My world just doesn't work without you in it."

After a few more beats of silence, a thought occurred to me, one that filled my chest and my body like a balloon. Everything about the idea felt right. *Yes*, I thought. *Now.*

I sat back up and faced Brandon, pushing my hair out of my face and wiping the tears from under my eyes. "I want to get married."

He raised a brow and smiled. "Well, I thought that was the plan."

I shook my head, causing my hair to fall back into my face. I spit it out of the way, which only made Brandon grin wider. Well, that was fine. I'd look like a hapless idiot anytime if it meant making him smile like that.

"No," I said as I blew another strand away. "I mean now. Tonight. Here."

Brandon frowned with confusion. "In the hospital?"

I nodded and sat up completely, suddenly consumed with the idea. "There's a chaplain and a chapel on the main floor. The chaplain could come up here, I know it, and we could ask one of the nurses to be a witness. We'd have to apply for a marriage license tomorrow in Atlantic City or someplace like that, but Brandon, I could take care of that, and—"

"Red," Brandon put in gently, turning me back to face him with a gentle finger on my chin.

I stopped talking.

"It's two-thirty in the morning, baby," he said with another small grin. "I don't think the chaplain is awake right now."

My heart sank in my chest. Of course. How stupid of me. Obviously it wasn't what Brandon wanted anyway. He wanted his friends and family, a real ceremony where we would announce our love for each other. Now that the campaign was done with, we were free to have the wedding we had originally wanted at the Cape, the kind with flowers and planning and whatever else went into something like that. He didn't want something quick, something the papers would cry about as a bad choice too fast. I should have known.

"But Red?"

I looked back up at him, all the negative thoughts still swirling around my head. My right hand automatically started toying with my ring.

"Let's wake him up," Brandon said with eyes so wide I thought I might fall into them.

366

"Really?" I whispered, clutching my fingers together.

Brandon pulled both of my hands to his mouth and kissed my knuckles, one after another. "There's nothing else I'd rather do today than become your husband, Skylar. Will you marry me in the morning, Red?"

I gazed at him, locked in his wide blue stare. My ring sparkled in a stream of moonlight seeping through the blinds. This man was my everything. I had been his from the first moment I'd seen him, bound to him for always. And by some miracle, he was mine too. I hated that it took me so long to accept it, as he seemed to have done from the beginning, but now we were here. I could see our life together unfolding before us, and I wanted nothing more than to start it. Right away.

"Yes!" I whispered back fiercely. "A thousand, a million times, *yes*!"

Brandon pulled me close for a firm kiss, but it quickly turned into something much more involved, despite the fact that we had to be careful not to disturb his incisions. We stayed like that for what seemed like hours, licking, nibbling, savoring each other's lips and tongues. For once I wasn't thinking of anything that was, or anything that might be. I was only thinking of us in this moment. I wanted nothing more than this.

"In the morning," he kept saying in between kisses. "In the morning, you'll be mine."

With every kiss, I tried to tell him the words that came from my heart, not my head. He didn't need to make me his. I already was.

* * *

In the end, it was more like what we'd planned originally than I thought it would be, only without the backdrop of the Cape. My dad put on his best black pants, white button shirt, and the one tie he owned to walk me down the aisle of the little chapel in the bottom of the hospital. Bubbe brought flowers and blintz. Jane, who had flown in as soon as she had heard of the shooting, had picked up an early

367

version of my wedding dress, which luckily didn't need much more than a few pins to hem the skirt.

It was the only part of the previously planned extravaganza that had felt like mine. In the midst of the bombast—the flowers, the band, the massive church venue and the press coverage—my dress was only for me. Simple, cream-colored satin that hung from my shoulders with delicate straps, draped almost casually over my breasts and down my hips in a bias-cut that recalled the classic style of the thirties, the dress allowed me to move freely. A light matching shawl provided the modesty required by a church wedding, but without the pretense of a cathedral, I could keep my shoulders bare.

After Kieran had pushed me out of Brandon's room so one of the nurses could help Brandon into a suit, the hospital staff let me use an empty hospital room to get ready. Jane pulled my bright red hair back into a simple chignon at the base of my neck, and had done my makeup lightly, letting my freckles shine through with just a bit of mascara and a pop of lip gloss.

"He doesn't want anything fancy," she murmured to herself, almost admiringly as she worked. "The most beautiful thing in the world to that man is you."

Our small circle of people—the handful of friends and family we considered ours—all stood tall, a few even wiping tears away while I walked slowly up the aisle of the tiny chapel.

But I couldn't see them. I could only see Brandon, smiling that massive smile I didn't think I'd ever seen shine brighter.

"You look beautiful," he whispered as I came to stand next to him in front of the chaplain.

I shrugged, but I couldn't shutter my own goofy smile. "It's not fitted properly yet. She thought she had until the spring, you know."

"Quit it," he said, although his mouth quirked up. "You stopped me in my tracks the first time we met. You could do it with your face painted green."

He'd given me variations of the compliment several times before, but it never failed to make me glow. "Likewise, Mr. Sterling."

Brandon's grin practically split his face in half, and I thought he was going to break tradition and kiss me before the ceremony. Then the chaplain cleared her throat.

I looked at Brandon. "Are you sure you're okay to stand for this long so soon after surgery?"

Brandon just rolled his eyes. "Red, I'm going to stand at my own wedding. You just worry about saying your vows."

"Um, are we ready?" the chaplain asked with a kind smile at both of us.

I stuck my tongue out at Brandon. We *would* start bickering at our own wedding.

Brandon raised a blond brow. "I've been ready for this my whole life."

So on we went, no muss, no fuss. In its own way, it was perfect: no frills, just us, the people we cared about, and only our love to fill the small space. We spoke the traditional vows, one after another, echoing the chaplain's words even as we watched the love shining through each other's faces.

"Do you have rings?" asked the chaplain, causing me to look at Brandon with panic.

"Oh no!" I squeaked. "I forgot rings!"

"Don't worry, Red. I got it."

Brandon accepted two velvet boxes from Margie, who then darted back to her seat.

"How did you..." I started as Brandon handed me one holding a simple men's platinum ring. "We literally decided to do this five hours ago. What jewelry shop is open at three a.m.?"

"Hey," Brandon said with shrug and a bashful expression that basically wrung out my heart. "If my money can't open Cartier early for my girl, what's it really good for?"

"All right," said the chaplain. "Repeat after me..."

So we did.

I slid the ring over Brandon's finger, enjoying the shivers that traveled down my spine as I intoned, "With this ring, I thee wed."

Brandon's smile was so wide I thought it might cause a power outage. And I gasped when he took out my ring, a white filigree band that was simple, yet intricate all at once.

"With this ring," he said in a voice that quavered, "I thee wed."

He slid the ring onto my finger, a snug fit next to the eternity-band-turned-engagement ring. Even when making his proposal, he had always meant forever. It had been forever with him from the start.

"I now pronounce you man and wife," said the chaplain. "You may kiss—"

She didn't get to finish before Brandon lifted me off the floor into a kiss that caused everyone in the room to whoop loud enough to reach the rafters.

"Do you love me yet, Red?" he whispered against my lips.

I pressed my forehead to his and closed my eyes. "Always."

Epilogue

Brandon

I scratch at the equation on my desk, but something's just not right. Is it the function continuity conditions? Or is it the basic physical model invalid? I really can't fuckin' tell.

I sigh and pick my cell phone up to dial the one person I know who could help me. Shit, he's going to love this. He'll take it as another excuse to badger me into going back to school. I'm not going to lie, I've thought about it. But I'm still enjoying my life at home too much to take on something like that.

"What is it, Bran? I'm a little busy right now preparing for class."

"You are not," I retort. "It's four-thirty in the afternoon. You're busy sneaking a can of PBR before you go home to Mom."

Ray, who I've only just started getting used to calling Dad, is silent. But I can hear the telltale sip of beer.

"Fine," he says. "What is it?"

"Can you open the shared drive?" I ask as I snap a picture of the problem I've been working on. Quickly, I upload it to a cloud folder. "Something's up with the new formula. I need your help."

He's as gruff as ever, but I take it with a grain of salt. Ray was never one to show emotion, but as I've gotten to know him better over the last five years, I've learned to understand just how he thinks and loves with his head, not his heart. It's times like these that have done it. No matter where he is or what he's doing, he'll drop just about anything to help with my projects.

Skylar's right, as she is way too much of the time, the cocky little minx. She always said that Ray would like my crazy inventions, the ones I finally took out again after we moved fully into the Brookline house. I remodeled the entire attic as my lab, and after I showed Ray some of my ideas, he started helping with the math side of things. Enough that we were able to get a few prototypes built a few years back. Since then, Sterling Petersen Lab was born. Ten years ago, I wouldn't have wanted to go into business with Ray to save my life. But things are different now. Now, we're really family.

"Is this for the ultrasound mapping or the baby monitor?"

I can hear him twisting in his chair and clicking through windows in his office, and soon we're off, launching into a discussion of math that would send most people to their graves with boredom, but which Ray and I both love. This is the one language we both speak. It's the one thing that makes me his son more than anything else. I just wish I hadn't fought it as long as I did.

Before I know it, it's almost five o'clock. My equation is fixed, and I've got at least five more ideas sketched out on a piece of paper. I could start on a sixth, but I hear the rumble of a car pulling into the driveway. I glance out the window, and I can see bright hair the color of the autumn leaves in the orchard shining through the window of the Prius she insists on driving herself every day to work. Ridiculous woman. We still have David on staff, but the poor guy spends more of his time carting me and Jenny around in an SUV than driving the Mercedes, which Skylar insists makes her look like a stuffy rich lady. Which is about the time when I point out the fact that she fulfills two out of three parts of that description, but only because pissing her off usually means tackling each other in the pantry or somewhere we can snag a moment of privacy in our busy house.

I glance at my watch, the new Garmin Skylar bought me last year for my birthday. It's nowhere as nice as my Rolex, but she teased that I'd get addicted to watching my heart rate and steps throughout the day. I'll be damned if the woman wasn't right.

"Time's up," I interrupt Ray while he's going on about a spectral domain solution, which seems to be applicable, but right now means absolutely nothing to me anymore. "Wife's home. Let's pick this up tomorrow."

It's five o'clock on the nose, and I'm half-jogging down the stairs when I hear the front door open. Skylar's home between four and five most days, since she's finally learned to get up to exercise with me in the mornings and goes to work early in order to be home to see me and Jenny. She still grumbles for a solid hour, but she's not complaining about the way I usually wake her up. And I don't mind the griping—but watching her run around the reservoir in skin-tight leggings makes it worth it.

Normally, we're not in such a hurry to see each other. She'll find me in the living room reading to Jenny, or sitting at the counter while Ana starts dinner. But this is different. This is Friday night. Our night.

Fridays are when Sarah and Danny take Jenny for dinner and a sleepover, the night before Christoph and Annabelle arrive for the weekend and our spare time is suddenly swallowed up by Little League games and swim meets. It's the one night of the week when the house belongs only to Red and me and we can do whatever we want, wherever we want. Don't get me wrong—I love my daughter. I love her so much, I decided to work from home instead of building a new office for the lab. She's got red hair and a sharp mouth, just like her mom. If Skylar's my sun, then Jenny's my moon, and my entire world revolves around these two women.

So yeah, I'm crazy head over heels for my daughter. But I need her mom.

I can hear her heels on the wood floors, clipping toward me at a furious pace. I vaguely remember her slipping on the red ones this morning, the ones I tried to give her once before, but which she only accepted after we were engaged. The damn things still drive me crazy, still remind me of when I wanted her so badly I was ready to throw out my reputation, her reputation, put my entire company at risk just to kiss her in the middle of my office. Actually, I think with a smirk, not much has changed.

Luckily, she's since let me do that, and much more, several times over in hers. Now that she's the boss, she's less worried about what people will think. Although I did notice that when she chose offices for the firm, she made sure that hers had absolutely no windows her colleagues could see into.

She tackles me right when I hit the bottom of the stairs, and my arms wrap around my wife like I haven't seen her in weeks, not hours. She's just as starving as I am. In a second, I have her up against the wall, causing two of the family portraits in the hall to fall sideways. I hike her tight skirt over her hips and affix my mouth to hers while she tears at my shirt.

"Uhhhhh," she growls as her hands make contact with skin.

It's the same sound she makes every time she touches my abs. I may be over the hill at forty-three, but I'm making damn sure I don't look it. *That's right, baby,* I think with a smirk. *You love it.*

373

Then her tongue does that thing where it twists around mine like she wants to eat me whole, and I can't think at all. All I can do is unbutton my jeans, let out the goddamn pipe she causes down there, and shove it in with everything I've got.

"FUCK!" she cries out loud enough to echo through the entire house.

Her hands tear at my hair. It's that slight line between pleasure and pain that gets me every time and only makes me harder.

"Jesus, Red."

I can barely breathe, I want her so bad, even though I'm already balls-deep inside her. Two palms full of the sweetest, ripest ass a man could ever want; a strawberry-shaped mouth that's currently sucking on my lips like a Jolly Rancher. That leaves...I look down.

"Take off your shirt," I say in a voice that's more of a growl than a request. Somehow, I lift her up, urge her legs around my waist, and get us over to the countertop in the kitchen, which was magically built at exactly the right height. I pull out, much to her disapproval, but keep myself right at her juncture, teasing but not entering.

Red smirks. She loves it when I order her around this way, toy with her body and her mind. I can't get away with it any other time, but when it comes to sex, we both know who's the boss.

I look at her shirt, which is untucked, but not unbuttoned. "Now."

With a sly smile that makes me throb against her, she lets go of my hair and slowly unbuttons her blouse, one agonizing button at a time. She loves to play with me, and even though it's fucking torture, I love it too. Like a man in a trance, I'm spellbound while she undoes the last button and pulls the black silk away.

And...shit. I have to close my mouth so I don't drool.

She's wearing that black thing I like—no, love—the one that's see-through so that I can see the way her perfect fucking nipples pop out like damn berries when she's all turned on. She doesn't know it; if I said something, she'd get self-conscious about it. But Red's nipples are her tell. The second she's turned on, it's like the room temperature just dropped by twenty degrees. When she was pregnant...forget about it. I feel dirty just remembering the thoughts I had about my pregnant wife, even though she was sick the entire nine months. Does that make me a pervert? Maybe. I don't really care.

I lean in slowly, and nip one breast through the lace. She arches into my touch and hisses.

"I said off," I order as my teeth latch to the other side. "That meant everything."

This time she's happy to obey. Red has even less patience than I have, especially by the time Friday rolls around. It's not that we can't have sex when our daughter is in the house—*fuck*, no, we'd go crazy—but by this time, it's been six full days of sneaking into the closet or the shower to mask the noises neither of us can keep tamped down. Six days of praying I'll have the presence of mind to kiss her when she comes, because my girl is fucking hopeless at staying quiet when I make her lose her mind. Unfortunately, it's one of my favorite things to do.

The bra-thing (I don't know what it's called—just that I like it) falls to the floor, and now I'm the one who's speechless, struck again by the beauty of this woman—my woman. Her breasts are a little fuller now, her hips a little wider after having a kid. She's even got a few tiny creases at the edges of those beautiful green eyes, and when I want to piss her off, I point out the few threads of gray she's gotten since Jenny was born. But none of that matters—every time I see her, all I can think is that I'm the luckiest son of a bitch alive. The smartest, wittiest, kindest, most beautiful woman in the world is in front of me, and she's all mine.

"Brandon," she whispers, bringing my eyes back up to meet those endless emerald beauties. I swear to God, the woman sees right through me.

I can't help it. I kiss her again, suck on her lips, first the top, then the bottom.

"Finally," I murmur. "It's been too long since this morning."

I'm having a hard time breathing; that's the effect she has on me. We've been married for five years, and I still have no idea what it is: jasmine? Tea? Something sweet and totally hers. Whatever it is, it's like crack to my dick.

Luckily, I seem to have the same effect on her.

"Off," she mutters, yanking hard enough at my shirt that I think a button or two pops off. I can't tell you how many times I have to send my shirts back to my tailor to replace buttons.

"Now," she demands when I don't move fast enough.

375

I have to stifle a chuckle. She's usually such a damn chatterbox, but when she's turned on, Red can only speak in one-word sentences. It's how I know she's *really* ready to go.

"Is this what you want, baby?" I ask in that low voice I know really gets her going. She says I growl like a lion. I don't know. I can't really control it. These things come naturally around her.

I pull off my shirt, letting her see the body I know she loves. It's just a body to me—big, annoying, with a few more aches and pains these days—but I do my damnedest to keep it up, if only to see that look on her face when she touches it in the flesh.

She brushes her fingers across my abdomen, scraping slightly with her nails. Her fingers pause over the scar on my left side, the one left by the knife that came way too close to ending things. I shudder. She knows exactly how to get me going too.

I slip a hand into her hair—the red hair she cut off a year after Jenny was born, when she finally had the balls to start her own firm with Kieran, Eric, and a few other people we poached from what used to be Sterling Grove. It's going well now, but it meant some seriously long hours in the beginning. In a way, it was good timing––I got to stay at home with my daughter and let someone else bring home the bacon while I figured out what I wanted to do with the three billion and change I walked away with after breaking apart my old life.

"I need a haircut," Red mumbles as I tug on the ends.

It's growing out again, just past her shoulders.

"Looks good to me," I say back as I dip down to suck at that spot on her neck that drives her crazy.

I'm not going lie; I miss it long, mostly because I like grabbing it in situations like these. But I'm telling the truth when I say she'd stop traffic in a garbage bag. Why does she think I still keep a driver around? I can't be trusted around heavy machinery when I see her in a skirt.

She's lost in a trance, her hands exploring me as she pushes my pants down with her feet. I kick them off with the rest of our clothes. She can't speak when she's like this, but her eyes glow. I love her glass face. I love that I can see every damn thing she thinks on it, especially when she's worshipping me.

Not bad for an orphan kid from Dorchester who never knew love. Red shows me with every single look.

376

Finally, she can't take the waiting anymore, and neither can I. She's been working long days getting the new firm set up, and the last two times we tried to do this, Jenny walked in to our room looking for her stuffed narwhal. That's right, my kid doesn't have a teddy bear or a stuffed dog. No, I had to go all over half the Eastern seaboard looking for a stuffed fuckin' narwhal because my daughter just had to have her own "water unicorn" after reading a book about them at school. Do you even know what a narwhal is? Do you know how hard it is to find a stuffed version of a weird looking whale with a giant spear coming out of its nose?

But the look on her face...she's too much like her mother, that's what she is. Everything shows, and when she's happy, she lights up the goddamn room. So, a narwhal it was.

"Hey."

Skylar's hand on my chin yanks me out of my trance. It's too easy to get lost thinking about my kid, but the second I hear that voice—that throaty, low voice that filters through my dreams day and night—all I can think about is her. And then her lips are back on mine—that heart-shaped mouth that gets her into trouble—and I can't think at all.

My hands move on autopilot. It's crazy, after all this time, five years together, and every part of me still knows instinctively how to please her. She's always been a book I can read this way, before we even spoke. They say that time dulls the senses, but for us, it's only gotten better. I know how to push her. I know how to make her feel better than she ever has, every single time.

With Skylar, it just comes naturally.

"Please," she breathes, hot and heavy against my lips. *Fuck*, I love it when she begs.

"What do you want, baby?" I whisper into her ear as I press just a little bit into her.

I've already given her a taste, and now she wants it. Bad. I nip the upper edge of her earlobe. She shudders, her thighs clenching around me. I almost come right there. *Fuck*, I need to be inside her again.

"You," she says, barely able to get the single word out. "Just...you. In me. *Now*."

She doesn't have to ask me twice.

I start to move slowly, but my girl is impatient tonight, jerking her hips against me, seeking a pace I'm not quite ready to give—mostly because I won't last long enough for her to come with me. She leans back on the counter, and fuck me, it's like she's serving up her body on a fucking platter for me. I reach down and brush her clit softly with my thumb, exactly the way she likes. Her body jumps in response, and eventually she starts to hum in time with my hips, thrusting back against me to take me as deep as she can.

Like I said: sexiest fucking thing on the planet.

"Come on, baby," I growl as I wrap an arm around her waist to leverage myself deeper. "I want the neighbors to hear you tonight."

I keep the insistent pressure going with my thumb while I pick up the pace with my hips. She moans and bites my shoulder as she collapses forward, all hot breaths and goosebumps. That breathy sound just about undoes me, and before long, she's shaking in my arms herself.

"Oh *God*," she cries as her body starts to tense up. Her fingernails dig into my back, and I feel her contract around my dick. I could lose it right now, but she's not quite there yet, and I want us to come together. Just...a little...bit...more.

"BRANDON!" she shouts as her body explodes around me, and thank fucking God, because I can't hold it back any longer either.

I shatter completely, cry her name as I empty myself into her. The woman makes me feel like I don't exist anymore—like there's no more Brandon, just this nameless core inside me whose only purpose it to give itself to her. I belong to her. I always did, even before I met her.

Slowly, gradually, we return to reality. The kitchen reconstructs itself around us—the familiar white marble, the atrium furniture, the wood floors that should probably be refinished sometime soon. But it's all a little blurry when I'm with her.

I pick my shirt off the ground and help her wrap it around her shoulders with a smirk before I locate my boxers. When I stand back up, Red is watching me with a queer look on her face. She's looking at the scar on my side—the one from the knife wound I took almost five years ago now.

While the rest of her face is still relaxed in a post-orgasmic daze, her eyes are slightly watered over. I know that look. It's the look that says I better get over there right fucking now.

"Hey," I say as I pull her into me. "I'm good. You're good. I'm here."

As much therapy as I've been in over the past few years to dig through my issues, Red is still dealing with her own traumas. The deeply ingrained trust issues that come from her mom and dad's neglect of her over the years. She doesn't like to hear it, but Danny was neglectful too. You can't have addiction nearly ruin your life and not fuck up your kid at least some.

But it wasn't until after Jenny was born that the panic attacks started. Paranoia plus postpartum blues is not a pretty thing, my friends, let me tell you. It didn't matter that Messina was dead and his organization had fallen apart without him—she was terrified his friends would come after us again, that someone would take Jenny the way they'd taken her. Lucas and Craig have been permanent fixtures in our family since the night Messina died.

It took her a while to come to terms with the fact that she was suffering from PTSD of her own—not as blatant and horrific as mine, but there nonetheless. Now that she knows it, the attacks, just like my nightmares, have become less and less frequent. And if I'm around, I can usually head them off using the same tool she uses with me: simple touch. I don't sing, though. Both she and my daughter have made it *very* clear that I have absolutely no musical talents.

After a moment, Red sits up and dabs at her eyes.

"I'm good," she says. "I'm good now."

I brush away the loose hair at her forehead and then kiss her. "Okay."

Then I step back, since Red usually wants a bit of space after these kinds of moments. I ramble around the kitchen, getting her a glass of wine, me a beer. She watches me from her perch on the counter, oblivious to the fact that even in my now-button-less shirt, her hair a slightly tangled mess from my hands, she's still the most beautiful thing I've ever seen.

When I turn back, she's grinning at me, like she sees something funny.

"What?" I ask as I come back around and hand her the wine.

She takes a sip and then combs back my hair with her fingers. "You need a haircut too."

I close my eyes and lean my face into her hand, enjoying the way it feels. "I thought you liked it long."

"I do. But this is getting a little nuts. You're starting to look like a hippie."

My eyes pop open, and I give her a fake glare that makes her giggle before I turn on the accent I know she secretly loves. "Let's shave it off, then. I'm from Dorchester, honey. We don't do no hippie shit."

She laughs, then tips her head up for another kiss. This time I take a little more, tasting her wine-soaked mouth fully. Damn. And I'm ready to go all over again.

But I step back, much to her obvious disappointment. I want to savor the night, not charge through it like a racehorse. "How was the day? Did you find a new office space yet?"

That's really all it takes to distract her. Red really can't ignore a question. She starts talking about the day spent with realtors, which clearly drove her crazy since she'd rather be seeing clients. But the firm is growing. They took on five new associates this year and just landed a huge client (alongside Sterling Petersen Labs), one that's big enough to allow them to dedicate a full thirty percent of their time to pro-bono cases. It's a lot of work, but I can tell she loves it. Red struggled for so long to figure out what she wanted to do with her career, but in the end, it became clear: she just wanted to be her own boss. The space to soar on her own terms.

"Also," I said as I reach around her to the stack of mail on the counter. "This came today. The kids both got into Billings."

At that, Skylar's face lights up. It's been rough with her siblings over the last five years. They settled into Andover pretty quickly, but it's always been clear that they needed a better home than a boarding school. We take them on weekends and over their vacations, when Janette will visit us at the Cape during the summer, but it's not enough. Those kids need a family. They always have.

When Maurice was put on the equivalent of house arrest for the French version of the Bernie Madoff scandal, we thought we saw an in. Janette had promised Skylar and me guardianship rights in exchange for paying their way for school. But Janette's just as wily as her husband—maybe more. She figured out that the kids were a way into Skylar's life and that we weren't going to abandon them no matter what. So guardianship went out the window, and we just

380

didn't have the bandwidth to fight it during the years after Jenny was born.

Until this year, when we finally took it to court. And won.

Skylar takes the letter from me and scans over the acceptance. She looks up with a grin that makes her freckles scrunch over her nose. It's so wicked cute, I can't handle it.

"So it's settled?" she asks. "They're coming here to live with us?"

I grin back. Christoph still hasn't totally lost his French accent, and even at eleven, he still hangs on every word I say. Annabelle isn't so attached—at thirteen, she's starting to want to do her own thing more and more. I know it will be a big change for them, going from essentially being on their own most of their life to living in a house with structure. But they both adore their little niece, and they never seem to want to go back to school when they visit.

"Oh God," Skylar says with a sudden hand at her chest. "I just realized something. We're going to have a teenage girl in our house. And she's cute." She looks up at me with wide, mischievous eyes. "It's going to be good practice for when Jenny starts bringing home boys."

At that thought, the smile drops from my face, and I feel like my hands just lost their feeling. Red immediately starts laughing.

"Oh God!" she crows as she bends over on the counter. "Your face! Oh shit, poor Jenny!"

"You mean poor Jenny's boyfriends," I say as I push a hand through my hair. "Christ. I do *not* want to think about that right now."

Skylar just keeps laughing even harder after I shoot her a dirty look. She takes another sip of her wine. "Oh, I almost forgot to tell you. I got a call today from Maria Frazier."

At that, I perk up. Maria is the social worker we've been working with. At first I was pretty reticent about working with the state again—not after the experiences I had as a kid. But Maria has single-handedly won me over to the hard work that so many of them do. The woman is a saint.

"What did she say?"

Red grins and puts her hand on my chest, right over my heart. "It's official, babe. We're going to meet him next Wednesday."

We thought about having another kid. Jenny was a surprise—one that came along in spite of the IUD. A good one, one that we were both over the moon about, but a surprise nonetheless, who came almost a year to the day that we were married at the hospital. But when we talked about another, Skylar was always more hesitant. I don't blame her—you would be too if you spent nine whole months tossing up every meal you had. But we didn't want Jenny to be an only child, so the conversation always came back to another idea: adoption.

There were so many kids out there, kids like me. Kids who didn't have loving families, or who came from ones so fucked up they couldn't get what they needed from their parents. And when we both talked about it, the idea of giving at least one of those kids a real home started to sound better and better. A place where they could get that thing Skylar and I had both always wanted—real, unconditional love.

"Grab my purse," she says gesturing toward the hall where she dropped her bag.

I smirk at her. I know her game—she just wants to stare at my ass when I walk away. When I return, she quickly opens her email.

"Nine o'clock on Monday morning," she said. "We'll have another interview, and if that goes well, we'll meet him then." She swipes again, and looks up at me, green eyes glittering. "Here he is."

In the email, there's a picture of a little boy who's maybe two. He's got dark hair and dark eyes, a round face that should be rounder, which makes me wonder if he's had enough to eat. His hair is cut awkwardly, like it was done too fast with a pair of kitchen scissors. But I can tell he's smart. There's a brightness in his eyes that makes it clear he's the kind of kid who notices things all the time.

"What's his name?" I whisper as I brush a thumb lightly over the picture. I'm almost afraid it might disappear.

Skylar kisses my shoulder and leans her head on my shoulder. "Luis. His mother was a single mom. Venezuelan refugee. I guess she got wrapped up into drugs when she got here—she overdosed a few weeks ago. He's..."

She drifts off, and I know she's thinking of my mother, of the way she abandoned me in the same way, over and over again. But it doesn't bother me to think about right now. All I can see is Luis.

And in that moment, I only feel one thing. There's that swelling in my chest, the same one I had the second I saw Skylar sitting in my windowsill, the moment I watched my baby girl come into the world. For all this kid is a stranger, I know he's my son. And no matter what he's been through, what he needs to live a healthy life, how hard that might be for him to accept, I'll always be there for him. I'll always love him. Because that's what fathers do.

"He's perfect," I whisper.

"He is," Skylar agrees as she looks down at him with me. "There will be some things to sign, and we'll need to appear in court. But soon, he'll be really and truly, legally ours."

"Ours," I repeat, and my voice is full of awe and wonder. How could he be anything else?

THE END

Need more of the spitfire world?
Get the first book of Matthew Zola's story here on special:
www.nicolefrenchromance.com/theotherman
AND
Get the free prequel here:
www.nicolefrenchromance.com/thescarletnight
Jane and Eric's story is available now! Get it HERE:
www.nicolefrenchromance.com/thehatevow
Keep reading for sneak peeks of both stories.
Thank you so very much for taking the time to read the Spitfire Series. Reviews can make or break writers, so I hope you will consider leaving an honest review.
xo,
Nic

The Other Man

An Excerpt

Nina.

Nina Astor.

Was here.

In this apartment.

Staring at me with the *exact* same expression she'd worn just before I kissed her for the first time. Lips partially opened. Jaw dropped an inch or so. A dewy sheen over her plump bottom lip.

Kiss me, she seemed to say.

And I couldn't. Fuckin'. Move.

"You two know each other?"

Eric's voice knifed through the tension, and with regret, I watched Nina assume a mask I'd noticed her cousin take several times. Family trait, apparently. She smoothed her dress—a fitted white thing that was conservative but for a tasteful, yet mouth-watering slit to just above her knee—and turned to pick up a binder she had set on the entry table.

"We've met." Her voice was calm as she crossed the room to stand by the couch. "It was at the fundraiser for Juan Ramirez, wasn't it, Matthew?"

I couldn't stop staring at her legs long enough to answer.

"Nina, wine?" Eric asked from the kitchen.

She nodded, though she didn't look up. Not at him. And certainly not at me.

Finally, I managed to move enough muscles to swallow and clear my throat. It wasn't easy. "Oh. Yeah, um, yes. Yes, that was probably it. Good to see you again, doll."

I couldn't help it. It slipped out. The seemingly harmless moniker, but one that had come as naturally to me with her as breathing. It was special, "doll." The name my grandfather used to use for *Nonna* when he was still alive. The one that made her blush well into her seventies. The one that made her his.

Not everyone grows up with that kind of model for a relationship. But I did. My parents were good for fuckin' nothing, but the two people who raised me, staunchly Catholic Italians who took on five kids in the Bronx, had been in love with each other since they were teenagers and stayed in love until my grandfather's last breath.

"Doll," he called her, even then, like he was about to whisk *Nonna* off to see Frankie Valle at the Copa. And she'd blush and chatter at him in Italian, like they were still just kids. Fools in love.

Maybe I should have been more careful. But the second I met her in that goddamn bar two months ago, Nina was "doll" to me. For better or for worse.

Nina's expression remained just as focused on the binder, but a tinge of pink colored her cheeks. *Good*, I thought. At least I wasn't the only one feeling something here.

Eric returned with Nina's wine, and we all watched awkwardly as she took a very long drink. When about half the glass was empty, she cleared her throat too.

"Ah, yes. Yes, it's nice to see you too, Matthew."

She looked me over for a few seconds longer than necessary. I fought the urge to drag her out of the apartment like a fuckin' caveman. Again, not an easy feat.

Nina blinked, like she had only remembered where we were, and turned. "Actually, Jane, this isn't purely a social visit. I have a dreadful favor to ask you."

I drained my wine, transfixed by the way Nina's skirt rode up her thigh as she sat beside Jane. You would think it had been three months since I'd gotten laid, not three damn days. You would have thought I'd never seen a woman's legs before tonight. All I could think about was the way her skin felt under my hands—velvety and smooth, taut and responsive. I remembered sliding my palms up those limbs, memorizing the lean curves of muscle and bone as I went. Up, up, up to the promised land waiting between them.

As I sipped on my wine, I could barely even make out the conversation. Something about a gala. An event Nina desperately needed Jane's help with. Fancy rich people shit.

It only reminded me of the fact that I was the odd man out here. Eric and Nina were old money. The sort that didn't know anything different. Jane was from more middle class stock, but if this

385

apartment was any indication, she'd taken to extreme wealth like a fish in water, shitty taste in wine aside. Being a de Vries obviously had its benefits.

That was when it hit me. De Vries. Nina was a de Vries. She was the granddaughter of one of the oldest families in New York, an genuine heiress to a shipping dynasty.

In other words, my polar opposite.

Get your copy here: **www.nicolefrenchromance.com/theotherman**

Also by Nicole French

The Other Man

Nina Astor gave me one red-hot night, then disappeared like a ghost. Three months later, fate drops her in my lap.

The only problem?

She's beyond off-limits, and we're worlds apart.

I'm a street savvy prosecutor with a bit of a dark side.

She's the daughter of a dynasty and property of the scum of the earth.

And her owner just happens to be the subject of my next investigation.

Nina thinks I'm on the right side of the law, but she's forgotten one thing:

When it comes to her, I'm not a good man.

To claim her as my own, I might sell my soul to the devil himself.

True be told…when it comes to Nina Astor, maybe I already have.

Read here: www.nicolefrenchromance.com/theotherman

The Hate Vow

Eric de Vries. Looks like millions. Worth billions. A body like the David with a mind to match.

Unfortunately for this wayward heir, to keep his money, he needs a wife. And of all the women in the world, he chooses me.

Too bad I've hated him for five years, since he took all my tears and tossed me away. The guy slept his way through half of New England and discarded women like hotel toiletries.

Been there. Done that.

Still...what would you do for twenty million dollars? Would you wear the dress? Fake a smile for the man who broke your heart?

Or would you run far, far away?

Yeah, that's what I thought. I'll see you at the church.

387

Start the series here: www.nicolefrenchromance.com/quicksilver

The Discreet Duet

Fitz Baker was the world's biggest sex symbol. Until he disappeared.

Fed up with the trappings of fame, he traded his world of Hollywood for a quiet life on Newman Lake. He was perfectly happy living as an island. Until he met her.

Returning home with nothing but a failed music career, all Maggie Sharp wants is to rebuild her life. A life that doesn't involve the surly, arrogant mountain man now living across the lake.

Still, there's something about Will...something familiar. Something Maggie can't quite put her finger on...

She only wanted the spotlight.

He gave up his life to escape it.

The real question is if they can remain discreet.

Start the series here: www.nicolefrenchromance.com/hollywoodsecret

Bad Idea

Repeat after me: stay away from the hot girl. The beautiful girl. The f**king ray of sunshine in the middle of your delivery route.

Layla Barros is everything I never knew I wanted. Everything I'll never have.

She's an innocent young student.

I'm a convicted felon.

She's rich girl from a nice family.

I've got nothing but a broken home.

But if I'm an addict, she's my drug. I can't stay away, even though I know I'll ruin her in the end.

She might be the girl of my dreams, but I was always a bad idea.

Start the series here: www.nicolefrenchromance.com/bad-idea

Acknowledgments

First and foremost, I'd like to thank my mom for her sense of romance and whimsy. If it hadn't been for the years and years of watching chick flicks and reading romance novels together, I probably wouldn't have the sense of optimism needed to write romance in a world like today's.

Secondly, I'd like to thank my husband and my family for giving me the support I need to write, even if it's just for twenty minutes a day while the kid is taking a bath. Writing kept me sane in these first crazy years of our life together, and it keeps me present moving forward too. I love you, always.

There are a lot of people who also took the time to help with the production of my first novel. Sarah, for her lovely advice on plot development and Yiddish. Don, for his exclamations when I told him I was attempting my first novel, and that it was actually genre fiction to boot. And more than anyone else, Burton, who was my final beta reader and legalese extraordinaire. Couldn't have written half the book without you. Thank you, friend! Jenny, who swooped in to help polish the later edition and let me lecture her on commas, and to Emily Hainsworth and Judy Zweifel, who have become absolutely indispensable in making all my books shine—thank you SO much.

And most importantly, **I want to thank you, the reader.** Skylar and Brandon's journey can't continue without your support and investment. If you enjoyed their story, **I would so, so, so appreciate your review on any of the online retailers through which you purchased this book.** I can't do this without you, lovely readers, who are the real muse of these stories.

About the Author

For more information about Nicole French and to keep informed about upcoming releases, please visit her website at www.nicolefrenchromance.com/.

Join my newsletter: bit.ly/NicoleFrenchNewsletter

Join my Facebook group for daily interaction with Nicole and excerpts from new works:
http://facebook.com/groups/nicolefrenchromance
Check out my Goodreads Page!

CPSIA information can be obtained
at www.ICGtesting.com
Printed in the USA
LVHW090403031121
702256LV00004B/132